HEAD GAMES

ALSO BY THOMAS B. CAVANAGH

Murderland

HEAD GAMES

THOMAS B. CAVANAGH

THOMAS DUNNE BOOKS

ST. MARTIN'S MINOTAUR NEW YORK

This is a work of fiction. All of the characters, organizations, and events portrayed in this novel are either products of the author's imagination or are used fictitiously.

THOMAS DUNNE BOOKS.
An imprint of St. Martin's Press.

www.thomasdunnebooks.com
www.minotaurbooks.com

ISBN-10: 0-312-36132-7
ISBN-13: 978-0-312-36132-7

First Edition: January 2007

10 9 8 7 6 5 4 3 2 1

For my father, who faced down cancer and beat it

HEAD GAMES

CHAPTER 1

I have a tumor in my head. I call it Bob.

Bob is the boss. He controls everything I do. He is the first thing I think of when I wake up in the morning and the last thing I think of before I finally drift off at night.

If I drift off. Too many things to ponder in the dark, wee hours, when there's nothing to do but think. See, Bob isn't much of a sleeper. Although, the doc tells me that'll change. Evidently, Bob will eventually become a quite relaxed son of a bitch, sleeping for much of the day, resting me up for my big, inevitable nap.

Bob's generous to a fault. Shares everything with me. Take these nuclear headaches. Bob gave me those. Doc says that they're from the increased intracranial pressure—less and less room for a constant amount of cerebrospinal fluid. Seems Bob is doing some remodeling inside my skull, adding on to his digs, maybe a game room or a den. The ever-expanding Bob needs his space, squeezing my brain juice till it can't squeeze no more. The big question is, how far down into my gray matter does his basement go?

Don't tell him I said this, but Bob is kind of a prima donna. Always has to be the center of attention. See, he's stretching out his tendrils into my brain like tree roots, short-circuiting my synapses, forcing himself into my consciousness even when I try to keep him out. I can't go five minutes without thinking about him. Putting on my socks. Taking a leak. Eating my Cheerios. I can feel him in there, a strawberry-sized lump of malignant cells, scrunching down in my cerebrum, getting comfy, putting his feet up on the coffee table. I can even feel it when I nod, not too heavy, about the same weight as a golf ball.

The doc says I can't actually feel the tumor. I'm imagining it. He said it's all in my head. I told him, "No shit."

Without a doubt, Bob is the most significant relationship in my life right now. He may be the most significant relationship I've ever had, which probably says more about me than I'd like to admit. But he's not happy just with me. He's reaching out. My former coworkers. My ex-wives. My daughter. My friends. He's become a presence in their lives, too.

Hey, Bob's a regular social animal. He wants to get to know everyone, even complete strangers. I was in the grocery store the other day buying six boxes of Twinkies—after all, at this point, what the hell do I care about fat grams and calories? Anyway, the cashier kind of looked funny at all the Twinkies and then up at me. I said:

"Hi. I have a brain tumor. How are you?"

I regretted it, of course, as soon as I saw the look on her face. She was maybe eighteen. Maybe nineteen. She didn't know what to say. Grown men I've known twenty years—toughest cops you'll ever meet, who've seen more up-close tragedy than ten average lifetimes— even they don't know what to say. What did I expect some stranger, a kid, to say? She probably went home and cried. I felt like crap.

Other times, I look around and see people going about their days, running errands, shopping for shoes, eating lunch, whatever, and I realize like an epiphany that they *don't* have brain tumors. I can't even remember what that was like. They all look like freaks to me now. And, what's worse, they don't even know Bob's there. Oblivious to Bob! How can that be? Bob is a palpable force that radiates from my head, lying like a blanket on everything I see, everything I think about, everyone around me. It consumes me. My friends feel it. My family feels it. I can't believe that everyone doesn't feel it.

Not long after I was diagnosed, when the shock of it was still seared into my consciousness like a brand, I was at a red light, looking at the drivers around me, amazed at their ignorance. Finally, I couldn't take it anymore. Next to me was a skinny white kid, bleached hair, in a torso-hugging tank top, sitting in a tricked-out

Honda CRX. He was nodding his head, lips pursed, to a rap bass beat that poured out his open window and pounded my ribs all the way in the next lane. I cranked down my window.

"Hey!" I shouted.

No response.

"Hey!" This time louder. The kid rolled his head back and tilted it toward me, giving me the insolent look that can only be found on seventeen-year-olds and ex-wives.

"I have a brain tumor!" I shouted over the bass. No reaction from the kid. I'm not sure what I expected or why I even felt compelled to talk to him. The light turned green and before he lurched down the street, he flipped me a lackadaisical middle finger.

I mentioned this to Cam—a mistake, I know—and her reaction was that it says a lot about me that I won't talk to my family or go to the support group recommended by the neurologist, but I'll talk to some strange delinquent on the street.

I'll say this. I respect that kid. He gave me no bullshit about what he thought. He taught me an important lesson, too, although I'm still deciding exactly what it was. Maybe not to feel so damn sorry for myself. Maybe to understand that the whole world doesn't revolve around me. Maybe that nobody gives the proverbial rat's ass about my terminal cancer except me. All valuable lessons, sure. But most of all, he stood up to Bob. He told Bob to fuck off and drove right out of Bob's life forever. I envied that kid. He's my new hero.

When I got my diagnosis, I transformed instantly into "the guy with the tumor in his head." Gradually, though, I'm slowly morphing into "the tumor with the guy around him." It's true. When people who know about the cancer look at me, they don't see me first. They see Bob. I can tell by their pained and uncomfortable faces, their awkward attempts at small talk (someone actually said to me recently, "Is it hot enough for you?"), their feeble efforts to be supportive. They mean well and I don't blame them for being awkward and uncomfortable. But don't tell me that *I'm* the one making them uncomfortable. It's all Bob, baby, and I'm just along for the ride.

When the phone rang, I was in my apartment, eating the last of the Twinkies, sitting on my couch in the dark, eyes closed. It sounds pathetic, I know. Sitting alone in the dark, no music, no TV, eating Twinkies, just me and Bob. But I haven't had any desire to listen to music for a while, and I think that, given my limited time left here on earth, watching *Fear Factor* would be a waste of it. Of course, sitting in the dark eating Twinkies isn't exactly carpe diem. What can I say? I'm full of contradictions. It's what makes me complex.

I let the phone ring until the machine answered.

"Michael. Mikey. It's George Neuheisel. Listen, I want to talk to you about something. It's kinda urgent. Call me back as soon as you get this." He left his number. I didn't recognize it.

I hadn't heard from George in a long time. Since before I left the job. Actually, not since before *he* left the job. There was really only one reason why he could be calling me. He'd heard from someone about the new roommate in my skull and felt compelled to call. I got a lot of those calls recently, and they all went about the same. Hang in there, Mikey. You're a fighter. You can beat it. We'll keep you in our prayers. Does it hurt? Let me know if there's anything I can do. Blah blah blah.

Again, I know they mean well and I appreciate that they actually had the courage to call—more than a few hadn't called, like they might catch cancer from me through the phone—but, I was over it by now. None of them knew how to end the call. More than one got emotional and started crying. It just wasn't doing anything for me, so I stopped answering.

But, still . . . George's call was a little different. It almost sounded like he wanted to discuss something specific. Maybe I owed him money. And what was with saying it was urgent? Was he afraid I was gonna die before I decided to return his call?

The more I thought about the message, the more I got the itch to call him back. I picked up the receiver and placed it back in the cradle twice before I dialed the number. George answered on the third ring.

And nothing was ever the same again.

"Seriously, Mikey, it's good to see you."

I opened my eyes. George's hulking six-foot-six frame stood over me.

"Christ, George," I said. "This is most comfortable goddamn chair I ever sat in."

George smiled. "Calfskin leather. Imported from Italy."

I was in the reception area of Global Talent Inc., melting into a buttery soft leather waiting chair. I wasn't kidding. This was the most comfortable chair I had ever rested my plebeian ass in. It was like a womb.

"See why I left the job?" George said with a smile, offering a hand and hoisting me up.

I saw, all right. Besides the chair, the floors were marble—also probably imported—the walls were trimmed in a rich cherry, and, sitting behind a massive chrome receptionist desk, was a young blonde who was so beautiful it hurt my eyes to look directly at her. George led me down a hallway lined with framed photographs of celebrities. Singers mostly, but a few actors, too. I recognized them all, even if I didn't know all their names. Each was posing with a short, goateed man in a black baseball cap.

Amazingly, George hadn't aged at all in the five years since we'd last seen each other. Hair still a sandy brown, cut short without a trace of gray. Square face. Thick neck. Wire-rimmed glasses that made him look like a biker professor. He was still a physically impressive dude. Besides his height, his build was more muscle than fat, and I was reminded why he would be so valuable as a bodyguard for Global Talent.

It was kind of a joke at the time. I mean, on the surface, why would someone leave a job as an up-and-comer in a metropolitan police department to become a bodyguard for a bunch of teenyboppers? It seemed like a step down. But after fifteen minutes in that glorious chair, I was ready to chop off a pinkie toe to get some more of that imported leather. Plus, I found out later that George had upped his salary to close to ninety grand a year when he made the jump. And now he was no longer just rank-and-file. He was the VP of security for the entire agency. I guessed his salary had jumped to $150K or more.

He escorted me into his office, which boasted a dramatic view of downtown Orlando's Lake Eola. I could see the afternoon traffic snaking around the lake, the joggers, the dog walkers. It was another sunny June day in Central Florida, with the mercury topping ninety-seven degrees and the humidity at an arid 84 percent. We sat in front of his desk in a couple of high-priced leather-and-chrome director's chairs. These were a far cry from the seats in the reception area, but still better than anything in my apartment.

"You want somethin' to drink?" George said. "A Coke? Cappuccino?"

"Uh, you got a regular coffee?"

"Sure." He pressed a button on his phone and asked some assistant named Gary to fetch me a cup of joe: cream, no sugar. He looked up at me. "So, how you feelin'?"

"Me? Oh, I'm swell," I said. "Thanks for asking. You?"

"You wanna talk about it?"

"Would you?"

A beat. "Okay, then let's talk business."

I blinked at him. He didn't invite me here to talk about Bob? It took a moment to sink in. It was a refreshing change of pace and one I wasn't expecting. Well, if he didn't want to talk about Bob, what *did* he want to talk about? Apparently, he was just getting to that.

"One of the boys is missing," he said.

"Boys?"

Gary appeared silently through a back door with my coffee in a large Global Talent mug. I thanked him and took a sip. The coffee was as tasty as the reception chairs were comfortable. Hazelnut or something. Gary slipped out the way he came in and George pursed his lips.

"Maybe I should back up," he said. "What do you know about Global Talent?"

"A little. The same as most folks, I suppose." I told George what I knew. Global Talent was a talent management company. It showed up in the local papers every so often, usually when one of its clients got a Grammy nomination or something. George filled in the rest. Global's clients were mostly kids, plucked from the ranks of the local theme-park performers and cadre of kid actors and singers working at Orlando's Disney and Nickelodeon soundstages. The kids were packaged into groups, taught some synchronized dance moves, and marketed relentlessly to the buyers of *Tiger Beat* magazine. The place was owned by Mario "Eli" Elizondo and competed with the other Orlando-based teen-talent empires, Johnny Wright's company and Lou Pearlman's Trans Continental. Wright managed some of the hottest performers around, including Justin Timberlake and Britney Spears. Pearlman was famous for creating 'N Sync, the Backstreet Boys, and O-Town. I had heard of some of these artists. Some I had no clue about.

"Our hottest act right now is Boyz Klub," George said. "Spelled with a *z* and a *k*. We broke them first in Europe, and the reaction was phenomenal. Their first album here in the States went platinum and they've just recorded their second. It goes on sale next month, the release timed to the start of a major concert tour. Everything's great except for one thing: one of the Boyz is missing."

"What do you mean 'missing'?" I said.

"Gone. AWOL. No one's seen him for over a week." George leaned forward onto his massive knees. "Here's the problem. If we don't find him, the whole tour's in jeopardy. That puts the album in jeopardy. That screws our marketing deal with Pepsi. And McDonald's. We're not just talking millions at risk here. It's tens of millions. Maybe hundreds of millions."

I nodded thoughtfully, as if I had some inkling of the high-stakes world of pop music. "You have no idea where he is?"

"TJ is . . . ah, TJ's a free spirit. A good kid, really. Kind. Thoughtful. Never let the fame go to his head. But he's got a different drummer, man." George sat back and rubbed the bridge of his nose. "He did this once before, after we got back from Europe but before our first U.S. tour. Showed up at the chartered jet ten minutes before we were supposed to leave. He'd been in the desert *meditating* for eight days. He looked like shit."

"So what are you worried about?" I said. "What makes you think he won't do the same this time?"

"We don't know. He didn't tell anybody he was leaving, didn't say where he was going, or when he'd be back. With so much at stake, people like to have assurances."

"Okay, George. Let's cut to the chase."

He narrowed his eyes at me, a hint of a smile at one corner of his mouth. "I want you to find him."

I figured as much. No way. "Look, Georgie—"

George held up both index fingers. "Don't say anything yet. I can make it worth your while."

"Money ain't exactly my biggest concern right now."

"Really? What are you living on? You quit before your twenty years were up. You got no retirement. I don't remember you as the investing type. So, what? Just drawing down your savings? How long will that last?"

"Long enough."

George pursed his lips and considered me. "What if you actually live for a while? Happens all the time. Praise Jesus, the doctors gave him six months and here he is five years later. You want to be sick *and* broke?"

I didn't like where this was going. He said he didn't want to talk about Bob, but here I was—again—talking about him. "Look, George, I appreciate the concern, but you don't need to worry about me."

George leaned forward again. "What about Jennifer? Don't you want to leave anything for her?"

I wasn't about to discuss my daughter with George Neuheisel. It pissed me off that he even dared to bring her up. "Why me, George? Hunh? I'm not even a licensed PI. I'm a retired cop with cancer in my brain. I'm probably the last guy you'd want for a job like this."

George sat back again. Took a deep breath. "You're the best cop I ever worked with and that's a fact. The tightest investigator. Remember when we needed to find that kid for the Ramirez trial? Everyone said he was gone, man. Invisible. But you found him, dude. That was all you. And what about 'Juan the Don'? Hell, that practically made you famous. Picture in the paper. CNN. They even put you on Discovery Channel."

"That wasn't me. That was a reenactment."

"But it was *about* you. What you did. Don't worry about the license. You can go on the Global payroll. Security consultant or something. And, yeah, there are some good PIs in town. With my budget, I could even afford the best from out of town. But we need to keep this very low profile so we don't spook the sponsors. And I've got a gut instinct that tells me you're the guy. I believe in fate, Mikey. Maybe God put that cancer in your brain so you'd quit the department and be available for this job. Who knows."

Yeah. If that was really God's plan, I wish He would've just hit me with a bus and been done with it. George had really become a myopic crackpot. Did he really just suggest that my terminal cancer had a reason, and it was to put me in a position to help him find a runaway millionaire kid who likes to meditate? I just stared at him.

"You're nuts. Really, George. You're over the edge."

"Mikey. Think about it. Don't say no yet. Think about Jennifer."

Now I took a deep breath. "How much?"

"You find him and it's fifty grand."

I let out a low whistle. That was well above the going rate for any private investigation I had ever heard of.

"It gets better," George said. "You find him before the tour starts and there's another fifty. You find him before the tour starts *and* make sure he's on the plane, you get two-fifty large, plus expenses."

I blinked. Had I heard that right? "Two hundred and fifty thousand dollars?"

"This is very important to Eli."

"Damn, George."

"Think about it, Mikey. Just think about it."

Oh, I'd think about it, all right. Whether I wanted to or not.

CHAPTER 2

I was late, as usual. If there was one thing that Becky could count on during our marriage, it was that she could never count on me. But she was quiet as I stepped up to the table. She had become a lot more tolerant since Bob showed up. Plus, no matter how much I deserved it, she tended to bite her tongue whenever Jennifer was around. Not that it really mattered. Jennifer was fifteen years old and well aware of her dad's shortcomings. I greeted them both and slid into the booth.

It was Becky's idea. With Bob's arrival and the doctors unable to give me any kind of accurate timeline, Becky thought I should spend some quality time with Jennifer, before it was too late. I protested. I'm sure that the last thing Jennifer wanted to do with her summer vacation was spend it with her dying dad, whom she didn't even like very much. On top of everything else, let's add resentment to Jennifer's long list of unresolved feelings about me.

But Becky insisted and I'd learned long ago that when Becky gets squared on an idea, she'll make it happen sooner or later. Arguing only prolonged the inevitable. So I acquiesced and agreed to meet them at Bennigan's for dinner and to pick up Jennifer for a four-week visit to Bob-Land.

"Mike . . . Hi," Becky said, starting to rise. "How are you?" She winced, obviously not intending to ask that question. Before she could apologize, I held up a hand.

"I'm good," I said. "Don't get up. You guys order yet?"

Becky gave me a sad smile as I slid into the booth across from them. "Just drinks," she said. She elbowed Jennifer, who finally met my eyes.

"Hi," Jennifer said.

"Hey," I replied, and was struck by just how much Jennifer looked like Becky. Both had brown hair with red highlights, Becky's cut shorter than Jennifer's shoulder-length style. They each had an attractive, thin face with a rounded chin and tapered nose.

Becky was still beautiful. The only signs of aging were the little crinkles at the corners of her eyes, which somehow made her look more beautiful in a mature, confident way.

Jennifer was growing into an attractive woman in her own right. At fifteen, she was still coltish with gangly limbs, but I could see the woman she would become. Once the braces came off and she grew into her frame, she would be a knockout.

Jennifer continued looking at me before glancing back down at the table and taking a sip of her diet soda. That was when I remembered the only part of me that she had inherited—her eyes. She had wide-set, brooding eyes the color of sunlit emeralds.

The waiter showed up, a kid barely older than Jennifer, and took our orders.

The whole point of this dinner was for Becky to hand off Jennifer. Once we said hello and ordered, we had pretty much exhausted the possible topics for conversation. Becky and I were used to uncomfortable silences. They had been a staple of our marriage. But I felt bad for the kid.

"So how was school this year?" I said and sipped the beer I had ordered.

Jennifer twisted her lips, chewing the inside of her cheek. "Fine."

"You're gonna be a junior, right?"

She fiddled with the crumpled wrapper from her straw and sighed, a sigh that said I had guessed wrong and she knew I would. "Sophomore."

"Right." I nodded and winced inside. "Driver's ed this year. That's cool."

She looked up at me through her eyebrows and clicked her

tongue. I got the message. Don't use words like *cool*. Don't try to talk like me. Don't try to "relate" to me. Fine with me, except I was using *cool* long before you were even born, kiddo.

"They don't have driver's ed anymore," she said.

"What? Since when?"

She shrugged and sipped her soda, looking away at the televisions behind the bar.

"Budget cuts," Becky offered.

I nodded and took another sip.

"Jennifer made the JV soccer team," Becky said.

"Oh, yeah?" I said. "That's great." Another sip. "Really great." If Jennifer heard me, I couldn't tell. Clearly the silent commercials on the bar TVs were a lot more interesting than me. I looked over at Becky and raised my eyebrows, an *I told you this was a bad idea* gesture that I knew she would understand. She exhaled and shot me a defiant look to keep trying.

Maybe later. "How's Wayne?" I said as nonchalantly as I could, taking another sip.

"He's fine," Becky said, equally nonchalant.

"Bone business doing well?"

About two years after our divorce Becky had met and married Wayne Graddo, by all accounts a decent guy. Wayne was an orthopedic surgeon and made way more jack than I ever would as a city cop, even as a detective. They—Becky, Jennifer, Wayne, and, on alternating weekends, Wayne's two younger boys—lived in a five-bedroom house on a lake in Windermere. Becky drove a Lexus SUV and, since she didn't have to work, devoted her considerable free time to worthy causes such as literacy and homelessness. When Becky remarried, it had stung. Not so much because she was now with another man but more the fact that she had clearly traded up. Guys' egos are amazingly selective. We all think we're the alpha catch and that any woman should feel lucky to have us. But when confronted with a truckload of empirical evidence that Wayne was clearly better than me in all measurable criteria—salary, emotional maturity, looks, parenting skills, golf handicap—it was pretty hard to swallow.

"Wayne's doing fine," Becky repeated. "He just opened a new office on Semoran."

"Yeah? What's that mean, a new summer house in the Carolinas?"

Becky shook her head. "Mike . . . don't. Not now."

"He already has a summer house in the Carolinas," Jennifer said, still watching the televisions behind the bar. I took a long pull on the beer and drained it.

The food finally appeared and we were saved from more charming conversation by the busywork of eating. When I was done, I excused myself to the men's room. I washed my hands and splashed water on my face, staring at myself in the mirror. I needed a haircut. There was now more gray than brown on my scalp, and I always thought a trim made me look younger. But who was I kidding? I was forty-two years old, not quite six feet tall, and 195 pounds. I was on the downslope of life and looked it. Dark bags under my eyes. Soft cheeks. Receding hairline. Brain tumor.

I ran my fingers over the area of my head that had been shaved for the biopsy. The hair had mostly grown back in the patch over the left ear, but I could feel the little scar, still tender from the procedure. How much time did I really have? The doctors all tried to avoid the question. They hated being wrong, even if they were wrong on the good side, because it just illuminated how powerless they really were. But none of the estimates gave me more than a year.

When I returned to the table, I saw that Becky had already paid the check and they were waiting for me by the front door. We walked out together.

"Jenn, why don't you get your bag?" Becky said, clearly a signal that she wanted to talk privately to me for a moment. Jennifer headed for the Lexus without a word. I watched her, saying nothing. This was Becky's show and she should have the first line.

"Don't blow this, Mike. That's your daughter. Think how you'll want her to remember you. How she'll describe you to her children someday."

"She'll describe Wayne."

"Mike, please . . ." Then I noticed that Becky was crying, trying to hold it back. But now the emotions were starting to bubble out faster than she could keep them in. "It's not fair."

I nodded. "For once, I think we agree on something."

Becky wiped her eyes and reached for my hand. She placed her other hand on my cheek. It was warm and soft. "I always . . ."

"I know," I said. "It's okay."

Then Becky hugged me, a desperate hug driven not from passion but from fear. A clutching embrace where she could bury her sobs in my shoulder. I rubbed her back and tried my best to avoid looking at Jennifer. After a moment, Becky recovered and suddenly broke away, saying nothing more, and strode purposefully toward Jennifer, who stood with her duffel next to my pickup. Becky grabbed her arm and leaned in close, whispering something to Jennifer, some last-minute instruction. Jennifer made no response, only looked at her feet. Becky shook Jennifer's arm slightly and the conversation was over.

In another few seconds Becky was in the Lexus and on her way out of the parking lot, offering one last furrowed glance at me through the tempered windshield. Then she was gone.

I unlocked the truck's passenger door and Jennifer climbed wordlessly into the cab. By the time I slid into the driver's seat, she had pulled out a portable CD player and earphones. I cranked the ignition.

She looked out the passenger window and spoke. "If you think you're gonna suddenly be Father of the Year or something, like some lame after-school special . . . it's way too late for that." She put in the earphones, cranked up the volume, and leaned back, eyes closed.

I put the truck in gear and thought, that's my girl.

The evening went about as well as dinner until nine thirty, when Cam showed up with a large pepperoni pie and a bottle of Chianti.

"Cam," Jennifer said. "Thank God you're here." They embraced.

After my divorce from Becky, Camilla Thackery-Hart and I had been married for four whirlwind years before we, too, divorced, almost two years ago. But we had remained friends—actual, honest-to-God buddies. Better friends now than when we were married.

Cam had blond hair, long, bronzed legs, and full lips that parted to reveal a crooked smile that contained just a hint of mischief. After being humbled by the quality of Becky's new husband, my ego had come full circle from thinking I was God's gift to wondering what in hell a woman like Cam saw in me. But Cam was and would always be a mystery. Her continuing interest in me was just part of the puzzle.

"Here," Cam said, digging in her large designer purse. "Have you seen this one? You *have* to see this one. You haven't seen it yet, have you?"

She produced a DVD of some teen romance I had never heard of and Jennifer's eyes lit up.

"Oh my God . . . ," Jennifer said. "You're such the bomb." She snatched the DVD and headed for the living room. It was no wonder that Jennifer gravitated toward Cam. Where Becky represented stability and domesticity, Cam was spontaneous, brash, and reckless. She was also eight years younger than Becky, which added to her mystique. A statuesque beauty, Cam dressed in designer clothes, usually black, and was always up on the latest pop culture. I saw more of Jennifer during my marriage to Cam than I had since she was four years old. Cam taught Jennifer how to put on makeup. Took her shopping and bought her a pair of Prada shoes. Since our split, I had hardly seen Jennifer at all. Divorcing Camilla was just one more of my many transgressions.

"Michael William Garrity," Cam said, laying a palm on my kitchen counter. "You look like crap."

"Nice to see you, too," I said.

"Here, have a slice. Seriously. Your hair's too long. You look exhausted." She glanced down in my garbage pail and spotted the Twinkies box. "Nice. I see that you're finally trying that new all-Twinkie diet I've read so much about. How's that going?"

"Cam . . . ," I said, smiling in spite of her chiding.

"No, seriously, Michael. How's that Twinkie diet going? Did your doctor recommend that?"

"Yeah. Eat two Twinkies and call me in the morning."

"That isn't going to help you."

"No kidding." She knew what I meant. Nothing was going to help me.

She sighed dramatically and looked me in the eye for a long moment. Then she shoved a slice of pizza into my mouth and kept pushing until almost the whole piece was crammed in, grease oozing down my chin. She was laughing, and if my mouth weren't full of scalding hot pizza, I would have been laughing, too.

"It's the newest thing," she said as I tried to chew. "The all-pizza diet." She took the pizza, the Chianti, and an empty glass into the living room to join Jennifer in front of the TV.

Cam was the buffer that Jennifer and I both needed. The evening passed pleasantly and the movie wasn't even as bad as I thought it would be. Jennifer loved it. Cam and Jennifer lounged on opposite ends of the couch, their legs lying casually parallel to each other.

When the movie ended, Jennifer and Cam talked a little about movies and boys, some of which I would probably rather not have heard. Jennifer showed such little regard for my role as her parent, she spoke as if I weren't even in the room. I know, being as absent in her life as I was, I had no right to feel protective, but it's still hard to sit and listen to your daughter describe some boy in her algebra class as "such a hottie." I tried not to listen, concentrating instead on the Chianti and channel surfing.

My ears perked up, however, when Jennifer mentioned her new favorite band, Boyz Klub.

"They are *so* cute," she gushed. "Especially TJ."

"What's so great about Boyz Klub?" I asked. An awkward silence fell over the room. They looked at me like I had just farted.

"You wouldn't understand," Jennifer said.

"That's a given," I said. "But all the same, I'm curious. What's so great about them?"

"They're four cute guys," Cam said. "Who can sing and dance."

"Yeah," I said. "But there are a lot of bands like that. What makes Boyz Klub any better than, say, the Backyard Boys or—"

"Back*street* Boys," Jennifer corrected.

"Right. Them. Or that other one, y'know . . ."

"'N Sync," Cam said.

"Yeah," I said. "Them."

Jennifer exchanged a look with Cam to confirm that I was really serious. Cam raised her eyebrows. *If he really wants to know, tell him.*

"Backstreet Boys are still okay," Jennifer said. "I mean, they're kinda cute and all, but they're getting old and married and stuff. I still listen to 'em, but Boyz Klub are younger. More on the edge."

"They all sound the same to me," I said.

"They would," Jennifer said with a roll of the eyes.

I couldn't let it go. "Aren't they all part of the same marketing machine? I mean, don't the same people write all their songs and record them and manage them and—"

"You are *so* wrong," Jennifer said with a little too much defensiveness. "Boyz Klub write almost all their own songs. They sound *totally* different."

"Okay. Relax. And you like TJ?" I said.

"I guess . . ."

"You mentioned him by name."

"So?"

"So, what makes him the one you mention by name?"

Jennifer chewed the inside of her cheek. "Why are you asking me all this?"

"I'm curious. I want to know more about your interests."

"Bullshit," Jennifer said.

I opened my mouth to chastise her use of profanity, but couldn't come up with anything that didn't sound hypocritical. While I hesitated, the phone rang. Jennifer looked at her watch.

"That's Gwen," she said, bounding up. "I'll take it in my room." And then she was gone, barricaded behind the closed door of my guest bedroom.

Cam tilted the last drop of Chianti out of the bottle into her mouth. She looked at me and smiled.

"Well, this is going well," I said.

"She's fifteen," Cam said.

I sighed and rubbed my face. When I took my hands away, Cam was still looking at me.

"What?" I said.

"You mind if I stay tonight?"

My eyebrows went up. "What about Ted?"

"Todd." She threw her head back and exhaled loudly. "Todd is a work in progress. I just don't have the energy anymore."

"So he's gone?"

"Adios, muchacho."

"And . . . what, you think you can just snap your fingers and I'll sleep with you?"

Cam made a show of placing the bottle on the coffee table and sauntering over to me. She plopped down in my lap and put her arms around me.

"Something like that," she said.

"I have some self-respect, you know."

She kissed my forehead. "I know."

"I'm not some boy toy at your beck and call."

Her lips brushed my cheek. "Of course not."

"I'm your *ex*-husband. Ex."

"Rhymes with *sex*," she said, and pressed her lips against mine.

CHAPTER 3

Cam and I had been sleeping together about once every three months for the past year. It was actually kind of nice and I didn't feel as cheap as I should have. Cam always initiated it—I wouldn't have the nerve or be willing to risk the rejection. Plus, I never knew when she was between her many relationships.

I opened my eyes and the digital clock on my nightstand read 3:42. My head was killing me. The headaches were always worse in the mornings, gradually improving as the day wore on. Bob was raging this morning. My skull felt like it was in a pneumatic press.

I swung my feet onto the floor and inhaled sharply, concentrating to keep my head up. Leaning down increased the pain. Putting my head between my knees would be enough to make me pass out. I braced myself and shuffled around the room with my eyes half-closed. When I reached the other side of the bed, I noticed that Cam wasn't there. The door to the bathroom was ajar and a thin bar of fluorescent light spilled onto the floor.

I inched closer to the door and saw Cam's bare foot through the gap. Her toes were painted a deep burgundy. I heard sniffling.

I took another half step. In four years of marriage I couldn't recall a single time I had heard Cam cry. She had gotten emotional, sure, but I was now hearing true, old-fashioned sobs for the first time. I had a pretty good idea why she was crying. And why she was doing it in the middle of the night when she thought I was asleep.

I stood there for another moment like some kind of audio voyeur, listening to her cry, before I turned around and slipped back to bed. Bob would have to wait. I closed my eyes in a futile attempt to reclaim sleep. It seemed like a long time before Cam came back to bed, but for all I knew it was only a few minutes. I heard the bathroom light click off and felt the bed sag as Cam crept under the blanket. I didn't hear any more crying. Not even a sniffle.

I assume I eventually did drift back off to sleep because when I opened my eyes, the sun was peeking through the blinds. I reached a hand back and didn't find Cam so I knew she was up. Bob was wishing me his favorite "good morning" by continuing the headache from earlier.

Slowly, I swung my legs out of bed and steadied my hand on the nightstand. Two deep breaths and I pulled myself up and found the bathroom. As I walked, I felt the nausea from the pain welling and I made it to the toilet just as my guts erupted.

As I came out of the bedroom and into the three-foot-by-three-foot nook that pretended to be a hallway between the two bed-rooms, I paused. Just around the corner, Cam and Jennifer were at the kitchen table. I heard spoons clinking on bowls and cereal-box liners being crinkled. I pressed back against the near wall so they wouldn't see me.

"You should just ask him," Cam said, obviously chewing.

"I don't think he wants to talk about it," Jennifer said.

A pause. "Probably not. But you should ask him anyway."

"I don't know . . ."

"Look, he has cancer and that sucks for everyone, especially him. But you're allowed to have questions," Cam said. "He may not want to answer. But you have a right to ask."

"I don't even know exactly what kind of cancer he has." I heard Jennifer open and close the refrigerator.

"You mean what kind of brain tumor?"

"Yeah," Jennifer said. "I mean, I suppose there's more than one."

"There are lots." I heard Cam sigh.

Now Jennifer paused. "Is his bad?"

"Yeah. Not the worst, but it's pretty bad." Cam cleared her throat. "There are four classes of severity and your dad's is a class-three, the second-worst. It's malignant, which means it's life-threatening and he'll eventually die if it isn't treated."

"Do they know . . . ," Jennifer said. "I mean, when do they say . . ." She didn't know how to ask the question.

I imagined Cam shrugging, a gesture I knew well. "Maybe a year. Probably less. And the last few months won't be very nice."

There was a fairly long silence, maybe thirty seconds or more. I couldn't tell if they were still eating. I didn't hear any more clinking or chewing. Jennifer finally spoke.

"So what's he gonna do about it?"

Another pause. "*That's* the question you should ask him. That's what we all want to know."

I jiggled the bedroom door handle and closed it loudly enough that I knew they would hear it. Then I turned the corner and stepped into the kitchen.

"Morning," I said.

They greeted me and I noticed that both of them had only eaten half of their bowls of Cheerios. Jennifer put hers in the sink.

"I have to get ready for work," she announced, and disappeared into her bedroom.

Cam studied me. "How you feeling?"

I poured a cup from a pot of coffee that Cam had thoughtfully made. "Peachy."

"Headache?"

"Just the usual wake-up call," I said, then sipped.

She crossed her arms, considering something. She looked typically stunning this morning. Black pantsuit, probably Gucci, which made her blond hair even brighter.

"I want you to take something," she said, standing and opening a large black briefcase on the counter.

"Cam, you can't do that."

"I know I have some in here," she said to herself. "Ah. These." She held out two small, blue boxes of pharmaceutical samples. The product label read Zuraxx.

"You do remember that I'm a cop."

"Ex-cop. Like ex-husband." She continued holding the boxes out. "Are you going to arrest me or take the pills?"

Handing out prescription-medication samples to anyone except doctors was an excellent way for her not only to lose her job as a pharmaceutical sales rep but also wind up in a cell. But, after a moment's hesitation, I took the pills from her.

"They're new," she said, closing up her briefcase. "For migraines. If they work, I can get you more."

"Thanks." Cam knew that the prescription painkiller that my neurologist recommended was about a hundred bucks for a week's worth, with no generic alternative. They worked pretty well, but I didn't have an unlimited supply of cash, so I often skipped a dose.

"Hey, Jen!" Cam called. "You almost ready? I've got an appointment." She turned to me. "I offered to drop Jennifer at the mall for work."

Jennifer emerged from her room and headed for the front door. Cam gave me a peck on the cheek and squeezed my arm.

"When are you off?" I yelled after them, meaning Jennifer. But they both turned back. Cam smiled as if she were remembering the familiar morning scenes of our marriage: me coming in from a graveyard shift and her rushing out the door to appointments.

"Four o'clock," Jennifer said.

"You need a ride?" I said.

"Dunno. I'll call if I do." And then they were both out the door, two estrogen blurs rushing down the stairs to the parking lot.

I stood there for a moment, struck by the sudden silence of the apartment, empty except for me and Bob. I decided a shower would be the first order of business, followed by a hearty breakfast of Zuraxx and coffee.

When I stepped back into the little hall alcove, I saw Jennifer's door half-open. In her room, I noticed a small stack of CDs on the dresser. I debated a moment, assessing the level of privacy I was about to invade, and stepped into her room.

She had been here less than twenty-four hours and the room was already a disaster: clothes strewn all over the bed, a quantity of cosmetic supplies to make a movie star jealous, hairbrushes, lotions, *Seventeen* and *Teen Beat* magazines, and shoes. More shoes than she could wear in a year. I stepped over to the dresser and flipped through the CDs. The second one in the stack was *Welcome to the KlubHouse* by Boyz Klub.

I studied the faces of the four young men who smoldered on the jewel-case cover. One of them was the prodigal TJ, although I had no idea which. Turning the case over, I read the titles of the tracks. They all seemed the same to me. I couldn't tell which were ballads and which were up-tempo, if they even classified music like that anymore. At the bottom of the back cover was a colorful invitation to join the official Boyz Klub Fan Klub.

As I looked at the case, my eye was caught by Jennifer's open purse sitting on the dresser next to the CDs. Before I could even stop myself, my finger was poking into the purse. I rationalized that I was looking for drugs, making sure my little girl was clean. But the truth was that I was snooping for information. Some clue or totem that would help me understand what kind of person she was. I didn't know my daughter very well, and that realization had left a dark, empty spot in the center of my chest, made more pronounced since yesterday afternoon. And our relationship wasn't exactly a TV sitcom where I could plop down on the couch and say, "What's on your mind, kitten?" Finding a copy of *Catcher in the Rye* or a SAVE THE WHALES button or a love note from a boy might fill that emptiness just a little, might help me decipher just who this Jennifer Garrity was. And, hey, I also wanted to know if there was a condom in there. I'm not sure if I wanted to find one or not.

I didn't find one.

My probe was interrupted by the sudden appearance of Jennifer in the doorway.

"I can't believe you!" she shrieked, eyes wide with rage.

"Jennifer—," I replied lamely.

She charged into the room and snatched the purse. "You find anything good?"

"Sorry."

"How 'bout my work ID?" She held up a name-badge pin defiantly. "It's a good thing I forgot it or I wouldn't have had to come back and help you go through my personal, private things."

"Jennifer—"

"You wanna know what's in here? Huh? How 'bout some gum?" She threw a pack of cinnamon gum at me hard enough that my chest stung. "No? Not what you wanted? How 'bout lipstick?" She chucked a metallic tube of lipstick at my head. I barely dodged it and heard it smack loudly into the wall behind me. "Not the lipstick? I know! You want my goddamn tampons! Here!" She hurled two tampons at me, and, inexplicably, I caught one.

"I hate you!" was her final comment on the matter before she turned and ran out of the apartment.

I took a deep breath. Looked down at the tampon in my hand. I placed it carefully on the dresser next to the CDs, which I restacked into a neat pile. I stepped out of the room and gently closed the door behind me.

I popped two of the Zuraxx and drained the cup of coffee. A minute later the phone was in my hand. A minute after that I was talking to George Neuheisel.

"George," I said. "It's Mike Garrity. I'll do it. I'll find the kid."

"It's so fucking unprofessional, I could vomit."

Other than a perfunctory greeting, those were the first words I ever heard from Mario "Eli" Elizondo. He was a short guy, maybe five-five. Maybe. He looked to be on the downside of forty, close to fifty. His hair and the mustache and goatee around his thin mouth were unnaturally black. A little too black for the wear on his skin. He was trim and wiry and gestured in jerky motions when he talked. His eyes were dark and narrowed into slits when he paused to think or waited for you to answer one of his questions.

He was sitting behind his barge of a desk. I was across from him in another of Global Talent's many imported, luxury ass-rests. The office was stupidly large, like something out of a movie. The wall to my right was almost completely glass, overlooking the buildings and parks of downtown Orlando. The opposite wall was a giant grid of state-of-the-art electronic gear. Television monitors, stereos, receivers, speakers, whatever. I had no idea. I don't know my woofer from my tweeter. I just knew there was some serious change invested in that wall of media.

The wall behind the desk was covered in photos of celebrities managed by Global Talent, celebrities that Global Talent would like to manage, and other celebrities that Eli had happened to grab for a quick photo op. Sprinkled in throughout the photos were framed gold and platinum albums from Global Talent artists.

I wasn't sure if Eli expected some sort of response to his statement. I looked over at George Neuheisel, who sat next to me, for some guidance. But his undivided attention was completely focused on his boss. Apparently, George didn't want to miss any of the wisdom from Mount Eli.

"Yeah," I offered.

Eli nodded, jerking a finger toward me. "He knows what's at stake here. He knows very well. That kid—" Eli stopped himself as his face flushed with sudden anger. "That kid doesn't have a grateful bone in his body. When I found him, he was making eight-fifty an hour singing songs in the park dressed like a fish. A fish!"

George nodded. Amen, Reverend.

Eli continued, "Now look at him. He's a millionaire. A millionaire!" The arms were jerking wider now, opening up. "How many twenty-two-year-olds have fourteen million in the bank? Not too fucking many, let me tell you." I knew the little speech was over when Eli slammed both palms down on his desk with a flat smack. His nostrils were flared as he looked from me to George and then back to me.

"We'll find him, Eli," George said. "Don't worry."

Eli nodded, more to himself than us. "Tell me how."

George looked at me expectantly. As a point of record, George and I had not yet discussed the details of the case. About five minutes after I'd walked into the office, George announced that Eli was thrilled I was coming in to help and wanted to meet with me right away. So here I was. I had no idea how I was going to find the kid. I wasn't a PI. I suddenly felt I had made a big mistake accepting the job. I was in over my head.

"I'll need some background," I said. "Everything you have on him. Addresses, phone numbers, bank accounts, credit cards. A guy like this, with the financial resources at his disposal, could be very tough to find. He could be drinking a daiquiri in Tahiti right now, paying all cash, and we'll never find him." Eli's eyes narrowed at me. "The way to find a guy like this isn't to follow the money. If he's smart, there'll be no money to follow. You find a guy like this by talking. Friends, family, girlfriend, bandmates, rabbi, whatever. Someone knows where he is, and that someone can be convinced to tell us."

Eli was motionless for a moment before he nodded again. "And how exactly," he said deliberately, "do you convince them to tell us?"

I shrugged. "Depends. Maybe we come up with a magic number with a dollar sign in front of it. Maybe we lean on them a little. Maybe we buy 'em a puppy. Everyone has a different button."

Eli nodded knowingly, his face expressionless. "Who do you want to talk to first?"

"Dunno. You tell me. You know him. Who *should* I talk to?"

Eli and George exchanged a look. Eli's head bobbed once.

"His mother," George said.

Now it was my turn to nod. "I'll need a list of everyone you can think of and how I can get in touch with them. Plus, I'll need to get into his house or apartment, if possible."

"George'll arrange it." Eli took a breath. "Will you want to interview the other Boyz?"

"The band?" I said.

Eli's head went down and up again.

"I would think so," I said.

"Okay. I suppose you will. We're just in final rehearsals, and with TJ missing, everything's been kind of tense. George'll get you in touch with them so it doesn't interfere. The last thing we need right now is another distraction." Eli leaned onto his desk. "We'll need you to sign a nondisclosure agreement. Any personal information you get about the band must remain private. For their own safety. They have some pretty enthusiastic fans."

"You wouldn't believe if I told you," George said.

"Plus," Eli said, "the band has a very specific image. All information released about them is tightly controlled. Disclosing any information about any of the Boyz outside our standard communication channels is off-limits. Even a little inconsistency or inaccuracy can tilt the image and jeopardize a hundred-million-dollar sponsorship deal. This tour must not be compromised." The eyes narrowed again. "You understand what I'm saying, right?"

"Everything stays in the family," I said.

Eli smiled. His teeth were perfect and white and in no way grown in his own mouth.

CHAPTER 4

TJ Sommerset loved his mother. Otherwise, he wouldn't have bought her a forty-five-hundred-square-foot cottage on a golf course in exclusive Isleworth. Located in southwest Orlando, Isleworth was the home of sports stars and movie actors, surgeons and magnates. It had to be quite a culture shock for Mrs. Sommerset, formerly of a rented duplex in lower-middle-class Pine Hills.

George arranged a meeting time and, presumably, a clearance through the impressive community gate. The guards were polite, but I saw them eyeing my beat-up truck as it sputtered past.

I had been inside the Isleworth gates once before, investigating a racketeering case while on loan from the Orlando Police Department to the Metropolitan Bureau of Investigation, or MBI, a multi-jurisdictional task force that covered a variety of Central Florida vice and organized crimes. The guy we were investigating ended up being found guilty of laundering a boatload of heroin money through a series of successful T-shirt and souvenir shops in the more touristy parts of town.

A perfectly manicured road wound through the community, with colossal Mediterranean-style mansions sprinkled on either side. Some were on the water. Most were on the golf course. A half dozen or more PGA heavyweights lived in here somewhere, including Tiger Woods and Mark O'Meara. Baseball stars with winter homes, movie actors with local roots such as Wesley Snipes—the neighborhood was a veritable who's who in Central Florida.

I followed George's directions and pulled into a long brick driveway that could have been a road itself. The drive led up to

Mrs. Sommerset's humble abode, a six-bedroom cottage overlooking a lake. A moment later I was stepping up the cobbled walkway to the front door, wondering just what the hell I was doing.

I rang the bell, which chimed three deep, resonant notes as if from an ancient European cathedral belfry. A few seconds later, one of the ornate, oversize double doors opened to reveal Mrs. Arlene Sommerset.

The surprisingly lovely Arlene Sommerset. I didn't know what to expect, but I guess I'd pictured someone older. I pegged her a few years past me, mid to late forties, and soft-featured in a pleasing, feminine way. Her hair was light brown and cut short but stylish, as was her outfit of khaki capri pants and a white T-shirt. Her brown eyes looked both young and old at the same time. She had a disarming, sincere smile that she offered as soon as she opened the door.

"You must be Mr. Garrity," she said softly, with the slight twang of an old-Florida Southern accent.

"Mike."

She led me through the house, which was decorated expensively, though tastefully. The heroin-money launderer had loaded his mansion with garish modern art and animal-print rugs. In contrast, the Sommerset décor wasn't meant to impress. It was meant to be comfortable and inviting, which it did with $10,000 sofas and a TV the size of my bedroom wall.

"Can I get you a drink?" she said as we passed through the kitchen. "Iced tea?"

"That would be great. Thanks."

I sat in the living room, looking out over the patio and the pool to the manicured lawn and small lake beyond. Arlene Sommerset brought my drink and sat in a nearby chair.

Even if I hadn't gone through a quick briefing on the band (and TJ in particular), I would still have been able to tell which of the four Boyz was her boy. Mother and son had similar faces, although TJ's was thinner. Same tanned complexion. Same eyes that hinted at both innocence and experience. Looking at her, seeing his face in hers, I realized how gentle and feminine his features were.

"You're here about TJ," she said evenly, as a statement, while I took a sip of freshly brewed iced tea.

"Yes, ma'am," I said, falling back on habitual cop politeness. "Everyone at Global Talent is concerned. They asked me to help."

"Arlene," she said, echoing my request to be called Mike. "Okay. What can I do?"

I paused a beat and opted for the direct approach. "Where is he?"

Her eyebrows went up. "What makes you think I know?"

"Don't you?"

She considered me for a moment. "Did you want lemon in your tea? I completely forgot to ask. We have the most wonderful Meyer lemon tree in the backyard."

"No, thanks. This is perfect."

Clearly she wasn't worried about her son's sudden disappearance. Dusting off an old cop trick, I paused, looking at her pleasantly but patiently. A particularly effective interviewing technique is the skillful use of silences. Most people are uncomfortable with silences and will talk just to fill them. I waited, sipping my tea.

"I don't know where he is, Mr. Garrity," she said finally, meeting my gaze. "And, even if I did know, I don't think I'd tell you."

"Oh? Why not?"

"Because Eli Elizondo couldn't care less about my son, except for his ability to line his pockets."

I nodded, not doubting her for a second. "As I understand it, TJ is contractually obligated for this tour. He's missing rehearsals, promotional events, photo shoots. He's costing the company money."

"The amount of money he's made for that company, they owe him some downtime before he goes back into the machine for two or three years."

"I was told it was an eight-month tour," I said.

"U.S. Then there's Japan. And Australia. And Europe. Then the awards shows on TV. A new album. Recording sessions. Shooting new videos. Interviews. It's a roller coaster with no end. Sometimes you just have to step off the ride so you don't throw up."

"He's pretty well compensated for the hassle."

"He made enough money on the first album that he'll be rich the rest of his life. He was smart with his money. He doesn't need more. What he needs is a vacation."

I drained the tea. "Arlene, I understand. I do. But the company is worried. They have a lot invested in this tour and no one's heard from him in a couple of weeks." I could hear a faint clinking noise, which I realized was the ice in my glass. Looking down, I saw my hand trembling slightly.

"He'll be there," she said. "Before the tour starts."

"Perhaps we could call him on the phone, get him to tell us that. Have him tell Eli that. It would make everyone feel better." I heard a high-pitched hum, very soft, from somewhere nearby. I glanced around and didn't see anything.

"I told you. I don't know where he is."

"I think you do." The hum was growing louder and it dawned on me that it was coming from inside my own head.

Arlene Sommerset frowned at me. "Like I said, even if I did, hull poor dunn liffer nash ven."

I blinked at her. Her mouth was moving but the sounds coming out were completely unintelligible. I blinked again and saw her expression change. She leaned forward, a question crinkling her brow.

Her face grew smaller as the edges of my vision darkened. I swallowed and heard my glass of ice shatter on the tile. I felt her fingers on my forearm. She spoke again, now sounding like a recording at half speed with long, stretched vowels. Muffled, like under a pillow.

I pitched forward off the couch. The darkness at the edges of my vision expanded and, a moment later, swallowed me whole.

"Mike? Are you with us? Mike?"

I opened and closed my eyes a few times, making sure they worked before I tried to figure out where I was. I held them open and determined that I was lying on my back, staring up through gauzy vision at a textured ceiling with a nice oak-and-brass paddle fan.

It was Arlene Sommerset's voice I heard.

"Mike?"

My mouth was parched, but I was able to croak out an audible "Yeah . . ."

"Are you okay?"

"I dunno," I said, trying to sit up. She pushed me back down, a little too easily.

"Relax. Don't move. You're probably still groggy and feel like you got hit by a truck."

That was a pretty accurate description. My joints ached and muscles throbbed. And I had a hard time focusing my eyes.

"Here," she said, offering me a flexible straw in a glass. I put my lips on the straw and drank a long pull of cool water. It helped. A lot. "Just relax. Close your eyes. You're okay now."

I wanted to get up. Get out of here and go home. I was embarrassed and more than a little scared. But even more than that I was exhausted. Against my better judgment, I followed her suggestion and closed my eyes.

When I opened them again, it was still light out, so I couldn't have been out that long. Although my body still told me that someone had crumpled me up like a piece of paper and then unwadded me, I felt considerably more like myself. I sat up on the couch, rubbed my eyes, and looked around.

Arlene Sommerset was not in the room. A puffy, little white dog sat on the floor, panting at me curiously. I regarded it with a raised eyebrow and eased myself into a standing position.

"Good morning," Arlene Sommerset said, walking through the kitchen, drying her hands on a dish towel.

"Morning? Jesus. How long was I out?"

"Just an expression. You've been asleep a little over an hour. You still thirsty?"

"Yeah . . ."

"Orange juice would be good." She opened the closet-sized refrigerator door. "I've got some fresh squeezed in here somewhere."

I noticed a fresh Band-Aid on the heel of my palm. It was tender to the touch. I winced.

"You cut yourself on the glass," Arlene said. "When you fell. It's not bad. I cleaned it out for you."

"Thanks." I took two steps toward her. "Listen, I'm really sorry about—"

"So," she said, looking into the fridge, "is it epilepsy or brain cancer? Or something else?"

I froze, surprised by the question and the casualness with which it was asked.

"Ah, here it is." She emerged from the fridge with a plastic pitcher of juice and poured me a glass. She walked it over, and as I took it, she said, "So?"

"Cancer."

She nodded. "Primary or secondary?"

"Primary."

"C'mon. Sit down. Drink your juice."

She led me back to the couch and sat next to me. I took a sip. I could tell it was fresh squeezed. Sweet and pulpy.

"You called George?" I said.

She shook her head. "I didn't call anyone."

"Not even 911?"

"You opened your eyes and spoke to me within a minute or so. I knew it was over. The best thing for you was to just rest awhile."

I took another small sip of juice. "How did you know?"

She smoothed a wrinkle in her pants. "My husband had liver cancer. Very advanced by the time we found it. Before the end, it metastasized to his brain as a secondary tumor. He had seizures, too. I got to be something of an expert."

"I'm sorry."

She nodded appreciatively. "It was harder on TJ. He was only twelve at the time. He saw his daddy convulsing on the floor more than once."

"Did I . . . convulse?"

She offered a reassuring smile. "A little. Not so bad."

"I'm sorry you had to see that. And that I broke glass all over your floor. I—"

"It's okay. Drink your juice."

I did as instructed. Then I placed the glass, carefully, on the coffee table.

"Are you on any meds for it?" she said. "Arthur was on Tegretol for a while. Dilantin, too."

I shook my head. "This is my first. I knew they were likely, based on . . . the tumor's location." I almost said *based on Bob's location,* but caught myself. I wasn't sure I could adequately explain Bob to Arlene Sommerset.

"You need to call your neurologist. Tell him that it's started."

It's started. Or, more accurately, it's ending. I nodded slowly and could feel Bob in there like a peach pit, smiling at the big show he'd put on, planning his next performance.

"You shouldn't drive," Arlene said. "I'll take you."

"No—"

"Or I could call a cab—"

"No. I'll be okay. I'll get home. Put my feet up. Go see my doctor in the morning. You've done enough. I'm sorry I bothered you."

She walked me to the front door, but stopped before we reached it.

"Why are you looking for TJ?" she said.

"Global needs him for the tour."

She shook her head. "I know why *they're* looking. Why are *you*?"

A pause. "If I find him, I'll make a lot of money."

She regarded me coolly. "So it's about the money."

"Isn't everything?"

"No, Mr. Garrity, I don't think it is." She opened the door. "And I don't think you think so, either."

I took a step. "A man in my situation has priorities other than money, right?"

"Something like that. I do have some experience with this. When Arthur died, we didn't have two pennies to rub together. But all the money in the world wouldn't have made any difference."

I passed through the door and started down the cobbled walkway to the driveway. After a few steps I stopped and turned back.

Arlene Sommerset was still in the open doorway, hand on the knob, watching me leave.

"If you talk to TJ," I said, "tell him that I know a girl who would really like to meet him."

"I'll tell him. If I talk to him." She watched me for a moment longer, then slowly closed the door.

CHAPTER 5

When I got home, there were two messages on my answering machine. One from George asking how the interview with Arlene went, and one from Cam. I played Cam's twice.

"Michael William Garrity. What the hell were you thinking? Just when I think you can't do any more to damage your relationship with Jen . . . She's beyond pissed, y'know, and I can't say I blame her. She says she won't stay with you tonight and refuses to call her mother. Said she'd sleep on the street first, and I think she actually means it. I'll put her up at my place tonight. Have a heart-to-heart. She'll be back under your roof by tomorrow. Just stay outta her room, 'kay? Go in there again and it's justifiable homicide. Thanks again for last night. Gotta run." Beep.

So it was just me and Bob for the evening. I called George back. Told him that Arlene said she didn't know where TJ was. I wasn't convinced she was telling the truth. He told me he had prepared the background file I wanted and I could pick it up anytime tomorrow. Then he reminded me of the tour start date. Again.

The next call was to my neurologist's office. I talked to the scheduler and got an appointment for first thing in the morning. Then I got a highball glass from the cupboard and filled it with Jim Beam. I downed the drink in three large gulps, standing in my kitchen. I poured another and brought it with me to the living room. By the time the second glass was drained, I was out cold, snoring fitfully on my couch.

I woke the next morning, still completely dressed—even my

shoes—and noted pleasantly that Bob had spared me the usual skull-splitting wake-up call today. Probably sleeping late after his big show yesterday.

An hour and a half later I was in an exam room in the doctor's office. My neurologist, Dr. Tanner, came in hurriedly. He was about my age but with chiseled features and in better shape. He wore glasses that slipped down his nose. When he looked up at me over those glasses, as was his habit—his eyes serious with more knowledge about my health than I'll ever have—my stomach always did an *Oh, shit* spin.

He greeted me and took a moment to review my chart, flipping pages and nodding. He ran me through the usual battery of tests: penlight in the eyes; follow the finger (my favorite); look over here, look over there; count backward from one hundred (he always stops me in the low eighties); touch your nose; etc.

He asked about the biopsy scar on the side of my head, an inch and a half above my left ear. Poked at it. Seemed satisfied it was healing okay.

"Tell me about the seizure," he said.

I did, as much as I could, considering I didn't remember any of it. Mostly, I remembered the sensations just prior: the trembling, the hum in my ears, that I suddenly couldn't understand the English language.

"Those are called auras," he said. "Hints that a seizure is imminent. A lot of people never get any warning. If this is your pattern, you're actually lucky." Yeah, I thought, some people win the lottery, I get auras with my seizures. Whoopee. He continued, "An aura will help you prepare for it. If you're driving, stop. If you're standing, sit down. Get away from hard surfaces or sharp objects. Basically, safeguard yourself."

He reminded me that the brain's temporal lobe, where Bob lives, is involved with the understanding of sounds and spoken words. I may run into more episodes where I can't understand what people are saying. He recommended that I carry a card with a short explanation that I can hand to people when it happens.

He wrote me a scrip for an antiseizure medication and went through the impressive list of possible side effects: double vision, impaired balance and coordination, dizziness, drowsiness, tremors, headache, and nausea. He told me to keep track of any side effects and let him know. There were a lot of drugs on the market and sometimes it took a few tries to find the right one for an individual patient. He instructed me not to drive until I got the meds.

Then he looked up at me over the top of those glasses and I knew what was coming.

"So what do you want to do, Mike?"

I said nothing, silently wishing we could go back to follow the finger.

"It's been a couple of weeks since the biopsy," he continued. "Have you given any thought to the treatment options we discussed?"

"Not really."

"Every day it takes to decide is a day your tumor is getting bigger."

"I'm aware."

"A grade-three astrocytoma needs treatment as soon as possible. It'll eventually turn into a grade-four and then growth will accelerate rapidly."

"None of the treatment choices you gave me were exactly good."

"You have a brain tumor, Mike. Nothing about it is good." He closed the folder that held my chart and leveled his gaze at me. "You know, of course that not making a choice *is* a choice."

I knew.

I decided not to tell anyone about my new party trick. If Cam or Becky or even Jennifer knew about the seizure, it would only worry them. I'd try the medication, and hopefully they'd never have to see one. I could feel Bob's disappointment.

After filling the scrip I headed over to Global Talent, where I met George in the lobby. He handed me a surprisingly thick folder.

"The best I could do on short notice," he said. "We don't have credit card numbers or any personal financial information. All we have are records of salary payments and expenses. Tax withholdings and stuff."

"What about friends?" I said, flipping through the pages. "Who would he disappear with?"

"What friends? TJ's kind of a loner. Keeps to himself. Writes a lot. He wrote almost half the lyrics for the new album. Last time, when he vanished into the desert, he was all alone."

"There's nobody I can talk to? Nobody he might confide in?"

George shrugged. "I swear, I've never seen him hanging out with anyone but the other Boyz. To be honest, this gig is pretty all-consuming. Once they taste some success, most of our clients don't have time for old friends. Too many planes. Too many hotel rooms. They drift away."

"There's no one from his pre–Boyz Klub life he might get back in touch with? Seems like a stretch."

"Maybe, but I don't know 'em. Wait—I do remember a cousin or something. I met him once or twice at a concert, but never saw 'em hanging out. Freddie or Eddie or something. Kind of a hanger-on."

That's all George had on friends. This kid was going to be tough. I'd look up the cousin. And I'd definitely be back to Arlene Sommerset's house once I had more to go on. I hoped to pick up a clue or two by scrubbing through the file. Surely TJ had some kind of social connections.

"I did get you this," George said, reaching into his pocket. He produced a silver house key on a Boyz Klub key chain. "His apartment. We have keys for all the guys, in case we need to get in there while they're on tour. We also help out with a cleaning service, pest control, perks like that. It makes them more available for work."

I took the key and a remote for the community security gate.

"What kinda car does he drive?" I asked, pocketing the key.

"Nothin' fancy. Late-model VW Jetta. White, I think. No—yellow. Before you go, let me introduce you to the Boyz. In case you need to interview them later."

He walked me down the hall, past the pictures of Global clients and Eli glad-handing celebrities, to a door marked REHEARSAL STU-DIO. A red light blinked above it. I followed George through the door.

We stepped into an anteroom for observers and walked past comfortable chairs to the large glass pane that looked into the dance studio. Beyond the glass was an expansive room, brightly lit, with pale hardwood floors stretching from wall to mirrored wall.

Inside the studio, music pounded at a volume that popped my eyes open. Five people were in the room: the three Boyz, a male choreographer, and a female assistant. I recognized the Boyz from the album cover. To my right were Ben and Holden. Then there was a gap where, presumably, TJ was supposed to be. On the other side of the gap was Miguel. All three of them moved in impressive synchronization, performing athletic dance moves while the choreographer clapped hands in rhythm and counted loudly. Legs kicking, arms swinging, the dance looked like a stylized fight, a hip-hop update to *West Side Story*.

Through all of the moves, Holden sang the lyrics into a small headset microphone. I realized that he wasn't lip-synching for the dance rehearsal, he was actually singing. I may not be the biggest fan of their bubblegum music, but I can appreciate talent when I hear it. This kid was talented. Not only was his voice strong and soulful, he was able to deliver the vocal goods while performing acrobatic dance moves that would have had me wheezing in thirty seconds.

Miguel turned left when he should have turned right, and the choreographer shouted, "No!" The assistant cut the music. The choreographer chastised Miguel and demonstrated the proper turn, insisting Miguel mimic him.

"Concentrate, Miguel," the choreographer said. "Concentrate. Okay, let's take ten and come back for 'All I Got.' I'm still not happy with the thing at the end."

"Come on," George said, and gestured with his head. I followed him into the studio. George quickly introduced me to the three Boyz before they took advantage of their break, explaining that I was going to try to get in touch with TJ.

"Good," Holden said. He was tall and sinewy, with curly, close-cropped blond hair. He took a swig from a bottle of water. "When you find him, do me a favor and kick him in the ass."

"Better yet," Ben said, "let me." Ben was shorter than Holden, but solid. He obviously spent a lot of time in the weight room. His thick brown hair contrasted against his pale skin. He wiped a towel across his face.

"Did you talk to his mom?" asked Miguel.

"Yeah," I said. "She didn't know anything."

Miguel nodded. He was about Ben's height, but thinner, with a taut, dancer's frame. He had an olive-toned Mediterranean complexion, and his shaggy black hair hung down over his eyes.

"Good luck, dude," Holden said, finishing his water and walking out of the studio. The other Boyz followed him. Miguel hesitated for a half step before he reached the door, but then disappeared into the anteroom.

"So what's next?" George asked.

"I think I'll do a little apartment hunting," I said.

CHAPTER 6

TJ Sommerset lived in a nice but unspectacular condominium complex on the west side of town, nestled among the landscaped upper-middle-class, ranch-style homes and the strip-mall plazas with Publix supermarkets and Pier 1 Imports.

I used the remote George had given me to open the security gate and parked my truck in front of TJ's building. I was surprised that, given his popularity, TJ wasn't barricaded behind some impenetrable fortress. But the Palm Terrace condominium complex was quite nice and, when constructed, was one of the few in the area to retain a number of tall, moss-draped oak trees, which provided both cooling shade and some degree of privacy.

The key worked as promised, and soon I was standing in TJ's living room. It was a two-bedroom floor plan, airy and spacious. Fireplace in the living room, decent-sized kitchen. He had very little furniture, probably because he spent most of his time on the road. A nice flat-screen TV sat in an ordinary entertainment cabinet, but what looked like an expensive stereo dominated the wall opposite the living room's solitary couch.

I took a quick tour to make sure I was indeed alone. I was. The master bedroom was neat except for a rumpled pile of clothes in a laundry basket on the floor. I couldn't tell if they were dirty or clean. The closet door was ajar. Peeking in, I saw a few shirts and pants hanging, but not even a week's worth. There were a lot of empty hangers. Looked like he packed a full suitcase before he split. I stuck my hand in the pockets of the clothes in the closet and in the laundry basket, but they were all empty.

The bed was a queen and was neatly made. I methodically checked under the mattress, the pillows, and the box spring for something. Anything. There was nothing. A quick search of the lone nightstand netted me two unopened condom wrappers, some loose change, and a few *Tiger Beat* magazines featuring Boyz Klub on the cover.

The master bath was also neat. It looked like the tub had even been scrubbed. There was nothing of note in the medicine cabinet, the drawers, or the linen closet, unless you're into spare rolls of toilet paper.

I made my way back to the living room and poked through the entertainment cabinet. A handful of DVDs. Not a bad collection, which included the original *Godfather,* the latest *Star Wars* and *Lord of the Rings,* and a few Gene Kelly flicks. I recalled something that George had told me about TJ. He was a student of his profession. When he needed inspiration for some new dance moves in a concert, he always returned to the masters: Gene Kelly, Fred Astaire. He also loved Gregory Hines, Savion Glover, and vintage Michael Jackson.

TJ's CD collection was equally eclectic. He appeared to have every album Billy Joel ever released, along with Elton John and Paul Simon. Mixed in were a few Red Hot Chili Peppers, Britney Spears, Backstreet Boys, Bob Dylan, Johnny Cash, and Don McLean. Just the thought of this mismatched musical gumbo gave me a headache.

Before leaving the living room, I ran my hand under the couch and between the cushions. Nothing.

Next I headed for the kitchen. The pantry was sparse. I found a clipped bag of potato chips and opened it. I popped a single chip in my mouth. Soft and disgusting. These had been here awhile. Meaning he had probably been gone for a while. I rolled the bag back up, replaced the clip, and put it back on the shelf.

I pulled the lever for the kitchen faucet and the pipe sputtered for a beat before spitting the water out. No one had used this sink in at least a few days. The validation of my assessment came when I spotted that the refrigerator was unplugged and both the fridge and freezer doors were ajar. They were empty and no longer cold. So not only did that confirm that TJ had been gone for a while, but it also bolstered the assumption that he'd left of his own free will.

Abductees don't typically take the time to unplug their refrigerator before being whisked away. And, in my experience, abductors don't either.

I perused the small guest bath and, finding nothing, made my way into the second bedroom, which was currently functioning as an office. A computer sat on an IKEA desk. Papers were scattered all around the room. I picked one up at random.

Lyrics were written on it. There were dozens of pages, each containing song fragments.

I pressed on the computer and was able to boot it up without a password. I scrolled through some of the file listings. There was a folder called "Songs in progress," containing more files of lyrics. He had a couple of computer games loaded.

Double-clicking his Internet connection soon landed me on his home page, the official Boyz Klub Web site. I looked in the saved addresses by clicking the arrow in the address bar, hoping to see if he'd recently accessed a travel site or did some research about where he might go. But the drop-down list was empty. A quick check of the browser settings revealed that TJ preferred to have his cache and history cleared every day. I looked at his bookmarks. Nothing there either. Just a handful of favorite sites, mostly songwriting pages or official sites for his boy-band competition.

I shut the computer down and began rummaging through the desk drawers. Finally, I found something that might help, if I could pull a favor from an old friend. I found some old statements for both a credit card and a checking account. I scribbled the bank names and account numbers on a piece of paper.

I also found a letter addressed to TJ from some charity called Journeys of Hope. Apparently, TJ had donated $20,000 to the group and they were "very grateful for the generous gift that will provide happiness to some families who desperately need it." The letter was signed by the executive director, Marian Cooksey. I jotted down her name and contact info from the letterhead.

The last thing I saw before I decided to stop invading TJ's privacy was a small stack of photos. They were mostly of the last Boyz Klub tour: the guys clowning around backstage, Ben and Holden crossing their eyes for the camera, Miguel sleeping shirtless in a hotel bed, roadies setting up a show, landmarks from cities they had visited. The Space Needle, the HOLLYWOOD sign, Bourbon Street. There were a few pictures of the desert, but there was no way I could tell where it was. Somewhere in the vast southwestern corner of the United States. To this day, nobody knew exactly where in the desert TJ had gone. The pictures provided no definitive clues. Still, I slipped the stack of photos into my pocket.

I left the apartment as I'd found it and locked up. I drove around the parking lot, looking for a yellow VW Jetta. I didn't find any. Before I split the complex, I stopped by the condo office and spoke to the manager. I explained that I was from Global Talent and had a message for TJ Sommerset. After talking my way through the question of why the management company didn't know where to reach their client, the manager finally said he had no idea when TJ was coming back. When he went on tour, he was sometimes gone for months. Global sent a monthly check to cover the rent.

"Funny thing, though," he said. "Last time we saw him, he gave us a check for four months' rent."

"He never did that before?" I asked.

"Never. And, coincidentally, that pays up his lease. Are you guys gonna renew for him?"

"I'll have to ask." I left a note in an envelope for TJ to call me immediately and scratched out a short, awkward explanation why. It was a waste of ink. TJ Sommerset was long gone from Palm Terrace, and I was pretty sure he had no intention of coming back anytime soon.

I spotted the blue Mustang right away, trailing behind me after I left the condo complex, but didn't think anything of it until it pulled into the plaza parking lot behind me. As I walked into the Starbucks, I tried to get a look at the driver, but the glare from the oppressive Florida sun on the windshield obliterated any hope of seeing inside. I shrugged it off, vowing to see if the car was still there when I left.

I got a big, strong cup of coffee and found a quiet table in the back to read over the file George had prepared. It was mostly a press kit for Boyz Klub, but it provided me with some rudimentary background. George had added some comments throughout to flesh it out.

Before I had left for TJ's apartment, George and I spent an hour or so going over some additional information about the band. Most of my questions were about relationships between the band members, between them and Eli, plus any other significant players in the band's life. We had talked in a large Global conference room while a publicity intern sat at one end of the table forging the band's autographs on a stack of eight-by-ten photos, using a different color marker for each member.

My interest was in learning as much as possible about why TJ felt compelled to disappear without a word. George insisted that he was just a temperamental-artist type, but I found that hard to buy at face value. I figured his disappearance was probably related to his relationship with someone. Somebody he wanted to get away from or maybe even someone he wanted to get closer to. So far, I was still sticking with the assumption that no foul play was involved. No one seemed particularly concerned about his safety: not his mother, not Eli, not the band. In fact, Eli and the band had basically been pissed.

I sipped my coffee and flipped open the folder. In addition to the papers was an advance copy of the new Boyz Klub album: *Boyz Life*. I opened the CD jewel case and skimmed the liner notes. TJ had thanked his mom. Setting the album aside, I began reading, sorting out the information I'd gotten from talking with George and combining it with the data in the background file. Between the two a picture was starting to emerge.

TJ was the youngest of the four, but when the age range for all of them was between twenty-two and twenty-four, that wasn't saying much. He was born in Orlando and made his way through the hit-or-miss quality of the Orange County school system. He started working at the theme parks while still in high school, clawing his way up from concessions to character performance to successful auditions for live stage shows. TJ sang and danced for two years as historical figures, film characters, cartoon animals—whatever the role required.

Eli Elizondo plucked him from the theme-park stage during an open call for a new band that eventually became Boyz Klub. According to George, TJ had genuine talent. But, so did most of the other folks toiling away in Orlando's open-air matinee choruses. What TJ had going for him was an indefinable look that Eli was searching for. A sultry innocence that could make teen and preteen girls squeal. What TJ also brought with him was a burning ambition to be more than just part of another pretty-faced boy band.

He wrote songs and lyrics and pushed the envelope of what Eli wanted the band to be—sometimes to the point of ugly public arguments. TJ claimed that Madonna was still Madonna because she'd evolved and grown out of her bubblegum image. She changed and reinvented herself. If she hadn't, TJ claimed, she would have ended up no different from Cyndi Lauper: a nostalgia act with a couple of old pop hits and irrelevant today.

Eli couldn't give a crap about evolving. He wanted Boyz Klub to deliver what the demographic wanted. And the demographic wanted cute guys singing benign songs and dancing in sync. Eli didn't want controversy. He didn't want edgy. He wanted a formula. It was a source of continuing friction between him and TJ.

TJ's relationship with the other band members was hot and cold. There were periods where they all seemed to get along great. There were also stretches where any one of them would be on the nerves of one or more of the others. Given the amount of time they spent together, under pressure, dealing with the rigors of travel, it was a wonder they didn't all kill each other.

There was nothing George could tell me that pointed to any single event—an argument, a practical joke gone bad—that would have driven TJ away without letting someone know. If everyone weren't so surprisingly unconcerned, my first instinct would be to suspect trouble.

George had nothing on romantic relationships, and whatever preband friendships TJ had were apparently vaporized by his meteoric rise to fame. Except for his mother and the cousin, TJ had no other local family.

His mother's parents were deceased, and after his father's death,

TJ had lost all contact with his father's parents. Regarding aunts and uncles, it was the same story—no interest or contact, except for this mysterious cousin. It seemed unlikely that TJ was hiding out with extended family.

What about Arlene? Could TJ be camping out with Mom in the big house in Isleworth? I had no idea. I supposed it was possible, but unlikely. If we were to follow TJ's previous pattern—if you could even call one prior instance a pattern—he was probably in the desert again or somewhere equally remote. At this point, my Tahiti scenario was as likely as any.

Finding this kid was going to be tough, if not impossible. With his secrecy and unlimited resources, if he didn't want to be found, he wasn't going be found. All he had to do was be smart and avoid an electronic trail. If he did that, he was invisible. A ghost.

I pulled out the piece of paper I had written TJ's bank and credit-card account numbers on. It represented the only bread crumb I had yet found, and I had no idea how stale it was or if it even led in the right direction. But it was all I had.

I punched a few buttons on my cell phone and listened to the warbling ring. A moment later I heard Jim Dupree's resonant baritone answer.

"This's Dupree."

"Big Jim. Mike Garrity."

A surprised pause before, "Hey, G. What's up?"

"I need a favor."

"Oh, yeah? This a big favor or a small favor?"

Big Jim Dupree had been my partner at OPD for three years. We joined the department at about the same time and had immediately hit it off. Physically, we couldn't be more different. Jim was African-American and clocked in at a towering six foot five, 270 pounds. But our personalities clicked. He had a smart-ass sense of humor that jibed with mine and an equal passion for removing scumbags from decent society.

We both made detective within two years of each other and had overlapping tenures on the Metropolitan Bureau of Investigation. I had trusted him with my life many times and wouldn't hesitate to do so again, should the need arise. Too bad Big Jim wasn't also a neurosurgeon.

"Don't know," I said, answering his question. "Probably a big favor."

"Huh," he said noncommittally. "How you feelin'?"

"Okay. Good days and bad days. You know."

"Yeah. . . . When you comin' back?"

"I'm out, Jim. I'm out for good."

"Damn. Never say never. You take care of business. Beat that shit. Get better and come back. I'll keep your desk free."

I chuckled. "What're you gonna do, sit on it?"

"If I have to. You come back and see ass prints on your desk, you'll know." I could hear the smile in his voice. "So, what's this big favor? You wanna date my sister?"

"I need to check some activity on a credit card and bank account."

There was a long pause.

"You got a problem with one of the ex-wives?" Jim said.

"No. They're both cool. This is somebody else."

"Anyone I know?"

"I doubt it," I said. "Some freelance work I picked up."

"Do I want the details?"

"Probably not. It's nothin' shady. At least I don't think so. That's one of the reasons I want the accounts checked."

"And what's keepin' you from goin' down to the credit bureau your own damn self?"

"You mean besides the fact that I'd have to forge a consent signature? And that happens to be against the law?"

Jim snorted, knowing as well as I did that nobody ever checked those signatures. People ran unauthorized credit checks every day.

"Yeah," he said, " 'sides that."

"Well, I can't afford the five grand if I get caught. But, mostly, I'm afraid the name on the account might get recognized. I'm trying to avoid attention."

"Oh, yeah? This somebody famous?"

"Yeah. With a certain crowd."

"Who is it?"

"TJ Sommerset."

"Never heard a him."

"It ain't your crowd. I figured that if the check came through the department, it had a better chance of staying quiet."

"Maybe, maybe not," Jim said. "Say I do this, what're you gonna do with the info?"

"Try to figure out where the guy is. He's a runner and I've been asked to find him."

"And suppose I give you this info and you do find him. Then you pass that along to whoever asked you. Any chance the runner winds up with a toe tag?"

"Nothin' like that. This is straight up. I wouldn't take a job like that."

"You could be gettin' played."

"No chance," I said. "This is clean."

"Parents looking for a runaway?"

"Not exactly, but you're in the neighborhood."

"Y'know," Jim said, "last time I checked, you didn't have no PI license."

"This is kinda under the radar."

I could tell Jim liked that. "Okay, James Bond, gimme the numbers."

I read him the credit-card and bank-account numbers, along with the other particulars he needed. Name, address. Jim said he'd see what he could do and would get back to me.

"This gonna put you in a spot?" I asked, knowing that every credit check shows up in a management report. Jim could get asked some uncomfortable questions if he got caught running a check on someone not part of an active investigation.

"I got a few favors owed me," he said. "Let's just say you're lucky you have cancer or I'd probably tell you to go jump in a gator pond."

"You're the best, Jimbo."

"Ass-kissin' don't suit you."

"So," I said, "what's your sister's number?"

"I wouldn't wish that on either one of you," he said, and promptly hung up.

I drained the coffee and gathered up the file. As I stepped outside, I glanced down the row of cars and saw that the blue Mustang was gone. In another minute, I was in my truck and pulling out of the parking lot. I made a quick stop at Home Depot for a couple of things, then swung into Publix to pick up a rotisserie chicken for dinner.

Three blocks later I spotted it, trailing two car lengths behind me. I kept going, my eyes flicking up to the rearview every few seconds to see if it was still back there. It was. I changed lanes, and a few seconds later the Mustang followed. Without signaling, I abruptly turned right at a Vietnamese restaurant and watched the Mustang make the same reckless move.

I learned two things: one, I was definitely being followed, probably by an amateur; and two, there was only one tail on me. If I were being tracked by a pro, he wouldn't have pulled an obvious move like that turn. If I hadn't made him before, that decision would've put a big red flag on top of his car. Likewise, if I were being tracked by a team, the Mustang would've never followed me like that. It would've kept going and I'd have been picked up by another of the team's unknown number of surveillance vehicles, trackers peeling off and on seamlessly to avoid detection.

I decided to stick to my original plans and headed home. I wondered how far the tracker would go. Would he follow me into my apartment parking lot? Would there be a confrontation? Who was this dude?

I parked in front of my building and debated whether I should make a move. Doing so would eliminate whatever advantage I might have by knowing I was being followed. I decided that, unless confronted by the tracker, I'd play along until I could figure out who was on my tail. Or why.

I went upstairs and, from my living room window, watched the Mustang pull into my parking lot. It circled my building three times before it turned back onto the road and drove off. I squinted and strained, but couldn't get a read on the license tag. I didn't own a pair of binoculars. Never needed them until now.

I picked up the phone to call George. If that A-hole Eli had someone on my tail, I was going to be pissed. There would only be two reasons. Either Eli wanted to use me to find TJ's trail and then have his own man locate him to avoid paying me the big check, or he didn't trust me. Whichever, I didn't want anything to do with it. My medical condition afforded me the luxury to piss away a quarter-million-dollar opportunity without regret.

If it wasn't Eli who was behind the tail, then I had no other ideas. Things could get interesting.

However, before I could dial, there was a loud knock on my front door. I dropped the phone and crouched down. Every time the Mustang circled, it was out of view for several minutes. Plenty of time for a hidden passenger to slip out.

I removed my nine-millimeter Glock from the holster in my nightstand and made my way slowly to the front door. I peeked through the peephole but saw no one there. I backed around the side of the entry and stood in the archway to the kitchen, pistol raised.

"Who is it?" I ordered.

The answer that came back filled me with both relief and apprehension.

CHAPTER 7

"It's me!" came the voice through the door. Female. Annoyed.

Jennifer.

I opened the door and saw her in her green FOOD COURT shirt, name badge pinned to the front.

"I forgot my key at Cam's," she said, stepping in.

"You okay?" I asked, looking past her at the outdoor stairway that led down to the parking lot.

"Yeah," she said with equal amounts of annoyance and confusion.

"You alone?"

"Yeah . . . Jesus!" she yelped when she saw the gun in my hand.

"It's okay," I said, closing and locking the door.

"What the hell?"

"Nothin'," I said. "How'd you get home?"

"Gwen drove me."

"What kind of car does Gwen drive?"

"What's going on?"

"Nothin'. It's okay. What kind of car?"

"A Sentra. You're freaking me out."

"Sorry. I'll put this away." I disappeared into the bedroom and replaced the Glock into the holster. I made a mental note to start carrying it, concealed, until I knew who my new friend in the Mustang was.

"Why did you have your gun?" Jennifer said when I returned to the living room.

"Paranoia. If you're a cop long enough, you get a little jumpy."

"Looks like you got out just in time."

"Not soon enough," I said.

Oddly enough, the tension created by greeting her armed completely dissipated the tension I'd expected when she returned. My ill-advised foray into her room was suddenly far less important than whether I was going to shoot somebody.

"I got a chicken for dinner," I said.

"Okay."

I boiled some carrots and threw a couple of potatoes in the microwave. Although still a little awkward, dinner was almost pleasant. We made small talk, mostly about her job at the mall. A couple of times I almost apologized for poking through her purse. But the timing never seemed right and I didn't want to snap the thin line of civility we were balancing on.

"Listen," I said, "I got this today." I opened the Home Depot bag and pulled out a door dead-bolt kit encased in plastic. "It's for your room. It's got two keys and they're both yours."

She took the kit and studied it. I couldn't read her face but I almost detected a slight nod.

"I didn't want to open it before you got home," I said, "so you could see I didn't copy the keys. I was gonna install it tonight, unless you want to get it rekeyed."

"No, that's okay."

"Then I'll put it in tonight." It didn't look hard to install and I certainly had the tools for it. My tool kit was one of my most prized possessions. It had come with me after I'd been kicked out of the only two houses I had ever owned, and it had survived the sticky fingers of lawyers through both divorces. The longest relationship I've ever had has been with my cordless Makita drill.

"I'll get the dishes," Jennifer said.

I nodded. If the dead bolt was my lame attempt at an apology, then washing the dishes was her acceptance of it. We were speaking in Garrity code, but at least we were communicating.

I helped with the dishes. When we were done, I found my shoulder case and dug around in it.

"I have something else for you," I said.

Jennifer looked skeptical, but remained silent. I found the CD of the new Boyz Klub album that George had given me and handed it to her. It took a moment for it to register. But then it clicked and her eyes widened.

"Oh. My. God." She looked at the back of the jewel case and then up at me. "Do you realize what this is?"

"Yeah. The new Boyz Klub album."

"This isn't even available yet. You can't even buy it until next week."

"Yeah."

"Oh. My. God. How did you get this?"

"I know a guy."

"A guy? What guy?"

"A guy. I used to work with him."

"I can't believe this. I just—I can't believe this."

"Yeah," I said.

"I gotta call Gwen. She's gonna die. I mean, she's gonna *die*."

Her eyes still boring into the CD case, holding it with both hands, Jennifer started toward her room. After a step she stopped and turned back.

"This is really cool," she said. "Thanks."

With a smile on my face, I headed for the Makita.

"All right, G. Who's this runner, really?"

Big Jim Dupree sat across from me in a downtown coffee shop positioned in the shadow of the SunTrust skyscraper. He had a hand the size of a dinner plate resting on a sealed manila envelope.

I closed my eyes and took a deep breath. I had a hard time watching Jim take manly bites of a blueberry muffin, crumbs sprinkling onto the table. I'd discovered, to my dismay, that the antiseizure meds made me nauseous. Plus, Bob had the skull jackhammer going full speed this morning.

Normally, given how I felt, I would never have agreed to meet Jim for coffee like this. But he'd called early this morning and told me he had the info I was looking for. If I wanted it, I needed to get it in person.

"Garrity?" he said, after I failed to respond for a moment. "You okay?"

I opened my eyes. "Yeah," I said, and felt the wave of nausea subside.

"You sure?"

"Yeah." I stirred my black coffee. I nodded at the envelope. "What did you find?"

"Who's the runner?"

"Just a kid."

"A damn rich kid. Who?"

"Like I said before, his name's TJ Sommerset. He's in a band called Boyz Klub. One of those all-boy deals from Global Talent."

Jim nodded. "George Neuheisel."

"He hooked me up. Asked me to find the kid before their upcoming tour started. He kinda went AWOL."

Jim opened his mouth and inserted the remaining two-thirds of the muffin. A couple of chews and it was history. He slid the envelope across the table at me.

"Don't know if this is gonna help or not," Jim said.

"What's the quick and dirty?"

Jim shrugged. "Boy's got a fifty-grand limit on the credit card, but there's been no activity—at all—in the last two weeks. Before that, goin' back a ways, mostly furniture and big-screen TVs and shit. A computer, too."

I thought about the furnishings at Arlene Sommerset's Isleworth mansion. TJ not only bought her the house, but filled it up, as well.

"What about the bank account?" I asked.

"That's the interestin' part. Dude's got almost seven hundred grand in the bank. 'Bout a week and a half ago, he withdraws almost a half a mil. Cash."

I let out a low whistle.

"Damn right," said Jim. "Dude can get himself pretty good and gone with that kinda coin."

"He took off once before. Nothing in there that might tell me where he went?"

Jim shook his head. "Like I said, don't know if this is gonna help or not. But it was fun reading." Jim drained his cup of coffee. "You say he's a kid?"

"Twenty-two. Worth maybe ten million from the first album, with a new one about to be released."

"Ten million. Damn. Maybe *I* should call Georgie. I got a good voice. Sing every week in the church choir."

"You don't exactly have the look Global goes for."

"What're you sayin'? My tan's too dark?"

"I wasn't thinkin' that. But, now that you say it, all their bands do seem pretty pale. No, I was thinkin' more about your, uh . . . Face it, man, you weigh more than all four of those Boyz Klub kids combined. My advice: keep the day job."

Jim shot me a mock-angry look and a knowing smile. "I'm still saving your desk, G. Place ain't the same without you."

"Please. Don't waste your time."

"Ain't no waste of time to sit on it while I'm working. Gotta sit anyway."

"Then don't waste your ass. I'm sure you could put it to much better use."

"Doubtful, bro," said Jim. "Doubtful."

It was a reception area, but a far cry from the reception area of Global Talent. A couple of secondhand chairs sat along a hand-painted wall decorated with appliqué stickers of local theme-park characters. One-half of the room was filled with kid-oriented para-phernalia: tiny chairs, plastic bins of toys, puzzles, dolls, and a small TV with an older Sony PlayStation attached.

The suite looked like it had once been a doctor's office, complete with sliding-glass window at the receptionist's desk. The window slid open and a sandy-haired guy in his late twenties poked out.

"Mr. Garrity?" he said. "Marian said she'll be right with you. You want a soda or something?"

"No thanks," I said, and returned to the seven-month-old *Ladies' Home Journal* in my lap. The day was getting better. Although not exactly what I'd hoped for, the information Big Jim had provided had been helpful. My nausea of earlier in the morning seemed to have subsided, and Bob's famous "brain pain" had been reduced from a piercing stab to a dull ache. And, as a bonus, I was now learning all about Celine Dion's brave battle with infertility.

A few minutes later a door opened.

"Mr. Garrity?" It was Marian Cooksey, executive director of Journeys of Hope. She was late fifties, early sixties, African-American, and short—maybe five foot three—but seemed taller in her bearing and heels. Her demeanor was businesslike, but unhurried, and after two seconds with her I had no doubt that she was in charge.

"Mike," I said, shaking her hand.

"You mentioned that this was about TJ?"

"Yeah. I'm from Global Talent and I just have a few questions."

She offered a genuine smile. "Of course. We can talk in my office."

She led me through the adjoining hallway, past photos of kids posing with theme-park characters: Mickey Mouse, SpongeBob, Goofy, Shamu. I saw a couple of shots of young girls standing with TJ.

Journeys of Hope arranged free Orlando theme-park vacations for terminally ill children and their families. Creating memories to last a lifetime, however long that might be. It wasn't lost on me that the kids in the pictures were probably all now dead.

We walked by several small offices where young workers talked on phones. Sitting in one office, chatting with a worker, were two adults and a young girl with a completely bald head. My hand involuntarily touched my biopsy scar.

This visit was definitely a long shot, but besides the few financial records, the letter from Journeys of Hope was the only real lead I'd found in TJ's apartment. Marian Cooksey led me into her office, a cramped but cozy space filled with inexpensive furniture. She cleared some papers from a chair and I sat. She left the door open and sat next to me in the other guest chair, one leg crossed precisely over the other.

"So TJ's finally changed his mind?" she said.

"Pardon?"

"I assume that's why you're here. I've been telling him for ages that he should be more open about his charity work. He would set such a positive example, and honestly, the publicity wouldn't hurt our fund-raising."

"He never wanted the publicity?"

She shook her head. "He said that wasn't why he was doing it. It wasn't about him. You should make that very clear in whatever promotion you intend to do. He was very sincere. To him, it's only about the kids."

"Can you describe his involvement with Journeys of Hope?"

"It started when one of our kids asked to meet him. She was a fan. As soon as he learned about us and what we did, he became actively involved. He made himself available whenever a client asked to meet him. I recall one time when he flew back on a red-eye from Los Angeles in the middle of shooting a music video, just to spend an hour with one of our kids. Then he was back on a plane by lunchtime. He probably didn't sleep for three days."

"I didn't know that."

"Nobody does. He told me once that it was the least he could do. That these kids didn't have time to wait for his schedule to clear. Of course, he's also provided us with significant financial support."

"And what do you consider significant?" I said.

She wagged a finger at me. " 'Whoever sows sparingly will also reap sparingly, and whoever sows generously will also reap generously.' TJ Sommerset has been generous with more than his time. Several times a year we get a check from him for anywhere from twenty to fifty thousand dollars. It makes a huge difference to a charity like ours, believe me."

"I'm sure it does."

"Even with the parks donating hotel rooms and admissions, these types of trips are usually beyond the reach of our families. Most are racked by medical expenses. Each of TJ's donations allows us to serve between four and ten families. There are probably twenty-five families whose entire trips were funded solely by TJ."

"He's made quite a difference."

"He's a blessing. A gift. And I'm glad he's decided to take his light out from under the bushel basket."

I paused, wondering how much longer I could deceive this

woman before the floor collapsed under the weight of my guilt and I plunged straight to hell. "Do you think," I said slowly, forming the thought in my head, "that TJ's interest in Journeys of Hope comes from the loss of his father as a child?"

This time it was Marian Cooksey's turn to pause. "I don't know. I wasn't aware that he lost his father as a child."

"Liver cancer."

She nodded slowly to herself, letting just a bit of her weariness show, a weariness of watching far too many people die at far too young an age.

"We all have our reasons, Mike." She took a breath that seemed to clear the weariness aside. "So what changed TJ's mind? The last check?"

"Last check?"

"He didn't tell you? Well, it did come anonymously as a money order, but it's from his bank. I just assumed . . ."

"May I see it?" I asked.

"I suppose . . ." Marian Cooksey got up and rummaged through a desk file drawer. "I have copy in here. Ah." She pulled out a file folder and handed me a photocopied money order dated a week ago. It was made out to Journeys of Hope.

The amount was $300,000.

"It arrived the other day," she said. "No note. No return address. I just assumed it was from TJ. I've tried calling him several times over the past few days but haven't reached him."

I handed the photocopy back. "Is that unusual?"

"Not really. Although, he usually gets back to me within a day or two, depending on what he's doing."

"Have you ever gotten a check that size before?"

"Never."

Marian Cooksey and I chatted for a few more minutes, but I started to itch to get out before she realized I wasn't being completely honest. I left her both my cell phone and the main Global number if she had any questions or information, or if she got another big check. I told her that Global was still deciding how to proceed and needed to discuss any publicity with TJ first.

After saying good-bye, I lingered alone for a moment in the waiting room, examining the bins of toys against the wall. Then I wrote Journeys of Hope a check for a hundred bucks, placed it on the receptionist's desk, and slipped out the door.

The Journeys of Hope offices were on the fourth floor of a worn-down medical complex. I debated taking the unventilated stairs but quickly discarded the notion as unnecessarily masochistic. I pressed the call button and waited for the rickety elevator to rumble up from the first floor.

One of the downsides of a career as a cop is a pathologically heightened sense of suspicion. You tend to see many perfectly innocent situations as potentially nefarious. The shifty-looking kid lingering in the back of the 7-Eleven. The department-store shopper with the ridiculously large purse. It's a tiresome way to live, always expecting people to act their worst, and a contributing factor to cop burnout. But the flip side is that the very same paranoia can sometimes turn out to be right, giving you a few seconds extra to prepare or react.

I saw the guy from the corner of my eye, leaning over a water fountain a few steps from the elevator. I didn't know why, but my spider sense was seriously tingling. Looking back on it now, I should have heeded that suspicion and done something. Grabbed him. Threatened him. Shot him.

Something.

But I didn't. At the time, I didn't know. How could I? I shrugged it off. Besides, I wasn't carrying a weapon at the time.

Instead, when the elevator chimed, I stepped calmly in and watched him lean up from the water fountain and step into the box with me. He was a big dude, at least four inches taller than me, in his late forties, early fifties, with an unruly shock of dyed black hair. Deep-set eyes, buried under a heavy brow. He was dressed in dark slacks and a fluorescent green golf shirt that was so bright, you could read by it. The Day-Glo shirt was stretched across his girth, topped with a blue blazer. Neon business casual.

I hit the first-floor button and the doors wheezed closed. We each assumed the standard elevator position, facing forward, saying nothing, like at a line of urinals. As soon as we started our slow descent, however, Mr. Day-Glo spoke, still looking forward.

"So, Mike," he said in a voice higher and more nasal than I would have expected. "How goes the search?"

I paused for a breath's length. "Who wants to know?"

"A friend." He turned and took a single step toward me. "Actually, a friend of a friend."

I quickly sized up my situation and it wasn't good. No escape. Him between me and the alarm button. The elevator continued its glacial, vibrating descent.

"That's far enough, pal," I said.

He took another step, which, in the confined space, put him right in my face.

"Any leads?" His breath was polluted with cigarettes and stale coffee. "The clock's ticking, Mikey."

"Back off, or—"

"What? What are you gonna do?" He placed a hand into his blazer and rested it under one arm. I saw the shadowy glint of a pistol handle. I tensed my body, preparing to grab his arm and launch a knee into his groin. I was unarmed, my Glock sitting uselessly in my truck's glove compartment. I had foolishly questioned the appropriateness of bringing a nine-millimeter semiautomatic weapon into the Journeys of Hope office. Without a weapon or even the obligatory can of cop pepper spray, I knew my only hope was to make a decisive, dirty move.

"You gonna find him?" he said. "I suggest you find him soon."

I contracted my thigh muscles, preparing a preemptive blow. In the instant before I struck, the elevator suddenly chimed and the door opened onto the second floor. An elderly couple stood there expectantly in the hallway.

Day-Glo took a half step back and we both watched the stooped woman assist the even more stooped man, lifting his walker over the gap in the elevator threshold as they entered. Just as the doors closed, I slipped out of the elevator and bolted across the hall to the stairs.

I tore down the steps three at a time and pushed out into the parking lot. A few seconds later I was in my truck peeling out onto the road. I saw no one exit the building and no one following me. I took a quick look around for a blue Mustang, but didn't see it.

Once I was a few miles away and the adrenaline began to subside, I got mad. Really mad. Pissed. Goon-style intimidation never sat well with me, and this was a classic case. *A friend of a friend?* If my guess about the friend's identity was right, he was going to get a goddamn scorching earful.

CHAPTER 8

"So, Mikey, can you be there tonight?" George said through the phone receiver.

"Screw you," I said, glancing at Jennifer watching TV in the living room.

"What?"

"You heard me. Tell Eli to go find him himself. Or have his goon do it."

"What are you talking about?"

"Just stop it, George. You're insulting me."

"Mikey, seriously, what the hell are you talking about?"

I took a sip of a freshly poured finger of bourbon. "Are you telling me you don't know? Are you really telling me that?"

"Mike. This is me. What happened?"

I took another sip and exhaled deeply through my nostrils. I decided to give George the benefit of the doubt. I relayed an abbreviated version of my encounter in the elevator.

"Mike, that wasn't us. I swear."

"Right."

"Seriously. I swear."

"Maybe not you, George. At least, I hope not. But it stinks like Eli, I'll tell you that."

"No way. He doesn't operate like that."

"Bullshit."

"I'm telling you, Mike. It isn't Eli. I don't know . . . Maybe it was a reporter, or paparazzi or something. If the tabloids found out about TJ being gone, or even suspected it, they'd offer you a lot of money for a scoop. That's why Eli's paying so much. It has to be more than they'd pay."

"He wasn't paparazzi."

"You'd be surprised. They'll do anything. Bribe, threaten, lie, cheat, steal . . . Intimidation is a routine tactic for them."

"I don't know . . ."

"Why would Eli do that? Why would he risk driving you away? We need you, Mike. I'll talk to Eli and make sure he had nothing to do with it. Besides, he'll want to know if the tabloids smell blood so he can come up with a cover story. Really, Mike, we need you. Just give me until tomorrow morning to talk to him. You'll see. Tomorrow morning, okay?"

I finished the bourbon and felt the will to argue melting away. "Okay . . ."

"Good. Great. So, listen, I think we might have a lead."

"Oh?"

"Can you spare a few minutes tonight?"

"Tonight?" I repeated, looking again at Jennifer watching TV.

"Just a few minutes, but I think it's important."

George gave me the particulars and I reluctantly agreed. I jotted them down and then told Jennifer I had to go out. I'd be back before ten. Apparently, Gwen was busy tonight so Jennifer planned on staying home, listening to the new CD, maybe surfing the Web, chatting online with friends, or watching some MTV. So much for the modern teen to do, so little time.

Still, I hesitated. Even if Eli and George had nothing to do with my friend in the elevator, this was, after all, the whole reason Jennifer was staying with me—so we could spend time together. Running out chasing TJ wasn't going to improve our relationship.

But since last night things were going okay. Well, at least we weren't fighting, which was epic progress in our relationship. Maybe a little space would heal any lingering anger over my purse safari. So I left her a frozen lasagna and jumped in my truck.

As I drove downtown, I periodically checked the rearview for the blue Mustang or any other car that seemed to be going the same direction for a little too long. But no one was tailing me.

A few minutes later, I was standing outside a restricted-access door of the TD Waterhouse Center, known locally as the O-rena. I ran into an old cop buddy working off-duty security who slipped me into the tunnel. I made my way up into the arena where the Orlando Magic and the New York Knicks were in their shootarounds on the floor. The stands were about half-full as folks arrived and made their way to their seats.

When I was first diagnosed with cancer, the docs gave me the whole spiel about statistics: survival rates, incidence of occurrence—I don't even remember half of it. But one stat that had stuck with me was incidence of occurrence. Over forty thousand people are diagnosed with a primary brain tumor each year. That's about fourteen for every hundred thousand people. Whenever I saw a large crowd of people—at a sporting event, a concert—I couldn't help but wonder who in the crowd had a brain tumor but didn't know it yet.

That's what popped into my mind as I scanned the half-empty arena. Soon those seats would all be filled, and there was a decent chance that someone watching the game tonight had his or her own Bob germinating in their brain and didn't know it. Maybe he would never know it, or not know it in time to do anything about it. Maybe it was the woman wearing the blue baseball cap. Or the guy eating the hot dog. Have another hot dog, pal. And a beer. Enjoy 'em while you can.

I continued scanning the seats and finally saw Holden and three other young guys coming down the stairs into the lower bowl. I made my way over to them and stepped up just as they sat in their third-row, center-court seats. Holden looked up at me, probably taking me for a fan, his countenance pleasant but wary. But then my face must've clicked for him because I saw the wave of recognition wash over him. Almost imperceptibly, his body relaxed and he smiled.

"Dude, you made it," he said.

"Yeah," I said. "George called and said you needed to see me."

Behind us I heard a high-pitched gasp. I glanced around and saw a group of three teenaged girls. One pointed in our direction while the other two bounced excitedly on their toes.

"Maybe we can go somewhere else," Holden said, not turning around, but clearly aware that he had been recognized.

You're the one who wanted to meet at a professional sporting event, I thought to myself. Now you want privacy? But I kept my mouth shut. I gestured with my head and he followed me down the stairs to the floor.

My off-duty buddy got us around the corner and into the locker-room tunnel. There were people around, mostly press and Magic staffers, but it was much more private than the stands.

"So, what's up?" I said.

Holden fished in the back pocket of his jeans and produced a folded greeting card. Without a word he handed it to me.

On the front was a black-and-white image of a country lane that forked off into two directions. I opened it and read the text.

Life offers us many paths. Some are easy. Some are hard. Some are dead ends that force us to retrace our steps and start over. And some lead us upward to the clouds, and beyond, to our dreams.

At the bottom was written in a steady, cursive script, *Stay true to your path. TJ.*

I looked on the back but there was nothing more.

"When did you get this?" I asked.

"Today," Holden said. "That's why I called George. I figured you'd want to see it."

"Why did he send you a card?"

"No clue. Why does TJ do anything?"

"So, there's no occasion?" I asked. "No birthday? Anniversary of the band?"

"Gimme a break."

"He ever send you a card before?"

"Not like this. We'll sign cards for each other when it's some-one's birthday, but that's from the group."

"Where's the envelope?" I said.

"The envelope? For the card?"

"Yeah. Let me have that, too."

Holden shrugged. "Sorry, dude. I think I pitched it."

"Can you still get it?"

"Huh?"

"Is it gone forever or just sitting at the bottom of your kitchen garbage can?"

"I dunno. I think I opened it at the studio. It's probably in the Dumpster by now."

I rubbed my face. "Okay. Did you look at the postmark? Where was it sent from?"

"Jeez, dude. I didn't know there was gonna be a test."

"Think, Holden. This is important. Where was this sent from?"

"I don't know," he said, his voice crisp with an edge of irritation. "I didn't look. Knowing TJ, it was probably from fucking Neptune."

"Hey, Holden!" a deep voice called out behind us.

"Yo, D!" Holden said, embracing the chest of one of the Magic players, a lanky black guy with an easy smile. The player was at least a head taller than us. He had been walking with the rest of the team back to the locker room to prepare for player introductions. He and Holden chatted for a few minutes about an upcoming celebrity charity game.

"It's for the kids, man," the player said before he disappeared down the hall.

Holden looked back at me with an expression that suggested he'd forgotten what we were talking about. I held up the card to refresh his memory.

"You get anything else?" I said.

"No, dude. Just the card. We done here?"

"Where do you think TJ is?"

"If I knew that, he'd be here now." Holden leveled his gaze at me, telling me that he was done with the conversation.

"Okay," I said. "Let me know if you get anything else."

"You'll be the first," he said, and walked back up into the stands.

I pinched the card between my fingers, staring at it, trying to squeeze some meaning out of it. TJ was telling us something. There was a reason he sent this. Was a pattern emerging? The card, the big check to Journeys of Hope, if that was indeed TJ's doing . . .

Was he just being TJ, as Holden implied? Or was he sending a message? Feeling sentimental? Saying good-bye? Did he have no intention of coming back?

Too many possibilities and too little evidence. I read the card again, but didn't divine any answers. I heard the Knicks being introduced and headed down the hall toward the exit. The thunderous music "for *your* Orlandooooo Magic!" boomed through the building. Before the players were introduced, I was out the door and into the humid night air.

"Morning, Bob," I mumbled aloud, my voice a hoarse croak at five thirty in the morning. The pain in my head was intense, a searing stab that cut behind both eyes. Bob didn't reply, but I knew he heard me.

I also knew I wouldn't be getting back to sleep, so I showered and made a pot of strong coffee. I popped a couple more of Cam's Zuraxx and tried to sit very still at the kitchen table, closing my eyes in a vain attempt to numb the invisible knife in my skull.

I don't know how long I had been sitting there, but when I opened my eyes, I saw Jennifer watching me from her bedroom doorway. I couldn't read her expression. She seemed cautious, maybe curious, maybe concerned. Maybe all three. Maybe none.

"Mornin'," I said.

"Morning." Jennifer went around the table and grabbed a mug from the cabinet. She poured a cup of coffee and stirred in some milk and sugar. I said nothing as she sat at the table and sipped. But she noticed me watching her.

"What?" she said.

"Nothin'."

"I drink coffee all the time, y'know."

"Okay."

"Lots of kids do. All my friends."

"Good."

"There's no age limit on coffee, like alcohol."

"Yeah."

We sat silently for a moment, just a coupla pals hooked on the bean, sipping our joe.

"Does your mom know you drink coffee?" I said.

I caught her in midsip. She froze, looking up at me over the rim of her mug. I had my answer. I smiled. She smiled back.

There was a knock at the front door that startled me. The wall clock said 7:12 a.m.

Jennifer and I exchanged a look. From the expressions on our faces, neither of us was expecting anyone. I thought about grabbing my Glock, but didn't want to spook Jennifer again. I pushed up from the table and peeked through the door peephole.

I groaned to myself and wondered if I could get away with pretending we weren't home. There was another loud knock, followed by a muffled voice calling, "Hello?!" I opened the door.

"Hi, Wayne," I said.

Jennifer's stepfather stood on the mat holding a toiletry bag. His face twitched into an awkward smile. He was as handsome as I remembered, tan and athletic, wearing a crisply pressed white shirt and a dark silk tie.

"Hi, Mike. Hope I didn't wake you."

"Nah," I said, stepping aside so he could enter.

"Wayne!" Jennifer exclaimed, immediately putting her coffee cup on the table and pretending it wasn't hers. Wayne's eyes darted over the scene. Two cups of coffee. A fifteen-year-old girl. He looked at me with a question in his eyes. There may have been an accusation and a judgment in there, too.

"You want some coffee, Wayne?" I said, closing the door. "Just made a fresh pot."

"Uh, no. Thanks."

"Well, if it's not my famous coffee, what brings you by at seven in the morning?"

He held up the toiletry bag. "Some stuff for Jennifer." He handed it to her. "Your mom found some vitamins and makeup and stuff you left at home. She asked me to drop it by on my way to the hospital. We wanted to make sure you had it before we left."

"Thanks," Jennifer said.

"Left?" I said.

"Becky and I are taking a few days at our place up north. Didn't she tell you?"

I shook my head. "Must've slipped her mind."

"Well, she's been under a lot of stress. You know. With everything."

"Yeah." I almost smiled. I was supposed to feel sorry for Becky because of the strain my terminal cancer has put on her. That pretty much summed up our marriage. "You want some breakfast? Cheerios?"

Wayne offered a polite smile. "Thanks anyway."

"I'll put this away," Jennifer said, and took the bag into her room.

"How you feeling?" Wayne said as soon as we were alone. I saw his eyes take in my shabby apartment. He was cool, didn't change his expression, but I knew that somewhere inside he winced.

"I'm fine."

"Headaches?"

"Sometimes."

"You still seeing Joe Tanner?"

"Yeah."

"He's good. You could do a lot worse."

"He seems okay," I said.

"Has he figured out a treatment plan yet?"

"Still working on it," I said as Jennifer came back into the kitchen.

"Sure you can't stay?" she said to Wayne. "I'll make you some eggs."

"Thanks, kiddo, but I'm late for work."

I escorted him to the door and locked it behind him. I occurred to me that my daughter had never offered to make me eggs. This morning I had been promoted to the position of adult with whom she can share her secret coffee habit, but I had a long way to go before I reached the exalted status of Saint Wayne. It pissed me off.

Sure, I knew my problems with Jennifer were my own doing, but it pissed me off, all the same.

"Get dressed," I said.

"What?" Jennifer said.

"Get dressed. We're going out for breakfast. Then I have plans for us this morning."

CHAPTER 9

I had the two-thousand-calorie, triple-cholesterol platter at Denny's. I put some extra grape jelly on a buttered biscuit and crammed it into my mouth. The encounter with Wayne had stirred something within me. Anger. Jealousy. Hunger. For the first time in a long while I was truly hungry. And, most surprising of all, Bob backed off on the headache. Maybe it was the food.

Jennifer picked at her omelet. She had hardly touched it.

"Whassamatta?" I said, my mouth full of biscuit. "You not hungry?"

She shrugged. Sipped at her OJ.

I swallowed the biscuit. Gulped the last of my coffee and gestured at a waitress for a refill. I gazed a moment at Jennifer and took a deep breath.

"Listen, you probably have some questions . . ."

She looked up at me and inhaled sharply, frozen. By her deer-in-headlights expression, I assumed she thought I was talking about sex.

"Y'know, about my cancer."

Her expression softened, but just barely. "I guess," she said, shrugging.

"What do you want to know?"

"I dunno . . ."

I raised my eyebrows, an attempt at encouragement. That it was okay to ask.

She shrugged again, pushing a piece of omelet with her fork. "Does it hurt?"

"No. The cancer doesn't hurt. Not yet. But I do get pretty bad headaches. See, around the brain is a cushion of fluid." I gestured an imaginary halo. "As the tumor gets bigger, it takes up more and more room, squeezing the fluid into a smaller and smaller space. As the pressure grows, the headaches get worse."

"What happens when there's no more room?" she said, still looking down at her plate.

"They can drain some fluid off to relieve pressure. But, really, by the time the tumor is that big—at least with my kind of tumor—headaches will be the least of my problems."

"What kind is it? The tumor." Jennifer put the fork down, but still wasn't looking at me.

"There are lots of different types of brain tumors. Some are even harmless. They grade tumors like mine in four levels, with four being the worst. I have what's called an anaplastic astrocytoma. It grew out of cells called astrocytes. My tumor is a grade three." I paused, trying see what kind of reaction I was getting. Jennifer's face was blank. Purposely blank. She was listening but pretending it was no big deal. "The doctors told me I could expect to live for another year or so, maybe more, depending on what the tumor decides to do. Grade threes usually turn into fours, also called gliomas. Once that happens, it usually goes downhill pretty fast. The last couple months will be kinda rough."

The waitress refilled my coffee cup and moved on. Jennifer poked the fork back into her eggs. "What do you mean . . . *rough*?"

"When the brain goes, so does your . . . personality. You can lose muscle control. You forget things. Your mood can change. You can lose the ability to talk. You may not be able to control your behavior at all. I don't know what'll happen. So far the most I've had are the headaches. But I also had a seizure. I'm on medication, but I expect it'll only get worse."

Jennifer shifted her weight and rotated her glass of juice. Her face puckered a little.

"I'm not trying to make you uncomfortable," I said. "Just thought you might have some questions. And I want to be completely honest. But we can talk about something else—"

She looked up at me. "So what are you doing about it?"

Stopped me cold.

"Can't you, like, take a pill or something?" she said.

"You mean treatment?"

"Yeah. Can't you *do* anything about it?" Her gaze was direct. Withering.

"It's complicated. Surgery is usually the first choice."

"So?"

"So, it's not so cut-and-dry. Even if they do go in, with a grade three, they almost never get it all out. Which means the tumor grows back. And, it usually comes back at a higher grade. Plus, the tumor's location is risky." I pointed at the biopsy scar on the side of my head. "It's not right at the brain's surface. They'd have to dig a little to get at it. The surgeon says that not only is there a ninety percent chance they won't get it all, but there's a fifty-fifty shot I'll suffer permanent brain damage either way. I could end up a vegetable."

Jennifer was silent for a moment, thinking about what I'd just said. "But what choice do you have?"

I hunched my shoulders. "It's up to me. I could also choose radiation or chemotherapy, which are mostly used as follow-ups after surgery. They can blast radiation right at the tumor or even surgically implant irradiated wafers. But, really, those just prolong the inevitable. They may slow the tumor down, but they won't stop it."

"So . . . surgery is your only choice."

"No . . ." I stirred a spoon in my black coffee.

"What else?"

I didn't say anything for a long moment, wondering just how honest I was going to be. It looked like she was about to get the total-honesty package.

"What else?" she said again.

"I could do nothing."

She furrowed her brow, confused. Then realization dawned and her expression changed into disbelief. "You mean give up?"

"I mean, let nature take its course."

"You mean give up." This time she said it as a statement.

"You have to play the cards you're dealt," I said, sounding

suddenly, inexplicably, like a Kenny Rogers song. "If you've got a bad hand, you can bet all you want but you'll still lose. Best to know when you're beat and cash out before blowing all your chips."

Jennifer stared at me for another few seconds, mouth slightly agape.

"You're not even going to *try* to fight?" she said, her lip curled in disgust.

This time it was my turn to look down at my plate. How do you explain to a fifteen-year-old—your daughter—that there really wasn't much worth fighting for? You had burned out at your job five years ago. The cancer was a blessing because it finally gave you an excuse to quit. You'd suffered through two failed marriages and had finally accepted that marriage as an institution just didn't work for you. You lived in a shitty little apartment that was no better than the one you had in college. You had no investments. No significant savings. No obligations. Parents long dead. No siblings. Your only child didn't like you very much. The thought of trying to salvage your relationship with her seemed way too hard when you had another thirty years of life to endure. Now that it was down to a few scant months, it just wasn't worth the effort.

She wouldn't understand if I tried to explain it. It would sound like I was wallowing in self-pity, which, admittedly, was pathetic. But I didn't feel sorry for myself. Honestly. At least I didn't think so. I just knew who I was and what my life had become. When I thought about it, I realized that Bob had arrived right on time. Some cosmic force—God, the universe, karma—had taken measure of my life and decided that, on balance, I was better off gone. Who was I to argue?

But Jennifer wouldn't understand that. I didn't even think I could express it adequately. Instead of trying, I merely shrugged again and looked down at the table.

With a small shake of her head, Jennifer turned back to her omelet and took a bite. We were silent for a moment. The sounds of the restaurant seemed incredibly loud. Silverware clinking. A guy coughing. A cell phone ringing. A baby crying. A plate breaking back in the kitchen.

I punctured a link sausage with my fork and skated it lazily around my plate. I couldn't bring it to my mouth. Putting down the fork, I pushed the food away. My ravenous appetite had vanished. And I could feel Bob's coffee break ending as the skull jackhammer went back to work.

Fortunately, I caught George on my cell phone while Jennifer was using the restroom. George had just arrived at the office and swore again that Eli had nothing to do with my new elevator friend. Apparently Eli was concerned and wanted to know more about it. When I asked George if I could bring Jennifer to the office, he told me "no problem." In fact, he'd even set up something special for me.

After talking with Holden at the basketball game the previous night, I figured it was time to sit down with the rest of the Boyz. If Holden had received a card from TJ, I was willing to bet my left ear that Ben and Miguel also had. Maybe some Global staffers, too. If I could get a postmark and compare the messages, I might have a general location and deduce some sort of pattern. At least as a starting point.

I hadn't yet told Jennifer where we were going. I planned to surprise her. Wayne might have the Lexus, the vacation place in the mountains, the relationship with my daughter, but I could deliver the idols of her youth. If this went well, it was a moment that she would remember the rest of her life. The heroes we have as kids are the most important we'll ever have. They are the heroes of innocence and wonder and possibility, before life shines the harsh light of reality on us. And them.

I pulled into Global's downtown parking garage. Jennifer asked a few questions, which I refused to answer, while we rode the amazingly quiet elevator upward. Realization seeped in for her when we walked into the opulent Global Talent lobby.

I asked the gorgeous receptionist to ring George. A minute later he appeared and escorted us down the hall, past the celebrity photos on the wall, to the door marked REHEARSAL STUDIO.

Jennifer's eyes were wide now. She had to have guessed what was going on but refused to believe it. She looked at me and I tried to stifle my grin. George opened the door and Jennifer's mouth dropped open.

"Oh . . . my . . . *God*," she said, her hands quivering at her sides.

Just as before, through the glass, I could see the three Boyz rehearsing a set of acrobatic dance moves with a choreographer. I put a hand on Jennifer's elbow and guided her into the room. Then I positioned her in front of the glass, where she stood with one hand over her mouth, the other trembling, her breath coming in rapid pants.

George pulled me aside where she couldn't hear us.

"She doesn't know about TJ, does she?" he whispered.

"Don't worry," I said, shaking my head. "I just want her to say hi and maybe get a quick photo while I'm interviewing Ben and Miguel."

"Okay," George said, looking up through the glass wall. "I'll grab Ben first for you and introduce Jennifer to Holden and Miguel."

"Thanks, George. I appreciate it."

"Yeah. No sweat." He slipped into the rehearsal studio.

I stepped up next to Jennifer. "You okay?"

"I can't believe this," she said, unable to tear her eyes from the glass. "I can't believe this. I can't believe this." She was still trembling.

"I'll just be a few minutes."

Finally she turned and looked up at me. Her face was intense, but utterly confused. The question was unsaid but clear: *How the hell did you do this?!*

"George is VP of security for the band. We used to work together at OPD."

The music stopped and Holden finished singing, stretching out the last note, eyes closed, voice full of emotion. Jennifer was at risk of a genuine old-fashioned swooning.

I saw George chatting with the three Boyz and the choreographer. They all looked over at us at the same time, and I sensed Jennifer's spine stiffen next to me. George waved us into the studio.

"C'mon," I said, and took Jennifer's elbow again. I led her into the studio, which was much cooler than it looked through the glass. The group was standing in the middle of the blond hardwood floor.

"Guys, this is Jennifer Garrity," George said as we approached. "Mike's daughter. She's a big fan."

To their credit, the Boyz knew how to connect with their fans. Holden, Ben, and Miguel each greeted her and made her feel welcome. Jennifer was borderline apoplectic. She managed a couple of stammering "Hi"'s and avoided any major teenaged embarrassment.

I handed George my thirty-five-millimeter camera, which, amazingly, I had actually remembered to grab from my apartment before I'd left. He nodded and shook a thumb at a door on the other side of the room.

Ben gave Jennifer a smile, exchanged a look with me, and headed for the door.

"I'll be back in a minute," I said to Jennifer, and followed Ben through the door.

CHAPTER 10

It was a combination dressing room/locker room/country club. It was ten times nicer than either of my previous houses and on a whole separate planet from my current apartment. Thick pile carpet, marble vanities, massage table, therapeutic spa, the works. Ben grabbed a Gatorade from a cooler and flopped into a couch along one gilded wall. He mopped his head and neck with a small towel.

"George said you want to talk about the card," he said, running his fingers through his dark, curly hair.

"Yeah," I said. "Did you get yours yesterday, too?"

He nodded. Paused. Then shook his head. "I swear I don't know what goes on between TJ's ears."

"Can I see it?"

"Sure." Ben pulled himself up. He opened a door that led, presumably, to a private changing area and returned a moment later with an envelope.

The postmark was Orlando, the west side of town. Not too far from Isleworth. Three days ago. Either TJ was still local, availing himself of the services of the U.S. Postal Service, or someone had mailed these for him. Maybe dear old Mom. I would definitely be back to see Arlene Sommerset very soon. Maybe today.

I opened the card. This one featured three images in a landscape orientation. To the left was a hairy brown caterpillar. In the center was a cocoon hanging from a branch. On the right was a rainbow-colored butterfly. I opened the card. The text inscription read:

Fulfill your destiny.

Underneath, TJ had written, *Be all you can be. Always believe in yourself. —TJ*

"Any idea why he sent it?" I asked.

Ben shrugged. "I think he's trying to be inspirational. TJ's kind of, y'know, sensitive."

"What do you mean?"

"Y'know. He's real emotional. Happened before the last tour, too. He came back from the desert talking about his cleansed spirit and chakras and stuff."

"Did he send you a card like this then?" I said, holding it up.

Ben considered a moment. "No. Don't think so."

"So this is different."

"Yeah. I guess. I just figured it was a new twist on the same old."

I made a noncommittal grunt. "Where do *you* think he is?"

"Probably back in the desert. Or in some cave with his legs folded. Hell if I know."

We chatted for another minute or two, but I had everything useful out of Ben I was going to get. We stepped back into the dance studio.

Holden, Miguel, and the choreographer were teaching Jennifer to perform the dance moves in the number they were rehearsing. She stood between the two Boyz, while the choreographer stood in front. All three faced the mirrored wall, stepping in unison.

"One two three, left," said the choreographer. "Twist, kick, three four. Arm, elbow, head, right. Good, Jennifer!"

I froze, struck by the sight of my daughter dancing between the Boyz. A vision flashed in my mind of Jennifer, ten years older, in a white gown, dancing at her wedding reception. The vision was gone in an instant, but I felt my heartbeat quicken. It was a scene I would never live to see.

Ben stepped around me and walked back to the group. But I was immobilized. If I moved, I was afraid my knees would buckle and I'd crumble to the floor.

George clicked a few shots with my camera of Jennifer dancing. Then he nodded to Miguel. Ben took Miguel's place in the routine and didn't miss a step. Jennifer glanced over and saw me. Her eyes were wide and she was trying desperately to hide an ecstatic grin. She looked as if she'd just won the lottery.

Miguel passed into the room behind me. I couldn't stop watching Jennifer. Her gangly fifteen-year-old frame was surprisingly graceful. I felt that, in some indefinable way, I was witnessing the end of her childhood. It was a moment I didn't want to end, as delicate as a soap bubble. If I looked away, the bubble would pop and be forever gone.

"Hey, man, you coming?" It was Miguel in the doorway behind me.

"Yeah," I said, watching for another moment and then closing my eyes.

Miguel sighed deeply and his lips formed a pained smile.

"I don't know," he said.

"What d'you mean?" I asked. "You don't know if you got a card or you don't know where it is?"

He sighed again. "I don't know if I should show you."

I furrowed my brow. "Yeah? Why not?"

Miguel got up from the couch, the same one Ben had sat on, and paced back and forth. Finally, he said, "It's personal. TJ sent it to me, not you."

"Look, you wanna find him or not?"

"Of course."

"Then where's the card?"

Miguel stopped pacing and looked hard at me. He wasn't angry. He was struggling internally, trying to decide what to do. Then he vanished into his private dressing room and came back out with a card in an envelope. Same postmark date and zip. I pulled out the card.

It was a black-and-white image of an urban sidewalk. A crack ran down the middle. Sprouting up through the crack, forcing its way through the concrete, was a bright yellow rose, the only color in the picture. Inside, the text said:

Never give up. Never.

TJ had written, *Never give up. Always remember. —Thomas James.*

I read it twice. This card was basically the same as the others. But different, too. The signature, for one thing. Thomas James, not TJ. Why?

The flash of a memory. TJ's apartment. The photographs I took from the office. There were several images of the band, but . . . but the only band member featured alone was Miguel. And now Miguel was the one to receive the card with the special signature. Coincidence?

Something was scratching at the back of my mind, a notion that I couldn't yet form. What was it?

"What are you supposed to always remember?" I asked.

Miguel looked at his feet. "I'm really not sure," he said softly.

"Nothing specific?"

"I don't think so."

The photographs flashed in my mind again. The only band member in a picture by himself was Miguel. There was something else . . .

"Why did he sign it Thomas James?" I asked.

"That's his name."

"If you say so. I've only ever heard him called TJ."

"What do you think TJ stands for?" he said, finally looking at me, a glint of irritation in his eye.

"Yeah, but nobody calls him Thomas James. Right?"

Miguel looked down again.

"Right?" I repeated.

"I do," he whispered, almost to himself. "Sometimes."

And then it hit me. In the picture of Miguel alone, he was asleep in a hotel bed. He was shirtless, eyes closed, wrapped up in rumpled sheets.

I sighed.

"Look," I said as gently as I could, which probably wasn't very gentle. "I'm not here to pry into your relationship with TJ. It's none of my business. But Eli's hired me to find him before the tour starts, and if you have any information about where he's hiding, you need to tell me. I promise I'll keep my mouth shut about everything but where he is."

"*Eli,*" Miguel said, disgusted. "Eli's the one who drove him away. If something happens to TJ, it'll be on Eli."

"Whoa. Wait a sec. Slow down. Eli knows about you and TJ?"

"Knows? Of course he knows. He's the one who forced me to—"

Miguel caught himself, fighting back a surge of anger, probably wondering how much he should say to me. But his blood was up, making him want to talk, and I knew I would have a short window to get whatever info I needed.

"What did Eli force you to do, Miguel?"

He put his face in his hands. "He's right. I know that. I mean, look who buys the records and the magazines. They're all girls. They have this image of who we are. If we don't deliver what the audience wants . . ." Miguel rubbed his eyes.

"So what did Eli do—tell you two to knock it off or the band was gonna dissolve?"

"Something like that. Except he came to each of us separately." Miguel smiled to himself. "TJ told him to go to hell."

I took a step toward him. "But you didn't."

Miguel's smile faded. "I know these boy bands only last so long. We've got a year or two, maybe more, before something new comes along. I plan to milk it for all it's worth before it's gone. I don't want to do anything that'll end it early."

I took another step. "So you went to TJ and told him it was over."

Miguel nodded, the memory clearly painful. "He told me I was a coward. And a liar. I told him that we could wait. Boyz Klub would run its course. We could start over then. He said it would be too late. That I would have already lost my soul."

"So he was pretty mad?"

"At first. But I know he was hurt." Miguel wiped a tear from his left eye. "So was I, man. But what could I do without risking everything? What could I do?"

"When was this?"

"Couple weeks ago. A few days later he disappeared."

"Where is he, Miguel?"

"I don't know, man. I wish I did."

"Come on, Miguel. Where is he?"

"I don't know!" he said, his voice rising. But he appeared to be less angry at me than generally frustrated that he didn't know. I think I believed him. "We weren't exactly talking when he left."

"Okay. Okay." I sat in a lounge chair across from him and rubbed my temples, trying to organize my thoughts. I took a deep breath and let it out slowly. "Do you have *any* guess where he could be?"

Miguel shook his head wearily. "I've tried, man. I've thought until my head aches. If I knew, I'd probably have gone to him myself."

I laid my head back on the top of the chair cushion. My thoughts were racing. I quickly tried to assimilate this new twist. "When you said that Eli knew, that you blame him, you also said that if anything happens to TJ, it'll be Eli's fault. What do you mean? What could happen to TJ?"

Miguel's face contorted and I thought he might bawl. He reached back and produced a folded piece of paper from his pants pocket. He handed it to me.

"This came in the card," he said, grimacing.

I unfolded it and read TJ's meticulous penmanship:

Some days bring sunrises and some days bring sunsets. And each day is filled with greetings and partings. Good-byes need not always be sad. Although I believe that there could have been more, I celebrate the time we did have together. And I cherished being an artist and expressing myself through music. Now that I'm gone, try to remember me like that: as an artist. I'll soon cast off my chains and finally, thankfully, be rid of the burdens placed on me by society . . . by expectations . . . by life. What will lift my wings and carry me skyward is the memory of your breath upon my cheek and our voices raised together in song. Adios, Miguel. Do not forget me.—Thomas James.

When I finished reading, I looked up and saw Miguel watching me intently, his face pained. Clearly, he wanted to know if I understood. I think I did.

It had been a while, and I don't ever recall reading one with quite so much imagery, but I was pretty sure I recognized a suicide note when I saw one.

CHAPTER 11

George told me that no one else at Global Talent had received a card from TJ. Only the band. But, clearly, Eli knew more than he was letting on.

I left a dazed Jennifer in the reception-area lounge. She was still on an incredulous high after meeting and dancing with the members of her favorite band. I expected the big question of why I was meeting privately with Ben and Miguel, but she remained quiet. She appeared to be savoring her moment, making it last longer, like Cinderella humming a happy tune on the way home from the ball. Besides, the pissed expression on my face probably discouraged open discourse.

I strode down the lush hallway covered with photos and ignored the assistant manning the desk outside Eli's palatial office.

"Hey—," she said as I whooshed past. I leaned on Eli's door and pushed into the office.

He was standing in front of the window wall, hands on hips, talking to himself.

"I don't give a rat's ass what she says. I won't play those games. We're in L.A. on the fourteenth and she needs to book us now or we go with another show. . . . No. . . . I said *no*!"

Then I noticed the thin cord hanging from his ear and realized he was talking on the cell phone tucked away on his belt. I felt the presence of the heavyset assistant behind me. Still talking, Eli saw us from the corner of his eye and turned his head.

"Well, then have him call me," he said, looking directly at me. "I'd love to talk to him. . . . No, that's not confirmed yet. . . . Soon. If I knew when, I'd say so, goddamn it. Hold on." His eyebrows went up at me. "You find TJ?"

"We need to talk," I said.

"You're damn right." Eli nodded at the assistant, who backed out of the office, closing the door. "Hey, Billy, I gotta call you back. Ten minutes. . . . I know. . . . I *know*. Don't go anywhere. I mean it. . . . Yeah."

He pressed a button on the phone and narrowed his eyes at me. "So what's up, slick? George tells me someone approached you."

"I think we have a problem."

"No kidding. If the press suspect TJ's missing, just wait until the rumors start flying. It's probably already on the Internet message boards. That's why you gotta find him now. To nip all the nonsense in the bud."

"Were you gonna tell me about TJ and Miguel, or was this some sort of test?"

Eli opened his mouth, already preparing some smart comment, when my question smacked him in the teeth. He closed his mouth. Removed the cell's earphone. Then he sat in a chair and sighed, holding the arms and leaning back.

"Shit," he said. "You're good. I've managed to keep that a secret for more than a year. I can only think of five people who know. I don't even think Ben and Holden know." I said nothing and sat in a chair opposite him. "How did you find out?"

"It doesn't matter. Didn't it occur to you that TJ ran off right after you told them to knock it off?"

"Sure."

"And you didn't think it was important enough to tell me?"

"Tell you?" He stifled a mirthless chuckle. "I struggle for a year to keep that a secret and I'm supposed to blab it to some guy off the street five minutes after I meet him? George doesn't even know, for crissakes. I wasn't gonna say anything in front of him. And now look. Somebody's already leaked that he's missing."

"Is that why you hired me? TJ wasn't exactly gonna take your call, or anyone's from Global. You thought someone from the outside might be able to reach him."

"Generally. Plus, George said you knew what you were doing. Seems he was right."

"It's hard for me to do my job if you're hiding things from me."

"Hiding? What does TJ's sex life have to do with this? Just tell me where he is, not who he's doing."

I leaned forward onto my knees. "There's a big difference between running away to recharge your batteries and running away to escape your life. In this kinda case, motive can be everything. The *why* could tell us *where*."

Eli shook his head. "Okay, Einstein. Now you know why. Tell me where."

"Maybe if I knew this from the start, I'd have found him by now. At the moment all I've got is a general suspicion."

"So, go get him, slick."

"What else don't I know?" I said, giving him a pointed look.

"What else is there *to* know? You already found the one thing I was trying to keep secret. Anything else is small-time next to that."

"Let me be the judge of what's small-time."

Eli shook his head again. "There's nothin' else." He paused, then looked sideways out the window. "It's no secret TJ and I didn't get along. We argued over the types of songs we should record. About how the music videos should be shot. Everything. And, privately, we argued about him and Miguel. TJ's a major pain in my ass."

"But you're willing to pay me a quarter mil to find him."

"This is bigger than me. Bigger than TJ. This is corporate sponsorship. This is megamillions. This is a sold-out worldwide concert tour. This is . . . an industry." He took a deep breath. "Whether I like it or not, I need TJ on that tour. He gets twenty percent more fan mail than the other members of the band. For God's sake, don't tell them that. They couldn't possibly read all their mail so we only give them selected stacks to look at. But I get the stats. I know." Eli paused and rubbed his face, an atypically weary gesture for his normally frenetic manner. "I need an innocuous, *heterosexual* TJ on that plane when we kick off the tour. And I need you to find him."

I expected him to punctuate his last statement with a jaunty *slick* or *ace* or *Sherlock* or something, but he didn't. He just looked at me with hangdog eyes, uncharacteristically vulnerable. I suddenly believed that he didn't honestly know who the guy in the elevator was. Eli seemed to have aged ten years since I'd walked into the office.

I seriously pondered quitting. As I've said before, terminal cancer imbues in one an incredibly low tolerance for bullshit. The money would be nice for Jennifer, but it wouldn't do me any good in my pine box. I could walk away.

But then I thought about Miguel's note. If that really was a suicide note, and it wasn't already too late, I was the only chance TJ had. I now had a new reason to find him: to save him.

I had quickly grown to admire TJ in the past few days and believed the world would be a lesser place without him. And I couldn't bear to think about what his death would do to Jennifer, let alone the millions of fans just like her.

I considered telling Eli about the note, but I couldn't think of what good it would do. Even if I found TJ alive, it seemed pretty clear he was through with Boyz Klub. Based on what I'd learned about TJ's character, I didn't think he'd be persuaded to change his mind. Eli was on the road to some serious expectations adjustments. Even if I managed to find TJ, the only victory would be if he was still actually breathing. I got up from my chair and looked down at Eli.

"I'll find him," I said. "I suggest you pray I do before it's too late."

He nodded slightly, mistakenly thinking that I was talking about the start of the concert tour.

Jennifer was quiet as I pulled my truck out of the parking garage and onto a busy downtown street. The tall bank buildings stood like glass canyon walls on either side of us and reflected our passing in distorted, staccato frames.

"I'll drop you at the apartment and then I've gotta go out for a while," I said.

Jennifer was looking out the window. With her face turned

away, I couldn't see her expression. She remained silent, but she radiated an energy—an electric charge—that was palpable inside the cab of my truck.

"Jennifer?"

"Okay," she said, still looking out the window.

I made my way through the grid of one-way streets until I found the on-ramp for I-4, Orlando's aortic artery. I pulled out onto the highway and immediately braked to avoid a flatbed truck full of lawn equipment.

"Why did you talk to Ben and Miguel alone?" Jennifer asked. Her tone was mild, idly curious.

I was expecting the question. "George asked me to do some background interviews of the band. Routine security stuff. George and I go way back at OPD. Honestly, I think he gave me the job because I have cancer."

"And Holden?"

"I already interviewed him." I checked my mirrors before changing lanes. I was also performing a habitual scope for the blue Mustang. So far, I didn't see it.

"TJ, too?" Jennifer said.

"Actually, no. He's next."

"Have you met him? TJ?"

"Not yet."

Jennifer sighed and paused, looking again out the window. "I wonder what he's like," she said lazily to herself.

So do I, I thought.

"Where was he today?" she said.

"Dunno. Maybe he was sick."

"Maybe." She continued looking out the window, basking in the day's experience but coloring it with a thin coat of regret for not having met TJ, too. She was quiet for the rest of the drive home.

I pulled into my apartment parking lot and got out to walk her up.

"That's all right," she said. "I've got my key."

"Okay." I stopped on the sidewalk. I would've preferred to walk her up. I was still a little concerned about the blue Mustang and the creep in the elevator. But we appeared to be alone and I understood her need for her adolescent space.

She took a half step toward the stairs, I thought, then threw her arms around me and laid an ear against my chest.

"This was the best day of my life." Ordinarily, I would've characterized a statement like that as a childhood exaggeration. But I knew it was true. There would be other days for her that would be more significant and more joyous. But for now, today, this was truly the best day of her life. It was a memory that she would carry with her always, to be pulled out and reviewed fondly from time to time.

And I felt grateful that I had been able to give her this gift that would last the rest of her life.

"Thanks, Dad." She held on just a little too tight and a beat too long. Enough for me to wonder if this moment had more to do with my cancer. Then she let go, quickly wiping a cheek.

"You gonna be okay for lunch?" I asked.

"Please." She rolled her eyes.

"What about work? You got a ride?"

"I'm off today."

"Oh. I'll try to call when I know when I'll be home."

"Sure. Whatever. I'm cool. Would you drop off the film while you're out? Do the one-hour and get, like, quadruple prints. I'm gonna show *everybody*."

"Um, yeah, okay."

"I've *gotta* call Gwen."

I watched her—half girl, half woman—bound up the stairs. I got back in my truck and sat for a moment, taking deep, measured breaths. The sharp sting of tears seeped into my eyes and I was afraid I might actually sob, something I hadn't done since I was a kid.

Since being diagnosed with cancer, I had gone emotionally numb. Hell, who was I kidding? I had gone emotionally numb years ago, probably shortly after Becky and I got married. Maybe even before Jennifer was born. But now here I sat in my truck, on the verge of a genuine outburst. Orlando's June heat saved me as the cab quickly turned into a convection oven.

I turned over the ignition, cranked up the AC, and pulled out into the street. For the first time in a long time, I flipped the radio on and found an old Eagles tune.

Desperado, why don't you come to your senses? . . .

I reached over and turned up the volume.

CHAPTER 12

The uniform at the Isleworth guard shack was waiting for me, clipboard in hand.

"Hi," he said cheerily. "Who are you here to see?"

"Arlene Sommerset." The guard asked my name and I gave it.

"Is she expecting you?"

"I don't know. Probably not." I'd tried calling Arlene from my cell phone on the ride over, but I only got her machine.

The guard popped back into the shack and punched some keys on a computer. A few seconds later the gate swung up and the guard poked his head out.

"Okay, Mr. Garrity. You're on the list. You know where you're going?"

"Uh, yeah."

"Have a nice day."

"Thanks." I nodded and pulled through the barrier. The list? I figured that getting through the gate was a hopeless mission. But Arlene Sommerset had put my name on her permanent admittance list.

That was a definite surprise.

As I drove through the Mediterranean-styled mansions and putting-green manicured lawns, I pulled out my cell phone. I took a fortifying breath and punched in a familiar number. A moment later, I heard Big Jim's baritone voice through the receiver.

"This's Dupree."

"Big Jim."

A pause. "G. This's gettin' to be a habit. You might as well come back and sit at your desk, as much as we seem to be talkin' lately."

"I have another favor. Can you run a check of the hospitals and morgue? New arrivals."

"You still lookin' for your skip?"

"Yeah."

"Thought you said I didn't have to worry 'bout no toe tags on this deal."

"Just covering all my bases. I have a hunch he may not be in the best frame of mind and may try to hurt himself."

I imagined that I actually heard Jim shaking his head. "I don't like what I'm hearin' here, G. It's makin' the back of my neck itch. That ain't good, bro."

"Just let me know what you find. Especially John Does who fit the physical."

"I'm scratchin' my neck right now, bro. Can you hear that? I'm gettin' a bad, itchy feelin' 'bout this *case* that George Neuheisel pawned off on you. Maybe you should just walk away."

"Too late, Jimbo. I'm already in—what the hell?" As I turned the corner onto Arlene Sommerset's street, I saw a low-slung, red Mazda MX-6 in her driveway. A male figure was peeking through one of the house's side widows.

"Say again, G?"

"Gotta go, Jimbo. I'll talk to you later." I pressed off the phone and parked the car two houses down, where I still had a view of the figure. Although I was still too far away for a really good look, I could see enough to observe that the figure was not TJ. The hair was lighter and there was at least thirty pounds more on the body. But he was young, probably close to TJ's age, wearing a dark blue sweat suit and high-top sneakers. I watched for a few minutes as the kid looked in another window, knocked on it, then looked again.

He worked his way to the front door and rapped it with his knuckles. Then rang the bell and knocked once more. He peeked through the sidelight windows next to the door. He looked like he was getting increasingly frustrated.

The kid stepped past the door and crept his way around the other side of the house, out of my view. I reached under my seat, found my nine-millimeter Glock, and shoved it under my shirt into the back of my jeans. I hopped out of the car and strode quickly to Arlene's house.

I went around the opposite side of the home, moving deliberately through the thick St. Augustine grass. It crunched softly under my feet as I stepped. I glanced into each window as I went past and saw no indication that anyone was home.

I reached the back of the house, where a huge screened swimming pool sat, complete with a whirlpool spa and bubbling waterfall. I peeked around the corner. Through the screen I saw the kid in the sweat suit coming around the other side. He stepped through the deep grass, squinting into the lanai.

"Hey!" he called in a nasal voice. "Hey! Anybody home?" He tried the screen door but it was locked. He pounded the doorframe with the bottom of his fist, and the aluminum clanged loudly, echoing across the pool.

If this kid was a burglar, he was the world's worst. I slipped back around the corner and traversed the landscaping to the front yard, where I crossed the street and slid quietly into my truck.

Okay . . . so who was this kid? My guess was that he knew the Sommersets, Arlene or TJ or both. He called out like he expected them to know who he was. Plus, he was inside the gate. With celebrity neighbors all around, one did not easily sneak through the security gate at Isleworth. If he was merely a garden-variety Boyz Klub fan, he would have been stopped and pounced on long before he made it to the house. Was he a neighbor? A close friend? If he didn't live here, was he also on the Sommersets' permanent-access list?

Which might make him who? A boyfriend? Arlene's? TJ's? He seemed way too young, and tacky, for Arlene, and TJ had just gotten out of a serious relationship with Miguel. Both seemed unlikely scenarios.

Wait a sec—George mentioned a cousin. I hadn't found time to follow up on the cousin yet. This kid might be him. So what to do about it? I immediately decided against a direct approach.

As a cop, when I was in the midst of an investigation, especially a major one for the Metropolitan Bureau of Investigation, it was always a difficult call knowing when to meet an issue head-on and when to sneak up on it from the side. There were advantages to both. In this case, I felt the sneaking-up option to be the most prudent. This cousin might know where TJ was and confronting him might make him clam up. Following him, on the other hand, might yield pay dirt. I jotted down the Mazda's tag number.

It took a few minutes for the kid to come back around the house. He continued to check every window and to beat on the front door. I slumped down in my seat and flashed back to a thousand other stakeouts I had sat vigil on. They were boring, uncomfortable propositions, but, despite that, I had felt alive, purposeful. Especially at the beginning of my career. I was truly doing good in the world, removing some very bad guys from decent society.

Drugs. Prostitution rings. Gambling. I had been a lead investigator on a case that had resulted in the arrest and conviction of Juan "the Don" Alomar, a local mob crew chief and boss of the major bookmaking operation in Central Florida, run from the back office of a used-car lot on East Colonial Drive. Used cars were a cash business and it was easy to launder money through that front.

I had been thinking more about this case since George had mentioned it during our first meeting in his office. It was a big deal at the time. Newspaper articles. An interview on CNN. And, of course, the reenactment on a Discovery Channel investigations program. I had endured more than the usual amount of ribbing in the office, but, in retrospect, it was probably the pinnacle of my career. Everything from that point on was a process of slow decay, my attitude and passion for the job wearing way like a stone under a continual drip. At the time, though, the Alomar case represented all the reasons I'd first entered law enforcement.

Alomar was a San Juan transplant, known in Puerto Rico for gambling and providing a safe haven for the mob's drug-smuggling mules headed for the mainland. He was run out of Puerto Rico when one of the mules got busted and things became too hot. He, like so many from that Caribbean U.S. territory, found his way to Central Florida and reestablished operations. Alomar's was a branch office of the Angelino crime family of Paramus, New Jersey, and my evidence had cranked up at least a half dozen FBI investigations of some serious wiseguys up North. It was a big collar, probably my biggest, and put the squeeze on illegal gambling from Daytona to Tampa. It even sent a popular legal gambling ship from Port Canaveral into dry dock.

Nailing guys like Alomar had made me feel that I was making a difference. But somewhere along the line, that fire burned out. I'd arrest a guy only to see him right back on the street again in a few weeks. I busted one pusher twelve times for the same thing. Too much time spent with the very worst society had to offer. Being a cop is a job where no one's ever happy to see you coming. It skews your life perspective. Makes you cynical and jaded. I'm sure it didn't help my marriages. My gut grew cold and the job became a grind of routine and repetition. I stayed in for a long time after that, even after I realized I had burned out, mostly because I didn't know how to do anything else.

My marriages had failed. My parenthood had failed. I defined myself by my career. My work had given me purpose when the rest of my life was crumbling around me. So, if I wasn't a cop, who was I? Even though I had grown to hate the job, if I quit, I might cease to exist. And then Bob showed up with a brand-new identity for me.

Cancer Guy.

Sitting here now, I tasted the dormant but familiar flavor of investigation. It was a sensory memory, the scent of professional mission. I hadn't felt it in a long time.

The kid opened the Mazda's driver's door and dropped into the seat. He fired up the engine and squealed out of the driveway. I put the truck in gear and was right behind him.

There was scant traffic on the Isleworth roads, but, with so many landscapers and plumbers and exterminators continually working in the neighborhood, the sight of a pickup truck was hardly suspicious. I followed the red Mazda back through the neighborhood and emerged right behind it on the other side of the security gate.

The Mazda turned right onto Conroy Road, so I did, too. I let a little separation grow between our vehicles to avoid obvious detection. From the edge of my vision, I saw a flash of blue.

My eyes darted up to the rearview mirror and there was the goddamn blue Mustang bearing down on me like a locomotive. I hadn't seen it when I'd pulled out of Isleworth. I was busy watching the Mazda.

I instinctively pushed down on the gas to avoid being rear-ended, but the Mustang kept coming. In front of me the Mazda suddenly leapt forward, the kid in the sweat suit accelerating away like I had Ebola. My eyes jumped back to the rearview where the Mustang was about to crash my bumper and send me fishtailing into a retention canal. At the last possible moment, the Mustang veered left, swerving out into oncoming traffic.

A loaded dump truck appeared from around a bend, heading straight for the Mustang. I gripped the steering wheel and stood both feet on the brake, the antilocks shuddering, fighting to maintain control. The Mustang squealed and jerked back in front of me, spraying road pebbles across my windshield as the dump truck thundered past us on our left.

Then the Mustang lurched away, screaming after the Mazda. I mashed my foot down on the accelerator and took off after them both.

My old truck groaned and protested, but managed to maintain the distance between me and the Mustang. The Mazda swerved recklessly, careening between and around cars in a frantic attempt to escape the Mustang. But the Mustang kept gaining.

Ahead of us I saw a traffic light turn yellow. The Mazda blew under it just as it flipped red. The Mustang was right behind, flying through the intersection at close to eighty miles an hour. A crossing white minivan squealed to a crooked stop to avoid being smashed.

I leaned on the brake and heaved to a stop. Ahead of me, through the crossing cars, I saw the Mustang and Mazda changing lanes, darting back and forth in their dangerous chase. If I didn't get through this busy suburban intersection in the next few seconds, I would lose them.

I nosed out into the intersection and heard a few angry horns blaring. After a moment, the oncoming cars instinctively slowed, seeing my truck halfway in their lane. It was the opening I needed and I floored the accelerator.

More furious horns sounded as cars in the farther lanes squealed to a stop. I pulled the wheel hard left to avoid a gold Camry and bounced over the raised concrete curb of the median on the far side of the intersection. I thumped back into the street and leaned heavily on the gas to make up the distance to the Mustang.

We barreled through the streets of West Orlando's Dr. Phillips area. It was only a matter of time before the cops joined our game of tag.

The Mazda raced past the entrance to Universal Studios and for a moment I thought he might turn into the parking garage. But the Mazda kept going, seeing the line of cars snaking out from the admission gate. I guessed that the kid didn't want to get boxed in where he'd be vulnerable.

We all turned onto Sand Lake Road, luckily catching the traffic light on green, and zigzagged our way under I-4. Next we were on International Drive, a tourist-heavy part of town populated with myriad hotels, shops, restaurants, and the gargantuan Orange County Convention Center. Traffic would likely be too heavy on I-Drive for this chase to continue. Something bad would happen.

Unfortunately, I was right. Up ahead, I saw a row of red taillights waiting for a traffic light. The Mazda screeched hard to the right, skidding into the parking lot of a souvenir shop. He quickly accelerated, trying to regain control of his car, but it was too late. He plowed into a row of parked rental cars like a bowling ball into a fresh set of pins.

The cars slammed into each other with the same sound as a dump truck pushed over a cliff. The front of the Mazda disintegrated, compressing into itself.

The Mustang squealed to a halt next to the carnage. A familiar, hulking guy with a thick shock of black hair leapt from the Mustang and ripped open the Mazda driver's door, no easy feat considering the door was now an entirely new shape.

I swerved into the parking lot just as the big man was yanking the kid out from the Mazda. He picked the kid up with both paws and threw him against the back of the car. I saw a thin line of blood trickling from the kid's nose.

I shoved my truck in park, gripped my nine-millimeter, and was out the door.

CHAPTER 13

My neon-golf-shirt-wearing buddy from the elevator had a hand around the kid's neck now, squeezing so hard the kid's face was turning purple. He was saying something to the kid, something clearly unpleasant, but I couldn't catch what it was. I raised the Glock and pointed it in their basic direction.

"Hey!" I said in my former cop voice. "Playtime's over."

Not removing a finger from the kid's throat, the elevator goon turned his head slowly toward me. His lipless mouth was an expressionless fissure between his nose and flat chin.

"Fuck off," he said in his nasal voice.

"Let go of junior there," I said.

He didn't move. I focused my aim at his big square head.

"Let him go, sport. And keep your hands where I can see 'em."

Except for turning his head at me, the big guy hadn't moved since I'd arrived. His eyes were as hot as cigar ashes. Still motionless everywhere else, I saw his fingers slowly release the kid's neck. The kid flopped over onto his hands and knees, coughing and sputtering, a drop of blood plopping from his nose onto the parking lot asphalt.

"He has a gun," the kid said, wheezing.

"Where?" I said.

"His ankle."

"Take it," I said, maintaining my aim and gaze intently on Day-Glo's face. The kid looked up at me, hesitating. "Take it!" I ordered. "And slide it over to me."

The kid pushed himself over to the big man's leg and shoved the pant cuff up. A small .22 semiautomatic pistol was holstered above his right ankle. The kid fumbled with the safety strap but managed to extract the weapon.

During this, the big guy and I continued making the love eyes at each other. He remained motionless—a statue—but his eyes increased their malevolent intensity. My cop instincts were telling me that he was very bad news. I couldn't let my guard down for an instant.

"Slide it over," I said to the kid without looking at him.

The .22 bounced over the blacktop and skidded to a halt about eighteen inches from my toe. The kid pulled himself upright and leaned heavily against the trunk of his demolished car. His left hand clutched his rib cage and the wince on his face registered definite pain.

"Okay," I said to both of them. "Somebody tell me the story."

In my peripheral vision, I could see a couple of shoppers staring wide-eyed through the T-shirt shop window. In the clouds above I heard the boom of an afternoon thunderstorm rolling in from the west. It was immediately followed by a distant siren.

That was the kid's cue because he instantly turned and started running, his gait a limping struggle.

"Hold it!" I shouted, and was summarily ignored. The kid disappeared around the side of the shop. I debated going after him, but a little voice in my head told me not to turn my back on Day-Glo.

The big guy finally moved. He straightened himself up and rolled his shoulders, adjusting the lay of his bright orange shirt across his back.

"Okay," I said, "talk quick before the cops show up. What's goin' on? Why have you been following me?"

"You ain't gonna wait for the cops and you know it," he said, tilting his head and popping a vertebra in his neck. "You gonna hand my piece back?"

"Unlikely."

"You pissed in the wrong soup, brother." He started back toward the Mustang.

He was right about the cops. If I waited for them to arrive, I'd be hauled in with him. As it was, I only had a moment or two to slip away, and even then, I could still easily get nabbed. So, unless I wanted to actually shoot him, that meant I had to stand here like a limp wiener and watch him drive away.

Day-Glo backed his ass into the Mustang's driver's seat. "I want the money," he said. "And I don't care who I carve it outta. You. Him. Don't matter to me. But I'll get it. And somebody's gonna get carved." The approaching sirens were getting louder.

"What are you talkin' about?"

He narrowed his eyes at me. "You really that dumb? You better get yourself smart pretty fuckin' quick, Mikey."

"Who the hell are you?" I said, jabbing the barrel of the Glock at him.

"I told you. A friend of a friend." The Mustang's engine growled to life.

"You stay away from me, *friend*. I see you again—"

"And what? You gonna shoot me? Do it now, then." He lifted his chin farther out the driver's window, offering a clean shot of his Frankenstein head. He held it up for a beat while I stood there impotently. "Yeah," he said, and the Mustang started rolling. "You have a nice day now, Mikey. Enjoy your time with that little girl of yours." A moment later the Mustang melted back into the I-Drive traffic, slipping between lanes.

The sirens weren't far now. I snatched the .22 from the ground, trying to grab only the trigger guard and not lay a bunch of fingerprints on it, and leapt back into my truck. I pulled forward and slipped out the rear of the shop parking lot, turning onto an industrial service road that ran behind the I-Drive restaurants and shops and fed the distribution area of the convention center. I did a quick scan looking for the errant kid in the sweat suit, but he was nowhere to be seen.

A fat raindrop whacked my windshield with a sharp crack. Then another. They were soon followed by a brilliant flash of lightning and a thunderclap so loud that I flinched, my ears ringing. The raindrops were then joined by 10 billion of their siblings. An aggressive wind billowed mile-long sheets of plump droplets across west Orange County. It was a typical Florida summer-afternoon storm shower: a tempest of biblical proportions. I leaned heavily on the pedal and sped off.

The cops would be thick here in a few minutes. Probably Orange County deputies but maybe a few of my old friends at OPD, too. Depended on who was winning the jurisdictional politics at the moment. If I stayed smart, didn't speed, got out on the Beachline Expressway, and the storm stayed as torrential as it was starting, I had a shot of getting away.

And I needed to get away. I suddenly had a lot to do.

I had no doubt considerable effort was expended to find the Mustang and the Ford pickup that the witnesses surely identified. But the weather turned into an ally. In that storm, it was too difficult to mobilize a truly effective dragnet. And forget about calling in a chopper. I guessed that the officers (or deputies) on the scene figured they had the smashed Mazda and could easily track the owner down. They might even have grabbed him already. He was on foot, after all, and injured. Once the cops had him, they could figure out the rest of the sordid story. I wished I could.

I drove around for thirty or forty minutes before I found a Bennigan's restaurant and parked. The storm let up just enough to allow me to run from my car to the restaurant without scuba equipment. I planted myself at a high table in a dark corner of the bar, ordered a Scotch straight up, and tried to catalog my next steps.

First, the case . . . I still needed to get in touch with Arlene Sommerset. She needed to know about TJ's letters and my fear that he's a suicide candidate, if not already—God forbid—a victim. I'd left her a voice mail before arriving at her house. I now used my cell phone again to leave her another message to call me as soon as she could.

Next, the kid in the sweat suit. I assumed he was TJ's cousin, but that was just an educated guess. I needed some confirmation. He had somehow gotten through the Isleworth security, and it made sense that if he really was the cousin, he would be on the Sommerset access list. But why all the creeping around the Sommerset abode? He clearly wanted to get inside. Did it have to do with TJ? Or something else? It occurred to me that it was possible that Arlene was home the whole time but avoiding him. She might still be home, avoiding me, too.

Finally, Day-Glo and his blue Mustang. Clearly, the guy was a professional influencer. His demand for money. His threat to carve somebody up. The .22 on his ankle. A picture was taking shape, but it was way too ugly to hang on a wall. My best guess was that the cousin owed Day-Glo or his boss some money. But the cousin didn't have the money, and the usual result of such a situation was a scene like the one a little while ago in the parking lot. Perhaps I'd just wandered into the wrong place at the wrong time.

But Day-Glo knew my name. And had been following me. I first spotted him after searching TJ's apartment. Was TJ mixed up in this? Was this a more plausible reason for disappearing than Eli's interference in his and Miguel's relationship? Was Day-Glo following me to find the cousin? Or TJ? Or both?

Or was this about me somehow? The goon described himself as "a friend of a friend." Was it just an expression or did it have more significance? And why did he make a point to mention my daughter? It was an unambiguous threat.

Jennifer—I suddenly remembered her sitting alone in my apartment. My fingers quickly punched the cell's buttons and I heard the phone ring a few times. I let it ring, waiting for the answering machine to pick up. It never did. Five rings. Six rings. Finally, I heard a click followed by Jennifer's voice.

"Hello?"

"Jennifer, it's me. Your dad." I wanted to call myself Mike. I felt awkward referring to myself as Dad.

She had been on the other line with Gwen and had finally decided to answer the call-waiting tone. Gwen was probably still on the other line. I made Jennifer check that the front door and windows were all locked. I lied to her that there was a report of a rapist in the neighborhood and instructed her to stay inside. Only after she promised twice that she would did I hang up.

Or, despite his protestations, was the whole scene today still somehow tied to Eli Elizondo and Global Talent? Maybe he really didn't trust me to find TJ and had hired some PI on his own. Or maybe Eli wanted one of his own guys to shadow me, make sure I was doing what I was supposed to. Once I found TJ, the big man would swoop in and ensure he got on the tour plane. But why chase the cousin? To find TJ? And why risk pissing me off if I now knew about TJ and Miguel?

I needed information—some edge to give me an advantage. I'd managed to get both the Mazda's and Mustang's license tags. A DMV search would tell me who I was playing chase with. A call to Big Jim Dupree should enable that. I was getting concerned about going to the Big Jim well too often. I was on the verge of abusing our friendship. But I decided to call him anyway, later tonight. Maybe go over to his house with a bribe—a bottle of the good merlot he and his wife liked so much.

If the DMV check didn't produce results, I still held the .22 pistol. I could pull the serial number or have Jim lift some prints, if they weren't too compromised.

A second Scotch replaced the drained first and I ordered a bacon burger to accompany it. I hadn't eaten since breakfast at Denny's and was suddenly famished. I was halfway through the burger when my cell phone chirped.

"Hello?" I said, wiping ketchup from the corner of my mouth.

"Mr. Garrity, it's Arlene Sommerset. You wanted to talk with me?"

"Yeah. I'll be there in twenty minutes," I said, and clicked off the phone.

CHAPTER 14

I pulled into Arlene Sommerset's brick driveway. The last time I had been inside this house, Bob gave a command performance of the Seizure Follies. I didn't relish the idea of returning for a possible encore.

So far the antiseizure meds had been working fine, without debilitating side effects. The nausea was still severe but intermittent. There had been no more seizures since my last visit to the Sommerset manse. However, the doc had told me nothing was guaranteed. Another seizure was still possible and a different prescription might be necessary.

Involuntarily, I flashed back to what I remembered of the seizure. The confusion when I couldn't understand what Arlene was saying. The tunnel vision. The distorted hearing. The glass smashing on the tile. Pitching forward off the couch.

My hand froze on the keys in the ignition, about to shut off the engine. I distinctly remembered falling off the couch, the expensive Italian tile spinning up at me before I lost consciousness. Arlene told me afterward that I'd convulsed, presumably there on the living-room floor. Yet I awoke laying comfortably back on the couch.

How did I get from the floor back to the couch?

I didn't think that Arlene could have lifted me by herself. It was possible, I supposed, but I doubted it. I've lifted my share of unconscious bodies in my career, and it's a lot harder than lifting someone with some kick. Imagine a 185-pound sack of water. My guess was that Arlene had some help. Yet the only other resident of the house that I'd seen was that yippy little dog.

Which begged the question: Was there another resident that I didn't see?

I cut the truck's engine and made my way to the front door. Arlene answered it with a tired smile. She said nothing and stepped aside, indicating I should enter. I did and followed her into the family room this time. The family room was furnished with bright Florida upholstery and thick beige carpet. A gold-trimmed ceiling fan rotated lazily overhead.

We sat on separate couches across a glass-and-bamboo coffee table. There was no offer for something to drink this visit.

"So, what was so urgent, Mr. Garrity?" she said evenly.

"I'd like to speak to TJ, please."

"I told you before, he's not here."

"With all due respect, Mrs. Sommerset, cut the crap."

"Perhaps you should leave."

"Perhaps you should start telling me the truth. Is TJ here?"

"No."

"Was he here during my last visit?"

"No."

"Who helped you put me on the couch after my seizure?"

"What? No one."

"Look," I said, holding out both hands, a plaintive gesture. "My agenda has evolved somewhat. Yeah, I'm still looking for him, but the reasons are a little different."

"Oh?"

"The truth is, I'm concerned about your son's safety."

She narrowed her eyes. "What do you mean?"

"I believe that TJ may be considering harming himself."

Her brow creased. "What? That's ridiculous."

"Are you aware that TJ recently sent a series of cards to the other members of the band, offering farewell and inspirational messages?"

"So? If you knew TJ, that wouldn't surprise you."

I sighed. I was about to cross some invisible line of privacy and wondered if I was doing the right thing. I determined that I was—that I needed to in order to reach TJ in time.

"Your son was in a relationship with someone. Someone important to him. Eli didn't approve of the relationship and interfered, ruining it. Immediately after the breakup, TJ disappeared. And TJ also just sent this other person a special letter, a letter that looks way too much like a suicide note for me not to be concerned." I leaned forward slightly. "So I ask you again: Where is TJ?"

Arlene was silent for a moment, her eyes drifting down, searching inward. Finally, she spoke.

"Who?"

"I don't know if I should—"

"Who?"

"Arlene, that doesn't matter. What matters is that I find TJ and make sure he's okay."

She closed her eyes and clenched both hands. "Tell me," she said in a desperate whisper.

My head dropped and I exhaled slowly. "Miguel."

She absorbed that and nodded to herself. Then she opened her eyes and looked directly at me, her lips a taut line.

"Is TJ here?" I said, trying to be gentle.

"No," she said in a weary voice, and for the first time I believed her.

"Has TJ been here recently?"

Arlene swallowed with difficulty. "Yes." She winced, as if revealing this caused her physical pain. I felt sorry for her.

"You lied to me."

"I'm his mother."

I nodded. That seemed to be explanation enough.

"Where is TJ now?"

Before she could answer, the telephone blared loudly. Arlene hesitated, looking up at the ceiling, letting it ring twice before rising from the couch. She stepped into the hallway adjacent to the kitchen and answered it. She listened for a moment, thanked the caller, and hung up. She came back to the foyer and gazed into the family room at me. The blood had drained from her face. She looked nauseous.

"That was the guard gate," she said. "An Orlando police cruiser is on its way to my house."

The cylinders in my brain instantly started firing. This neighborhood was the jurisdiction of the Orange County Sheriff's Office, not the Metro Orlando Police Department. There were a couple of likely reasons why OPD was on its way. First, TJ was dead or injured and OPD had found him. They were on their way to notify the next of kin. Based on her countenance, this was what Arlene feared. Second, the cops had made the connection between the smashed Mazda on I-Drive and the Sommersets of Isleworth. They were coming by to ask a few pointed questions about the snooping kid. Third—

Hell, I didn't have time to worry about a third reason. My truck, the truck surely ID'd by witnesses, was sitting in plain sight in the driveway. I had to haul ass or hide. I leapt from the couch.

"Arlene, listen to me," I said. "There's a chance that these cops are investigating an incident that I was involved in earlier today. I didn't break the law or hurt anyone, but it's important that they don't know I'm here. If they find me, my search for TJ will be over. Do you understand?" She stared at me, confused. I gripped her arm. "Do you understand?" Finally, she managed a frightened nod.

I raced through the kitchen and tore open the door to the spacious, three-car garage. The temperature in the garage was like a sauna. I found the controls for the electric door opener and punched the button. The garage door whirred up and I ducked under it.

A few seconds later I pulled the truck into the garage next to Arlene's silver Jaguar sedan and pressed the controller to shut the door again. I felt my heart thudding in my chest, the adrenaline starting to surge, the heat popping beads of sweat across my forehead and neck.

My feet still in the garage, I waited with the kitchen door ajar, listening, inhaling the cool air-conditioning from within the house. There was a faint click behind me as the automated garage light shut off. I presumed that Arlene was still standing in the foyer, her guts tight with anxiety, waiting for the police to arrive with what might be the worst possible news about her only child. I thought about Jennifer and tried to put myself in her place.

I heard two car doors thump in the driveway, followed by the musical doorbell chime. Quietly, I closed the kitchen door and slipped back into the cab of my truck. If the cops got nosy and decided to poke around, outside the main house might be the best place for me to lie low. There, in the sweltering, darkened garage, I closed my eyes and waited.

Twenty minutes later I heard the car doors thump again in the driveway and the police cruiser pulled away. The kitchen door squeaked open and light spilled into the garage.

"Dear God," Arlene said. "It's an oven in here. Of all the places to hide. Come inside."

I was drenched in sweat, which made the cool air-conditioning of the kitchen feel like a restaurant freezer.

"You okay?" I asked.

"Look at you, you're soaked. Come on."

I followed her through a carpeted hallway to a side room. One of several guest bedrooms. But there was no bed in it. There was a small desk, some boxes, and a large walk-in closet. Arlene disappeared into the closet and rummaged through the hanging clothes.

"I never had the heart to get rid of these clothes," she said from inside the closet. "I gave away most of Arthur's stuff, but there were a few things I just couldn't part with. Here. This might work."

She emerged holding a shirt and a pair of khaki pants. She also held a pair of bright yellow swim trunks.

"He was a little shorter than you, but these might work in a pinch. I didn't keep any of his underwear, but I do have this swimsuit. He wore it during a family vacation in Key West the year before he died. Here." She handed me the clothes.

"Arlene," I said, taking the bundle. "What did the cops say?"

"After. Get out of those wet clothes. The bathroom is across the hall. You can wash up first."

I followed orders and stepped across the hall to the bathroom. I stripped out of my sweaty clothes and ran cold water in my hands, rubbing it on my forehead and across the back of my neck. After the stale, fermented air of the boiling garage, the chilled water on my neck was almost baptismal.

The pants were a little short at the ankle, but the shirt fit fine.

The swim trunks I now wore as underwear made faint rustling noises when I moved. I came out of the bathroom barefoot, carrying a bundle of my own sodden clothing. I found Arlene in the kitchen, setting down a glass of yellow-green liquid.

"Drink that," she said. "It's Gatorade. You need to replace your electrolytes."

Only when I took the glass and started drinking did I realize how thirsty I was. I gulped the liquid like I had just crawled in from the Mojave. I saw Arlene scrutinizing my attire.

"They're a little short, but not bad, all things considered." She stepped around the kitchen's butcher island for a better view of my ensemble. "Nobody's worn those clothes in ten years. If I don't look right at you, I can almost imagine Arthur standing here in my kitchen."

I drained the glass and placed it on the breakfast bar. "He never saw this house, did he?" I asked.

She shook her head. "TJ was only twelve when he died. Arthur never saw his son's success. This ridiculous house." She held up her arms and gestured at the room.

"What did the cops say, Arlene?"

She opened the fridge and retrieved the half-empty Gatorade jug. "Nothing about TJ," she said, pouring me a second glass. "Seems my nephew is in a bit of trouble."

I took the glass and sipped, sensing there was more, waiting for her to continue.

"I assume that you already knew that, though."

I nodded. "Is that what they wanted? To talk to you about the big scene on I-Drive today?"

"Sounds like it was quite a show."

I clenched my eyes and pinched the bridge of my nose. "Arlene, I have a lot of questions for you."

"Like what?"

I let out a breath. The pent-up questions shot out like machine-gun fire: "Like, who is this nephew? What's he gotten himself into? Why has some hired goon been tailing me all over Orlando? How do I fit into it? Did the cops ask about me?" I took a small step toward her. "Why did you put me on your guest access list?" Another step. "Most important, where the hell is TJ?"

Arlene's eyebrows went up. "Those *are* a lot of questions. Some have short answers and some have much longer ones. And some I don't have any idea what you're talking about. But I'll be happy to answer as many as I can."

"Good. That's good. Let's start with TJ."

"That's a short answer. I have no idea where he is."

"He didn't tell you?"

"No."

"No guess?" I said. "A hunch?"

"No."

"When did you last see him?"

"Three days ago."

"Here? In the house?"

"That's right."

"He was here, in the house, the day I had my seizure, wasn't he?"

"Yes."

I shook my head with new respect for Arlene Sommerset. She had lied as well as anyone I had ever interrogated, including professional street liars and Mafia-connected toughs trying to avoid a cell-block "accident." She was as cool as any of them.

"We need to reach TJ," I said. "As soon as possible."

"I don't believe TJ would commit suicide," she said, leaning a hand on the kitchen island. "I don't believe it."

"Arlene. Please. Just let me talk to him."

"I swear to you, I don't know where he is. He packed his things three days ago and said he was going to find some solitude. He didn't say where he was going or when he'd be back."

"Can I get a message to him?"

"Only if he decides to call me."

"I'm worried about his safety. He needs professional intervention. He needs to talk to a counselor."

"You know," she said, "for the record, he's well aware that

you're looking for him. If he wanted to talk to you, he'd just pick up the phone."

"If not me, have him call someone. A counselor. Please."

Arlene turned her head absently toward the counter window, staring over the pool to the manicured lawn. She sighed.

"What are you going to do about your brain tumor?" she asked, still looking into the backyard.

The question caught me off guard. It took me a second to regain my bearings. "I don't know."

"Can it be treated?"

"I don't know. Maybe. The odds aren't good."

She nodded to herself. "Mr. Garrity. You still have a lot of questions and I'm starting to get hungry. I get cranky on an empty stomach and that won't be pleasant for either one of us. Let's continue this conversation over dinner. My treat."

"Okay."

"But, please, go home and change first. Seeing someone else walking around in Arthur's clothes is about to make me cry."

CHAPTER 15

"Did you grab the wrong suitcase or something?" Jennifer said when I walked into the apartment. She eyed my outfit. "I mean, where's the flood, dude?"

She and Gwen were on the living room floor reading the liner notes of the *Boyz Life* album I had given her. Gwen was an alert, big-eyed girl with midnight-black hair.

"Long story," I said.

"Did you get the pictures?" Jennifer said.

"Yeah." I produced a set of one-hour drugstore prints I'd picked up before arriving home. They featured Jennifer's visit to the Global rehearsal studio this morning.

Gwen grabbed each one from Jennifer with increasing incredulity.

"Oh my God, Jenn. Look at you! Oh my God! Look, he's holding your hand!"

"I told you," Jennifer said.

Gwen sat up and looked seriously at me. "Mr. Garrity. You are, like, the coolest dad ever. No doubt."

I exchanged a look with Jennifer, searching for validation of the opinion. She gave me a furtive look, embarrassed, awkward. But she didn't roll her eyes and declare, *Yeah, right.* Which is exactly what she would have done a few weeks ago. I suppressed a smile and stepped into my bedroom.

Arlene suggested meeting at an Irish pub in Winter Park. I hadn't been there in seven or eight years, but I knew it well. Dark wood, Guinness on tap. A crowd of mostly upwardly mobile young professionals and rich kids from nearby Rollins College. I rummaged through my closet looking for the right clothes, wondering what I should wear, suddenly aware that I cared.

I couldn't remember the last time I was actually concerned about my wardrobe. Maybe when Cam and I were still married. Definitely not since Bob arrived and I left the job. I grabbed a pair of Dockers from a hanger and stared at them.

Why did I suddenly care about what I was wearing? Was it for Arlene? This was by no means a date. Far from it. So why should my wardrobe matter? I suppose I wanted to look presentable to her. I pondered for another moment before exhaling and tossing the pants on the bed. It didn't matter. Introspection has never been my strongest suit. Some primitive part of my brain was dusting itself off and exerting its influence. I decided to go with it.

After a quick shower, a collared shirt and sport coat finished the ensemble. I brushed my teeth and ran a razor over my chin. Jennifer promised not to leave the apartment or open the door for anyone. She and Gwen were making a frozen pizza and watching a movie. I nodded, wished them a good night, and locked the door behind me.

"Eddie is family, and you have to love your family, right?" Arlene rotated a half-empty bottle of Corona in a ring of its own condensation on the table. "Those are the rules."

She was wearing a pair of beige slacks and a hunter green sweater twin set. She looked lovely and I was glad I'd put on the sport coat, the first time I had worn one since becoming unemployed.

"What kind of trouble is he in?" I asked.

She shrugged her shoulders and sipped her beer. "Who knows? He smoked a lot of pot when he was in high school. His mother told me he gambles. Bahamas. Vegas. Maybe some shady stuff, too. I honestly don't know. It could be anything."

"How close are Eddie and TJ?"

"Not very. Eddie's a year older and they were buddies as kids, but they drifted apart the last few years. If you're wondering if Eddie would know where TJ is, the answer's no. And TJ wouldn't call him. I've advised TJ to stay away from him."

"Does your son always listen to his mom?"

"Mostly."

"I think Eddie's looking for him," I said. "He was snooping around your house today, trying to get in."

"Eddie's a user. TJ has a big heart and Eddie'll take advantage of him." She tore a corner from her beer label. "I called Carol, Eddie's mom. She has no idea where Eddie is. The cops have been to her place, too. She's worried, but mostly she's tired. This isn't the first time she's been visited by police looking for her son."

"Eddie's father is your husband's brother?"

"Yes. Like I said, family."

A blond waitress came by our table and delivered our entrées. We each ordered another drink.

"Has TJ helped Eddie in the past?" I asked. "Loaned him money?"

"Probably. I don't know. I wouldn't be surprised."

Arlene had no idea who the thug in the Mustang was. She'd told the cops the same when they'd asked. She also denied knowing anyone with an old Ford pickup. I thanked her for covering.

"It was selfish," she said. "I've changed my mind about you, Mike Garrity. As odd as it is to admit it, now I do want you to find TJ. I can't believe that he would hurt himself, but . . . He wasn't himself when he left the other day. He seemed withdrawn. Inside himself. I tried calling his cell phone but it's off. He's my only son. I need to make sure he's okay."

"Then I'll need your help. If you have any guess where he could be, any information, if he calls, if you hear from Eddie, anything, I need to know about it. I don't know how much time we have."

"I'll do what I can. He left three days ago. He was driving his Jetta." She put her fork down, bit her bottom lip. "What about . . . Miguel? Doesn't he know anything?"

I stopped eating, too. "No. He's worried. He feels guilty for what happened."

"Who else knew about them?"

"Not sure. Eli, definitely. A few close to him. Maybe a couple of others had suspicions. But they were very discreet." I took a breath. "I'm sorry I had to tell you."

"Don't be. I didn't know about Miguel, but I'm not surprised. I know TJ's gay. We never talked about it, but I knew. A mother knows. He knows I love him no matter what. I just . . . want him to be happy."

"I have a daughter. She's fifteen. We haven't always gotten along. Mostly my fault. But she's TJ's biggest fan." I wasn't sure why I was telling her this or what kind of response I expected. Arlene just nodded knowingly. "Why did you put me on the security list at Isleworth?"

Arlene considered and half smiled. "I knew you'd be back." The crooked smile seemed to imply that she hoped I'd be back. What was happening here?

Arlene promised to call her sister-in-law and get me some names of Eddie's friends. Maybe I could find him through some known associates. Maybe I could get some answers about Mr. Day-Glo in the blue Mustang. Maybe Eddie knew where TJ was. A lot of maybes.

I thanked Arlene for dinner and walked her to her silver Jaguar. She leaned against the driver's door and crossed her arms.

"I've done some research," she said. "I found some stuff on the Internet. If possible, surgery is almost always the first treatment option for brain tumors."

"Mine is in a risky spot."

"Risk is relative, Mike."

"Good night, Arlene."

"I'll talk to Carol and call you in the morning."

"Thanks again."

I stood in the parking lot and watched her drive away, the red taillights flowing into a river of red taillights on Fairbanks Avenue. Across the street was a liquor store. I went inside and bought a bottle of five-year-old merlot.

I realized that, like Eddie, I had also become something of a user. The wine was a peace offering. A token of appreciation for favors both past and future.

. . .

Lydia Dupree was surprised to see me. It had been a few years. She stood wide-eyed, her hand on her mouth. She quickly recovered and embraced me there on the front stoop.

"Oh, Michael. How are you?"

"Good, Lydia. Really."

"We've been praying for you." Her dark eyes were moist.

"Thanks."

She led me inside where Jim and the kids were watching a Magic playoff game on TV. The team had made a surprising push deep into the postseason. Jim saw me and stood, crossing the living room in three giant strides.

"Am I interrupting?" I said.

"Naw," Jim said. "Jameer twisted his ankle and we just blew an eight-point lead. Game's over anyway." He eyed the bottle-shaped paper bag in my hand. "What's this?"

"A bribe."

" 'Bout damn time."

We sat at the kitchen table and I relayed the story of my afternoon, leaving out that I now possessed the goon's .22 pistol. I did give Jim the Mustang's license tag. He wasn't personally working the Eddie Sommerset case, but he'd find out who was. Probably Orange County, not OPD. Jim would have to give the primary this info, but he'd see what he could run first and pass it along. He also promised to try to keep me out of it, saying he got a tip or something.

"I need to know who the Mustang's working for," I said. "What kind of mess I've stepped into."

"I'm gettin' that itchy neck, G," Jim said, scratching the bristly hairs on the back of his neck. "Not good, bro. Not good."

"I'm not ready to quit yet. I can't. Not until I find the kid."

Jim leveled a sausage-sized finger at me. "You're lettin' this get personal. What're you, some kinda rookie? What's the matter with you?"

"I know." I rubbed my hands over my face. I was tired. It had been an eventful day.

Jim studied me, a sour twist on his lips. "You okay?"

"Yeah . . . tired. The doc has me on some pills that make me puke. That's generally no fun." I traced a finger along a knot in the polished wood grain of the table. "I had a seizure the other day."

Jim was silent for a moment, his expression softening. Then he pushed his big body out of his chair and slapped my shoulder. "C'mon. I'll open the wine, make some popcorn. We'll watch the fourth quarter and see what the Magic have left. There's always hope for a miracle. Right?" He looked at me meaningfully.

"Sure."

I squeezed onto the couch between the Dupree kids. Jim and Lydia reclined on the love seat. The adults drank the merlot, the kids had juice, and we all polished off the bag of microwave popcorn. For the first time today—for the first time in a long time—I felt myself really relax, emotionally and physically, nestled in the bosom of the Dupree family.

And the Magic came back and scored the game-winning shot on a desperate three-pointer, just as time expired.

CHAPTER 16

Gwen had left by the time I returned home. Jennifer was still awake, sitting at the desk in her room, tapping away on her laptop computer. The blue glow from the monitor cast her in an ethereal light.

"Hey," I said, leaning against the doorjamb.

She looked up. "Hey."

"What are you up to?"

"Nothin'. Just a chat room."

"Chat room . . . What do you chat about?"

"Y'know. The usual. This one is for Boyz Klub fans. We talk about the new album. When concert tickets go on sale. Rumors like Holden dating Britney, before she got married. Stuff like that."

I nodded, silently wondering how those subjects could possibly sustain any conversation, online or otherwise.

"Huh. That's funny," Jennifer said, crinkling her brow at the monitor.

"What?"

"I wrote that I met the band today, and that it was totally awesome. But I still want to meet TJ. Most of the other people in the room wanted to know details. Y'know, what they were wearing, are they really as cute in person . . . But this one is different."

I crossed the room and sat on the edge of the bed behind her, peering over her shoulder. "What do you mean, different?"

"Well, most of the people in this room are regulars. But this one is new. Klubhopper1. I've never seen her before."

"Her?"

"Her. Him. I don't know. I just say 'her' 'cause, y'know, it's easier. This room is almost always girls. Anyway, she asked me to join her in a private room."

"What's that?"

"Regular chat rooms are open to everyone. Sometimes they even have a moderator. Everybody sees everyone else's messages. But you can also jump into a private room where you just talk to each other. Or you can go IM."

"IM?"

"Y'know, instant messenger. This Klubhopper person wants to talk to me privately."

"Why?" I asked, squinting my middle-aged eyes at the smallish font on the screen.

Jennifer read the last line on the monitor. "Says she wants to talk about TJ."

"Isn't that dangerous, going into a private room?"

"Nah. It's just talk."

"But you don't know who it really is. It could be anyone."

"And she doesn't know me either. I'm just Jenn405. Yeah, she could really be some forty-year-old perv or something, but it's not like I'm ever gonna meet 'em or anything. It's all anonymous."

"So, are you gonna talk to her privately?"

"I dunno. I guess." She leaned over the keyboard and typed out a response. A few clicks of the mouse and another tap on the keyboard and Jennifer stepped into a private room with Klubhopper1. As long as the conversation was purely digital, I told myself it was basically harmless. But it still gave me the creeps that my fifteen-year-old daughter was having conversations with anonymous strangers.

"She wants to know how I managed to meet the Boyz today," Jennifer said.

"Don't say too much. I can't compromise the band's security."

Jennifer typed a few lines. "Basically, I said that my dad knows somebody at Global Talent. That's all." A few seconds later a reply appeared, but I still couldn't read it. "Uh-oh," Jennifer said. "Creep-oid alert."

"What?"

"She wants to know my name. Probably a perv." Her fingers clacked at the keyboard. "I'm telling her to take a hike."

"What's she saying now?"

"Apologizing. Wants to know why I like TJ. She probably thought I could help her meet the band. Now she's backing off, afraid I'll log out."

I stared in amazement at my daughter. Fifteen years old and instinctively analyzing someone's secret agenda and motivations, probably accurately, based solely on a few words on a screen. She would be well suited for politics or diplomacy. Or law enforcement.

Jennifer typed a reasoned response to why she liked TJ, and I stood, heading for my own room. I was especially tired tonight after my showdown with Mr. Day-Glo and hiding out in Arlene's garage. It was a lot more activity than my recent routine of Twinkies on the couch.

"Don't stay up too late," I said.

"Yeah," she said, sending her message and waiting for the reply. I'd put one foot through the door when I heard her exclaim behind me, "Holy shit . . ."

I froze and turned back to her. "What is it?"

She read from the computer screen, "Does your father happen to be named Mike Garrity?"

"What?"

"How does she know your name?"

I quickly strode back behind the desk. "Who is that?"

"Klubhopper1. That's all I know. What should I say?"

I pressed my thumb and index finger against my forehead, trying to figure out how to play this. In a normal conversation, you could feign not quite hearing and maybe come back with a "Who?", trying to draw out some more information, a technique I had successfully used in various interrogations. But you can't pull that with an online conversation. I sat again on the bed.

"Dad? What should I say?"

I felt the fingers on my forehead start to tremble. Who was this Klubhopper1 and how did he or she know me? That she'd immediately made the connection to Jennifer disturbed me.

Then I heard a familiar high-pitched hum growing in my ears.

"Damn," I said. "Damn. Damn." The hum filled my ears, leaving no doubt regarding what was about to happen.

"What should I say?" Jennifer asked again.

"Jennifer, don't worry. I'm gonna be alright."

"What are you talking about? What should I type?"

"I'm about to have a seizure." My hand was shaking more violently now and the hum was getting louder. I lay back on Jennifer's bed, preparing as Doc Tanner instructed.

"Dad? What are you doing?" Jennifer's voice was strained, filling with panic. The edges of my vision blurred and began to darken. Jennifer's stricken face appeared in view. She said something that I didn't understand, maybe a repeat of "Dad," maybe something else.

"It's okay, Jenn." My hand shook uncontrollably. "Don't worry. Don't worr—" I felt every muscle in my body tense as I jerked upward, my back arching spasmodically. Then the darkness gushed in and submerged me completely.

"Dad? Daddy?"

Jennifer's blurred face came into a soft focus. She was sideways.

"Daddy! Can you hear me?"

I grunted. "Yeah . . ."

"It's okay, Dad. They're on their way." Her eyes were red and her cheeks wet. Her voice wavered with barely contained panic.

I looked past her and realized that I was no longer on the bed. My cheek rested on the rough fibers of the carpet. Jennifer reached toward me and dabbed my lip with a wet tissue. When she pulled it back, I saw a smear of pinkish blood.

The sight of the blood must've triggered my pain receptors because, as soon as I saw it, I felt a sharp sting in my lower lip. It throbbed in rhythm with my pounding heartbeat.

"Wha . . . ," I mumbled, unable to ask the question I wanted.

Jennifer was crying. "Oh, Dad . . . It's okay. . . . It's okay."

I closed my eyes, overcome by intense fatigue. From somewhere far away, like at the bottom of a well, I heard a loud knocking.

A moment later I felt hands on me, heard deep voices, Jennifer saying something. I felt myself being rolled over and an odd sensation of floating. I forced an eyelid half-open and saw the ceiling of my apartment scrolling by. Then I was out the door and tilting down the apartment-complex stairs. I closed my eye again.

When I next opened it, I was in the back of an ambulance, jostling slightly with the vehicle's motion. An earsplitting siren screamed intermittently. The intense examination light positioned over me was too bright to look at. I leaned my head and saw a young paramedic with a crew cut, speaking into a radio, calling out my vital signs.

"Hey, Mike," he said. "How you doing? Can you hear me?"

"Yuh . . . ," I mumbled.

He held my forehead and shined a penlight into each of my eyes. The light hurt. "Sluggish, but responsive. Here. Follow my finger."

Oh, boy. Follow the finger. But before I could play my favorite brain-cancer game, my eyelids felt suddenly heavy. So tired . . .

"Mike!" the paramedic called. "Mike! Stay with me!" I heard fingers snapping loudly in my ear.

I forced my eyes back open.

"Follow my finger." The paramedic moved an extended index finger back and forth across my field of vision. My reaction was slow, but I did follow it. "Good. We're taking you to Orlando Regional. Your daughter is up in the cab. Who's your doctor?"

"Tan . . ."

"Who? Come on, Mike. Help us out."

"Tan . . . ner."

"Tanner?"

I grunted.

"Okay. Good job. Just hang tight. We're almost there. Anybody else we should call? Your wife?"

I wanted to say, *Which one?* but only managed a guttural "No." I couldn't keep my eyelids open any longer. They came down like window shades, blocking out the harsh light.

I awoke in a hospital room. The first thing I noticed was the warm pressure on my hand. I lifted my head, with some effort, and saw

Jennifer's hand resting on mine. Her head was on the mattress of the bed, her face obscured by her brown hair.

"Hey," I said hoarsely.

Her head jerked up. She gawked expressionless at me for a beat before slipping her hand off mine.

"Hey," she said.

"Thirsty . . ."

"Yeah. Okay." Jennifer got up and poured me a styrofoam cup of water from a plastic pitcher on the bedside tray. I sipped it greedily. "They said not to drink it too fast. You'll make yourself sick."

"Who said?"

"Them. The nurses."

My muscles ached the same as after my first seizure. Like I had been beaten with a sack of oranges on every inch of my body.

"What time is it?" I cleared my throat.

"Dunno. Late. Quarter to one."

"Jesus," I mumbled. "I'm sorry, Jenn. I'm sorry you had to see that. Go through that."

Jennifer squeezed her lips together, twisting her mouth, fighting back her emotions. She made a quick nod, which I assume meant that she accepted my apology.

"I'm okay now. I'd like to go home." I looked around. I appeared to still be in the emergency room examination area. I hadn't been admitted. Yet.

"They're keeping you overnight," Jennifer said, regaining her composure.

"No—"

"I'll be okay. Cam's picking me up."

"You called Cam?"

"Yeah."

"What about your mom?"

"No. Not yet. She and Wayne are somewhere between here and North Carolina. I'll call her cell phone in the morning. She'll probably turn around and come back."

I shook my head. "I don't want her to come back. I'll be home tomorrow."

The curtain pretending to give me privacy from the dozen other poor souls in the ER whisked back, revealing a tall Hispanic nurse with a nametag that said Carmen.

"Hi, Mike," Carmen said. "How you feelin'?"

"Like new. Like I want to go home."

Carmen scanned my chart with pursed lips. "Thirsty?" she asked without looking up.

"I gave him some water," Jennifer said.

"Good girl." Carmen turned to me. "Never left your side, except when we kicked her out. Loves her daddy."

Jennifer looked away.

"When can I go home?" I asked.

"Probably tomorrow. We called Dr. Tanner and he wants us to admit you for twenty-four-hour observation. He'll be by in the morning. He might want to do a CAT scan. He's also gonna change your seizure meds. You been havin' a lot of seizures?"

"This was my second."

"No fun, eh? You work those muscles pretty good when you're thrashin'. We can give you a little somethin' for the soreness, if you want. How's the lip?"

She poked at my lower lip and it felt like a knife stab. I inhaled sharply.

"You bit it pretty good when you fell off the bed," she said. "Anything else I should know? Headache?"

"Not at the moment."

"Good. That's good. We'll get you admitted soon." She replaced my chart on the foot of my hospital bed. "You have another visitor. Pretty blond lady in a slinky dress. I can only allow one guest at a time, so if you want her to come back . . ." Carmen looked at Jennifer.

"That's Cam," said Jennifer. "I'll go back to the waiting room. She can come in."

Carmen put her arm on Jennifer's shoulder and led her out of the cubicle, pulling the curtain behind her.

"It's okay, sweetie," Carmen said. "We'll take good care of him."

The curtain jerked back again and Cam stepped in wearing a black cocktail dress. She gave me a weary look, affecting a slightly annoyed expression. But then the façade cracked and she burst into tears.

"Oh, Michael," she cried.

CHAPTER 17

"Hey, Cam," I said. "It's okay."

"You jerk," she said through tears, fishing desperately in her purse for a tissue.

"Yeah."

Cam blew her nose and flopped down into a guest chair. She propped an elbow on the chair's arm and rested her cheek against her palm. She sighed loudly.

"Y'know," I said, "I don't ever remember seeing you cry when we were married."

"You weren't dying then, you jerk."

"True. But it almost seems as if you still love me."

"Of course I still love you." She dabbed the tissue again at her nose. "You jerk."

"You just can't be married to me."

Another sigh. "No. I can't. You're a very hard guy to love, Michael. You're like some kind of love black hole. Sucking everything into the void and giving nothing back."

"Maybe I can change. My doctor says that the tumor might change my personality. Maybe it'll be an improvement."

Cam swallowed loudly and fought back another wave of tears. "Please . . . Why won't you treat it?"

I said nothing, instead looking down at my hands and studying the orange hospital band on my wrist.

"Jennifer is terrified," Cam continued. "She thought she was watching you die tonight. She was beside herself when she called me."

"I'll talk with my doctor tomorrow. He'll give me some new meds to stop the seizures. Jennifer won't have to see that again."

"You're not listening. You never listen."

"Will you watch her tonight?"

Cam nodded. "Of course."

We sat in silence for a few seconds. Cam stood and crossed the cubicle to my bed. She placed a hand on my cheek and leaned down. Then she kissed me gently on the forehead and embraced me, leaning awkwardly over the bed.

She tightened her grip and whispered, "You jerk."

Terminal cancer isn't all bad. Knowing you're going to die gives you an amazing ability to prioritize. If you knew that you had only a finite amount of time left on earth, how much of it would you spend scrubbing your toilet? Or flossing? Since I'd heard my diagnosis, I'd done neither.

At least that's how I rationalized to myself after the new CAT scan revealed that Bob had grown. Not a lot, but he had definitely grown. Tanner gave me his trademarked over-the-glasses look and told me that this wasn't a good sign. Gee, Doc, thanks for the newsflash. He gave me a new antiseizure scrip and told me I could go home later that afternoon.

About an hour after Tanner left, a priest leaned into my room. He was a young Hispanic guy with dark, neatly trimmed hair. He smiled at me.

"Mr. Garrity?"

"That's me."

"I'm Father Sanchez. Your admittance papers said you were Catholic."

"I guess that's true. I was."

He nodded and I spotted a rueful smile. "You mind if I come in?"

"I guess."

He sat in the chair next to the bed and leaned his elbows on his knees. Jennifer must have listed a religious affiliation when they brought me in. I raised my eyebrows at him.

"How do you feel?" he asked.

"Never better. That seems to be everyone's favorite question lately."

"That's probably understandable. Considering." He picked at a thread on his pressed black pants. "I take it that you're not a practicing Catholic."

"Well, y'know, practice makes perfect, and I'm not even close to perfect. So . . ."

"Do you want to talk about the tumor? I imagine that you're dealing with a lot of emotions right now."

"Thanks anyway, Father."

"Sometimes it helps just to talk. Say things out loud."

"Maybe later."

He nodded again. "My name's Luis. Luis Sanchez." He stood. "I'm around if you really do want to talk later. The nurses can get in touch with me. I'm a good listener. I don't judge. Please think about it." He considered me for a long moment. "Facing your own mortality is a terrible situation. But, a blessing, too, in its own way. I think I can help you, as I've helped others. Please. If you don't talk to me, I encourage you to talk to someone. I can even recommend a counselor, if you want."

I swallowed, suddenly struck by almost the same words coming back at me that I'd spoken to Arlene about TJ. Father Sanchez offered a sad smile and a nod. Then he was out the door.

I turned and gazed out the window, my thoughts empty, like a vast, treeless tundra. My eyes eventually fixed on a line of dark purple clouds that were brewing on the horizon. The daily thunderstorm was coming early today.

At about six thirty Cam and Jennifer showed up and sprang me from the hospital. After a day eating hospital pabulum, I was ready for some actual people food. So we hit a Mexican place on the way home and I ordered a burrito grande with extra sour cream. I knew my colon would pay for the indulgence later in the evening, but it was worth it.

When we got home, my answering machine was blinking like a road barricade.

George Neuheisel was on there three times, getting more agitated with each successive message. I only had a week left before the concert tour. He needed a status for Eli as soon as possible. He *really* needed to talk to me about the case. I erased them all.

Arlene left a message with Eddie Sommerset's phone number and address. She also provided the name of Eddie's best friend, who lived in an apartment on the south end of International Drive, between Sea World and Disney. I jotted down the info on a scrap of paper. Arlene also left me TJ's private cell number. I had found a different number in the file that George had given me, but it was out of service. I wrote down the new number.

Big Jim left a message, too. Said he hadn't been able to run the Mustang's tag yet, but he would. He wanted to make sure I was okay.

No message from Becky, telling me she and Wayne were driving back from North Carolina. Jennifer probably never called. Good girl. When the messages were done, I poured myself a tumbler of bourbon and eased onto the couch, where Cam and Jennifer were watching TV.

Cam eyed the drink. "Is that a good idea with your new medication?"

"Seems like a good idea to me." I took a sip. I looked over at Jennifer. "So, Jenn, have you been in your chat room today?"

"No. I've been with Cam or at the hospital since last night."

I nodded. "So, you haven't talked to Klubhopper anymore?"

"Club hopper?" said Cam.

"No," said Jenn. "I didn't even sign out last night. I just left her there by herself when the ambulance came. After a while, the system automatically times you out. She probably wonders what happened to me."

I took another sip. "Why don't you log in? See if you can find Klubhopper again."

"Really? Okay. That was weird last night, huh?"

"Yeah," I said. "Let me know what you find."

"What are you talking about?" Cam asked. I explained the strange question about me during the chat session last night and that I believed it was related to a case I was working on. "A case?" said Cam. "You're working on a case? I thought you quit." I gave Cam the *Reader's Digest* version of my current employment, skipping the car chase and the pointed pistol on I-Drive yesterday. She shook her head. "You really never cease to amaze. I don't know if taking on a case like that is a good idea for you, what with everything going on, but I guess it's better than sitting alone in your apartment, eating Twinkies."

I nodded. As usual, Cam was right. I finished the bourbon and put the glass down, feeling the warm liquor seep into my arms, relaxing me. Relaxing Bob.

"I'll go see if Jennifer's having any luck," Cam said, and left the room, clicking off the TV on her way.

I laid my hand absently on the side table, and it rested on the piece of paper with my phone messages. I picked it up. A moment later I was punching TJ's cell number into my phone. I heard the warbling digital ringing.

"Hey, Dad," Jennifer called from the other room. "Come here."

TJ's phone rang again and I knew he wasn't answering. I stood and started toward Jennifer's room. There was another ring and I was about to press the phone off when I suddenly heard TJ's voice answer. I froze in Jennifer's doorway.

"Hey, yo, this is TJ," the voice said, and I realized that it was a recording. "I can't answer my phone right now. I'm either rehearsin' or sleepin' or out clubbin' or just plain chillin'. Leave your piece after the beep. God bless."

The message was followed by a tone.

"Dad?" Jennifer said. "You coming?"

"Hi," I said into the phone, looking at Jennifer. "This is Mike Garrity. I would really like to talk to you. Just talk. That's all. Your mom gave me your number. She's worried about you. Listen . . . I know what Eli did to you. But it'll be okay. Just call me." I left my number and then hung up.

"Who was that?" Jennifer said.

"Nobody." I nodded at the laptop computer. "Any luck?"

"Yes and no. I poked into a couple of chat rooms, but she wasn't logged in. So I searched the user profiles and found her. See? Klubhopper1. No real information except that she's a fan of Boyz Klub. But it does list her IM address."

"Instant messenger," I said.

"Yeah. I can check if she's online. If so, I can pop her to see if she wants to talk. Should I?"

"Go for it."

"What are you going to say?" Cam asked.

Up until about thirty seconds ago, I had no idea. But now I had the beginnings of a plan.

CHAPTER 18

- **Jenn405:** wanna talk?
- **Klubhopper1:** HEY! where did you go last night? you bailed
- **Jenn405:** Yeh. kinda had an emergency. Sorreee...
- **Klubhopper1:** So. whatsup?
- **Jenn405:** we never finished chatting. I never answered your question.
- **Klubhopper1:** question?
- **Jenn405:** U know
- **Klubhopper1:** Right. your dad
- **Jenn405:** right
- **Klubhopper1:** so?
- **Jenn405:** So...
- **Klubhopper1:** IS your dad Mike Garrity?
- **Jenn405:** who wants to know?
- **Klubhopper1:** I do! LOL.
- **Jenn405:** who's Mike Garrity?
- **Klubhopper1:** seriously?
- **Jenn405:** seriously. who?
- **Klubhopper1:** nevermind.
- **Jenn405:** no, really. who is he?
- **Klubhopper1:** just a guy. sorry I asked.
- **Jenn405:** someone you know?
- **Klubhopper1:** nah.
- **Jenn405:** why do you wanna know?
- **Klubhopper1:** no reason. just curious.
- **Jenn405:** you can tell me

- **Klubhopper1:** forget it.
- **Jenn405:** R U sure?
- **Klubhopper1:** YES! Let's talk about Boyz Klub.
- **Jenn405:** OK
- **Klubhopper1:** did you *really* meet them yesterday?
- **Jenn405:** TOTALLY. it was awesome.
- **Klubhopper1:** but not TJ?
- **Jenn405:** no. wish he was there. he's the cutest.
- **Klubhopper1:** where do U think he was?
- **Jenn405:** don't know. sick?
- **Klubhopper1:** maybe he quit the band
- **Jenn405:** SHUT UP!
- **Klubhopper1:** could happen. bands don't last forever. look at the Beatles.
- **Jenn405:** look at the Stones
- **Klubhopper1:** boy bands don't last. sad but true.
- **Jenn405:** Boyz Klub will. They're diff'rent. Deeper.
- **Klubhopper1:** U really think so?
- **Jenn405:** most def. besides, I'd be depressed for a YEAR if TJ quit. I'd NEVER come out of my room.
- **Klubhopper1:** don't say that.
- **Jenn405:** it's true. *BIG SIGH* so what do you like to do for fun?
- **Klubhopper1:** usual stuff. y'know.
- **Jenn405:** Stuff like rehearsing or sleeping or clubbing or just plain chilling?
-
- **Jenn405:** Hello?
-
- **Jenn405:** RU still there?
- **Klubhopper1:** who is this really?
- **Jenn405:** what if I told you that Mike Garrity IS my dad?
- **Klubhopper1:** what if you did
- **Jenn405:** what would you do?
- **Klubhopper1:** Is he?
- **Jenn405:** Yeh.
- **Klubhopper1:** why should I believe you?

- **Jenn405:** Decide for yourself. What if I told you that he just took over typing and is talking to you right now?
- **Klubhopper1:** Is he?
- **Jenn405:** Could be. How do you know my name?
- **Klubhopper1:** A friend.
- **Jenn405:** A friend… Can you be more specific?
- **Klubhopper1:** nope
- **Jenn405:** Let me guess.
- **Klubhopper1:** whatever
- **Jenn405:** You got my name from your mom.

—

- **Jenn405:** Still there, Klubhopper?
- **Klubhopper1:** not for long
- **Jenn405:** Can we talk person to person?
- **Klubhopper1:** what for
- **Jenn405:** I want to make sure you're okay.
- **Klubhopper1:** I'm fine. for the first time in a long time I'm finally fine.
- **Jenn405:** Your mom's worried about you.
- **Klubhopper1:** leave my mom out of this
- **Jenn405:** She wants me to find you. She wants me to talk to you.
- **Klubhopper1:** you lie you lie you lie you lie
- **Jenn405:** It's true. I promise. Call her yourself.
- **Klubhopper1:** keep talking about my mom and I'm outta here
- **Jenn405:** Just call her. Tell her you're okay.
- **Klubhopper1:** whatever
- **Jenn405:** Why did you ask about me by name?
- **Klubhopper1:** just curious. You're poking your nose into a lot of places. My home, my work…
- **Jenn405:** Just looking for you. Let's meet for lunch. I'll buy you a sandwich and stop poking my nose around.
- **Klubhopper1:** ha ha. how do you feel?
- **Jenn405:** What do you mean?
- **Klubhopper1:** how do you FEEL?
- **Jenn405:** I feel OK.

- **Klubhopper1**: any more seizures?
- **Jenn405**: Yes. Unfortunately. One. Last night. That's why you never got an answer to your question about me. Thanks, by the way, for whatever help you might have been during the last seizure.
- **Klubhopper1**: yeh
- **Jenn405**: I know you have some experience with the whole situation. I know about your dad.
- **Klubhopper1**: lets not talk about that. 2 sad
- **Jenn405**: I also know about Miguel. And Eli. Everything will be okay. I think I can help you.

–

Jenn405: Hello? You there Klubhopper?

–

–

- **Jenn405**: TJ?

"What the heck is going on?" Jennifer said, reading over my shoulder. "Was that *TJ*? *TJ Sommerset?*"

I leaned back in the chair and looked at the ceiling. I blew out a long breath. I don't think I had exhaled since I'd taken over typing from Jennifer.

"I don't know," I said. "I think so."

I was worried that I had overplayed my hand. Mentioning Miguel and Eli both in the chat and on the cellular voice mail was a calculated gamble. It was meant to keep TJ a little off-balance, but also to reassure him that I knew what he was going through. I understood the situation and everything would be okay. But, if TJ wasn't ready to hear it, it could spook him and drive him directly to whatever action he may only have been contemplating until now. His sudden exit from our conversation didn't reassure me. I prayed I hadn't just made a tragic tactical blunder.

"How did you know it was him?" Cam asked, clearly stunned.

"I didn't know for sure. But, I just tried calling him on his cell phone and got his message. There was something on there about being out clubbin'. I heard it just as Jennifer was looking for this

Klubhopper person. Something clicked. I thought there might be a connection. Plus, somehow, he knew my name. It was a guess, but seemed worth a shot."

"Damn," Cam said, shaking her head.

"You have TJ's phone number?" Jennifer asked as if I'd just told her I had a direct line to the president. "You can just . . . *call* him?"

"Yeah." I looked back at the ceiling.

"His *mom* gave you his number?" Jennifer said, the volume of her voice rising with each new question. "And what was that about Miguel? And Eli? And his dad? And your first seizure? What the hell is going on?!"

I picked up my cell phone and redialed TJ's number.

"Are you calling him right now?" shrieked Jennifer. "Can I talk to him?"

As I expected, TJ wasn't picking up. I decided against leaving a second message. I'd done enough damage. I hung up and felt the air go out of Jennifer.

"Can I hear his message?" she asked. "Please?"

"Jennifer. Relax."

"You *have* to tell me what's going on. Right now."

"I don't have to tell you anything. Besides that, I'm not allowed. And besides *that,* it's none of your business."

"None of my business? You were talking on my account with my user name. That makes it my business."

"No," I said. "That makes it a favor. And I appreciate it. But we're done now. It's over." I stood.

"Where are you going?" Jennifer said.

"To bed. You wouldn't believe the day I had yesterday, and I didn't get any sleep last night in that hospital. Between IVs and machines beeping and middle-of-the-night CAT scans, I didn't catch a wink. I'm beat and I'm going to bed."

"I'm gonna try to find him again," Jennifer said, sitting down at her computer.

"Don't. I think I pissed him off. You'll just make it worse. He's long gone by now, anyway."

Jennifer ignored me and kept typing. Her sour face told me I was right. Klubhopper1 had logged off completely.

Cam left the room with me and we lay down, fully clothed on top of my bed. She brushed an askew strand of my hair over my ear.

"I don't even know where to start with you," she said.

My eyes were closed. "Let's start with 'good night' and end with 'good morning,' " I said.

She stroked my hair and I felt my body relax, sinking deeper into the cocoon of my bedspread. Even with my eyes closed, I knew she was watching me. The thought of it comforted me as I drifted off into a heavy, dreamless sleep.

Bob woke me the next morning just after 5 a.m. with an ice pick to the temple. I don't know if it was the intense headache or the new seizure meds, but I had a bad case of the queasies. I staggered out of bed and puked into the toilet, trying feebly not to wake Cam. You can cover a cough or stifle a sneeze, but it's pretty hopeless to barf quietly.

I washed my face and brushed my teeth, rinsing twice with blue mouthwash. While on my last rinse, I heard the phone ring in the bedroom. After a career as a detective, I had received my share of 5:30 a.m. phone calls. None were ever good news. Cam grabbed it on the second ring as I emerged from the bathroom.

"Hullo," she said, her voice thick with sleep. "Just a sec." She held out the phone to me, not moving her body or head, her eyes still closed. I took the receiver.

"Yeah?"

"Detective Garrity?" came the male voice.

"Not anymore."

"Right. Sorry. I knew that."

I recognized the voice. Nasal, breathy. "Igor? Is that you?"

"Uh, yeah. This is Ignacio."

Ignacio Colon was a technician at the Orange County Medical Examiner's Office. He was the body guy. He put them in the freezer. Took them out for autopsies or next-of-kin identification. Wheeled them to and from the autopsy room. It was morbid work, but he handled it professionally. So professionally, in fact, that he had acquired the unwelcome nickname of Igor, as an homage to Dr. Frankenstein's assistant. Everyone called him Igor. Even me. It was a reflex.

"So what's up?" I said. "It's kinda early for a social call."

"Oh—jeez. I'm sorry. I didn't realize—"

"It's okay. Just remember that normal people aren't ready for phone calls at five thirty in the morning."

"Right. Right. I'll remember." I could picture him nodding, making a mental note for future reference.

"So, what is it, Ignacio?"

"Oh, well, Detective Dupree, he asked me to keep a lookout for any new arrivals. John Does. Young white guys. If any came in, he wanted me to call you."

Uh-oh . . . I tried to swallow, but my throat was tight.

"I take it someone just came in."

"Yeah."

"Can you give me a description?" I dreaded the answer. The timing was right for TJ if I did indeed drive him to suicide last night. I was afraid that I had made a tragic screwup.

"Uh, y'know," Igor said, "maybe five-nine, five-ten. White guy, like I said. Young. Probably in his twenties, although it's hard to tell. No ID. Blue jeans. White T-shirt. Sneakers."

"What about his face? What color is his hair?"

"Yeah. That's the tough part."

"Oh? Why's that?"

"Well, on account of he's got no head."

Igor wasn't kidding. There was a clean—intentional—slice through the vic's neck. Nasty business. I walked slowly around the slab, a grimace on my face, studying the body.

He was a young male, about TJ's age. However, Igor was right. It was hard to tell. Complexion looked Caucasian. Maybe a light Hispanic, but probably Caucasian. I didn't see any identifying marks. No tattoos or piercings. The clothing was nondescript—jeans, T-shirt, and sneakers.

There was no way for me to tell if it was TJ. Same age, similar build, similar height. All maybes. All questions. Not ever having met the kid, I couldn't know. Arlene would know, but there was no way I was calling her down here for an eyeful of this grisly scene unless I was more sure than not. Right now, it was just a wild guess.

Still, the timing of the body's arrival placed a heavy weight around my neck. It was uncomfortably coincidental. But what about the decapitation? That didn't look like a suicide.

"Where'd they find him?" I asked Igor.

Igor stood across the slab, his arms folded over his chest. He was tall and unnaturally thin, with a hawkish nose and thick glasses. His dark hair was thinning on top and I could see a shine from his scalp reflecting the morgue's overhead lights.

"Hotel parking lot over by Universal," Igor said, using his thumb to push his glasses onto the bridge of his nose. "Tourist family found him when they parked their car."

"Very nice."

"Yeah. Not exactly in the brochure."

I leaned down and examined the hands. No visible defensive wounds or wrist markings to indicate ligature.

"So, what else can you tell me?" I asked, still scrutinizing the hands.

"Nothing official." I looked up and raised my eyebrows at him. I got the hint. He could let a few unofficial scraps drop. "Well, the ME still has to do the autopsy, but he took a quick look before you got here. Definitely homicide."

I stood. "I think I can guess the official rationale."

"Neck cut is too clean. It was no accident. And there's very little blood on the shirt collar or on the ground where they found him. Obviously, he was moved, but the ME thinks he was dead long before they started chopping."

"And they didn't find the head?"

"*Nada. No esta cabeza.*" Igor occasionally slipped into Spanish. Without the head, a positive ID would be difficult. Not impossible, just difficult.

"Any reported missings?" I asked.

"None that match. That I know of. You looking for somebody special?"

"Sort of."

"You think Marie Antoinette here is him?"

"Dunno. Hope not." I sighed. "Probably some runaway, lookin' for dope money, picked up the wrong john down on the Trail."

There was a brief pause as we both looked at the poor kid on the table in front of us.

"I always liked you, Garrity," Igor said, breaking the silence. "You were never a jerk like a lot of them."

"Thanks. . . . Who's the primary?"

"Joe Vincent." I knew Joe. He was a good detective. Could be a hard-ass sometimes, but he knew what he was doing. He definitely fell into Igor's "jerk" category.

"So, Garrity. Is it true? You got the cancer?"

"That's what they tell me."

He shook his head. "Too bad. I always liked you, man."

Well, that made one of us.

I thanked Igor and asked him to keep me posted. Then I stepped out into the parking lot, where the pink light of dawn was breaking over the tops of the palm trees. I squinted at it for a moment before turning away and climbing into my truck. As I cranked up the ignition, I thought to myself, I ain't dead yet, Igor.

CHAPTER 19

I tried calling TJ's cell phone again, but got his voice mail. As before, I chose not to leave a message. Next I called his cousin Eddie, using the number Arlene Sommerset had left on my answering machine. He wasn't home either. I decided against leaving a message for him, too, figuring he was on the lam and not returning calls. A voice mail from me would probably just drive him further underground.

I then called George Neuheisel's office number, knowing it was too early to reach him there. Counting on it, in fact. I left a message, informing him that I was well aware of the start date of the concert tour and that the "status" was that I was still looking. Click.

I turned my truck out onto the interstate and headed for the south end of International Drive, down past Sea World, but not quite to Disney. That was where Eddie's best friend lived, according to the message left by Arlene. I figured that if Eddie was crashing at this pal's apartment, hiding out, the odds were good that he'd actually be in residence at 7 a.m.

I found the apartment complex, a decent enough place called Harbor Bay. It was populated primarily by hourly service workers from the theme parks and surrounding hotels and restaurants. Young adults, scraping by, putting on happy faces for the paying tourists.

The friend's name was Milo. I walked up to his second-floor apartment and knocked loudly. There was a long silence. I knocked again and heard rustling on the other side of the door.

"Hey, Milo!" I shouted. "Open up." No response. I pounded on the door again. "Milo!"

A muffled voice in the apartment called back, "Dude, it's seven in the morning!"

"C'mon, Milo. Open the door."

"Who the hell are you?"

"Somebody you need to talk to. Be a good boy. Open up."

"Like hell," Milo said, still through the door. "I know a goddamn cop when I hear one. Go away. I ain't done nothin'."

"Milo, don't be like that. I just wanna talk."

"Fuck you. I'm clean."

"Milo . . ."

"No! Go away!"

I sighed. "It's about Eddie."

A long pause.

"Eddie who?"

"Gimme a break, Milo. This has nothin' to do with you. Just open up. I'll ask a couple of questions and be on my way. I swear."

"Ask your questions through the door."

"That's not polite, Milo. Look, you're a good friend. I respect that. But if you really wanna help Eddie, you'll open the door."

"Right."

"Eddie's in some trouble, Milo. You probably know I'm not the only one lookin' for him. But I'm the only one who wants to help. I'm not gonna arrest you or him or make any trouble. I just need to talk. That's all. Now, c'mon. Open the door."

There was another long pause followed by the click of the dead bolt. The door opened an inch and Milo poked his face out. He was a little shorter than me, with mocha skin and thick, loosely dreadlocked hair. He was shirtless, wearing only a pair of striped boxers.

"I need to talk to him," I said.

"He ain't here."

"Uh-huh." I leaned on the door and shoved my way into the apartment.

"Hey!" Milo shouted. "Dude!"

I moved quickly through the darkened living room, stepping over crumpled clothes and strewn pizza boxes. Past the kitchen and into the short hall. The master bedroom on the right was a disgusting pigsty, but no one was in it. I saw a big Ziploc baggie of marijuana next to some used socks on the dresser and a bong on the floor half-filled with dirty water.

I stepped into the master bath. The gray buildup on the tub made my lip curl. I recoiled, but not so far that I missed the pile of clothes in the corner. I poked at them with my toe and thought they looked an awful lot like the sweat suit I'd last seen Eddie Sommerset wearing. The clothes stank with mildew and were still damp.

Milo was in the bedroom when I emerged from the bathroom.

"You need to leave. Now."

"Where is he, Milo?"

"I don't know."

"When did you last see him?"

"Why should I tell you?"

"Because it's the right thing to do. Believe it or not, it'll help Eddie. Besides, if you do, maybe I'll forget about that huge bag of pot in your room. That's a quite a stash. Maybe enough to make a dealer charge stick."

"Come on, dude. You entered without a warrant. It's inadmissible."

"No. You opened the door. Invited me in. You shouldn't have done that."

"Asshole."

"Where's Eddie?" I said.

"He left. I don't know where he is. I swear to God."

"When?"

"Yesterday morning. Dude took my car."

"What kind of car?"

"Dodge Intrepid. Black."

"Where'd he go?"

"How would I know?" Milo sighed. "He was scared. I seen Eddie in trouble before, but this time he was really scared."

"What was he so scared of?"

Milo shrugged. "Who knows? With Eddie, it coulda been anything. My guess is that he owed money. Eddie gambled. A lot."

"On what?"

"Anything. But mostly sports."

Sports . . . There was no place legal in Orlando to place sports bets. A few years ago, if that was your jones, you would have had to get friendly with an outfit like the one run by Juan "the Don" Alomar, which I'd busted up. Somebody had obviously filled Orlando's bookmaking vacuum.

"Who does Eddie place his bets with?" I asked.

"That ain't my scene, dude. It was Eddie's deal. I got my own problems. I hadn't heard from him in a month or two when I get this call the other day. Wanted me to pick him up in the middle of a killer thunderstorm and let him hide out for a while. I said okay. He did the same kinda thing for me once. But, if this is serious, big-time trouble, I can't afford to get involved. One probation violation and I'm back in the joint."

"You know Eddie's cousin, TJ?" I asked.

"The singer? Nah. Never met him. But Eddie tried to call him while he was here. Don't think they hooked up, though."

I looked Milo in the eye. "You being straight up with me, Milo? On everything?"

"I don't want no trouble, dude."

"Alright. If Eddie comes back, you call me at this number. You might be saving his life." I wrote my cell number down on a piece of paper and turned toward the front door.

"Uh, dude, what about my stash?"

"What stash?" I said.

My brain gears were churning as I drove over Sand Lake Road to Eddie's apartment. Was TJ's disappearance related to Eddie's trouble? Eddie seemed pretty desperate to get in touch with his cousin.

Eddie lived in a nasty apartment complex on Oak Ridge Road called Tudor Court. It was a series of low-slung, two-story buildings with flat roofs, bars on the windows, and filthy tan paint peeling from the cracked stucco. A lone palm adorned one side of the entrance drive. A withered stump adorned the other side. The palm was yellowed and thin and, amazingly, seemed unable to cast any shadow whatsoever. Weeds sprouted through the cracks in the asphalt.

I parked in front of Eddie's building. As I swung open the truck's door, I caught a flash of black in the side mirror. Turning, I saw a black Dodge Intrepid parked behind me. I sauntered over and peeked inside. Nothing visible or identifying in the seats. However, the rear bumper sported a green decal declaring the owner a Harbor Bay resident.

I hiked up the bowed metal steps to the second floor of the building. The pungent smells of curry and garlic enveloped me as I made my way down the exterior balcony that served as a front hall. I reached Eddie's door and knocked.

No answer. After another moment, I knocked again. I peered into the front window, but couldn't see through the closed horizontal blinds. I knocked again. Silent as a tomb.

"Eddie?" I called. "Eddie! I'm here to help. I'm the guy who helped you the other day on I-Drive. Open the door." Still no answer. "I can help you find TJ!"

I figured if anything would get him to respond, it was that. But there was no answer. He was probably squeezing himself out the bathroom window right now. Not sure what to do, I placed a hand on the front doorknob. Even this early in the day, the scuffed metal was already hot.

I turned the knob, and surprisingly, the door opened.

With all the blinds closed, the apartment was dark. And hot. The AC was obviously off. I immediately doubted that Eddie was home. After just twenty minutes in Arlene's garage the other day, I was ready to expire. Eddie wouldn't be able to take an extended stay in this oven.

I made a quick pass through the apartment, which didn't take long. It was unoccupied. I opened the fridge. Checked the expiration date on the milk. Eddie had until tomorrow to finish his quart.

I rifled through the kitchen drawers, looking for an address book, a Post-it, a scrap of napkin with a note on it. There was nothing. Just a few ketchup packets from McDonald's and a pencil with the lead snapped off.

A similar search in the one bedroom and bathroom also yielded nothing. I found the Intrepid's keys hidden among the junk mail and crumpled laundry on his dresser. I took them back outside and opened the car. The interior contained a few fast-food wrappers on the floor and a pack of opened cigarettes in the cup holder. Inside the glove compartment was a small, black cell phone. I wondered if it was Eddie's or Milo's. Probably Eddie's. I picked it up and slipped it into my pocket. After cooking in the car, it was way too hot to hold at the moment. I'd figure it out later.

After confirming the trunk was empty, I closed up the car, returned the keys to the dresser, and got into my truck. With one last glance around for the blue Mustang, which was nowhere to be seen, I pulled out of the Tudor Court apartment complex and headed downtown to Global Talent.

For such a big, hulking guy, George was acting like a baby. He was scared shitless of Eli. And he wasn't alone. The whole Global Talent office had an uncool vibe, everyone stressed, no one safe from Eli's wrath.

The biggest contributor to Eli's black mood was the continued absence of his most popular band member with only one week left before the start of the concert tour. The new album hit the shelves in a few days. A lot of money was at stake, and all of it was in jeopardy.

George said nothing as Eli grilled me on the progress of my search. All I told him was that I was getting closer, but hadn't spoken directly to him yet. Eli wasn't happy. George looked like he might lay an egg in his shorts.

I checked in with Miguel, who was getting final adjustments to his concert wardrobe. He hadn't heard from TJ yet either.

On the way out, George reminded me that he was the one who'd brought me in, vouched for me. If I blew it, he was gone. He couldn't face going back into a squad car.

I nodded and told him I was still working on it, although I had pretty much abandoned hope of TJ actually returning to the band. Hell, I just hoped he hadn't killed himself yet.

In the truck, I tried calling TJ again with the same fruitless result. I pulled out into traffic and drove home, Mustang-free.

When I came in, I saw Jennifer on the couch, removing her

shoes. She was wearing a red T-shirt and a mall nametag, having just arrived home from work.

"I'm sorry," I said, remembering how early I'd left. "Did you need a ride?"

"Nah," she said. "Cam was still here when I had to leave this morning, and my friend Julie gave me a lift home."

"Short day?"

"Yeah. Bill just wanted someone for the lunch rush."

"What's that?" I said, pointing my chin at a cardboard box next to her purse on the dinette table.

"Dunno. It's for you."

"Oh, yeah?" I wandered over and peered at it. It was a regular brown cardboard cube, like what might be purchased at a mail-supply store, about the size of a standard hatbox. Written in black marker on the side was my name. No address. "Someone leave this outside the door?"

"Nah. Some guy at the mall gave it to me." Jennifer kicked off her sneakers.

"Some guy? Who?"

She shrugged. "I dunno. A guy. Said he was your friend. I figured you were expecting it."

I pursed my lips and touched an upper edge of the box with an index finger, turning it a half inch. Not too heavy, but something was definitely in there.

"What'd this guy look like?" I asked.

"Jeez, I dunno. He was just some guy. An older guy. Like your age."

"Jennifer," I said, starting to get a bad feeling. "Think. What color was the guy's hair?"

She sighed in annoyance. "Dark hair. Black, I guess."

"You see what he was driving?"

"No. He gave it to me in the food court, right before my shift was over." She crossed her arms. "So? What's in it? Why the third degree?"

A queasy feeling was in the pit of my gut like an elevator dropping too quickly. I knew what was in the box.

"Dad?"

I turned my back to Jennifer, blocking her view of the table. I used her keys to pop the tape and lifted the cardboard flaps.

I was right, of course.

Within the box was a large Ziploc freezer bag. And inside the clear plastic bag was the neatly severed head of Eddie Sommerset.

CHAPTER 20

"So why you? It your birthday or somethin'?"

Detective Salvador Diaz grinned at me with a crooked yellow smile. He had a solid, stocky frame, and the shoulders of his thin dress shirt pulled tightly when he leaned forward onto his knees. His eyes were inky black and hard.

"I honestly don't know," I said. We were in my living room, me on the couch and Diaz on my recliner. The crime-scene techs were wrapping up, the cardboard box and its grisly contents having been removed about twenty minutes earlier. There wasn't much for the techs to do, since this wasn't much of a crime scene. But, there was no denying I'd found a human head on my dinette table, and everyone had to go through their motions.

"Aw, c'mon, Mike," Diaz said, sitting back and affecting a sardonic smile. "You were on the job all those years. A detective. A couple tours with MBI. You tell me you don't have a *guess* why somebody picks you to get the boy's head?"

"I didn't say that. I just don't know anything for sure."

"Now we gettin' somewheres."

"What about my daughter?" I said, looking at the closed door of Jennifer's room.

"She's fine. Detective Crowley is with her."

Both Diaz and Crowley were from the Orange County Sheriff's Office, not the Orlando Police Department. Although my address says Orlando, my apartment sits just outside the city's jurisdiction in unincorporated Orange County, giving the sheriff's department control over the homicide. If the headless corpse that Igor showed me this morning turns out to be, as I suspect, the rest of Eddie Sommerset, an epic turf battle is on its way. With the body found in the city limits and the head found in the general county, the case was bound to be a political football.

Since Diaz and Crowley were Orange County, I didn't know them and I couldn't leverage much of my local law enforcement reputation to get a break. I knew a couple of the county guys from MBI assignments, but none were currently in my apartment. I had informed the partners of my own background.

When they arrived, Crowley and Diaz had split up to get independent statements from both me and Jennifer. Standard procedure.

But Jennifer was pretty upset. Upon realizing that she had been carrying around a human head—the head of TJ Sommerset's cousin, no less—she kind of freaked. I got her mostly calm by the time the uniforms showed up. But when Crowley pulled her aside, Jennifer gave me a look of such abject terror that I was momentarily paralyzed. I told her to relax. Everything would be fine. She didn't do anything wrong. Just tell the truth.

Crowley appeared to have a gentle touch. As a woman, she was probably better equipped to handle a distraught fifteen-year-old girl than Diaz or some other male detective. Even me. This wasn't a sexist observation. This was a fact. Most guys I knew in this line of work were a little jaded and unfazed by a few teenaged tears. I suspected that Crowley would at least refrain from browbeating her.

"I want to see her," I said.

"C'mon, Mike," Diaz said. "You know how this goes. We can't have you talkin' to each other until we get your full statements."

"I won't talk about it. I just need to see that she's okay."

"Mike . . ."

"I'm not talking at all, to you or anybody, until I know she's okay."

Diaz pursed his lips at me and finally sighed, waving a beefy hand at Jennifer's door. I rose and knocked on it, swinging it open before anyone inside could respond.

Jennifer was sitting on her bed. She was dry-eyed, but a few crumpled tissues littered the comforter. Crowley leaned against the desk. The detective looked to be in her midthirties, with dull, straw-colored hair cut shoulder-length. A few wisps of gray had popped up, and she had apparently made no attempt to hide them. She turned her head to me inquisitively.

"You okay?" I asked Jennifer. She nodded. "You need anything?" Jennifer shook her head. I looked over at Crowley.

"I'm just taking a statement, Mr. Garrity," Crowley said. "Give us a few minutes and we'll be on our way."

I nodded. Lingered for a beat. Looked over at Jenn. "If you need anything—at all—you let me know. Even if you're not done yet, okay?"

"Okay," Jennifer said in a small voice.

Crowley offered a reassuring smile and nodded for me to close the door. I did and returned to the couch.

"So," Diaz said. "Where were we?"

"I think I know who killed him."

"Please. Make my job easy."

I described the driver of the Mustang, the black-haired thug with the nasal voice.

"This guy have a name?" Diaz said, taking notes.

"I'm sure he does. But I don't know it." I gave him the Mustang's tag number. "And this . . ." I stood and disappeared into my bedroom, returning with a plastic bag containing the .22 pistol that Eddie had removed from the thug's ankle holster. "It's the shooter's. Not the murder weapon, since I had it before the kid turned up dead, but it's got a serial number and I bet you can pull some latent prints. Maybe get an ID."

Diaz's eyebrows went up. "Why don't you start at the start and tell me just what the hell is goin' on?"

Just what the hell *was* going on? I had to admit that I didn't know. But my mind instinctively began cataloging what I did know.

Eddie was into something bad, owed money to the wrong people. Shylock, drug dealer . . . Probably a bookie, according to his friend Milo. Must have been a lot of money to a very bad or well-connected dude. I knew quite a bit about the bookmaking business from my MBI work on the Juan Alomar sting, but I had never seen anyone get the guillotine for being upside down with his bookie.

I'd seen a few busted thumbs and a shattered kneecap, but it wasn't good business to whack someone who owed you. You may send a strong message to the rest of your clients, but you'll never get your money. And any serious outfit—especially a mob-connected crew—knew that they were part of a business and that there were consequences for poor financial performance. It didn't make sense to kill someone just because he owed.

So, why *did* they whack him? It was clearly a message hit. But meant for whom?

Me?

I got the box, so presumably, the message was mine.

Correction: Jennifer got the box. I had no illusions that her involvement was a coincidence. Obviously, they wanted me to know that they knew who Jennifer was, where she worked, and that they could get to her. Handing her the box to deliver to me was a threat.

Ultimately, they must want something from me. What? In my experience, all these guys ever want is their money. Whatever the marker was, I was pretty sure I couldn't cover it. They had to know this. They had to know all about my crappy apartment, my anemic checking account, maybe even my new friend Bob, draining down my meager savings to pay for doctors and drugs. I couldn't cover any serious debt, especially one serious enough to get you shot and decapitated.

Yeah, shot. In addition to the obvious trauma of a missing body, Eddie's forehead had been ventilated with what looked like a .38-caliber air conditioner. The gunshot probably occurred before the head was severed, administered close range, execution-style. It was my best guess, based on experience and the forensic tech's obvious search for gunshot residue on the face. If Igor's headless John Doe was indeed the rest of Eddie Sommerset, it would validate the ME's hunch that the vic was dead before he lost his noggin.

So, if it could safely be assumed that I was in piss-poor financial condition, and that fact was no secret, why did I get the gruesome message? Setting aside my obvious inability to pay, even on principle alone, why should I inherit Eddie's debt? I didn't even know the kid. I had never laid eyes on him before a couple days ago.

What could the wiseguys possibly want from me?

TJ . . .

Eddie had frantically been trying to reach his cousin for at least several days. It would probably be easy enough for the bad guys to find out my interest in locating TJ. In fact, as I recalled, I first picked up the Mustang tailing me after visiting TJ's condo.

The most likely scenario was that, knowingly or unknowingly, TJ had inherited Eddie's debt. But TJ had turned invisible before Eddie could reach him to bail him out. The bad guys figured that Eddie was a liability and, in business parlance, chose to write him off. But the debt stayed on the books. They would still get their money from TJ.

However, to collect, they needed to find TJ, who was conveniently missing. Enter a certain ex-cop with a tumor in his head, who just happened to be looking for him.

Christ, what did I walk into here?

Where the hell was TJ, and why, really, was he missing? Was it because of Eli's interference in his relationship with Miguel, or did it have something to do with Eddie? Was it both? Something else?

"Mike?" Diaz said, tilting his head at me. "You still with us?"

"Yeah . . ."

I gave Diaz the whole story, omitting a detail or two regarding the specifics of the standoff on International Drive. I'd broken a few statutes there and wasn't interested in getting busted. Diaz didn't press me, but he had to know there was more to it. I appreciated the pass he gave me.

"You got a PI license?" Diaz asked, taking notes, not looking up.

"No. I'm working as a consultant to Global Talent. Their payroll."

"Cute. But we both know you're doing PI work. I could stop you."

"But you won't."

"Oh, yeah? Why not?"

" 'Cause I've got a much better shot at actually finding TJ than you do. I have the background, I've done the legwork, and I've got contacts who trust me," I said, thinking of Arlene.

Diaz considered me skeptically. "I'll let you have a little more rope. Not much. But the deal is you bring me everything you get when you get it. No funny business."

"Of course. One more thing. I need to respect the request of my client and make sure everything stays quiet. If word gets out that TJ is missing, it could be very bad for him and his business."

"Sure. Whadda I care?" He pulled his stocky frame up from the chair. "But, like I said, any funny business and I'll go on TV myself and put up TJ's picture asking the public to call us with any information about his whereabouts. Do not mess with me."

"I get the message."

Jennifer's door opened and Crowley stepped out. "We're done," she said.

Diaz nodded and they both placed business cards on the kitchen counter. Diaz assured me he'd be in touch. When the front door finally clicked closed, I turned back and looked at Jennifer. She leaned against her doorframe, physically and emotionally exhausted. She no longer appeared upset, just drained.

"You alright?" I asked.

"Yeah. . . . It's just so awful."

I took a step toward her. "I know."

Her eyes pleaded with me. "Why?"

"I don't know," I said, taking another step. "The cops'll figure it out."

"Was he really TJ's cousin?"

"Afraid so." Another step. "I'm gonna keep looking for TJ."

"Can't you tell me what this is all about? What TJ has to do with it?"

"Not yet." I was right next to her now. We froze there for a long moment, not moving, finding some semblance of strained comfort in our physical proximity.

"It's just so awful," she repeated.

"I know." I reached out to her. She leaned into me and accepted the embrace, closing her eyes, and resting her head against my chest.

We stood like that for several minutes, not speaking, the only noise in the apartment our soft breathing. I felt her ribs rise and fall against mine as she inhaled and exhaled. Soon, the rhythm of our breathing synchronized, and we almost sounded like one person.

CHAPTER 21

When Jennifer retired for the night, I stayed up, making calls. The first was to Arlene Sommerset. She was upset about Eddie but not completely unprepared.

"We figured something like this was going to happen eventually," she said. "God, poor Carol."

"Listen," I said. "I found TJ, sort of. I think I talked to him last night in an online chat room."

"Are you serious?"

"Yeah. But it didn't go very well. He kinda hung up on me and I'm worried."

"I still haven't heard from him," she said.

"Keep trying to reach him. I've got a bad feeling that he has something to do with Eddie's problems and that's why I got the package today."

"No . . . not TJ."

"I dunno. I hope you're right. I'm still worried that TJ may harm himself, especially after last night. But now I'm even more worried that someone else may harm him first."

"The same people who killed Eddie?"

"Yeah. This is serious, Arlene. Serious as it gets. Get in touch with TJ and send him straight to the cops. He needs to get inside as soon as possible."

"Oh my God . . ."

The next call was to George Neuheisel at home.

"Jesus, Mikey, the cops? Did you have to call the cops?"

This, from a guy who not that long ago was a cop himself. "Uh, they sent me his *head* in a box, George. I couldn't exactly chuck it in the Dumpster."

"Yeah, alright. Yeah." I could actually hear him pinching the bridge of his nose. "What about reporters?"

"None yet." That was a surprise. It wasn't that often that a random head showed up in a box. The buzzards would soon start circling.

"Christ, don't tell 'em anything."

"Don't talk to me like I'm some rookie on a beat."

"Sorry. It's just the tour. Y'know, and Eli. There's a lotta pressure here. Once the press learns it's TJ's cousin, they'll be all over us. We gotta find him."

"Look, George, there's a chance TJ's mixed up in whatever got his cousin iced. I think that's why they sent me his head. They know I'm lookin' for him."

"Jesus . . ."

"If TJ's mixed up in it, the publicity will be ten times worse than the other stuff Eli's afraid will get out."

"What other stuff?" George asked.

"Just tell Eli. He'll know."

"What are you talking about?"

"I gotta go, George."

"Wait, Mike. Tell me—"

Click. I hung up.

Next I called Becky in North Carolina. I didn't have the number at Wayne's vacation house, so I tried her cell phone. She must have had it off because her voice mail picked right up. I left her a message to call me as soon as she could.

It would be best for Jennifer to remove herself from my general vicinity for a while. It concerned me that she was chosen to deliver Eddie's head. I didn't like the implication. I wanted Becky to return and watch her or make arrangements to send Jennifer up north.

I called TJ's cell phone again, figuring that it was another futile attempt to reach him. It was. His voice mail message came on.

"TJ, it's Mike Garrity again. Call me back, please. Something terrible has happened to your cousin Eddie and I'm afraid you may not be safe. If you don't want to call me, call your mom. This is not a scam." I left my number. Again.

I took the nighttime dose of my new antiseizure pills and lay down on top of my bed. I closed my eyes and waited for the dizziness. I had made the unhappy discovery that the main side effect of the new meds was a rolling dizziness that made me feel as if I were on the deck of an Alaskan fishing schooner. It wasn't bad enough to make me puke—yet—but it was extremely disorienting.

When Bob feels neglected, he throws a tantrum to get noticed. I believe he was jealous of my case, of Jennifer, of everything happening in my life at the moment that wasn't directly related to him. I'm convinced that's why the seizures started.

To keep him at bay, I wanted to lie quietly on the bed and spend some quality time, just me and Bob. Pay him some attention.

But that wasn't going to happen.

My apartment phone rang loudly on the nightstand, shattering the silence. The clock read 11:38 p.m. Like all cops, my home number was unlisted. Maybe it was Becky calling me back. I reached for the receiver.

"Hello?"

"Hi, Mike," said a nasal male voice. "Busy night?"

"You could say."

"You know who this is?"

"Yeah. My friend of a friend."

"So? You got my money?"

"Look, sport, I don't know anything about your money. I never even met Eddie Sommerset until the moment I met you. You got the wrong guy."

"I don't think so. You find the cousin yet?"

"No. The cousin is gone. I don't think he's comin' back."

"Wrong answer, Mike. You need to look harder."

"Why don't you just tell me exactly what you want? How much did Eddie owe you?"

"It ain't me he owed."

"Who?"

"A friend."

"Who?" I said again, the anger straining my voice.

"You don't need to worry 'bout that. You just need to find the cousin."

"I thought all you wanted was your money."

"Now you're gettin' it, smart guy."

"This is bullshit!" I barked. "Fuck you and fuck your friend. You stay away from me and my daughter or I swear I'll empty a whole clip into your ear. In case you haven't heard, I got terminal cancer. I got nothin' to lose."

"Wrong, Mike. You got plenty to lose."

And then he was gone, his nasal voice replaced by a click and a dial tone. I slammed the phone down onto the cradle, eliciting a reflexive ding. Pacing around the room a few times got my blood pressure out of the red zone but accelerated my dizziness. I lowered myself back onto the bed before I toppled over.

I found Detective Diaz's card and called him, giving him the gist of my conversation. He'd pull the last incoming number to my home phone, but I suspected it would be an anonymous pay phone in a parking lot somewhere. I had a feeling I was dealing with a pro here. I even suspected that the clumsy tailing by the Mustang was on purpose, making his presence known, starting the intimidation.

Before he hung up, Diaz told me that the Mustang's license tag was registered to a stolen Toyota Camry from Delray Beach. The serial number on the .22 pistol also came back as reported stolen. Both dead ends. They did lift some latent prints from the gun. A few, as they expected, were from Eddie, when he took it from the holster. But some others were on there, too, mostly partials, none pristine. They were running the prints through AFIS, but with only partials to work with, it might be a while before they got a hit, if at all.

Diaz also confirmed that it looked 99 percent likely that Igor's stiff belonged to Eddie's head. Let the jurisdictional politics begin.

"You might as well come back," said Big Jim Dupree, leaning on the hood of his unmarked OPD cruiser. "Hell, you're doin' police work anyway."

"I take it that you heard," I said, stepping off the bottom stair of my apartment building. As I walked over to him, I sipped scalding black coffee from a travel mug.

"Hell, yeah, I heard. I heard all about it. Joey V's gonna come see you, too."

"Great." Joe Vincent, the primary for Igor's body.

"Damn, G. What you doin' gettin' mixed up in big-time trouble? You promised me this was straight up."

"Yeah, sorry about that. At the time I told you that, I thought it was. But this case is an onion. Every time I peel back another layer, it stinks a little more."

"You got to get your damn self out."

"Workin' on it. Soon."

"Soon ain't soon enough."

I leaned next to him on the fender of the cruiser. Sipped my coffee. Looked out at the parking lot.

"You really find the boy's head in a box?" Jim said.

"Oh, yeah."

"Damn. That ain't cool." Jim scratched the back of his neck, going at it like it was covered in mosquito bites.

"Yeah," I said.

I took another sip and bid Jim farewell. I was dizzy again, probably too dizzy to drive, but there was no way I was sitting home on my ass. I'd called Cam early this morning—too early, since I'd woken her up, but Bob didn't feel like sleeping in—and arranged to meet her at a Starbucks on Kirkman Road before she made her rounds of the west side's doctors' offices.

As I left the apartment, I made Jennifer promise to keep the door locked and not to leave without calling me first. I didn't get any argument. She was a smart kid.

I pulled up to a red light and sipped more of my coffee. Nothing like a cup of coffee on my way to get a cup of coffee. The truck radio was off but I heard an odd, electronic chirp. Chirp-chirp. I furrowed my brow and looked around the cab. The chirp sounded again.

What the hell was that?

Chirp-chirp. It was coming from somewhere inside the truck. I poked stupidly at the radio knobs. Chirp-chirp. I leaned down and peered under my seat. There was some loose change and a few petrified french fries, but nothing that would be making the noise. Chirp-chirp.

Honk!

I jerked up to see a green light overhead and the traffic next to me rolling. Reflexively, I glanced in the mirror and saw an agitated commuter gripping his leather-wrapped Infiniti steering wheel.

I pulled through the light and spotted the Starbucks on the corner up ahead. Chirp-chirp. Damn! Where was that coming from? I turned the truck into the parking lot, pulling up next to Cam's black Porsche Boxster. The pharmaceutical sales biz had been good this year.

Cam spotted me through the window and nodded at me with her chin. I cut the truck's engine and paused, waiting to see if the chirping continued with the power off. Silence for a few seconds before—chirp-chirp.

I muttered a few choice swear words before stepping out.

"So? What's up?" Cam said, shaking cinnamon powder on a vanilla latte.

"I need a favor."

"Okay." We found a seat at a corner table.

"Can you watch Jennifer for a while? Until Becky comes back."

"Uh-oh. What happened? You didn't go through her purse again?"

"No, nothing like that." I told her about the package last night and my concern for Jennifer's safety.

"Of course," Cam said, her thoughts turning inward. "Of course."

"I'll talk to her today and arrange it."

"Okay."

Before we left, Cam asked me, "You want a muffin or something? My treat."

"No, thanks. I've actually noticed my pants getting tighter. That all-Twinkie cancer diet seems to have backfired."

Back in the truck, I was once again greeted by the electronic chirp-chirp, and it occurred to me that maybe it was bad news. Car bombs were not exactly unknown in the mob world, if that's what I was dealing with here. But why blow me up? If they were really counting on me to find TJ, exploding me into smithereens would be counterproductive. Plus, I had already driven the truck from my apartment to here without going boom.

Chirp-chirp.

So what was it? A listening device? If so, it was the world's worst. A GPS tracker? Maybe the bad guys were tracking my moves, following me. That seemed more likely, but I had never heard a GPS receiver or surveillance transmitter chirp like that.

I sat motionless for a moment, listening for it again. Chirp-chirp. Muffled slightly. Not right next to me. Maybe from the passenger side of the truck cab. Under the passenger seat? No luck.

The glove compartment.

I popped the latch to the glove box and it fell open. Chirp-chirp! There it was. A cellular phone. Not ringing, but chiming at regular intervals.

It was a cell phone, the one I picked up from the Dodge Intrepid at Eddie's apartment complex. I had completely forgotten about it. I pulled it out of the glove box and read the display.

There was one unplayed message, which was the reason for the chirping alarm. A text window asked if I wanted to call my (presumably Eddie's) voice-mail account. Why not? I pressed yes. It took a moment to connect. Fortunately, Eddie's cellular service, like mine, didn't require a security code. A digitized system voice provided the call stats. The message had come in last night, about the same time I was chatting with Detective Diaz.

I froze when I heard the caller's voice.

"Okay, Eddie," came TJ's recorded voice. "I got your messages. All six thousand of them. I can't take it anymore. Stop calling me. Whatever you want from me—or, should I say, however *much* you want from me—forget it. I bailed you out once, and it was one time too many. I'm making major changes in my life right now and, and . . . you're one of them. I'm sorry, dude, but the bank of TJ is closed. Whatever it is, you'll have to get it somewhere else. I have legitimate charities that I'd rather donate to. I really hope you work it out, cuz. You're a beautiful soul and are meant for more than the crap you're in now. I'll always be your family and I'll always be here for you spiritually, but please, don't call anymore if all you want is money. Peace, dude."

I played it twice more, fascinated, listening to the tone of TJ's voice. He sounded annoyed at first, but grew more disappointed and weary, maybe even sad. I couldn't decipher any specific clues regarding TJ's own situation or plans, except the cryptic reference to "major changes" in his life. Hoping to catch some background sound that might clue me into his location, I listened to it several more times. Nothing. No car horn, no background music, no boat whistle, foghorn, nothing.

I saved the message and hung up the phone. I debated calling Detective Diaz, or maybe even Joe Vincent, but something stopped me. They wouldn't glean any more information from the message than I did. And something told me that there was a reason I'd forgotten about Eddie's phone until this morning. I hadn't intentionally omitted it from my discussion with Diaz last night, but I decided to keep it to myself for a little while longer, not even sure exactly why.

The message from TJ was helpful in several ways. First, it told me that he was still alive or, at least, was still alive less than twelve hours ago. He hadn't yet offed himself or been found by Mr. Day-Glo. That was good.

Second, it confirmed my suspicion that Eddie was reaching out to TJ for money, as he had apparently done before. And TJ didn't seem to know what specifically Eddie wanted or why, which hinted that TJ had no involvement in Eddie's problems. TJ's running appeared to have more to do with Eli and Miguel than Eddie.

Of course, now, the reasons were academic. All that mattered was finding him or convincing him to come back for his own protection. I figured I should make another attempt to reach him and leave the obligatory message on his cellular voice mail.

I was still holding Eddie's phone and punched a few buttons, scrolling through the preset numbers until I found TJ's cell. I figured correctly that Eddie had it saved. I pressed CALL and put it to my ear.

A moment later it was ringing. I took a breath, thinking about the message I would leave, then heard a click on the other end.

"Dude, what're you pullin'? Everyone thinks something happened to you," came a young man's voice through the receiver.

TJ's voice.

CHAPTER 22

"You wouldn't believe the messages I've been getting about you, dude," TJ continued. "If this is a joke, it ain't funny."

My mind kicked into overdrive. TJ was live on the phone. He thought I was Eddie—why?—TJ was obviously screening calls, probably had caller ID. I was calling on Eddie's phone and TJ saw the incoming name and number. He had probably gotten several messages about Eddie since last night. He saw that it was Eddie calling and decided to answer.

But now what? I wasn't prepared to actually speak with him. It was completely unexpected and it knocked me off-balance.

"Eddie?" TJ said.

"TJ," I replied lamely, trying to think of something.

Long pause.

"Who is this?" TJ finally said.

"TJ. This is Mike Garrity."

Another long pause.

"Where's Eddie?"

"TJ, I have some bad news. The worst kind."

"Don't—"

"I'm sorry. Eddie's dead. He was murdered yesterday."

"No—"

"I'm sorry."

"I don't believe you."

"It's true. And I think you know it."

"No . . . ," TJ said, a twinge of emotion choking his voice.

"TJ, where are you now?"

"How did you get his phone?" TJ said, growing more upset.

"I found it while I was looking for him. I thought if I found him, I might be able to find you."

"How do I know *you* didn't kill him?"

"I didn't kill him, TJ," I said calmly, rationally. The more upset he became, the more reasonable I would sound.

"You're lying!"

"No, I'm not. You know as well as anyone the kind of stuff Eddie was into."

"Oh my God . . ." He was crying now.

"I know. I know. But, I want to make sure you don't end up the same. Tell me where you are and I'll come get you."

But TJ wasn't listening. He spat out his words between sobs. "Oh my God . . . He's been calling me and calling me. He wanted money. Is that why he's dead? The . . . money?"

"Yeah. Probably."

"Oh my God . . . If I had just . . ." He swallowed the rest of the sentence.

"It's not your fault, TJ. Eddie made his choices and they had nothin' to do with you. But I'm afraid this ain't over yet. You need to come home, where you'll be safe. Tell me where you are."

I heard him breathing heavily, trying to regain his composure, debating whether to tell me. I waited him out, figuring he was about to give it up.

"No . . ."

"TJ—"

"No . . ."

"I'm telling you the truth, TJ. Call your mother. Ask her. This isn't about Eli or Miguel anymore. I don't give a shit about that. You can quit the band, tell Eli to go screw himself. I don't care. But believe me when I tell you that some very bad guys are looking for you. If you won't tell me where you are, then please call 911 and tell the cops."

More breathing. "Nobody'll find me."

"These guys will. Eventually. Just tell me where you are. I don't care if it's Fiji. I'll come get you."

"No . . . they won't find me."

"TJ, please. You're not safe."

"I . . . I gotta go."

"Wait! Please—"

But he was gone. All that was left was dial tone in my ear.

"Damn!" I yelled, and smashed a fist onto the dashboard. "Damn!"

I dropped Eddie's cell phone and pulled out my own. I quickly called Arlene Sommerset. She wasn't home.

I left her a brief message, telling her about my conversation with TJ and imploring her to call him. Maybe she could get through to him. I reiterated my offer to go get him, no matter where he was.

I sat in my truck for a few minutes, feeling supremely frustrated. Figuring that I might as well keep the feeling going, I started the engine and headed for the offices of Global Talent Inc.

"I'd fire you, Garrity, if I thought it would make any difference," Eli said, his lips tight. "But it's too late now. You haven't found him and it's too late to bring in someone else. I'm fucked either way."

I said nothing. George sat next to me, chagrined, his eyes downcast. I looked over at him. He didn't meet my gaze.

Eli sat across from us, behind his huge desk. He closed his eyes and rubbed his temples. "This is all your fault," he said, looking up at George. "You vouched for him. Said he was an ace."

George leaned forward at his boss. "Eli—"

"Shut the fuck up, George. You said he could find anyone. You said going with him instead of that agency what's his name recommended would be quieter. Attract less attention. Less attention . . . ," Eli muttered to himself softly, almost breaking into a rueful laugh. Then he exploded, finger jabbing at George. *Now I've got fucking* Entertainment Tonight *calling about TJ's murdered cousin!*

So the word was out. I was surprised that the press hadn't found me yet. They would. Soon. They always did.

"You see these?" Eli said, scooping up a handful of pink phone messages. "They all wanna talk to TJ. Some are lawyers asking if he has representation! What the fuck does he need representation for, George? You're the fucking vice president of security! You're supposed to keep the little shits outta trouble. *This is not less attention!*"

"Hey, Eli," I said. "Relax."

He wheeled on me. "What?!"

"Relax. Havin' a tantrum isn't gonna help."

"What?!"

"So," I said. "Can I get one of those hazelnut coffees you guys have? They're tasty."

Eli's eyes bulged and apoplexy kept him from speaking. Throwing a non sequitur at him like that was meant to break his rhythm. Interrupt his tirade. It seemed to be working. Plus, I wouldn't mind one of those coffees. They really were tasty.

"Look," I said. "You can't blame George for Eddie gettin' killed. He had nothin' to do with it. Hell, I had nothin' to do with it and I ended up with the poor bastard's head on my kitchen table." They both just stared at me. I seemed to be speaking with some authority, and they were floundering for some direction, any direction. "And it's nobody's fault that TJ and Eddie were related. TJ's bad luck to have a scumbag cousin. He ain't the first, believe me."

There was a beat before Eli said, "I am so fucked."

"Probably," I said. "But havin' a hissy fit ain't gonna make it feel any better. Now, which do you want first, the good news or the bad news?"

Eli's head drooped. "Bad news? You mean *more* bad news?"

"Yeah. Sorry."

"Shit. Why not? Dump it all on me. Bury me in it, and if I'm lucky, I'll be crushed to death."

"Alright. The bad news is that even if I find him, I don't think TJ's comin' back. I think he quit the band."

Definitely not what they wanted to hear. The statement hung there, suspended over the desk, everyone staring at it, nobody wanting to touch it, like some dirigible turd.

"What did you say?" Eli finally said.

"Yeah, you heard me. I don't know it for fact, but my girlish intuition tells me he's done. You should start thinkin' about contingency plans."

"What're you *saying*?" Eli hissed. "That he *quit*? Are you *nuts*?"

"That's my hunch. And I think you know why." I met Eli's gaze directly. George cut his eyes back and forth between us. He had no idea what I was talking about.

"I don't believe it," Eli said.

"That's your prerogative." I decided not to mention the real bad news: my fear that TJ was contemplating suicide. It was too speculative and too inflammatory.

"What's the good news?" George asked. For such a big, hulking guy, his demeanor was meek—timid, even.

"Actually, I have two things. Whatever trouble Eddie Sommerset was in that got him whacked, I don't think TJ had anything to do with it. I don't think he needs any legal representation." I smiled. "Although, advice of counsel is always prudent."

"That's the good news?" Eli said. "That TJ isn't involved in his cousin's murder? That's our new threshold for good news?"

"If TJ is innocent," I said, "the Boyz Klub image and reputation remain intact."

"What the hell do I care?" Eli barked. "If TJ quits, there is no Boyz Klub! They could all be murderers and rapists, for all I care. The sponsorships are gone either way."

A real sweetheart, this Eli Elizondo.

"What's the other thing?" George asked. "You said there were two things."

"Yeah. I talked to him."

George didn't get it. "Him?"

"Yeah."

"You mean TJ?" Eli said, standing. He leaned forward onto his desk. "You talked to TJ?"

"Yeah. On the phone."

"When?" George said eagerly, grabbing my forearm.

Before I could answer his question or, more likely, tell him to take his big paws from my person, Eli's office door opened. His assistant poked her head in.

"Eli?"

"Not now!" Eli shouted, still staring at me.

"Uh," the assistant continued, "the police are here." That got Eli's attention. He swiveled his head at her. "They want to talk to you."

The door swung wider, and instead of seeing Orange County detectives Diaz and Crowley, in walked Orlando City detectives Joe Vincent and Gary Richards. They spotted me and George.

"Well, no shit," said Joe, smiling, looking at the two of us. "It's old-home week. Garrity, where you been? I been lookin' all over for you." I nodded a greeting at them.

"How you doin', Mikey?" Richards said with what appeared to be sincere concern.

"Eh," I said. "You know. Good days and bad days."

"Yeah," Richards said.

"So, Garrity," Joe said. "Can we go somewheres and talk? We got a lotta catchin' up to do."

Joe Vincent was about my age, with a full head of thick, salt-and-pepper hair and bushy eyebrows that could use a trim. He was in decent shape, still lifted a couple times a week in the department gym, but had gone a little soft since he'd left the patrol car a few years ago. I never knew him real well, but I got along with him okay when I was still on the job. He was a hard-ass detective, a pit bull who favored the direct, browbeating approach in suspect interviews. I wondered how he'd treat me now.

"So, no bullshit now, Garrity," Joe said, leaning back in the imported leather conference-room chair. "What are they like? The Boyz."

"Uh," I said, not expecting the question, "you mean the band?"

"Yeah. What're they really like?"

"They're okay, I guess."

"Assholes, right? They gotta be. You don't get that rich that young and not turn into an asshole. I know I would."

"I dunno," I said. "I only met 'em a couple times. They seemed okay. A lot more talented than I thought. I expected smoke and mirrors, y'know? But they're actually good."

"No shit." Joe Vincent smiled over at Gary Richards, who didn't return it. It was just the three of us in Global Talent's enormous main conference room.

Gary Richards was a couple years younger, with a thin, studious face. I don't think I could recall a single time I had ever seen him when he didn't look just a little sad, with his brows slightly furrowed, and the only smiles offered being of the wry, melancholy variety. I guess I couldn't blame him. Richards had lost his wife three years ago to breast cancer, leaving him a single parent of two kids under four years old.

"So, Mikey," Richards said. "Where'd they cut you?"

I turned my head and parted the hair over my ear so he could see the biopsy scar. Richards shook his head slowly.

"That's a bitch, man," said Joe. "A goddamn bitch, there."

"Yeah," I said, wondering how Bob felt about being called a bitch. "So why do I have to do this dance with you guys? I spent hours with Orange County last night."

"Jurisdictional bullshit," said Joe. "We found the body first, so it's our case. But they say the head trumps everything else. We say, get lost, the head is just another piece of evidence like you found a finger or a kneecap or something. They tell us to release the body. We tell 'em to shove it. They call the county commissioner. We call the mayor. Yada yada. It'll come back to us eventually, but I don't want the case to get cold while I'm waitin'."

Richards was staring at me, something going on behind those professor eyes. "Why you, Mikey?"

I took a deep breath and went through the whole sordid story again. I told them all the same things I'd told Diaz last night. I also told them I gave the .22 pistol to Diaz. I related the phone call I got from the "friend of a friend," as well as Diaz's information about the Mustang's tag and the partial print lifted from the gun.

The two detectives filled pages with notes. The only thing I held back was Eddie's cell phone, which remained safely in the glove box of my truck.

When I was done, they looked at each other. Something unspoken passed between them. Joe was the primary, but Richards clearly wanted to ask something. Joe sat back signaling Richards to go ahead.

"Thanks, Mikey," Richards said, his voice soft, unhurried. "We appreciate this info. We'll see what we can do to get the gun. Maybe run a ballistics on it and see if it was used in any other crime. But a couple things still trouble me." He paused, thinking about which one to ask about first. "You don't think TJ's involved?"

"No."

"Seems a stretch, though, to say the timing of his disappearance is a coincidence, wouldn't you agree?"

"I do agree. But I think that's exactly what it is."

"You really think," Joe Vincent said, "that TJ ran off because Elizondo came between him and his boyfriend? Risk those millions of dollars?"

"TJ is a person of deep convictions," I said. "You'd have to know him."

"But," said Richards, "I thought you never met him. How could you know why he ran?"

"I don't know. But I feel like I know as much about TJ as someone could without meeting him. I'm not pretending to have all the answers here. I'm just telling you my hunches. You can do what you want with 'em."

Richards nodded. "Please don't take offense. Nobody's questioning your abilities. We're just trying to understand."

"Was this common knowledge?" Joe said. "About TJ bein' a queer?"

"No."

"This couldn't be a blackmail deal? Go public with the big gay scandal?"

"It's possible, but I haven't found any evidence of that yet."

"And if it is," Richards said, "money would be the motive, right? You said the guy in the Mustang wanted money. TJ's money. So why kill Eddie? Send a message?"

"Because Eddie owed the money. TJ had bailed him out before and these guys expect him to do it again. Except nobody could find TJ and Eddie ran outta time. But they still plan to collect."

"So the million-dollar question is, who's your friend of a friend?"

I shook my head. "I wish I knew, guys. I never met the guy before."

"Who's he workin' for?" Joe demanded.

"I dunno."

Joe leveled a finger at me. "Don't you lie to me, Garrity."

"Fuck you, Joe. I ain't lyin'."

"Take it easy," Richards said.

"You think I haven't been tryin' to figure that out?" I said, growing pissed. "A friend?! What does that mean? Someone who sends a decapitated head home with my little girl? You think I don't wanna have a conversation with that scumbag? I've gone through every crazy angle I can come up with. Maybe it's somebody who knows someone here at Global. God knows, Eli probably has a Rolodex full of enemies. Or some friend of TJ's I haven't uncovered yet. Maybe the connection is me somehow. I probably arrested a thousand people in my career, including mob guys when I was with MBI. I bet there are more than a few people out there who did a little happy dance when they heard I had cancer. But what if it's TJ himself? Finally getting rid of his deadbeat leech cousin and setting up this game to throw us off the trail. With his money, he could afford a scheme like that. I don't have any goddamn answers. Everything I've told you is the truth. If you want me to keep my hunches to myself, fine. But if you're smart, you'll take advantage of my seventeen years on the job and listen to whatever the hell I want to say."

Joe Vincent looked unimpressed, his lips pressed together in a cynical pucker. Gary Richards spread his hands.

"Okay, Mikey," Richards said. "Is there anything else you want to tell us?"

"No." Then: "Yes. I want my cup of goddamn hazelnut coffee."

CHAPTER 23

I drank my coffee and finished up with Joe Vincent and Gary Richards. They'd spend the rest of the afternoon at Global Talent interviewing George, Eli, and anyone else who they thought might know something.

I stepped out of the building onto the humid downtown Orlando sidewalk to find a swarm of cameras buzzing and clicking in my face.

"Mr. Garrity!"

"Mike!"

"What's your connection to Boyz Klub?"

"Was TJ involved in his cousin's murder?"

"How did you discover the head?"

The press. Finally. Just doin' their jobs, I suppose, but it didn't mean I had to like it. I gave them my best sourpuss and pushed through to the parking garage. They barked more questions at me, two guys with video cameras actually following me down the cement stairs. But they soon got the picture that I wasn't talking and gave up, turning their attention back to the lobby of the building that housed Global Talent Inc.

I called Cam and she said that she was on her way to pick up Jennifer and take her to work at the mall. Jennifer had been called in. I didn't like her going out, even to her job, but I hadn't reached the point where I could really justify keeping her locked up. I promised to see her when her shift was over.

I tried calling TJ again, with no results. Before I knew it, I realized I was heading toward Isleworth. I decided to keep going.

I was still on Arlene Sommerset's access list, and the security guard passed me through into the wealthy enclave. A few minutes later I was in front of Arlene's door, ringing the doorbell.

There was no answer, even after two more rings, so I took a stroll around the house. As I came around the back of the house, I heard a soft splash. Through the patio screen I saw Arlene swimming laps in her pool. I knocked on the frame of the screen door. Her head jerked up.

"Hi," I said.

She said nothing, considering me for a moment before dipping her head back into the water and finishing her lap. She stepped up out of the pool and grabbed a chartreuse beach towel. She was wearing an attractive red-and-white, one-piece bathing suit, which complemented her body. Her skin was tight and smooth and she didn't appear at all self-conscious about her body, as some women do. I surprised myself by watching with a little too much interest the sparkling droplets of water rolling down her thighs and calves, her wet skin glistening in the sun. I realized that I was on the precipice of creepy and averted my eyes.

She covered herself with the towel and walked over to me. Expressionless, she flipped the lock on the door handle and turned away.

As she walked, she said, "You want an iced tea or something?"

"Yeah," I said, opening the door and following her to the lanai. She got a couple of drinks and sat at what was probably expensive patio furniture.

"Exercise helps me when I'm stressed," Arlene said, sipping her tea, leaning forward onto the glass table.

"You're stressed now?"

"I'm worried about TJ. He hasn't answered any of my calls or returned any of my messages. I don't know what I would do if anything happened to him. He's my whole world."

"I understand."

"How did he sound? When you talked to him, how did he sound?"

"Well, I've never spoken to him before, so I don't really have anything to compare it to, but he was upset about Eddie. It was a shock to hear it like that, from me, on Eddie's phone."

"Do you still think he might hurt himself?"

"I don't think so. I was never sure about that. Still not. But it's not my call. I don't know him. All I know is, he was upset." I took a breath. "I'm more worried about the danger from whoever killed Eddie."

Arlene turned and gazed out over the trimmed grass and at the lake beyond. Without looking at me, she said, "You have the most brilliant green eyes."

I didn't reply. I've never been good at compliments, which is how I took her statement. I swallowed a mouthful of iced tea.

"I know you're trying to help," she said, turning back to me. "I know you just want to protect my son." She put her hand on top of mine. "I'm sorry this has involved you personally. Your family. Your daughter having to deal with that. It's awful. Eddie caused a lot of trouble in his life. Even gone, he's still causing trouble." She leaned closer to me. "For some reason, I trust you, Mike Garrity. I want you to keep looking for my boy. I want you to bring him home safely to me." Her eyes locked on mine for a long beat.

Then she kissed me. Not one of those chaste, grateful-sister kisses on the cheek, but a full-blown face press with no ambiguity in its intention. I kissed her back, tasting the pool-cleansed skin, feeling the delicate, silky texture of her lips against mine.

She leaned back in her chair and drained her iced tea.

"I think you should go now."

"Yeah," I said, and finished my own glass.

"So what're we lookin' at here, Igor?" I said, flipping through the medical examiner's report. The good stuff was in the back, past the size of the gallbladder and the color of the pancreas, where the ME offered his summary of findings and conclusions.

Igor winced at my use of that name. I didn't mean to, it was just a habit. We stood in a small, colorless, locked office at the Orange/Osceola County Medical Examiner's building, which also handled the city of Orlando. The lights were low, the only illumination a pale yellow desk lamp. I wasn't supposed to be able even to see the autopsy report—the DA had asked for it to be sealed fearing a media frenzy. But Igor had palmed a copy for my perusal, which I appreciated.

"Pretty straight up," Igor said. "Toxicology came back negative. Stomach was empty. Boy hadn't eaten in a while. Cause of death was the big bullet in his forehead. Scrambled up everything inside his skull. Looks like a thirty-eight did the job, but no slug was recovered, so it's just an educated guess. GSR was thick on the skin. Point-blank, execution-style. Optic nerves are strained. Pressure in the head almost popped his eyeballs right out. Seen that plenty of times before." Igor shook his head, recalling the not-so-fond memories.

I skimmed through the medical mumbo jumbo, reading past the Latin, and found the conclusions. They jibed with Igor's summary.

"So when did they go to work on his neck?" I asked.

"Not sure. Not right away. Couple hours, tops. Lotta blood drained first. There wasn't very much blood around the neck wound, considering the location and . . . severity. They used a sharp knife, probably a big one, to cut the tissue, based on the cleanliness of the cut. Maybe some butcher shears severed the spine. Maybe a good set of tree pruners. They didn't chop off his head to kill him. That was just for fun."

"And you're sure the head fits the body?"

"No doubt. The tissue cut lines match up like a puzzle. Plus, we pulled a bunch of grass and vegetation from both the clothes on the body and the hair on the head. They match. Same kind of mud. Same sand. We'll run a full lab set on the dirt and vegetation, but I've seen it with my own eyes. At some point, the head and the body were both lying on the same patch of ground. My take is that they were still attached. Then the bad guys popped him and let him bleed for a while before pulling out the Ginsu. Also, the fingerprints from the kid's apartment match our headless horseman. That also puts the body with the head, which had a visual ID."

"Yeah," I said with full recognition that I was the one to offer the first visual ID. "So who ran the prints?"

"The ones what own the body, OPD. You know him. Joe Vincent. Big asshole. The other guys own the head."

"Anything else unusual?" I said, flipping some more pages in the report.

"Nada."

"So whose case is it? Who owns the whole corpse, OPD or the county?"

Igor shrugged. "Eeny meeny miny moe. The boy's dead. That's all that matters to me. Gotta get him cleaned up for the funeral. They wanna plant him tomorrow."

"That's pretty fast."

"The autopsy on the body was already done. The ME had already figured some sort of head trauma was the cause of death, based on the lack of any other injuries and no sign of bleeding when the head was severed. Once we got the head, it didn't take long to finish the report. Besides, the family wants closure. From what I hear, the boy was a handful."

I nodded and handed the file back to him, thanking him. I made my way out of the maze of cinder-block hallways that smelled of formaldehyde and latex. And death. Outside, I squinted up into the bright afternoon sun and inhaled the clean, unbloodied air. Hot again today. Mid-nineties. Eighty-five percent humidity with the daily afternoon showers on their way. I had been outside all of ten seconds, but the beads of sweat were already budding across my forehead. Summer in Central Florida.

Arlene would have the information on the funeral arrangements. I would definitely attend. The cops, both Orlando Metro and Orange County, would stake out the funeral, hoping that the killer would show. They both had my description of the Mustang and its driver. Teams of undercover guys, cameras with long-range lenses, maybe even a blue-and-white cruiser to spook a reaction, they'd be there in force.

I also thought that there was a better than average shot that TJ would make an appearance. And if both TJ and the killer were there, that was a situation I probably needed to insert myself into.

But why? I asked myself as I walked the frying-pan-hot asphalt to my truck. I didn't think TJ was coming back to Boyz Klub, so my shot at the big payoff from Global Talent was remote at best. And it was dangerous. I still didn't understand everything going on here, but I knew enough to realize that whatever it was, it was enough motive to kill Eddie Sommerset and send his head home with my daughter. The smart move was to stay as far away from the whole mess as I could get. Unfortunately, I was never the smartest guy in my class.

I could still taste Arlene Sommerset's lips on mine. She was counting on me to find her son and keep him safe. She was paying me nothing, but I felt a much stronger obligation to her than to Eli or George. I had also grown to admire and respect TJ. At least, I thought I did. I didn't *really* know him, but I cared what happened to him.

Plus, and if I was really being honest with myself, this was probably the strongest reason, if anything happened to TJ, it would break Jennifer's heart. I couldn't bear the thought of anything hurting her. Anything.

At some point, when Bob has finally had his way with me and I'm gone, Jennifer will likely have to deal with the emotional baggage of that. But, until that moment came, I would do everything in my power to prevent even the tiniest grain of hurt from touching her. If I had realized anything in the brief time she had been staying with me, it was that I had caused her enough pain in her life with my absence, as well as my apathy. From now until the end, I would do what I could to atone for that by wrapping her in a cocoon of safety.

And if that meant attending Eddie Sommeset's funeral and protecting TJ's life, even at the possible risk of my own, that was what I would do.

When I got to Cam's place, she and Jennifer were boiling pasta and ripping iceberg lettuce for a salad. Cam lived in an expensive condo in the trendy section of downtown Winter Park, just off the main drag of chic Park Avenue. Wall-to-wall, blond hardwood floors. Track lighting. Surround-sound stereo. Cam's décor was modern and tasteful: more Restoration Hardware and Williams-Sonoma than Home Depot and Sears.

Dinner was quiet, the events of the previous evening lying like a dark blanket over us.

"Jenn, you alright?" I finally asked, putting down my fork.

"I guess."

"You may have to give another statement," I said. "This time to the Orlando city detectives."

"What?" Jennifer looked stricken. "Why? Why do I have to go through all of that again?"

"It's complicated. And stupid. For now, they're gonna work from your statements to the county detectives. But they may want to ask you some more questions."

"I don't want to."

"I know."

"I don't wanna do it."

"I know," I said. "I'll do everything I can."

The three of us sat in silence for another minute, the only sound our forks clinking on our plates.

"Did you reach Becky?" Cam asked.

"Not yet," I said. "I left another message on her cell phone."

"Mom doesn't need to come home," Jennifer said. "I'm not a baby."

"No," I said. "You're not."

More silence. More clinking.

"Dad?"

I looked up from my twirled pasta.

"What does this have to do with TJ?" Jennifer asked.

I popped the spaghetti into my mouth and chewed, considering her question. I thought about what right she had to the truth. Considering that she was the one who'd toted Eddie Sommerset's head home from the mall, she was as entitled to the truth as anyone.

So I told her. I told her everything except the part about Miguel. Being gay was TJ's private life and not mine to share. But Jennifer got everything else.

She listened without interruption, without showing much emotion. When I was done, she sat looking at me, but not seeing me, lost in her thoughts.

Finally, she said, "I want to go to the funeral."

"No," I said.

"I'm going."

"No. It could be dangerous."

"With or without you, I'm going."

"Jennifer, it's not a good idea. I don't know who'll be there."

"I need to go," she said. "I don't know why. But I need to go. It'll help. No matter what you say, I'm going. You're gonna have to handcuff me to the bed to keep me from going."

I pursed my lips, squinting at her. I didn't think she was bluffing. And I didn't think she wanted to go to satisfy some looky-loo morbid curiosity. I think she was actually sincere. An amazing accomplishment for a fifteen-year-old.

"Okay," I finally muttered. "But you stay next to me the whole time and do exactly as I say."

Cam shook her head. "A chip off the ol' block."

I snorted and couldn't help but smile. I resumed eating. When I stole a glance at Jennifer, I could see her suppressing her own grin.

CHAPTER 24

Jennifer had brought her laptop to Cam's and we spent a little over an hour surfing the chat rooms and looking for Klubhopper1. He was a no-show. I tried TJ's cell phone again. No luck. He wasn't answering.

I spoke to Arlene, who had been leaving her own series of messages for TJ. She gave me the details for the funeral. She said nothing about our kiss, but it was there anyway. Awkward pauses and a curious reluctance—on both of our parts—to hang up. It was truly strange.

Cam didn't ask me to stay. It was just assumed. Especially with Jennifer also staying, I just slid as expected into the routine of occupancy.

I stood in Cam's master bathroom, brushing my teeth with a borrowed toothbrush, studying myself in the wall-sized mirror. None of the stuff on the counters was mine. Not the lotions or the makeup, the perfumes or the swabs. This was her bathroom, separate from me, totally and completely. I popped my seizure pills and headed into the bedroom to lie down before I became too dizzy.

Cam was already in bed, leaning against the headboard, reading a magazine. I lay on my back and stared up at the ceiling. My eyes were open. Bob wasn't sleepy.

"What are we doing?" I said to the ceiling.

"Hmm?" Cam said, still reading.

"What are we doing here?" I repeated to the ceiling.

Cam put the magazine down. "What?"

"I don't know what we're doing here."

"Michael, are you okay?"

"I mean, are we really divorced? Is that our reality?"

"Yes," she said. "We are really divorced."

"Then what are we doing here? Why am I in your bed?"

She hesitated, examining me. "Don't you like being in my bed?"

"That's not the point."

"What is the point?"

I sighed, still staring straight up. "You date other people."

"Yes." She knew enough of my social life not to say *So do you*.

"And that's not supposed to bother me?" I said, finally looking at her.

"I don't know. Does it?"

"I don't know. I think so."

"So . . . what, you want me to stop dating other people?"

I closed my eyes and let out a rueful chuckle. "Yeah."

"Is that what you want?"

"Cam, we're *divorced*. You can date farm animals if you want and I have no right to say boo."

"Do you want me to stop dating other people?" she repeated.

"How can I ask you that?"

"Then what do you want?"

I paused, thinking about the question. It was a good question, really cutting to the core of my concern. The truth was that I didn't know what I wanted anymore. My navigation seemed off. Did I want a relationship with Cam? Or Arlene? Or anyone? Or was it pointless, given my circumstances? What *did* I want? Perhaps the question really was, did I want to live or die? The answer to that might determine everything else.

But I couldn't articulate that to Camilla. I barely even understood it. So, instead I said, "Do you think we'll ever get remarried?"

That brought her up short, with an expression that might result after unexpectedly sitting on the wet seat of a public toilet. I thought I saw subtle flashes of at least four distinct emotions dance across her face. Shock. Pity. Love. Disappointment. She exhaled and I saw it all in her eyes.

"That's what I thought," I said.

"It didn't exactly work out before."

"Yeah. Plus, the terminal cancer makes a big effort kind of a waste of time, right?"

Now I saw the hurt in her eyes. I was sorry I said it. Not that there wasn't some truth in it. I just shouldn't have said it.

"That's not fair," she said, emotion catching in her throat. "You know this has nothing to do with that."

"Okay."

"I just don't think we're compatible like that. I need someone who . . . can give something back."

"Yeah. So, I ask again, what are we doing here?"

I thought she was going to get mad. The old, predivorce Cam might've let me have it, although I'm not even sure why. I was never exactly sure why she got so mad at me. For me, our married life was a constant adventure in anger discovery.

But this new Cam, the one who cries secretly in the bathroom in the middle of the night, was silent. Her eyes glistened and she tried to force a smile through her obvious pain. "I'm just . . . not ready to lose you yet." She placed a palm on my cheek. "I'm holding on to you the only way I know how. I'm . . . just so sorry."

"Yeah . . ."

She put her magazine aside and lay down next to me, draping an arm across my stomach, her face buried in my shoulder. We lay like that until she fell asleep.

Bob and I stayed up for a while, thinking.

I'm not sure how much sleep I got. A few hours. A few minutes. It all had the same effect. Bob roused me in the predawn with a good old-fashioned skull-splitter.

I got up and leaned on my elbows over the sink. I felt like I was going to puke, but I never did. I wish I had. I might have felt better. Bob managed to maintain just the right level of low-grade nausea to keep me miserable.

I took a shower, keeping one hand on the tile to stay upright. Then made some coffee, took a handful of pills—antiseizures, pain relievers, Flintstones vitamins, I don't even know anymore—and sat on Cam's balcony. The world was quiet. Every so often I heard a car door thunk, the early commuters heading off to work. But, mostly, the world was still, shrouded in a low fog that sat on everything like a layer of thick, puffy cotton. Car roofs, palm fronds, and the top of the bricked community mailbox seemed to bob on top of the mist. I sipped my coffee.

Today was the day they would bury Eddie Sommerset. By all accounts, his was a wasted life. But that was a harsh judgment, wasn't it? He had his good points, right? He had to. No book is a single piece of paper. Even Hitler had his mama.

At some point in the not too distant future, they would be planting me in the ground. What would they say about me? What would be the consensus? A wasted life? I hope not. Surely I had done some good. I had taken a lot of bad people off the streets and put them behind bars. Surely the world must be a little better from having had me around.

Since I had become involved in the search for TJ Sommerset (to which I had started referring, only to myself, of course, with the Hardy Boys title The Case of the Missing Boy Band Boy), I had been too busy to wallow in my own particular flavor of self-pity. I had actually gone for an hour or so at a time without thinking about my brain tumor. I don't want to say that I forgot about it, that wouldn't really be true, but I was able to push it into the background. Not focus on it. Not obsess about it.

I know it sounds ridiculous, but I really think that's what triggered the seizures. Bob was jealous and wanted some attention. I had something else to think about now and he responded like a petulant child. As I said, I know it sounds crazy, but I'm the one with the tumor, so cut a guy a little slack.

I felt the woozy light-headedness of the antiseizure meds descend like a light rain, misting over the nausea, melting into a combined glaze of total body discomfort. And the headache was still going strong. I drained the last sip from my mug, but didn't get up for a refill.

Somewhere, out there in the fog, TJ Sommerset was hiding.

From Eli. From his mother. From me. From whoever killed Eddie. From himself, maybe. From his life.

I wondered if I would find him in time. Not in time for the concert tour, although I guess, on some level, I still wondered about that, too.

Finding TJ had become inexplicably important to me. Something I needed to do before I was gone. For Jennifer. It had become some sort of twisted redemptive quest.

So, I sat there with my empty coffee cup and wondered if I would find him in time—in time to prevent my attendance at another Sommerset funeral. God, I hoped so.

I closed my eyes and steadied myself on the back of the pew in front of me. My glaze of nausea and dizziness was still thick. I hadn't barfed in church since I was six years old. It was a particularly unpleasant experience and I had no desire to repeat it now.

I felt Jennifer's hand rest on my back, a silent, meaningful gesture. A few deep breaths later I felt a little better and opened my eyes. I exchanged a wan smile with her. She gave me an oddly maternal pat on the back and removed her hand.

I surveyed my surroundings. Maybe forty or fifty people were in the Baptist church. I saw no sign of the goon from the Mustang. I did spot Gary Richards sitting on an aisle, looking appropriately sad, his usual expression. Arlene sat in the front with who I presumed was Eddie's mother, Carol. I only saw the back of her head clearly, but Carol appeared to be holding up stoically. No wailing. No hysterical crying. Just a quiet, dignified sorrow.

An organist played an old hymn, one of the usuals, "How Great Thou Art" or something, while the pallbearers escorted a white coffin down the center aisle, leaving it in front of the pulpit. Not surprisingly, Eddie's mother had opted for a closed casket.

A minister stepped up to the pulpit. He was younger than I expected. They always seemed to be silver-haired middle-agers. But he was in his midthirties, thin, and spoke with a voice that could have used a little more baritone to suit his profession. He reminisced about Eddie's passion for life. His zeal. His love of competition. His independent spirit. I gave the preacher credit. He did a masterful job euphemizing Eddie's vices to the point where they could have been virtues.

I continued looking around for TJ, periodically checking the entrances for a shaft of light that would reveal a door opening and a figure slipping in. But he was nowhere I could see. I caught Gary Richards doing the same sly checking.

I wondered if TJ might have shown up in disguise. If he did, I wasn't good enough to detect it. I hoped no one else was either.

I wanted to do a quick exterior check, see if I could spot a car parked on a corner or a mourner who looked out of place, TJ's yellow Jetta, anything that might point me toward either TJ or Eddie's killer.

"I'm gonna get some air," I whispered to Jennifer, and patted her knee. Then I stepped my way out of the pew and slipped outside.

The sun blasted me as I pushed out of the church. There was no relief looking down. The white cement of the steps and sidewalk reflected the overhead sunlight with a blinding brilliance. I squinted and came down the steps, moving off the sidewalk and onto a patch of unmowed St. Augustine grass.

Looking up and down the suburban street, nothing jumped out at me except the unmarked white van two blocks down. I pegged it for an Orange County surveillance team. One block in the opposite direction I saw a woman standing at the curb, leaning against a silver Ford Taurus, smoking a cigarette. I recognized her and stepped over.

"Hey," I said.

"Hey," said Orange County homicide detective Sharon Crowley. "How's Jennifer?"

"I think she'll be okay. She's inside now."

Crowley's eyebrows went up in surprise that Jennifer was at the funeral. Then she jutted her bottom lip and nodded slightly. A *way to go, kid* kind of gesture.

"You see anything?" I asked.

She shook her head. "Clean so far. We've got people in a perimeter all around the church. We've got electronic surveillance. We've got undercovers inside. We've got a half dozen patrol cars hiding five blocks away, waiting for the call for backup. We should be ready for anything."

I glanced around. No sign of anything suspicious. All this prep may have been a lot of setup with no punch line. "Yeah, but are you ready for nothing?" I said.

She took a long drag on the cig. "I did some checking on you, you know."

"Yeah?"

She nodded. "I have some friends assigned to MBI. One of them's been there awhile. Remembered you."

"Who?"

"Bill Urlacher."

I nodded. I remembered him. Eager, hotshot kid from the Sheriff's Department. But he was okay. I liked him well enough.

"How do you know Urlacher?" I asked.

"Long story. Too long. Let's just say that cops should never date cops."

"Yeah." If there was ever a motto that belonged in stone, that was it.

"Anyway, Urlacher says you're the real deal. Said that the Juan the Don bust was all you before the Feds took over." I didn't say anything. "Urlacher said you pissed off some family men in the tristate area. Said there was a bounty on your head."

"Rumors," I said. "Obviously I'm still here."

"I remember that case." Crowley looked at me and crinkled her eyes. "That was badass."

"Long time ago."

"I've done some checking on Eddie Sommerset, too. If your hunch is right, Eddie was in over his head to someone, probably a bookie. But there hasn't been a major gambling operation in Central Florida since you busted Alomar."

"That you know of," I added.

"True. There's an outfit in Tampa and the usual cast of characters down in Miami who we might want to consider."

"Or Eddie was layin' bets with someone out of state. Or offshore. This is the information age, y'know."

She smirked. I liked her smile. It was attractive with a no-nonsense directness. No overdone lipstick, no duplicity. "We just don't know enough yet," she said.

"Whoever it was, Eddie must've been in pretty deep to bring that kinda heat on himself." I glanced over at the van. "So why aren't you in your car? Aren't you afraid of spooking anyone who might show up? TJ? The bad guys?"

She shrugged. "I'd give 'em a lot of credit if they knew who I was. Plus, I did a radio check with everyone and got an all clear before I got out. Mostly, I just needed a smoke."

I glanced into the Taurus. Empty. "You don't smoke in the car?"

"Diaz asked me not to."

"I don't see him sittin' there."

"He says he can smell it in the seats." She hunched her shoulders again. "Your partner makes a request, you try to accommodate. It's a small car. Y'know how it is."

I did. The front seat of a surveillance car gets even smaller when you're sharing it with Big Jim Dupree.

"So where is my buddy Diaz?" I asked. "Other side of the church?"

She shook her head. "His kid is in a school play or something. He took a personal day."

I made a thoughtful face. "No kidding. He didn't strike me as the daddy type."

"No? He's got six kids."

"Yeah?"

"Yeah. Friend of yours is covering the back. Joey." She made a sour face.

"Joey?" Then I realized. "Joey V?"

"Yeah. Kind of a prick. Thinks he's my boss."

"That's him. Except nobody calls him Joey V to his face. He hates that."

Her smirk appeared again. "I'll remember that," she said, obviously filing that knowledge away for possible use at a later date. I liked her more and more. "We're still fighting over jurisdiction. But since this church actually sits in county territory, we agreed it was our show. Joey V," she said with more than a twinge of sarcasm, "didn't like it."

We were silent for a moment, each of us doing the slow rotate with our eyes, scanning the area for anything out of the ordinary. Crowley looked over at me.

"You know something, Garrity?"

I cocked my head.

"You don't look like the daddy type, either," she said.

CHAPTER 25

They planted Eddie Sommerset in a lovely spot, partially shaded by a big old live oak tree drooping with Spanish moss. The burial was well attended with most of the mourners from the church memorial service making the long trek through the suburban streets with their headlights on.

The crowd looked larger than it actually was with the attendance of the local media. The TJ Sommerset connection was too juicy to ignore. Microwave vans and print reporters hovered nearby, close enough to hear the minister's final words, but far enough away to claim some sort of faux respect for the service.

The few available seats were reserved for the family under a portable nylon awning, so everyone else stood. A lucky handful got a spot in the valuable shade of the oak. The rest of us, including Jennifer and me, stood exposed like rotisserie chickens in the scalding noontime sun.

Since we'd left the church, I'd felt my nausea and dizziness returning, building like an incoming tide. I also felt Bob knocking around in my skull, the headache still hanging on. Bob's idea of a tantrum. I felt crappy and was ready to leave.

I couldn't take any more antiseizure meds. In fact, they were probably causing the dizziness and nausea. I did have a couple of capsules of Cam's Zuraxx in my front pocket. I kept my hand in my pocket, fingering the pills, feeling the sweat emerging on my scalp and rolling down the back of my neck and forehead. The tie and the dark suit only made the sun worse. The texture of the pills, how they rolled between my fingers, reassured me, gave me some hope of feeling better at some point. However, there was no way to take them until the ceremony was over and I could find something to drink.

The casket lowered down to the bottom of the grave with the help of an automated winch that made a quiet whir as it unrolled the supporting straps. A few moments later it was all over and the crowd dispersed.

I put a hand on Jennifer's shoulder in what I hoped to portray as a paternal gesture, but was really more of an attempt at steadying myself so as not to fall face-first into the grave as we walked past back to the cars. When I turned, I found myself staring directly into a microphone and a NewsChannel 2 video camera.

"Mr. Garrity," said the attractive redheaded reporter. "Can you comment on your reaction to Eddie Sommerset's funeral, in light of your role in his murder?"

"What?" I said, squeezing Jennifer's shoulder for stability. Jennifer looked at me, her face confused, aghast. "I had no role—"

"Why did you receive Eddie's severed head?" the reporter continued.

"Look," I said. "Now isn't a good time." I closed my eyes to stop my vision from swaying. I opened them again. The reporter's eyes were wide, her brow raised in anticipation. In my peripheral vision I saw the horde of other reporters moving in.

"Why won't you answer the question?" the redhead asked.

Back in my days on the job I would have said "No comment" and told her to go jump in a gator pond. I had done exactly that countless times. But at the moment I was dizzy and nauseous. Distracted. I wasn't myself.

Instead, I said, "Seriously. Now is a bad time."

"Sure," the reporter said. "I understand. Come on. We'll step over somewhere a little better, out of the sun. We can take all the time you need." She took another step closer to me, reaching with her hand, trying to guide me away from the rest of the swarming media.

"No, you don't understand."

"I do, Mr. Garrity. I do. I'm sorry for jumping in like that. Let's step over here and you can have a moment to think about your answers." She turned to Jennifer. "Hi. I'm Kylie Harmon from NewsChannel 2. Who are you?"

"Uh—," Jennifer said.

"She's off-limits," I barked.

Kylie Harmon paused, cutting her eyes between me and Jennifer. "Okay. That's fine."

The clicking of machinery grew loud as the throng pressed in, everyone wanting to get a piece of my statement. Questions peppered in at me, but I couldn't make them out individually. All my faculties were currently concentrating on remaining upright. The cemetery grass below me felt like the rocking deck of a schooner. Sweat poured off me. I had to get out of this damn sun. I began breathing more heavily. I jammed a finger into my collar, trying to let some air through.

I tried to turn away, but Kylie Harmon leaned in close. "With an exclusive, you can have time to compose your answers. Say what *you* want to say." She put a manicured hand on my elbow. "Just say yes, Mike."

"I gotta get outta here," I mumbled, and tried to turn away— find some path through the crowd.

Kylie Harmon tightened her grip on my elbow, turning me back. "Come on, Mike—"

"Sorry," I whispered, and then puked all over her bright blue pantsuit. I doubled over convulsively, tilting forward like an automated lawn sprinkler and spraying a wave of vomit right at her. I heard her yelp in surprise and horror. Leaning over, my hands on my thighs, I watched her matching blue pumps stumble backward. I saw the contents of my stomach oozing down her slacks as she retreated.

Jennifer's hand was on my back. "It's okay, Dad. It's okay."

I coughed and spat, clenching my eyes open and closed. The collective gasp of the crowd subsided, replaced by amused tittering. They, of course, had gotten it all on tape.

Jennifer led me aside. Fortunately, the crowd parted without resistance and we found a shady spot under a different live oak tree. I sat and leaned back against the bark.

"Sorry about that," I rasped.

"It's okay." Jennifer produced a tissue from her handbag and I wiped my lips. I spat again, trying to remove the biting, sour taste of vomit from my mouth. No use.

"It's the meds," I said.

"I know."

I heard someone approach. It was Detective Crowley.

"Garrity?" she asked. "You okay?"

"In the pink." My voice was hoarse.

"You want me to call someone? An ambulance?"

"No. I'm fine. Just a little nauseous."

"You sure?"

"Yeah."

"Can you drive home?" She offered a wan smile to Jennifer as both a greeting and acknowledgment of her underage status.

"Yeah. I'll be fine. Go on. Go catch the bad guys."

She considered for a beat. "If you need help, I can have a uniform take you home or to the doctor or something."

"Thanks anyway."

Crowley turned and strode over to a small cluster of plainclothes cops, including Gary Richards, who looked concerned. I offered a little wave to tell them I was alright.

I closed my eyes again and leaned my head back against the tree. After a couple of deep breaths through my nostrils, I started to feel better. The puking had ejected my nausea, even if only temporarily, and the excitement had soothed Bob. The headache was diminished.

I heard footsteps approach in the grass and stop directly in front of me.

"You do know how to put on a show," said a familiar voice.

I opened my eyes and squinted up. "Jennifer," I said, "I'd like you to meet Mrs. Arlene Sommerset. TJ's mom."

We drove to a McDonald's three blocks down the street from the cemetery. It occurred to me that there is a McDonald's three blocks down the street from everywhere.

Arlene and Jennifer each ordered a meal, substituting a side salad for the fries. I got a large Coke to settle my stomach, although

I was feeling much better since my graveside eruption. The Coke came in a large collector's cup featuring the four members of Boyz Klub in jazzy poses. So far, McDonald's corporate in Chicago hadn't yet pulled the concert tour promotion, which had apparently just started.

"I'm so sorry for what you went through," Arlene said to Jennifer.

"Thanks," Jennifer said, concentrating on her salad.

"Check it out," I said, holding up the Boyz Klub collector's cup.

Jennifer reached her hand out and held the cup, turning it carefully, studying it.

"Where do you think he is?" she asked Arlene.

Arlene's eyebrows went up and she gave me a look.

"Jennifer knows I'm looking for TJ," I said. "And that I haven't found him yet." I relayed the story of how Jennifer had helped me connect with TJ online.

Arlene nodded. "I don't know," she said. "I've thought a lot about that recently and I just don't know. I wish I had locked my doors or something. If I had known there would be all this trouble, I would've kept him from leaving my house."

"That wouldn't have worked," Jennifer said. "If TJ really wanted to go, you couldn't stop him."

Arlene considered this. "No, I suppose you're right." She picked at her food. "You seem like you really know my son."

Jennifer shrugged.

"She's a fan," I offered.

"So, you think he's in a hotel or something?" Jennifer asked. "Couldn't you call around and see if he's registered?"

"Where would you start?" I said. "There are a million hotels in the world and TJ could be in any one of them. He can afford to go anywhere he wants for as long as he wants. And leave no trail."

"Besides," Arlene said, "he never stays in a hotel under his own name."

"Oh?" I said.

"For security. He always checks in under some alias. They do it all the time for celebrities. It throws off the stalkers and the paparazzi."

"What name does he use?" Jennifer asked.

"Depends. He changes it all the time. But he usually combines the first and last names of his favorite songwriters."

I sat forward and put down the cup. "What do you mean?"

"He'll combine Brian Wilson and Bernie Taupin into Brian Taupin or Bernie Wilson or something."

"And who are his favorite songwriters?"

"He has a bunch. Paul Simon. Billy Joel. John Lennon. Paul McCartney. Don McLean. Jim Croce. Dylan, of course."

"He likes seventies music."

"Not disco. But, yes, he appreciates good lyrics. Poetry. There are some more current artists he likes, too, but I don't know them as well."

I nodded. Sipped my soda. Jennifer crunched the last bite of her salad.

"I gotta go soon, Dad. I'm working the afternoon shift."

"Okay."

We cleaned up and dumped our trays. As we stepped outside, Jennifer turned to Arlene.

"If you talk to him—TJ—tell him that we want him to do the tour. Even if Boyz Klub is done afterwards, the fans want to see them together one last time. *I* want to. It would be sad if it all just went away without us being able to say good-bye. Y'know?"

Arlene put a hand on Jennifer's arm. "I know, sweetie. I know." She let go and looked at me. Her eyes pleaded for me to find him.

I nodded at her and wondered just how the hell I was going to do that.

CHAPTER 26

I dropped Jennifer at the mall for work and then sat in my truck for a few minutes, wondering what I should do now. I literally had nothing to do. With Eddie's funeral over, all my leads for finding TJ had dried up. Jennifer told me a friend was giving her a ride home, so I didn't even have to be back to pick her up later. My afternoon was completely free.

When I turned the wheel, my arm crossed my chest and I felt something in my suit pocket. My cell phone. I'd forgotten it was in there. Pulling it out, I noticed that it was off. I had turned it off for Eddie's funeral and, in all the excitement of barfing for the cameras, had neglected to flip it back on.

I pressed it on. I had two messages. The first was from Becky in North Carolina. She had finally gotten my voice mail and was returning the call. She wanted to know if everything was okay.

How exactly should I answer that? I dreaded telling her about Jennifer carrying Eddie's head home from the mall. No, Becky would definitely not take that well.

I decided that the best thing to do would be what I do best: avoid and ignore. The call back to Becky would wait until I was in a frame of mind to deal with the consequences. It was how I dealt with most issues during our marriage—and also our divorce, for that matter.

The second message was from George Neuheisel. He was clearly calling at the behest of his master. Eli was concerned about my lack of progress locating TJ. He wanted to know if TJ showed up at his cousin's funeral. He wanted a status on the investigation. He wanted my plan for finding him with less than a week remaining before the tour started. Mostly, he wanted me to come straight to the Global Talent offices and get yelled at.

I thought about that for a moment and decided, what the hell? I didn't have anything better to do.

Forty minutes later I again sat in Eli's office watching him have a red-faced fit. George sat passively next to me, lips pursed.

". . . not gonna get a single fucking penny!" Eli was saying. "You hear me? Not a cent! No TJ, no money!"

"I think by now I understand my assignment," I said.

"You better, asshole." Eli leveled a finger at me. "You better."

That was about all I could take. I snapped a hand out and grabbed the finger, twisting it up.

Eli chirped in sudden pain, "Eeef!"

George made a move to get up, and it was my turn to point at someone. I jabbed my finger at George.

"Sit down, George." He froze, knees bent, hovering over the chair. But he didn't sit back down. "Do it, Georgie, or I'm gonna pop his finger out."

Eli slapped his desk twice with the open palm of his free hand. "Sit!" he hissed through clenched teeth.

George sat.

"Good." I turned back to Eli. "Now you listen to me. Don't threaten me about money 'cause I don't give a crap. Haulin' my ass in here and screamin' at me isn't helpin' me find him. You wanna help me? Then leave me alone and let me work."

"Okay," Eli grunted.

I gave the finger a little twist and let it go. Eli's hand recoiled back to his chest where he cradled it like a wounded duckling.

"You're insane!" he said.

I shrugged.

"And you are so fucking fired. You hear me? Get outta my office!"

"You don't wanna do that," I said.

"Oh, yes, I do. I wanna do that as much as I've wanted to do anything in my life. Get out."

"Okay," I said, rising. "But who's gonna find TJ for you? Nobody you bring in now is gonna come up to speed fast enough to make any difference."

Eli's eyes bored into me. He was furious. Probably the thing that made him the most livid was that I was right. He had to keep me on the case. He had no choice.

He blew out a long exhale. "Don't you have informants or anything? Sources on the street who tell you things?"

I snorted and remained standing. "You watch too many movies. If TJ was a transvestite crack whore down on the Trail, then maybe I could dig up a source or two. But he's not. He's a millionaire kid with a broken heart who could be drowning his sorrows on the beach in Rio for all I know. And my worldwide network of wealthy superspies is a little thin these days."

"This isn't funny."

"No, it's not. A human head on my kitchen table is not funny. None of this is funny."

"So what're you gonna do?" George asked.

"I'm gonna keep lookin'. I'm gonna hope to get lucky. I'm gonna pray I find this kid before he hurts himself or ends up like his cousin. But first I'm gonna get the hell outta this office before it completely sucks out what little life I have left. If I were TJ, I'd run away, too."

I turned and strode out of the office. I went directly to the break room, where I poured myself a big mug of gourmet coffee. Then I waltzed out past the receptionist, taking the mug with me.

I sipped it all the way down the elevator to the third level of the building's underground parking garage. My truck was waiting for me halfway down the full row, next to a concrete pillar.

As I pulled my keys from my pocket, I became aware of a car approaching up the ramp. No, it sounded bigger. A truck. It turned the corner just as I reached my door.

It was a black Cadillac Escalade SUV, a behemoth under any circumstances but seemingly even larger now scraping just below the cramped, low ceiling of the garage. It slowed down, waiting for me to vacate my spot. I held up a finger.

The windows were tinted almost black and I couldn't see inside.

The front passenger window slid down and a beefy, sandy-haired guy leaned out.

"Just a sec," I said. "I'm leaving."

The guy nodded. "What's your hurry, Mikey?"

I froze. Oh, shit.

The Escalade's door swung open and the guy got out. "Take a little ride."

"Uh, thanks anyway." I quickly cut my eyes left and right. I was trapped between my truck on one side and a minivan on the other. Behind me was the concrete garage wall. The Escalade sat directly in front in what was my only real path of escape.

My nine-millimeter Glock again sat uselessly inside the cab of my locked truck, tucked under my seat. All I had was the stupid Global Talent coffee cup I now clutched.

The sandy-haired guy took a step toward me and I didn't hesitate. I hurled the mug at him and turned, planting a foot on my front tire and launching myself up onto the hood of my truck.

"Ow! Shit!" I heard the guy shout as I rolled across the hood. I thought I heard other doors on the Escalade opening. I righted myself and leapt from my hood onto the hood of a green Volvo, crouching to keep from smacking my head on the low ceiling. One more step and I bounded over the next gap, picking up speed, hitting the hood of a Civic.

Footsteps behind me now, on the concrete. I was alone on the cars, my pursuers chasing me from the unobstructed drive.

Another stride—another leap, now to a red Saturn. Rule number one—the rule always stressed in the women's safety-awareness classes at the community center—was to never, under any circumstances, *ever* get into the car. In the car, you're trapped, at the mercy of your attacker. The statistics showed that if you got into the car, you died. If you ran, you at least had a fighting chance.

Still moving. Another car, the sheet-metal hood buckling loudly under my running steps. Tires squealed as the Escalade joined the pursuit. I jumped again, landing hard on the hood, waving my arms to keep from falling. I propelled myself forward.

The footsteps were parallel to me now, pulling ahead. I had no plan for escape. I could see no fire exit, no stairs, no maintenance closet. And looming four cars ahead of me was a fifteen-passenger van with no hood to offer a purchase for my landing.

I hit a Mercedes hard and its security alarm whooped to life. Another leap and I thumped down on the hood of a Cavalier. Then I pulled up short and stopped.

Another guy appeared in the space between the last car and the passenger van. He looked Latin, not quite as big as the guy I'd thrown the coffee mug at, but still no slouch. The Latin guy pointed a large revolver at my chest.

Breathing hard, the car alarm wailing behind me, I knew I was cooked. More footsteps approached. I figured my only shot was to dive off the other side of the Cavalier and take cover behind it. Maybe I would get lucky and an OPD cruiser would round the corner on patrol before these guys blew my balding head off. Yeah, fat chance.

My calf twitched in preparation to jump, but before I could make a move, I felt my shirt being yanked from behind. I went down on my ass and slid backward. The sandy-haired guy shoved me to the concrete and stepped hard on my shoulder with a heavy construction boot. Brown coffee stains splotched across his dress shirt. His left cheek was red and puffy where the mug had connected. I might've broken something in his face. It looked like it hurt like hell. And he was none too happy about it. He hauled back a beefy fist to flatten my nose, but another big hand caught his forearm.

A familiar face leaned over me, and given the choice, I would've probably preferred the flattened nose.

"Now, Mikey," said Mr. Day-Glo, the black-haired goon from the Mustang, "is that polite? Someone offers you a ride and you throw a mug at him?" Today's ensemble featured an electric-blue golf shirt.

"You fucker!" screamed the sandy-haired guy. "I'm gonna kill you!"

"Very bad manners, Mikey. I'm ashamed."

Day-Glo grabbed my collar and hauled me to my feet.

"Let him go, you Greek bastard," barked the sandy-haired guy. "I owe him."

My—apparently Greek—friend from the Mustang sighed and looked at me. "Don't move."

There was nowhere to go. The Escalade sat idling at the end of the opening, blocking my escape. And now the Latin guy with the revolver stood waiting there, as well.

Day-Glo whirled on the sandy-haired guy, putting a thick hand on his throat. In an instant, a semiautomatic was in his other hand, pressing the barrel to the forehead of the bigger man.

"You do what I tell you," Day-Glo said. "And you keep your mouth shut doin' it. You're here for one reason, and that's to do whatever I say. You clear on that, slick?"

Slick said nothing, most probably because his windpipe was constricting.

Day-Glo released him. "Get back in the car. And keep your mouth shut." He turned back to me. "Sorry about that."

I didn't respond, instead eyeing the semiautomatic.

"Now let's try again, Mikey. Would you care to take a ride?"

I flicked my eyes from the gun to Day-Glo's face. "Sure, I'd love to."

The big goon broke into a wide, grotesque grin. "See? Manners. That wasn't so hard. After you." He grabbed the back of my collar and propelled me forward to the open back door of the waiting Escalade, thrusting me into the empty third-row seat. So much for not getting in the car.

I righted myself and sat up. Slick was in the front passenger seat, facing out the windshield. The Latin guy slid behind the wheel. Day-Glo positioned himself directly in front of me in the second row next to another, smaller man.

The smaller guy was in his mid-twenties, olive-skinned with close-cropped, black hair. His face was narrow, his mouth a taut, angry fissure. He glared at me over the back of the seat, his eyes furious—more than hot—molten with rage.

At first I didn't recognize him. But then it hit me. "Aw . . . shit."

The Cadillac started rolling.

"You know who I am?" the man said.

I nodded, looking down at my shoes. Some of this was starting to make sense now. But I needed to work it out. I needed time—

"Say it. Who am I?"

I looked up, meeting his gaze. "Juanito," I said.

Day-Glo's fist shot out over the back of the seat and caught me on the temple, knocking me sideways along the seat and tunneling my vision for a moment. That woke Bob up. The ache pierced like a spike behind both eyes and lingered.

"Don't call me that," Juanito said. "You especially."

"Okay," I said, sitting up and attempting to uncross my eyes.

Juanito then hit me with an open palm on the opposite cheek, snapping my head around. The just-healed cut on my lip from my most recent seizure reopened, and I felt the salty, metallic taste of blood on my tongue.

My first instinct was to lash back. Put a heel in Day-Glo's teeth and sink an uppercut into Juanito's chin. But I forced that impulse down. I was outnumbered, outgunned, and in their vehicle. This wasn't a fight I could win. If they wanted to give me a beating, then I guessed I was gonna have to take it. I just prayed that was all they had in mind.

"My name," Juanito hissed, "is Juan Alberto Alomar, the Third."

"Right," I said, wiping the back of my hand along my bloody lip. He could call himself the Queen of Sheba if he wanted, but he was still the only son of Juan "the Don" Alomar.

And I knew that this little car ride wasn't headed anywhere good.

CHAPTER 27

The Escalade bumped its way out of the parking garage and turned onto a bricked patch of downtown street. Alomar and Mr. Day-Glo considered me coolly for a few minutes. I said nothing, looking idly out the window, trying to commit landmarks to memory, to figure out where we were headed. Maybe I'd get lucky enough to describe to a 911 operator the route used to take me wherever we were going.

"You find him yet?" Day-Glo finally asked.

"Who?"

"Don't play fucking dumb," Alomar snapped. "The cousin. The singer."

"No."

Another few moments of silence. Alomar looked out the window, too.

"Where are we goin'?" I said.

They ignored me. My brain was churning, trying to make sense of this. Obviously, Juanito Alomar was my "friend" in Day-Glo's description of a "friend of a friend." With friends like these . . .

"Do you have any idea what you did to my family?" Alomar said, still gazing out the window. We were heading west on South Street, crossing under I-4. The neighborhood was quickly deteriorating.

"Look," I said, being careful not to call him Juanito. "Your dad was a bookie for the mob. Gettin' pinched is an occupational hazard. If it wasn't me, it woulda been someone else."

Alomar snapped back around, jabbing a finger at me. "You took him from us and killed him. You killed him, you bastard!"

"I, uh . . . ," I stammered. I couldn't recall ever killing anyone, especially the biggest criminal of my career. "What are you talkin' about?"

"My sisters had to grow up without their pop. No birthdays. No Christmas. My mother cried every night. She still cries."

I said nothing. He was heading down memory lane, and nothing I could say would make any difference.

"He never saw me play baseball my senior year. We went to the district finals. He never met my prom date." Alomar was breathing heavily now, the emotion taking hold. "Twice a year my mother would load us up into the car and drive to Kentucky or Virginia or North Carolina or wherever they had him that month. We'd get maybe an hour with him while an armed guard watched us. An hour for the whole family. But now we can't even do that."

"Did your father die?" I asked, trying to be gentle, not wanting another crack across the chops.

Alomar's finger was trembling now. "Lung cancer. They got him in the prison hospital up in Butner. He's too sick to talk on the phone. Can't get outta bed. They give him three months, tops. Those fuckin' prison doctors don't care. Why should they? He's just another inmate, right? Another spic scumbag. He complained and coughed up blood for months and nobody did a damn thing. When he finally collapsed in his cell, they decided, okay, maybe now we'll take a look. And by then it was too late. He was already a dead man. So now he lays there in his bed, wheezing, waiting to die. Praying to die. Can't talk. Has sores all over his body 'cause nobody bothers to change his sheets." Alomar swallowed. "And you're the one who put him there."

"Is that what this is about?" I asked. "What does this have to do with Eddie Sommerset?"

"My pop trusted you," Alomar continued. "He trusted you, man. *You* came to *him* to place bets. *You* were looking for the action. You fuckin' lied to him and set him up."

"I was doin' my job. So was he. Except his job involved gambling, extortion, prostitution, and drug smuggling. In the end, it was my job to arrest him. That's how it works."

"Tell that to my sister who had no one to take her to the father-daughter dance. Or to my other sister, who'll have no one to walk her down the aisle in November. Tell that to my mother, who you destroyed. Don't talk to me about your goodamn job." Another bout of intense glaring before Alomar looked back out the window. "I can't believe that, of all the people, it's you mixed up in this."

"Just what, exactly, is *this*?"

Day-Glo waggled the pistol. "Wrong question, Mikey. I thought I told you to get smart. You're tellin' us you don't know what's goin' on? After all this, you expect us to believe that?"

"I have a guess."

"We're listenin'."

I swallowed. "I assume you've reopened your father's business. Eddie was a customer and made some bad bets. Couldn't cover. Got a line of credit. Made some more bets, hoping to get outta the hole, but he only got deeper. Maybe he got more credit, based on a voucher from his rich cousin, who had bailed him out before." I looked directly at Alomar. "But you started to get nervous. This was your show now, not your dad's, and you couldn't afford a soft rep. Plus the growing red ink on the balance sheet was gettin' the attention of the home office up North. So they sent down . . . a consultant." I glanced meaningfully at Mr. Day-Glo. "To make sure things were handled. You decided it was time to call in Eddie's markers. But he was in too deep. And his cousin with the cash had disappeared. So Eddie ran. And you couldn't have that, right? It would be bad for business. So you start lookin', hopin' he'll find his cousin so you can get your payment, 'cause the cousin is the only one with the necessary cash. Along the way you learn that I'm also lookin' for the cousin, for a completely different reason. But it doesn't matter, as long as someone finds him. So you start tailin' me, too. Then you find Eddie and decide that you're tired of gettin' played. He's a weasel, and if you let him go, it's open season for everyone to start welshin' on bets. You need to make an example of him. To send an early message not to fuck with you. Smashin' his kneecap isn't enough. He's never gonna pay you anyway. So you make him the ultimate example. But the debt stays on the books and somebody's still gonna goddamn pay. The only one left is the cousin, who's still missing. And the only one with half a shot of findin' him is your old friend Mike Garrity." I paused, cutting my eyes from Alomar to Day-Glo. "So, fellas, am I close?"

They shared an expression that told me I was close enough.

Day-Glo raised the gun and pointed it about ten inches from my nose. "So where is he, smart guy?"

"I don't know."

"I'll ask you once more—"

"I told you! I don't know." The Escalade bounced over a set of railroad tracks.

Day-Glo lowered the gun, debating whether he should believe me.

"So," I said, "how much?"

They exchanged another look.

"It had to be a chunk," I went on. "To justify the result."

Day-Glo's expression hardened, zooming in on Alomar. The message was clear. This mess was because of Alomar's bad judgment, and he should be the one to admit the debt.

"One seventy-five," Alomar said.

I grimaced and nodded. That oughta do it. Poor Eddie never had a chance.

"Look, guys," I said. "I hate to tell you this, but I don't think I'm gonna find him. He's got millions of dollars and an itch to disappear. That's a strong combination."

"You'll find him," Day-Glo said.

"You're that confident in my abilities?"

"I am."

I snorted. "I wouldn't get my hopes up."

"I'm gonna get my money," Alomar said. "I don't care who it's from. The cousin. His mother. You. But I'll get my money."

"Leave the mother out of it. And leave me out of it, too," I said. "I've got nothin' to do with Eddie. I have no stake in his debt."

"You're in, Garrity," Alomar hissed, jabbing a finger at me. "You're part of this now and you better fuckin' find that singer. I want my money."

"What if I don't?"

"You will," Day-Glo said.

"Again, with the confidence. You do wonders for my self-esteem."

"Don't be a wiseass, Garrity," Alomar said, his eyes wide and crazed. "I'll take a hammer and knock out all your fuckin' teeth. You can still look for the cousin without teeth. I swear to Christ I'll do it."

I didn't doubt him for a second. The Cadillac came around another corner and I saw the shadow of the I-4 overpass slide across the truck. We were headed back to downtown.

Alomar lifted his chin. "Is it true? Do you really have cancer?"

The Escalade pulled into a bus loading area and parked.

"Yeah," I said.

Alomar nodded to himself. "Good." He looked me right in the eye. "I only pray that you die before my pop does." He turned away. "And that you suffer and your family suffers."

On that cheery note, Day-Glo swung the back door open and yanked me out onto the sidewalk. Then he opened the front passenger door where Slick sat in stony silence. The coffee stains on his shirt seemed to have darkened during the drive, and his crushed cheek was turning dark purple, swelling up and starting to shut his left eye.

"One shot," Day-Glo said. "You owe him one good shot."

Slick pulled his lumbering frame from the seat and stepped over to me, gripping a small metal rod in his palm. The rod was meant to make his punch harder, offer less give when his knuckles connected. I made a move to bolt, but Day-Glo whipped behind me, pinning my arms back.

A ham-sized fist shot out with alarming speed and cracked into my face, impacting my right eye socket with a force that snapped my head backward. Tiny pinpricks of yellowish sparkles danced in my vision for a moment before everything went black.

I was only out for a few seconds, but it was enough. That son of a bitch clocked me a good one and I knew I had a world-class shiner brewing. Add that to the bruise from the punch in the Escalade and the reopened lip from the slap, and I was becoming a poster boy for nonviolent confrontation.

I forced open a rapidly swelling eyelid while Day-Glo dragged me to a doorway. He unceremoniously dumped me on the stoop.

"We'll be in touch, Mikey."

A car door slammed. I heard the SUV peel away and turn a corner. I lay there in the doorway for a few minutes like some homeless bum. Footsteps came and went. People walking the city sidewalk, ignoring me.

I regained my faculties and pulled myself up. Leaning a hand on the brick façade, I poked at my upper cheek under the right eye and winced. Okay, that registered some definite pain. A sharp, raw, fresh pain. I prodded again and determined that my face still had structural integrity. Nothing was broken. But the way it was already swelling, I knew I wouldn't be posing for cover shots anytime soon.

The tip of my tongue dabbed at my split lip, and the pain made me involuntarily suck in a sharp breath. I spit a teaspoon of blood onto the sidewalk. Lovely. A dirty look from a passing woman in a business suit. I smiled at her and imagined holding up a sign that read WILL FIND MISSING BOY BAND MEMBER FOR FOOD. GOD BLESS.

I squinted up at the surrounding buildings, orienting myself. I was only two blocks from the parking garage of the skyscraper that housed Global Talent. I lumbered the distance and found my truck in the garage. The rearview mirror showed me the damage to my face. It looked bad, but I'd be okay. I knew that it would look even worse tomorrow.

I pulled out of the garage and let my mind stew on this latest development. Juanito Alomar had been a teenager when I'd arrested his father. I knew who he was. We had been watching him, too, as part of our investigation into the bookmaking operation. Juanito was officially employed by his father's car dealership, but we all knew his real job was to act as one of his father's bagmen. He'd take bets and collect payments, as well as make deliveries of customer winnings. He wasn't one of the enforcers, just a gofer for the business.

We had some evidence against Juanito, but, ultimately, the federal prosecutor decided not to include him in the indictment. He was a minor and under the influence of his father, the real target of the investigation. The prosecutor felt that not only would they have a hard time making the charges stick, but arresting the kid might make Juan the elder seem more sympathetic. So the kid walked away while his father went to federal prison.

The bookmaking operation dissolved. Someone bought the used-car dealership. The remainder of the Alomar family stayed low profile and out of trouble. Central Florida was a safer place for decent society once again.

But now Juanito was back, all grown up and running his dad's old operation. Apparently, he was involved enough in father's business while it was around to convince the leaders of the Angelino family up in Jersey that he could handle the responsibility. Wiseguys are like fire ants. You think you've killed them, but just wait a little while and a new nest pops up a few feet away, as nasty as ever.

So Juanito was the new mob bookie in Central Florida. He was also probably working his way back into the lucrative gambling cruise ships out of Port Canaveral. But he'd made an early mistake. He'd trusted Eddie Sommerset. Considering Juanito was likely on some sort of trial probation with the boys up North, the last thing he needed was a demonstration that he could be taken advantage of. It was bad business, and if mob guys defined themselves in any way, it was as businessmen.

Enter the enforcer from up North, our Greek friend in the Day-Glo golf shirts. His job was to make sure that Juanito collected, now and in the future. Eddie's execution served as an effective deterrent to other customers who might consider not paying. A head in a box was a much stronger message than a broken kneecap.

But the bosses up North still expected that debt to be settled. I imagined that Juanito had a lot riding on it. His credibility. His role in his father's old business. Maybe even his physical well-being. So he was intensely motivated to get the situation resolved as quickly as possible; so motivated, in fact, that he was willing to put his faith in the very man who'd arrested his father those many years ago to find the cousin. And now Juan the Don lay dying in a prison hospital in Butner, North Carolina, cancer slowly eating him alive.

I pulled the truck into my apartment parking lot and cut the engine. I took a deep breath and marveled at life's amazing symmetry.

Upstairs I found an ice pack in the freezer and pressed it against my swollen cheek. The pain was getting worse. Not to be outdone, Bob ratcheted up his headache, competing for the prize of most agonizing head pain.

I slouched in my recliner and leaned my head back, letting gravity hold the ice pack in place. After a few minutes, I decided that I better call Joe Vincent or Detective Diaz. Maybe both. They'd want to know about my little joyride in the Escalade.

I stood, found the last of Cam's Zuraxx on the kitchen counter, and swallowed them with water scooped from cupped hands in the sink. Then I turned to the phone. But I didn't pick up the receiver. I never got a chance.

The message light on my answering machine was blinking, and the display told me I had one message. I reached out my finger and pressed the play button.

It was a male voice, one I didn't recognize. But as he talked, the real message became clear and I felt my world suddenly crumble below me and cast me tumbling into the abyss.

CHAPTER 28

"Uh, hi. This message is for Jennifer Garrity. This is Bill. Y'know, your manager at the mall? Uh, I hope this is the right number. I have a note that this was where I could reach you this month. Anyway, I don't appreciate your little stunt today. I thought you were more responsible than that. You don't just walk out halfway through your shift without saying a word to anybody. Unless your mom was in a car accident or something, don't bother coming back. We'll send your last check in the mail. I hope the movie or whatever you did was worth being fired."

Click.

That was it. I played it again, praying that this was some sort of mistake, a bad joke. The time stamp on the message was about an hour and a half ago. Bill's voice repeated the same message in the same annoyed and disappointed tone.

My head started buzzing as my adrenaline surged. Jennifer was gone. It wasn't like her to walk out on her shift, especially without notifying anyone. She didn't call me. Maybe Cam—

I quickly dialed Cam's cell phone. It rang a few times and I worried that her voice mail would pick up. But then she answered, sounding hurried.

"Hello?"

"Cam. It's me—"

"Hi, listen, I'm in the middle of a presentation right now, can I call you ba—"

"Cam—did you pick up Jennifer today?"

"What? No. Really, Michael, now's not a good—"

"Did she call you?"

"Jennifer?"

"Yes. Has she called you today?"

"No." Cam paused. "What's wrong?"

"I don't know. I'll—I'll call you later."

I hung up. I had a bad feeling about this, the worst kind of feeling. I stood in my kitchen for a moment, paralyzed by it, wondering what I should do.

Maybe I was overreacting. Maybe the ride in the Escalade and the black eye had shaken me up too much.

This was probably nothing. Gwen probably came by with some friends and Jennifer decided to play hooky from work. Figured she could get away with it. She was fifteen, after all. I had done much more irresponsible things than that when I was fifteen. I forced a deep, calming breath. Don't panic, I told myself.

Call this Bill guy, I thought. Better yet, call Gwen. I'd probably even be able to talk directly to Jennifer. She'd apologize and promise to be more responsible. I'd relax and pour myself a stiff drink.

But my head was still buzzing and I knew that it was all wishful bullshit. I had to do something. If I stood in this kitchen for another second, my skull would explode. I looked at the phone and said, "Screw it."

I grabbed my car keys and sprinted out of the apartment.

I didn't just speed to the mall, I rocketed. I made the twenty-minute drive in just under ten minutes, weaving around traffic, blowing through red lights. I squealed my truck to a skidding stop in front of Macy's, leaving it parked askew in a fire lane.

I charged into the department store, quickly found the mall entrance, and raced to the food court. I dodged through leisurely shoppers—moms pushing strollers, teens grouped in a pack, senior citizens power walking. Some got out of the way and some got an accidental shoulder as I ran past.

The food court was an expansive tiled space with a variety of fast-food establishments around the perimeter.

I spotted the Gyro Connection, where Jennifer worked, and ran to the counter. A pimply boy looked up at me. His expression blanched when he saw my black eye.

"Uh, you wanna try one of our combo meals?" he said.

"Where's Bill?"

"Bill?"

"Bill. Your manager."

"Oh. Right." The kid turned and shouted into the back of the space, where the sandwiches were prepped. "Bill! Some dude wants to see you!"

A moment later a prematurely balding guy wearing a blue Gyro Connection polo shirt came out, wiping his hands on an apron. What hair he had left was dark, and his five-o'clock shadow was early and thick. It also looked as if he ate a few too many of his own sandwiches.

"Yes?" he said, narrowing his eyes at my shiner. "Can I help you?"

"Jennifer Garrity," I blurted.

"What about her?"

"Where is she?"

"Hell if I know. Who are you?"

"When did you last see her?"

"I dunno. When her shift started. She just up and left. We can't have that. It's unprofession—"

"When?" I barked. "Exactly when did you last see her?"

Bill hesitated. "Who are you?"

"I'm her father."

"How do I know that?"

Before I could launch myself over the counter and pummel Bill, the pimply kid spoke up.

"She said she was goin' to the bathroom."

"What?" Bill said.

"Jennifer. She said she was goin' to the bathroom and never came back."

"You didn't know that?" I said to Bill.

"No."

I turned to the kid. "She told you she was going to the bathroom but she never came back. Didn't that concern you?"

He shrugged. "I guess. It happens sometimes. You know."

I almost shouted my response. "It's never happened with Jennifer, has it?"

"No," the kid said.

"So why didn't you say something?"

The kid just shrugged.

"Goddammit!" I shouted. A few nearby patrons glanced over.

"What's going on?" Bill asked. "Is she alright?"

"I don't know, Bill," I snapped. "That's what I'm tryin' to figure out. I'll tell you this, though. If she's not alright, I'm coming back here and putting your face in the deep fryer."

The kid's eyes widened.

"Hey!" Bill said.

"She left her purse," the kid said.

"What?" I said.

"She left her purse."

"Go get it," I ordered.

The kid looked at Bill. "Don't we need, like, ID or something?"

My hand shot across the counter and grabbed the kid's collar. "Get the purse!" I hissed.

"Whoa—," Bill said. "Take it easy."

"Security!" the kid shrieked. "Security!"

More heads turned. A few people glanced over midbite to see what the commotion was all about.

"Let him go," Bill said to me. Then: "Go get the purse, Damon."

I released the collar. The kid, still eyeing me warily, shuffled into the back. He emerged a moment later carrying Jennifer's purse. I snatched it from him and poked through the contents. I produced a set of keys and held it up between white knuckles for Bill to see. In my other hand I gripped her wallet.

"Uh-oh," Bill said.

I threw them back into the purse and pointed a trembling finger at Bill. I was furious. But before I could unload on him, I heard and felt my cell phone ringing in my pocket. It brought me up short. Breathing heavily, I took a step back from the counter. The phone rang again. Bill and the kid stared at me fearfully, wondering what I was going to do next.

I took another step back and reached for my phone. For some reason, I kept my eyes on the two of them behind the Gyro Connection counter. I pressed the receive button and brought it to my ear.

"Hello?"

"Mikey, I think you've made enough of a scene here, don't you?"

My mouth went dry.

"It's not exactly wise to attract this much attention," Mr. Day-Glo continued. "Considering."

"Where is she?"

"We'll get to that in a sec. First things first . . ."

I wheeled around, scanning the food court for him. If I saw him, I had no doubt I would kill him.

I heard him laugh in my ear. "You're not gonna see me, Mikey. Unless I want you to."

I realized that he probably wasn't even here. He likely had a spotter, someone I didn't know, relaying info to him on another phone. I looked around for other people on their cell phones. There were at least a dozen. Probably more.

"I wanna talk to her," I said, my grip on the phone tightening.

"I'm sure you do. In your position, so would I. But, at the moment, what you want is irrelevant."

I stood, breathing heavily, biting my tongue. Lashing out wouldn't help. It could even hurt.

"Are you listenin', Mikey?"

"I'm listenin'," I replied through gritted teeth.

"That's good. 'Cause I'm about to give you the most important instructions you'll ever hear in your whole life. You better pay attention." Day-Glo paused, letting that sink in. "We want our money. You're gonna get us our money. And Juan wants the cousin, too. Juan thinks he's been hidin' from him and considers that rude. Juan thinks he needs a lesson in good manners. So, you'll personally bring us our money and the cousin."

"I've been workin' on the cousin. He's gone."

"You need to work harder."

"How much harder?" I asked, and closed my eyes.

"Ah. I was gettin' to that. You got twenty-four hours."

My stomach dropped. "Twenty-four hours?"

"Good listenin'."

"You can't be serious. That's impossible—"

"You better hope not. Our patience has run out. You'll bring us both the money and the cousin in twenty-four hours or we'll lose confidence in your abilities. Face it, if we don't think you can do it, we don't need you anymore. And if we don't need you, we don't need to waste our time with a weepy teenage girl."

"If you hurt her—"

"Save it, Mikey. Your parental outrage doesn't impress me. Now, don't get any clever ideas. We have people inside both OPD and the Sheriff's Office, not to mention the Feds. We're deeper in now than we've ever been. You breathe a word of this to the cops and it's over. You understand what I'm sayin' here? If you say anything, and I mean *anything,* we'll know. And we'll assume that means you won't be bringin' us our money. This is *not* a bluff. Trust me. If you call the cops, we'll make it extra bad for her. That's a promise I can keep."

"How am I supposed to find him in twenty-four hours? I've already been lookin' a lot longer than that with no luck. He could be in fuckin' Hawaii right now."

"I dunno. That's your job. But between you and me, you show up with the money but no cousin, Juan isn't gonna like that. Personally, I don't give a crap about the cousin. I just want my money. But Juan's the boss here now and he gets his say. And I understand he has a reputation to establish. So, that's the deal. The money and the cousin, in twenty-four hours, or we start workin' on your little girl."

"Jesus. Where the hell am I supposed to find a hundred and seventy-five grand?"

"Good question. If I were you, I'd start with the cousin. But I'd start pretty damn soon, 'cause the clock started tickin' when I called you."

"Where?"

"We'll call you when your time's up and tell you where. When we do, your job is to get in your truck and drive as fast as you can to wherever we tell you and deliver the money and the cousin. Then you leave. We'll release your kid and tell you where to get her. You find the money and the cousin and everything works out. Easy."

"And if I don't?"

A big sigh. "If you don't, then you'll be getting another cardboard box in the mail, won't you?"

"You son of a bitch. If you touch a hair on her head—"

"Manners, Mikey, please. Just get me my money. I'm pullin' for ya. Really. I'll be in touch. Make sure your phone battery's charged and make sure it's on when I call back in twenty-four hours. You do *not* want to miss my call."

"Let me talk to her," I barked. "I need to know she's alright."

"Say good-bye now, Mikey."

"Let me talk to—"

Click.

He was gone.

I let out an involuntary, guttural roar and squeezed the phone until my hand trembled. Then I swallowed and slowly lowered the phone, staring at it dumbly. Somewhere deep in the primitive-lizard part of my brain, I blamed the phone for the call I had just received. I wanted to scream and throw it with all my might at the enormous picture of a gyro glowing directly in front of me. I wanted to smash it with a mallet, to hurl it through the plate-glass windows, to grind the pieces between my teeth. I wanted to howl until my voice gave out. I wanted to lash out and destroy with an intensity I had never felt before.

But I didn't. Instead, I became immobile. Catatonic. I swallowed again. The phone's display said PRIVATE NUMBER. I blinked at it and finally looked up.

I stood there in the middle of the mall food court, surrounded by three hundred chattering people eating burgers and tacos, and I felt horribly, profoundly alone.

CHAPTER 29

Not knowing what else to do, I got back in my truck. I sat for a moment, feeling like I should drive somewhere. But where?

Maybe the Orlando Police Department headquarters. I could take Big Jim aside and tell him what was going on. But he would have to tell someone. Even if he wanted to, he couldn't keep it confidential. Not something like this. There would need to be a meeting. A red-team task force. A primary investigator. A logistics officer. A public affairs rep. A SWAT team on standby. A hostage negotiation expert. Since it was a kidnapping, he'd have to call in the FBI. There were procedures to follow. Protocols. A kidnapping like this was a big deal.

What Mr. Day-Glo had said about having people on the inside gave me chills. When I'd arrested Juan the Don a few years ago, we had discovered a disturbing web of informants and cops on the take. Two Orange County deputies, one OPD sergeant, a local ATF agent, an FBI agent in Tampa, and another in New York, all getting fat off mob money. At the time, it was a more than adequate network to get wind of a kidnapping task force. If Day-Glo was telling the truth about having even more assets on the inside now, then they would know about it almost as soon as I would.

If he was telling the truth. That was the central question. Sitting here in my truck, trying to decide what to do, it all hinged on whether I thought Day-Glo was bluffing. I had no doubt that he was telling the truth about hurting Jennifer. If he found out that I had gone to the cops, I knew that I would indeed receive Jennifer's severed head in a box. I clenched my eyes and shook my head, trying to jar the gruesome image from my mind.

But he might never know. If he was lying about his reach inside, then he would never know about the task force. I would also make sure I told Big Jim, and even the chief, that they might be compromised and to tightly control the information. But who was I kidding? OPD headquarters was gossip central. There was no way they would be able to put a lid on everything. Something would slip out, and if Alomar or Mr. Day-Glo had someone inside, it would be too late.

Was that a chance I was willing to take? Was I willing to gamble Jennifer's life on a guess that Mr. Day-Glo was lying? And, either way, was I willing to put her life in the hands of others, especially if I didn't trust them to keep their mouths shut?

It wasn't that I thought they were incompetent. Far from it. My former colleagues at OPD were professionals. They knew what they were doing and I respected them. I had spent my career in their ranks and knew that they would take Jennifer's kidnapping as seriously as if it were their own daughter. I also knew that not involving them risked not having all the intelligence I might need. For all I knew, they were already in the midst of a massive investigation of Juan Jr. and knew where he was right now. They might even have ongoing internal affairs investigations and could potentially know who the suspected informants were. Knowing who the informants were meant that they could be cut out of the loop.

But there was only one way to find out if they had that intelligence, and that was to tell them. This was a bad spot to be in. Whatever I decided, I wouldn't know if it was the right answer until it was all over.

However, I *was* dealing with a situation I knew as well as anyone. During the MBI investigation, in my undercover role, I had been accepted within the Alomar crime world. First as a customer, then as a low-level operative, recruiting other customers, being allowed access to information about other activities besides illegal gambling.

I knew these guys better than anyone else currently on the force.

No one was more qualified to talk to them, to think like them, to go up against them, than me. These guys were actually fairly simple to understand. Their motivations were greed and power.

I wouldn't get Jennifer back by having a SWAT sharpshooter put a bullet through a window. These guys were too smart for that.

Plus—and this was what it all boiled down to, wasn't it?—I *did* believe Day-Glo when he said he had people on the inside.

I had made my decision.

Maybe, if my time was running out and I had no other options, I'd call the FBI. There was no way I was telling Alomar that I didn't have the money. That would be Jennifer's death sentence. The FBI might supply me with the cash for a drop. They had done it before. Pay the kidnappers, stall for time, keep the hostage alive, and try to nab the bad guys after the drop. Maybe the Feds could even supply me with a TJ look-alike to accompany me. That was what I'd do when I had no other options. But, at the moment, I still had one other option.

I could find TJ.

I put the truck in gear and headed for Arlene Sommerset's house.

I had just pulled out of the mall when my cell phone rang, jolting me from my thoughts. My body gave a startled jerk and I fumbled in the seat to find the phone. The number had an 828 area code. I didn't recognize it. Fearing who it might be, I pressed ANSWER.

"Hello?" I said into the receiver.

"Mike, why haven't you called me back?"

I held my breath. It was Becky, apparently calling from the cabin in North Carolina.

"Becky," I said as a greeting.

"So what's going on? Is everything alright?"

There was a loaded question if I ever heard one. Hell no, every-thing was not alright. But I wasn't about to tell Becky that. If she had any idea the kind of danger Jennifer was now in, she would lose her mind. And she would never trust me to handle this alone. She would be on the phone calling every law enforcement agency, con-gressman, and senator. And she would not be satisfied until she saw

Tomahawk cruise missiles launched against enemy positions in and around Orlando. Telling Becky the truth might be the single fastest way to get Jennifer killed.

"Yeah," I said. "Sure. Everything's fine."

"Jennifer's okay?"

"Yeah."

"Can I talk to her?"

"Uh, no. You caught me in the truck. Jennifer's not here." Technically, this was not a lie. There was a pause.

"How's everything going?" Becky asked. "Between you two. Is it alright?"

"Sure. It's fine. We had a bumpy start, but, y'know, it's okay now."

"Good. I'm glad to hear that. This is important for both of you."

"Right. I know."

"Mike, I know you didn't want to do this, but—"

"Hey, Becky, I'm about to drive through a thunderstorm here. I should get off the phone. I'll probably lose you anyway."

"Oh. Okay—"

"I'll call you back tomorrow or something, okay?"

"Um, I suppose. I'd like to talk to Jennifer—"

"Sure. We'll call you back. How long are you stayin' up north?"

"Another week."

"Okay. Talk to you soon. Gotta go."

"Bye—"

I hung up, cringing at my blatant misrepresentation. I didn't like lying to her, but I didn't have a choice. I'd made my decision about what I was going to do to get Jennifer back, and Becky would never understand. When we were married, she barely trusted me to take out the garbage. She would never trust me to handle this.

But as I drove, I became more convinced that I was doing the right thing. Maybe it was ego or rationalization, but I honestly felt that going solo was the least risky course. I was an experienced law enforcement professional. I knew the Alomar operation better than anyone else. Plus, even contemplating the idea that I could be wrong was too horrible to imagine.

A few minutes later I pulled into the brick circular drive of the Sommerset villa in Isleworth. Arlene answered the door wearing dark blue sweats. Her evening lounging clothes. She was surprised to see me. And even more surprised by my punched-up face.

"Mike—my God. What happened?"

"Nothin'. I'm okay."

"What is it?" she asked, reading my expression. "Is it TJ?"

"Can I come in?"

"Of course."

We sat in the living room. She leaned forward, studying me with concern. I suppose I wasn't doing a very good job of masking my emotions.

"I need the truth, Arlene. This is critical. Have you heard from TJ?"

"What is it, Mike? You're scaring me."

"The truth, Arlene. I mean it. Have you heard from TJ?"

She hesitated and narrowed her eyes. "No."

"Do you have any idea, any wild guess, where he could be?"

"You've asked me these questions before."

"I'm asking again. I need to know."

"No. I have no idea where he is. Maybe back in the desert. I can't tell you any more than that."

I felt the air go out of me. I believed she was telling the truth.

"What's going on, Mike?"

I rubbed my face in my hands, feeling the tender bruise under my eye. "I'm in trouble, Arlene."

"How?"

"If I don't find TJ and produce a hundred and seventy-five thousand dollars in the next twenty-four hours, they'll kill Jennifer."

She blinked, not sure she heard me right. "What?"

I glared at her. She'd heard me alright.

"Oh my God. You're serious. Oh my God. Who?"

"Eddie's friends."

"Have you called the police?"

"No."

"For God's sake, why not?"

"Because it's quite possible that there are people inside the police department, and the FBI, who are actually workin' for the mob."

"No . . ." She shook her head. "You have to call them."

"I can't. I can't take that chance."

"How do you know?"

"I don't. Not for sure. But there's history there. It's just too dangerous. If I call and they find out, they'll kill her."

"What—what are you going to do?"

"Arlene, I'm desperate." I took a deep breath. "Can you get your hands on that kind of cash?"

"Me?"

"Yeah."

"All of it? One seventy-five?"

"Yeah."

"I—I don't know. I've never had to."

"Will you try?"

She swallowed and stared wide-eyed at me. She managed a slight nod. "I'll try."

I felt my eyes well with tears. I quickly blinked them away.

"Thanks," I said.

"What does TJ have to do with this?"

"I don't know exactly."

"Don't they just want their money?"

"They do. But they wanna talk to TJ, too."

"Why?" her voice was becoming shrill with concern.

"I'm not sure, Arlene. I just have to find him." I took her hand. "Look at me. I promise I won't let anything happen to your son."

She forced a weak smile through her trembling lips.

"How will you find him?" she asked.

"I'm still workin' on that."

She placed her free palm on my cheek. "Is there anything else I can do?"

"The rest is up to me," I said, shaking my head. "Although"—I released her hand and stood—"a coupla Hail Marys couldn't hurt."

CHAPTER 30

Two more calls to TJ from my cell phone were typically useless, each one connecting only with his voice mail. I left two urgent messages and raced back to my apartment, the truck's wheels barely touching the road.

Once inside, I found what I was looking for on the kitchen counter. Eddie's phone. The only time I had actually spoken to TJ was when I'd called him on his cousin's cell phone. Although TJ now knew that Eddie was dead and I had his phone, I was desperate. I realized that TJ would probably now ignore a call from Eddie's phone just as if it were a call from mine. Yeah, it was a long shot, but it was all I had.

I punched in the number and pressed SEND. A few rings later I heard the familiar sounds of TJ's voice-mail message. I cringed and clenched my jaw. My thumb jabbed the END button fiercely, also pressing the MENU button next to it. The phone's display screen changed to a scrollable list of choices: SOUND OPTIONS, ADDRESS BOOK, CALL DATA, TEXT MESSAGES, SECURITY, DIALING PREFERENCES. I blinked at the display for a moment, about to press the BACK button. But then I had an idea.

I pressed ADDRESS BOOK. I scrolled through the stored names and numbers. I recognized a few. Eddie's mother. TJ. I didn't see anything that looked like what I was hoping for: specifically, a listing for Alomar or one of his operatives. Eddie had probably been gambling illegally long enough to know some basics—such as always memorize your bookie's number and never save it in your phone. I thought that maybe I would get lucky and figure out where

Alomar was, giving me some type of advantage. Perhaps I could stake out the location, see if I could spot Jennifer, then decide whether to bring in the cops. I could call the SWAT team leader directly. It was unlikely he was compromised.

But it didn't look like I was gonna get that lucky. The address book was no help. I then wondered if Eddie was smart enough to delete his stored numbers. Most phones store all recent incoming and outgoing calls, even if they aren't saved in the address book. If Eddie had called Alomar recently, the number might still be in the call list.

I next pressed CALL DATA from the menu. On the submenu I chose OUTGOING CALLS. I cursed silently. For a kid who made a lot of dumb mistakes in his life, Eddie was smart about covering his tracks. The only outgoing calls stored were the two I had placed to TJ's cell number since I'd acquired Eddie's phone. Damn. Eddie had cleared the list before he died.

I pressed BACK and returned to the CALL DATA submenu. On most phones, the stored incoming and outgoing calls are cleared at the same time. But, just to be sure, I selected the INCOMING CALLS option. To my knowledge, there had only been one incoming call in all the time I had Eddie's phone—the call from TJ.

So, my hope faded when only one number appeared on the IN-COMING CALLS screen. I closed my eyes and tried to control my breathing. I leaned back against the kitchen counter.

Opening my eyes, I looked back down at the phone, hoping I had been mistaken. But there was still only the one number. I pressed BACK twice to return to the main menu. Just as I was about to select BACK again to reach the default phone display, my thumb froze suspended over the keypad. Something was wrong.

What was it? My subconscious seemed to be moving quicker than the rest of my brain. For some reason, I couldn't press BACK again. So I returned to the INCOMING CALLS screen and looked again at the one number displayed. The date and time were precisely when TJ had called the other day.

But the number was not his cellular number.

I hadn't immediately registered the difference. I had been expecting to see TJ's cell number, so that's what I thought I saw. Plus, and this was the part that made my hand begin to tremble, the area code was the same as TJ's cell phone: Orlando's 407. But the rest of the number was completely different.

Assuming that TJ wasn't calling on another Orlando-based cell phone I didn't know about, this implied that, as of the time he made the call, TJ was still in town. My heart began thudding in my chest. TJ seemed to be displaying a genuine reluctance to leave Central Florida. First, he had hidden out at his mother's house. Then, he had apparently remained in the area at least through a few days ago. Was it possible that he was still in town right now?

One way to find out. I selected the number and pressed the SEND button.

Eddie's phone told me that it was connecting. Then I heard it ringing. My heart pounded in my rib cage as the ringing continued. I let it ring for a long time. Twenty times. Thirty times. I had no idea. But it was clear that no one was answering. I disconnected.

When I was on the job, it was easy to run down a number and get whatever info I needed from it. But I no longer had that kind of access. I could ask for another favor from Big Jim, but to have him do it now, after dark, with the kind of urgency I needed, meant that I would have to tell him why. And I'd have to be honest. And he would have to do what he had to do and inform the proper folks inside the department. And Jennifer might soon be dead.

I wasn't ready to take that chance yet. There was another, simpler way.

A few steps later I was in my bedroom, pressing on the power of my seldom-used computer. It booted up and I double-clicked the icon for the Web browser. The computer had been a gift from Cam while we were still married, and according to Jennifer, it was now hopelessly out-of-date. But for the occasional letter or e-mail message, it suited me fine.

I punched up a search engine and quickly found one of a hundred Web telephone directories. I picked one that specifically mentioned a reverse phone-number lookup. I entered the stored number from Eddie's phone and hit SEARCH.

The site processed for a moment before returning an enigmatic

"The requested number is not listed. For advanced features, click *here*."

Not listed . . . I considered for a beat and clicked *here*.

A page informed me that additional number data were available only to registered members. Registration was free and easily accomplished by completing a simple, Web-based form. I agreed and supplied the information. Basically, they wanted my name and e-mail address. They could have whatever they wanted, for all I cared. Salary, Social Security number, shoe size, whatever.

I navigated back to the site's home page and retried the search. This time I received a slightly different response: "The requested number is not in our database. It is listed under BellSouth Corporation, Orlando, Florida."

BellSouth? Was TJ calling from a BellSouth office? They were all over town, but it didn't make any sense. Plus, it was unlisted. . . . I pondered this for a second before it hit me—

A pay phone.

I quickly returned to the search engine, and one short query later I found myself on an amazingly thorough site that offered locations for pay phones all across the country. It seemed to be someone's hobby gone berserk.

I found Florida in the menu and chose it. Then I entered the phone number again and clicked a GO button.

And there it was. A complete address. The phone was in front of a 7-Eleven on South Orange Blossom Trail in the heart of Orlando's red-light district. From my years in a patrol car and working cases, I knew right where it was.

I bolted from the apartment and peeled out of the parking lot, roaring down Sand Lake Road at highly illegal speeds. I made a squealing left turn onto OBT and raced through traffic, weaving around slower-moving cars. I slid in behind a Lynx county bus and got a faceful of diesel exhaust. The bus pulled away, revealing the 7-Eleven. I turned into the parking lot and idled, watching the phone for a moment, before deciding what to do.

A few ragged patrons entered and left the store, several taking swigs from a paper bag as they headed off down the sidewalk. This was a pretty dodgy neighborhood, populated by seedy strip clubs and hollow-eyed streetwalkers, both male and female. With so many transvestites making the rounds, sometimes it was hard to tell the difference.

I'm not sure what I expected—that TJ would just happen to make a call while I sat there or maybe he was hiding out by working the Slurpee machine inside—but, unsurprisingly, nothing happened. I cut the engine, got out, and approached the phone.

As I walked, I thought that if this were the movies, I would find a slip of paper wadded up in the coin-return slot with an address on it, leading me to TJ's precise location. But the pay phone's coin-return slot was empty, except for a mysterious greasy residue I wiped on my jeans. I examined the phone's surrounding canopy, looking for a scratched name or number that TJ might have left. All I found was a primitive depiction of male genitalia carved into the paint.

So much for the movies.

I picked up the phone's receiver and shook it stupidly, before replacing it in the cradle. This was hopeless. TJ was one of a dozen people who had used this phone in the last few days and I had no reason to suspect that he had used it more than once. The idea that I would be able to discern some clue from looking at it was preposterous.

TJ had probably been driving by, stopped to use the phone, then proceeded on his merry way. He was likely long gone a long time ago.

I decided to head inside and talk to the clerk. I'd show him a picture of TJ and see if he recognized him. Maybe TJ had hung around enough to get spotted. Maybe he bought a Snickers. I turned and pulled on the door. But I didn't go in.

Instead, my gaze landed on the building across the street and my mouth dropped open.

Of course. I should have remembered.

I didn't need to go inside and talk to the clerk. If TJ was still in town, I now knew exactly where he was.

The Rainbow Arms called itself a resort, and I suppose, technically that's what it was. But it was in no way a competitor to the myriad family-oriented resorts dotted across the Central Florida landscape.

The Rainbow Arms catered exclusively to a clientele with "an alternative lifestyle," mostly men.

There were two or three exclusively gay resorts in Orlando, the most notable—and reputable—being the famous Parliament House on north OBT. Even beyond the annual Gay Days event, the Orlando theme parks held a peculiar attraction for the homosexual community. And when they visited, they wanted to stay somewhere where they could be themselves, and where there was little chance of sharing a floor with uptight Midwesterners and toddlers wearing mouse ears.

The Rainbow Arms was located in the much seedier south OBT area. It had been raided a few times on vice charges, but the management couldn't really control what happened in their rooms. I knew it from my days on the job. It had a reputation of being looser than the Parliament House. A businessman with a wife and family in Omaha could check in under a false name, pay cash up front, and, for a few glorious days, finally act how he felt inside. There would be no paper record of his visit. As long as he provided some name and sufficient cash, there were no questions asked. He could walk a block in any direction from the front door and, for sixty bucks, find a date for the evening.

I knew instantly that this was where TJ was hiding. When I'd spoken to him on Eddie's phone, he'd said that nobody would be able to find him. And he was probably right. This was really the perfect place for a teen heartthrob to disappear. Nobody would suspect he would be staying at a gay hotel. It was inconceivable to everyone but a select handful of us who knew the truth. And this wasn't even the nicest gay hotel in town. For a kid with almost unlimited means, the choice of the Rainbow Arms would further throw pursuers off his trail.

Standing there in the 7-Eleven parking lot, I realized that it was a brilliant choice. Hiding right here in town in the last place anyone would suspect.

I hurried across the road, avoiding the barreling traffic, and made my way under the covered circular drive. In the early sixties, long before it became a gay resort, this had probably been a swinging vacation joint. The art deco architecture was so old it was stylish again, and the sea-foam-green paint looked as if it had been applied at least ten years ago. I pushed through the frosted-glass doors and into the lobby.

Speckled linoleum covered the floors. A small sitting area was separated from the registration counter by three chrome columns. Through the glass walls on the opposite side of the lobby, I could see an illuminated pool in the center of a darkened courtyard of hotel rooms. A few men were night swimming, but the courtyard was mostly empty.

I approached the counter, where a tired-looking guy in his early fifties leaned reading a newspaper. His face was lined and his hair was a little too blond. He lowered the paper as I approached and raised his eyebrows. He surveyed the shiner on my eye but, to his credit, said nothing.

"Hey," I said.

"Hey."

"I wonder if you can help me."

"We'll see."

"I'm looking for a guest."

"Oh?"

"Have you seen this guy?" I produced an ordinary family photo of TJ provided by Arlene. I didn't think a Global Talent publicity shot would be taken seriously. The guy scrutinized the picture for a moment.

"Cute. A little young for you, though."

"Have you seen him?"

The guy shrugged. "I don't know. I been here fourteen years. They all start to look the same. Sorry."

"I think he's checked in under another name. If I gave you a list of names, you think you could tell me if you have a guest who matches?"

The guy made a face. "Look, bud, if he wanted to see you, he'd tell you the name himself. And if he's the one what did that to your face, I'd say you're better off without him."

"How about Joel?"

The guy sighed. "Last name or first?"

"Last."

A few clicks on the computer. "Sorry."

"Simon."

"Last name again?"

"Yeah."

"Nope. You get one more, but only because I'm a romantic at heart."

"Taupin."

"As in Bernie?"

"Yeah."

A few more taps on the keyboard. "Strike three. *Che sarà, sarà.*"

"I have a few more names."

"I'm sure you do. But that's it. I think you should give it up."

I suddenly became aware of the inexorable ticking of a clock in my head, counting down the seconds until Jennifer ran out of time. If I dwelled on it for more than a second, it was like a great boulder on my chest, constricting my breathing, crushing the very life out of me. I swallowed.

"It's a matter of life and death," I said.

The guy shook his head ruefully. "It always is, honey."

"Please. This is important. Would this make a difference?" I laid a fifty-dollar bill on the counter. The guy eyed it. "Would two?" I placed another fifty next to it.

"Amazingly enough," he said, finally blinking, "that makes no difference at all. One of the things our guests like about the Rainbow is our privacy. Many of them don't want anybody to know they're here. We start breaking that confidence and it's bad for business." He considered me for a moment and leaned slightly across the counter. "Look, take one of those Grants and go buy a ticket to the show. It starts in twenty minutes. Most of the guests come to the show. It's one of the main reasons they stay here. Maybe you'll get lucky and see him in the crowd." He leaned a little closer. "But if you do, don't make a big scene. You make a big scene, I'll have to get Henry to remove you from the premises. Believe me, you don't want that. Henry has . . . anger management issues. You understand what I'm saying?"

"Yeah. Thanks," I said, sliding one fifty back off the counter. The guy put his hand on the other.

"Good luck, loverboy. You'll need it."

He was certainly right about that.

CHAPTER 31

I approached a pale, emaciated guy in a tuxedo, standing at a podium on the far end of the lobby. A poster on a nearby easel advertised:

The World Famous Rainbow Arms Trans Gender Extravaganza!
Featuring Lady Ursula, Miss Mabel, and Jasmine.
Special appearance by Naomi, performing the classics:
Cher, Celine Dion, Barbra Streisand, and Liza Minnelli.

I pursed my lips at the easel and stepped up to the podium.
"One," I said.
"Twenty-five."
I handed him the fifty and took my change. I stepped through a purple velvet curtain into a dark nightclub. A raised stage dominated the far wall. In front of it were a dozen or more cocktail tables. A small shelf lined the surrounding walls for the standing crowd. A long bar covered the majority of one side of the room.

Most of the tables were full and a good crowd lingered around the shelf on the perimeter of the room. Everyone was drinking. Waitresses in bow ties circled through the tables, taking orders and delivering drinks—the only women I had seen since entering the hotel.

I found an empty seat at the end of the bar and ordered a club soda. I tried to sip it casually as I scanned the room for TJ. The light was crummy and the crowd shimmered with movement, so it was hard to get much of a bead on anyone. I grabbed my glass and started circulating.

The room had a light, anticipatory mood. Once I got away from the bar and into the tables, I saw that quite a few women were actually here. I assumed, anyway, that they were women.

The rest of the room was dominated by gay men. Some were in couples, but most were mingling in their own large groups. And, just like in any other crowd, some were quiet and reserved, while others were loud and obnoxious.

I made three circuits through the room, taking a different route each time. I accidentally bumped a few elbows, brushed a little too close to both men and women, and drew several stares at my swollen face, but I never saw TJ. I was pretty confident that if he were in the room, I would've found him. I made my way back to the bar. My seat was now taken, but I squeezed through and leaned on the counter.

I finally caught the attention of the bartender, a bald guy with graying temples and tired eyes.

"Another soda?" he asked.

I laid TJ's photo on the bar. "You ever see him in here?"

He studied the picture for a beat, then flicked his eyes back up at me. "Lemme see your badge."

I reached in my pocket and produced another fifty. I laid the bill on the bar next to the photo. "I ain't a cop."

He considered that for another moment, before picking up the photo and studying it again, this time with more interest. While he was looking at it, the lights dimmed and a heavy bass beat thudded throughout the room. Colored lights flashed at the stage, where a curtain now hung.

The bartender put the picture back on the bar. I waited for him to speak, but he just looked at me, deciding something. He turned his head and spotted two waitresses queued up at the register, waiting to fill orders. So he said nothing. Even if he had spoken, I would've never heard him over the music anyway. The bartender palmed the fifty and slid it into his shirt pocket. Then he held up a finger for me to wait. He moved down the bar to tend to the waitresses.

I held my breath. Maybe the guy actually knew something. Or maybe he was just scamming my fifty bucks.

"Ladies and gentlemen! Welcome to the 'Paradise Arms Trans Gender Extravaganza!' "

The voice came from the stage, where a tuxedoed guy held a wireless microphone and grinned at the crowd. He strutted back and forth in front of the red curtain, eyebrows raised, nose crinkled. He described the show about to begin, and the crowd responded as each performer's name was mentioned. They were clearly celebrities in this world, even if they were completely anonymous in mine. Then again, what did I know? Until recently, I had never heard of Boyz Klub, they of the triple-platinum debut album.

"So, without any further ado, let's get this mother started! Leading things off tonight is none other than the Queen of the Scene, the Blonde from Across the Pond, England's very own . . . *Lady Ursula!*"

The curtain parted and the emcee slid offstage just as the music slammed into Patti LaBelle's disco standard "Lady Marmalade." Then out strutted a beautiful, albeit quite tall, blond woman in a slinky sequined cocktail dress. She moved surprisingly well on the spiked high heels and belted out the song's lyrics in a passionate— sexy—voice.

I had to blink twice to remind myself she was a man.

The crowd went berserk, some leaping to their feet, most singing along. Lady Ursula fed off the energy and worked the stage, as well as the crowd, like a Vegas pro. She was very good. I was staring dumbstruck at the spectacle when I felt a tap on my shoulder.

It was the bartender. He leaned over and shouted next to my ear.

"He never comes to the show. I don't think he likes the crowds. I usually see him in the afternoon, when the place is almost empty. Orders Seven and Seven."

"You see him today?" I shouted back.

The bartender nodded meaningfully.

"You got a room number?" I asked.

He hesitated and glanced around. Seeing nobody looking for a drink—everyone was watching Lady Ursula—he jerked his head to the side, indicating for me to follow. I did.

We went through a rickety door into a cluttered, brightly lit office. I could still hear the music, but now, at least, it was somewhat muffled, allowing us to have a semblance of a conversation.

"Whadda you want with him?" the bartender said, folding his arms.

"I'm looking for him."

"No shit. Why?"

"That's personal."

He eyed me again, taking in my bruised cheek and eye. "Don't tell me you're a couple. You do that and I'll know you're lying."

"Okay. He left home a few days ago. His mother is worried. She asked me to help."

"His mother, huh?" He seemed skeptical.

"You wanna call her yourself?"

"So what do you plan to do, drag him outta here? Lock him up until he stops being gay?"

"It's not like that. She doesn't care. She's just worried." The bartender continued to glare at me, a sour twist on his lips. "Look, all I wanna do is talk to him. Ask him to go home, or at least call her. That's all."

"He seems like a decent kid. I don't want him harassed."

"Neither do I." I held up my palms plaintively. "So, the room number?"

The guy's expression softened slightly and he sighed. Turning, he opened a drawer in the office desk and pulled out a stack of register receipts. "If I find out you're lying, I'll get Henry to make your black eye look like a hangnail." He flipped through the stack of receipts, looking at each one. Halfway through he stopped. "Ah. Here it is. Seven and Seven." He turned to me, holding the receipt at his side. "What've you got for the room number?"

He clearly wasn't satisfied with the fifty bucks I'd already supplied. He wanted some extra consideration for the room number. If he was legit, it was money well spent, so I peeled out another Grant and handed it to him. Just don't tell me he cared at all what happened to TJ. If he did, he wouldn't sell his room number for any price.

"Four seventeen," he said.

"No offense, can I see that?"

He paused, then handed me the receipt. It was an order for a single 7&7, and the room number was indeed 417. I handed it back to him.

"So is he a writer or something?" he said.

"Why?"

" 'Cause he's always writing. Comes in, has a drink, spends the whole time scribbling in a notebook."

"Yeah," I said. "What's the quietest way to the main hotel?"

"Follow me."

I trailed him out a side door in the office and down a cinder-block hallway. Several doors lined the hall, each adorned with a painted gold star. In one open doorway I caught an unsettling glimpse of a shirtless man wearing dark panty hose, a large red wig, and full makeup.

The bartender led me out a crash-bar door at the end of the hallway, and we emerged at a side corner of the main courtyard. The three sides of the hotel loomed around the palm-landscaped central swimming pool.

I thanked the bartender and slipped into the shadows of a stairwell. The room doors all opened onto exposed walkways overlooking the pool, organized something like a concealed motor lodge. In its pre-Disney heyday, this was probably an attractive resort for the Florida-bound Northerner. Palm trees, swimming pool, kind of like a secret lagoon. Of course, this was not only before Disney and the other theme parks arrived, but also before this neighborhood turned into the urinal of Orlando, featuring heroin junkies, crack dealers, and hookers. It's a fantasyland in its own right.

I padded silently up to the fourth floor of the six-story building and started down the exposed hallway. I was starting at room 401, which likely put TJ's room somewhere not quite to the corner, where the building turned at a right angle and ran parallel to the main lobby and nightclub.

I slowed slightly, considering my next move. After so much time spent with such little progress, this was all now happening at a whiplash pace. What exactly did I plan to do—stroll up, knock on the door, and announce my presence? That might spook him.

Should I stake out the room and wait for him to poke his head out? I didn't have time to sit and wait. He might be asleep already, or out for the evening. Or maybe he never left his room except for his daily 7&7 in the afternoon. By the time he left the room, it might be too late. No, I needed to practice a proactive investigation strategy.

I could bribe a housekeeper to open the door or at least get him to answer. But that assumed I could find one and that he or she could be bought. I was still thinking about it when I strolled up on room 417. The curtains were drawn, but I thought I saw a light on inside. My heart began thudding in my chest and I sensed the same adrenaline buildup that I'd always felt while on the job, just before I stormed a room.

I took a few deep breaths, trying to calm down. I had so much riding on this. My daughter's life depended on me making the right decisions, taking the right actions. I leaned my ear carefully against the door. I couldn't hear anything. Another deep breath and I straightened.

I swallowed, said a small silent prayer, and rapped a fist on the door.

A waited a second before I said, "Housekeeping!"

I knocked again.

I tilted forward, turning my head just a bit to listen. I still heard nothing on the other side. I saw no rustling of the curtains if anyone was peeking out.

I knocked again, this time more sternly. Just as I lowered my hand, I caught a glimpse from the edge of my vision of a figure approaching me. I looked over at the figure, turning my head slowly, as if underwater.

An overweight, middle-aged guy shuffled by in a bathrobe, ice clunking in a plastic bucket. He avoided my gaze. Probably in Orlando for one of our many conventions, but staying here unbeknownst to the wife back in Peoria. I watched him trundle down the walkway and disappear into a room several doors down. When I turned back, I looked out over the railing down at the pool. There were a couple of swimmers, but it seemed mostly empty, any crowd presumably drawn to the drag show inside.

I took one last glance at the door of room 417. Light was still visible through the peephole, meaning nobody was looking out at me. The curtains were limp. I needed a new plan. I headed down the stairs to the pool. From down there, I could plant myself somewhat inconspicuously in one of the deck lounge chairs and still have a clear view of TJ's room. Until I thought of something else, I figured I could stake it out and maybe get lucky.

I found a spot in the shadows on the opposite side of the pool that offered an unobstructed view of the fourth-floor walkway. If someone approached room 417 or came out, I'd see. I folded my hands, settled back in my chair, and began watching.

Suffice to say, I didn't see much. After a while, however, I did notice a small gathering, maybe a half dozen or so guys, sitting together under a gazebo at the far end of the pool just hanging out, drinking some beers, and listening to music. Keeping my eye on room 417, I stood and casually wandered over to the gazebo. They were all pretty young. Twenties or early thirties. Perhaps TJ was in the crowd—the music might be a draw for him.

As I approached, I quickly realized that the music wasn't coming from a CD or an iPod. One of the guys had a guitar and was strumming it. He had his head lowered, his shaggy brown hair hanging down over his eyes. I could see a goatee on his chin and a day or two of stubble on his cheeks. He was thin and wore a blue T-shirt over faded jeans with a ragged hole in one knee. I took a step closer.

The guitar player added some vocals to his acoustic music—and my knees nearly buckled. I recognized the voice. When he looked up, there was no doubt. He had a mop of shoulder-length hair and a scruffy beard, but the eyes were unmistakable. Arlene's eyes.

I sidled two steps to my right to pretend to lean against a gazebo post. The song ended and the group offered some casual applause. I stood frozen there, my muscles tensed, my mind racing. What was my move? How should I play this?

I remained motionless through two more songs. The music was very different from anything on a Boyz Klub album. Alternative. Edgy. Even cynical. More Green Day than Backstreet Boys. There was real passion in his playing.

The last song finished and the remaining few listeners downed their beers and wandered off. The guitar player looked sideways at me, as if suddenly realizing that I didn't quite belong. The honking shiner on my eye probably didn't help.

"You're good," I said.

"Thanks," he said warily. He stood and gripped his guitar by the neck. "Well, g'night." He turned to exit the gazebo, keeping his head down.

A second elapsed. It felt like an hour.

"TJ—," I said.

Without looking up, he dropped the guitar and bolted.

CHAPTER 32

"TJ! Wait!" I shouted and took off after him. "Wait!"

My foot caught on a gazebo step, sending me hard to the ground on my elbow. A sharp jolt of pain zapped through my upper arm and into my shoulder.

I pushed myself up and sprinted after him, little twinges of pain reverberating in my arm like electric shocks. TJ leaped over a deck chair and sprinted down the long edge of the pool. I was several yards behind him. Too far. And the kid was fast. He'd quickly put some distance between us if I didn't do something.

But what? Shout for someone to grab him? Right. Pull my Glock and cap him in the leg? I can't believe the thought actually entered my head. I blame Bob.

We tore across the patio, knocking chairs and plastic drink tables aside. I shouted at him again, but it was pointless. He wasn't listening and he wasn't stopping no matter what I said. The two remaining swimmers looked up curiously at the commotion.

TJ reached the stairs to the rooms upstairs and hesitated. He could go to the right up the stairs or left into the hotel lobby. He paused long enough for me to make up a few steps of the gap between us. I altered my angle toward the lobby to cut him off. I figured he'd try to get out of the hotel and into the darkened streets beyond.

But he didn't go right or left. Instead, he charged straight ahead. The door I had originally come out of, the one that led to the nightclub backstage, was ajar. A waitress stood at the edge of a Dumpster sneaking a cigarette. She had propped a plastic chair in the door so she could get back in.

"TJ! Stop!" I shouted, running after him.

TJ reached the doorway, stole a glance back at me to confirm I was still in pursuit, and barreled over the chair.

"Hey!" the waitress said, jumping back. "You can't go back there!"

The door started closing and I spent a half second wondering if it automatically locked when it shut. I assumed it did or the waitress wouldn't have gone to the trouble to prop it open. I didn't think I would make it before it shut. Just as the handle edge of the door swung into the frame, I jammed my fingers into it. It hurt as much as you would imagine, but after my beating in the Escalade, and now my potentially fractured elbow, it was small potatoes.

I whipped the door open and stumbled over the chair. TJ was ahead of me in the cinder-block hallway. I could hear the thumping music from the club. Still moving, TJ turned around and saw me coming after him. When he turned back, he ran right into Cher. TJ knocked her flat on her ass.

"Watch it, bitch!" Cher barked in a deep baritone.

"Sorry—," TJ said, and stepped over her.

By now I was almost on him. I hurdled the fallen diva and swiped a hand at TJ's blue shirt but came up empty. The kid arched his back and ducked left into an open alcove. I was right behind him and followed him up a small set of wooden steps and into the side wing of the nightclub stage.

The music was louder here, almost deafening, pounding a familiar disco song I couldn't name. TJ didn't stop running. He flew out past the wing curtains and onto the brightly lit stage. I didn't stop either.

The performer looked at us dashing across her (his?) stage. But she was a pro, not missing a line in the song. She swung her silver-sequined hips and shook her long blond mane, keeping perfect pitch, but eyeing us with a mixture of curiosity and fury.

The crowd let out a collective gasp when TJ flung himself off the stage, skidding into a nearby table and sending a round of drinks smashing to the floor. I made a somewhat less dramatic jump and followed him through the maze of tables in the dark club. The crowd gaped at us, realizing that what they were witnessing was not supposed to be happening, but unsure if they should do anything about it.

TJ was almost at the entrance to the club, which led out into the hotel lobby. I was a few steps away on the other side of a table. In my peripheral vision I saw a hulking shadow moving quickly toward me. This, I assumed, was the infamous Henry, and I had no intention of getting beaten up any more today. I put one foot on the seat of a chair and launched myself onto a cocktail table.

I sprang from the table and landed in front of the club entrance. Henry was still charging after me, building up steam, but my course over the table had bought me an extra few steps.

TJ disappeared out the club's door and I popped out after him. I saw a blue blur in jeans tearing out the hotel's main glass doors. I couldn't afford to let him out onto Orange Blossom Trail. He could easily vanish into its dark underbelly.

I pushed through the front door and TJ ran straight out into traffic.

"TJ! No!" I screamed.

Tires squealed and cars swerved. Two vehicles ended up with their front bumpers less than a foot apart. Miraculously, no cars actually hit each other, and TJ was unscathed. I took advantage of the shocked pause of the moment to rush across the street after him.

He was pretty shook up, breathing heavily, sweat running down his face. He backed away from me, working himself toward the parking lot of the 7-Eleven. He held up a hand for me to stop.

I didn't stop, but I slowed, raising my palms. He turned his head to look down the sidewalk, coiling himself for a break. I couldn't allow that. In an open run, TJ would surely outdistance me and be gone in a block or two.

"TJ—it's okay. I'm not gonna hurt you." I kept moving toward him. "We've spoken on the phone. I'm Mike Garrity."

He didn't stop backing up, but his brow furrowed.

"What do you want?" he said between breaths.

"I need to talk to you. I—I need your help." I swallowed and stopped. A sudden wave of emotion caught me and I fought back tears.

TJ saw that. "Help with what?" he said, still stepping backward.

"It's my daughter. Jennifer." I rubbed a hand over my face, trying to keep my composure. "If you don't help me, she's gonna die."

He stopped moving and put down his arms.

I hadn't eaten all day, so we found an IHOP and ordered a nighttime breakfast. Sausage and eggs for me, oatmeal and fruit for TJ. I relayed an abridged version of recent events, starting with the first phone call from George Neuheisel and ending with us sitting eating breakfast at 10:30 p.m. He knew some of the story, having witnessed my first seizure and talked to me online and through Eddie's cell phone. But, mostly, he was quiet, listening to me talk, sipping a cup of coffee.

"Okay," he said. "Now you've found me. What about the money? Where are you getting that?"

"Your mom."

TJ nodded, a resigned smile glinting across his face. With his long hair and unshaven face, he looked nothing like the clean-cut young man on the album covers. He was grittier. Older. Wearier. I was surprised that the bartender even recognized him from the picture. But sitting here in this booth, just a few feet away, I could see the boy in there. I could also see Arlene's feminine features, her long nose, her high forehead, her piercing eyes.

"I should call her," he said.

I nodded.

"She likes you, you know," he said.

"Pardon?"

"My mom. She likes you a lot. Maybe some of it is sympathy because of your cancer, like my dad, but I think it's more than that. I can tell. She really likes you."

"I like her, too."

He cocked his head, considering me and my worthiness for his mother. Then he broke off his gaze and sipped his coffee.

"So these are really bad guys," he said, looking down. "The ones who killed Eddie?"

"Yeah."

"They did that to your face?"

I nodded.

"And you really think they'll hurt your daughter?"

"I do."

TJ poked his spoon at a blueberry in his oatmeal. "And what, exactly, do they want me for? I mean, if you deliver the money, what do I have to do with it?"

"Good question. My guess is that Alomar is pissed and wants to shake you up. He thinks you and Eddie have been tryin' to stiff him."

"I knew nothing about it."

"Alomar doesn't believe that."

"So he's going to make me some kind of example?"

"Listen, TJ." I put my hands flat on the table and looked him straight in the eye. "I need you to come with me, to get me in the door and deliver the money. But I have no intention of leaving you with them or trading you for Jennifer. I haven't got all the details yet, but I'm workin' on a plan. I promise I won't let anything happen to you. I know you don't know me, but I'm asking you to trust me."

An awkward silence bloomed between us and I thought TJ might get up and walk out of the restaurant.

"That's a nice speech," he finally said. "But not necessary. I have no problem coming with you. In fact, you'd have to tie me up to keep me away."

This wasn't the reaction I expected. It was too easy. It made me suspicious. I decided to put myself in the role of devil's advocate.

"Aren't you concerned?" I asked.

He shrugged. "Sure. But this mess was Eddie's fault and he was my cousin. And I ran away so nobody could find me, which only made things worse. So now your daughter is the one who might suffer, and I need to do what I can to make it right."

I thought about this for a second. "I have a confession. I read the note that you sent to Miguel." His eyes met mine. "I was a cop for a long time, and when I read it, I figured I was reading a suicide note."

He put down his spoon. "Really?"

"Yeah." I waited, saying nothing else, narrowing my eyes.

"Well, I'm still here."

"Yeah. I see that. And I'm glad. I was worried. Your mother was worried."

"My mom read the note?"

"No. But I gave her the gist."

He put his elbows on the table and leaned his face into them. "Ho, boy. What did she say?"

"She didn't think you'd kill yourself, but she was worried all the same."

"No. About Miguel."

I took a deep breath. "Look, I don't wanna get between you and your mother—"

"Too late, man. What did she say?"

I relented. "Not much. She was surprised it was Miguel, but she wasn't really surprised, if you know what I mean."

"I think so."

"She said she knew. A mother knows."

"So she didn't, like, freak out or anything?"

"She was just worried about you. You left so abruptly, she didn't know what to think."

"I was upset."

"Upset enough to kill yourself?"

"Like I said, I'm still here."

I filled my mug from the coffeepot that the waitress had thoughtfully placed on the table. "Tell me if I'm close here. . . . You were upset. You had been fighting with Eli about creative issues. You were in a relationship with someone you cared about, and then Eli came in and destroyed that. You have more money than you'll ever spend, and you were still miserable. Your passions got the better of you and you wrote that note, fully intent on eating a bottle of Valium. Or worse. But it's a hard thing to kill yourself. It sounds romantic when you think about it, full of drama and a sense of immortality. But when it comes down to actually doing it, that's a whole different story. As the days went by, it got harder and harder. But now I show up and ask you to come with me into one of the most dangerous situations you can imagine, and you're all gung ho. Yeah, this is Eddie's mess and you vanishing didn't help. But maybe this is a coward's way to get yourself killed." I sipped my coffee. "And won't they all be sorry then?"

If he laughed or got angry, if he denied it or made a joke, I would have doubted my theory. But his silence confirmed that I was in the neighborhood.

"I don't want to die," he said softly.

"Are you sure?"

He nodded slowly.

"Okay," I said with a twinge of recognition for the irony of my role in this conversation, given my present ambiguous relationship with the uninvited resident in my brain. I brushed it aside. "You still wanna come with me?"

He nodded again.

"Good. 'Cause this'll be dangerous enough without a death wish, and I'm gonna need your help if I have any hope of pullin' it off."

CHAPTER 33

When we walked together back into the lobby of the Rainbow Arms, the desk clerk spotted us and shook his head, smiling. He had obviously seen me chasing TJ out the door earlier in the evening, and now here we were strolling together back through that very same door. I couldn't be sure, but I thought I heard him humming "That's Amore."

We retrieved TJ's guitar and went up to his room. The room was a disaster, littered with dirty clothes and food wrappers. There were two full-size beds, one of which was covered in papers scribbled with notes and lyrics. An open guitar case rested on the dresser.

"Sorry about the mess," TJ said, and grabbed some papers, attempting to bring some order to the chaos.

"I'm gonna use the phone." I dialed Cam's apartment.

"Hello?"

"Hi, Cam, it's me."

"Goddamn you, Michael Garrity. Where are you?"

"I'll get to that. But first, I need you to do something for me."

"No, first you tell me what the hell's going on. Where are you? Is Jennifer with you? What was that call about this afternoon?"

I took a deep breath. "Cam, calm down. Listen to me. I need your help. I need you to do me a favor. And I need you to do it without a lot of explanation."

"This better not be some kinda joke, Garrity."

"No joke, Cam. I swear. This is the most important thing I'll ever ask. If you still love me at all, you'll do it and not ask any questions."

There was a long pause. I could hear her breathing.

"Are you in trouble?" she asked.

"Yeah."

"What do you need?"

"Go to my apartment and get my seizure pills. They're on the counter in my bathroom. When you leave, look around for anyone watching. When you drive out, make sure no one follows you. Make some extra turns, double back, see if anyone follows. If so, go home and call me."

"Jesus, Michael. What's this about?"

I ignored the question. "If you think you're clean, then drive straight to the Rainbow Arms on south OBT, just off I-4. You know where it is?"

"I—I think so."

"Put the bottle in a brown bag and leave it at the front desk. Tell the attendant it's for Mr. Mathers in 417. Got that? Mr. Mathers."

"Mathers . . . Okay."

"If you think of it, maybe a clean pair of boxer shorts, too. You may not hear from me for a few days, but I'll call you as soon as I can."

"God, Michael, are you okay?"

"I'm fine."

"Whatever you're doing, for Christ's sake, be careful."

"Thanks, Cam. I owe you."

I hung up. I didn't want to leave the Rainbow premises until I absolutely had to. First, I didn't want to lose sight of TJ. I had finally found him and I had no intention of letting him go. Second, Alomar and his neon-golf-shirt-wearing wiseguy were probably trolling for me, hoping to catch the scent of my trail. Maybe they could cut me off and get what they wanted without me. And, if they got what they wanted—namely the money and TJ—then I had no leverage and Jennifer was in even more trouble. I couldn't risk being seen and followed.

But I needed my meds. When I delivered the money tomorrow, I couldn't risk collapsing into a jerking convulsion. So Cam would have to help me, even if the lack of information was killing her.

The plan was for TJ and me to hang out for the next seventeen hours until I got the call from Mr. Day-Glo and the curtain went up for the show.

"I should call my mom," TJ said, stuffing an empty Burger King bag into the trash can.

"Use your cell phone. And keep it short. The cops are probably listening on her land line, so call her cell. They think you might be connected to Eddie's murder. We don't want them showing up here all hot and bothered."

"Okay." He picked up his phone. He went into the bathroom for some privacy.

I didn't know what I was going to do with TJ for the next seventeen hours. To be honest, I didn't care. There were some things I needed to do in the morning, including a phone call to North Carolina, but there was nothing I could do now.

I lay down on one of the beds and closed my eyes. But I didn't sleep. For the first time in close to thirty years, I actually prayed.

I remember Becky sitting on the floor of Jennifer's room when she was a toddler, holding her hands together and reciting bedtime prayers. I never participated, but often observed from the doorway. When Jennifer asked once why Daddy didn't pray, Becky answered, "Mommy prays for Daddy," which was absolutely true.

I didn't even really pray when Becky was pregnant. Sure, we heard about possible complications and the dangers inherent in childbirth, but they were all remote, abstract possibilities. People had babies every day without problems.

I now also knew that people lost babies every day. And, faced with the concrete possibility of losing my only daughter, I prayed with all my heart. I prayed with an intensity that I had never felt before, even as an altar boy before my faith withered. I was terrified of what might happen to Jennifer, and I wanted nothing more than her safe return. Nothing.

I didn't care what happened to me. I would gladly accept death at this moment if it would ensure Jennifer's safety. Bob was insignificant compared to this new threat. I shuddered at the thought of what Jennifer must be feeling. The fear. The uncertainty. I was furious at my helplessness and I prayed to a God I had long since abandoned for help.

Whatever the sacrifice, I would make it. Whatever the personal cost, I would pay it. I would do whatever I had to.

TJ stepped out of the bathroom, putting his phone on the counter.

"She says hi," he said. "She's working on the money. She should have it in the morning before eleven."

"That's good. Did you tell her where you are?"

"No. I just told her I was okay and that I was going to help you."

I nodded and sat up, leaning against the headboard. He sat on the other bed and placed his guitar into the open case.

"What are you workin' on?" I asked.

"This?" He held up the guitar.

"Yeah."

"Just some songs. That's what I do. I write songs."

"I liked the couple I heard downstairs. Different from Boyz Klub, that's for sure. Y'know, my daughter thinks you're a genius. That your songs are somehow more . . . I dunno . . . *substantial* than 'N Sync or the Backstreet Boys. I think I may finally understand what she meant." I moved over and sat on the edge of the bed. "What else you got?"

"You don't want to hear any more of my songs."

"Yeah. I think I do."

TJ pondered this for a moment. "Okay," he finally said, and placed the guitar on his knee. "This is what I'm working on now. It's not done, so it's still pretty rough. Anyway . . ."

He dragged his hand across the strings and closed his eyes. His fingers were long, delicate, and danced across the frets. The music they produced was arresting in its simplicity. The song was melancholy without being maudlin, about a lost love reflected on from the distance of many years. He didn't have all the lyrics yet, but a sentimental chorus repeated several times.

When he was done, he held the final note for a beat, his eyes still closed, a twenty-two-year-old lost in a world of middle-aged regrets. Finally he emerged by blinking himself back to the hotel room.

"That's great."

"I'm still working on it." He placed the guitar back in the case.

"It reminds me of Paul Simon. Something like . . . 'Old Friends' or 'Still Crazy After All These Years.' You know 'em?"

"Yeah. Thanks. I love those songs."

"I can see why you and Eli might have creative differences."

TJ snorted. "Not so great for synchronized dance moves, huh?"

I offered him a weak smile. "So what are you gonna do?"

"What do you mean? About the band?"

"Yeah."

He shrugged. "I can't go back. Eli. Miguel. There's just too much baggage, y'know?"

I nodded. "But what about the tour?"

"What about it? That's why you started looking for me, right? Eli wanted me on the tour." He shook his head. "Baggage, man."

"I don't give a shit about Eli anymore, or his money. I just want Jennifer back. I'm askin' about *you* and the tour. About the commitment you made."

"Commitment? What commitment? Eli's probably already found a replacement. I think there's an automatic penalty in my contract with Global. So, Eli will take his money, but I don't owe him any more than that. The price of my freedom, man."

"Not Eli. I mean a commitment to your *fans*. To Jennifer. Do you have any idea how hard she'll take it if you quit?"

"I—I can't stay in that band. I can't live that lie anymore—not with who I am and not with my music."

"I *am* talking about who you are. You said it in your note to Miguel, and I saw it with my own eyes downstairs. You're a musician. An artist. Whether it's in a boy band or at a gazebo in front of five strangers, you need to perform. I saw it in your eyes. You have a gift. And a passion." I sighed. "I lost that passion a long time ago. When you have that . . . I dunno . . . I think you—you need to hold on to it for as long as you can. Because it fades. And when it's gone . . . it's just very hard to get back."

TJ eyed me, unsure. "Are we talking about you or me?"

I rubbed my face. I was suddenly very tired. "Look, you do what you want. All I care about is my daughter. But, it seems to me that there's plenty of reason to go back, at least for one last hurrah. Think about Miguel. He needs you back, as a bandmate if nothing else. You have a lot of fans out there, including my daughter, who would be crushed if you just vanished. Their support made you rich enough to walk away. Don't you at least owe them a good-bye? But, most importantly, you're a performer. You need to be onstage. Don't douse that passion. It's the essence of who you are. If you disappeared, I think you'd dry up. Half the Boyz Klub songs are yours anyway. If it were me, I'd ride the wave a little while longer, maybe a farewell tour or something, and lay the groundwork for the next chapter in my career."

"I don't know . . ." Then he muttered to himself, "Alanis Morissette started out on Nickelodeon . . ." TJ fell silent and I let the silence hang between us. "You want that bed tonight?" he finally asked, nodding at the bed I was resting on.

"Doesn't matter."

"I'll take this one. I'll call down to the desk and have them send up a toothbrush and razor for you."

"Thanks."

"So, you ever share a room with a fag before?"

"Not that I recall."

"Aren't you worried I'm going to make a pass at you?"

"Should I be?"

"You're not exactly my type."

"Then we should be fine." If Miguel was his type, then I could almost be described as the polar opposite.

We readied ourselves for bed, taking turns at the sink. When a bellman delivered the toothbrush and razor, he also delivered my antiseizure meds and a bag containing clean underwear and a T-shirt. There were also a couple more blister packs of Zuraxx. Good old Camilla. I could only imagine the chuckle the front-desk clerk was now having.

TJ and I hit our respective beds, killed the lights, and lay in the dark stillness of the room for a minute.

"Hey, Mike?"

"Yeah?"

"What's your plan for tomorrow?"

It was a good question and the exact subject I was pondering when he asked it. My plan was simple but risky. And it was still evolving. But TJ was a major part of it. And he asked.

So I told him.

CHAPTER 34

Bob woke me early, a little after six, with an ache like a car parked on my head. I pulled myself up and felt along the bed to find my way to the bathroom sink. The room was still dark with the heavy vinyl curtains pulled.

The sink was open to the rest of the room, adjacent to the tiny space that housed the toilet and shower. As I came around my bed, I saw a sliver of light from under the bathroom door. TJ was in there.

I flipped on a light and leaned on my elbows over the sink, fighting the rising nausea in my throat. I splashed a palmful of cold water on my face and took a few deep breaths. I popped two Zuraxx from their blister packs and swallowed them with another cupped hand of water.

The bathroom door opened and TJ emerged amid a puff of steam. He was wearing only a towel and his face was once again clean-shaven. His long hair was brushed back, making it appear short again. He looked very much like the album-cover TJ. A shirtless album-cover TJ.

"You okay?" he asked.

"Yeah," I croaked.

"Headache?"

I grunted.

"My dad got those. Near the end." Then he realized what he'd just said and quickly added, "Sorry."

I gave him a wince and a shrug meant to say *Whatever,* but I'm not sure he got it.

I shuffled into the bathroom to take a leak, which made my

bladder feel better but did nothing for my headache. When I came out, TJ was dressed.

"You up for breakfast?" he asked.

"Maybe coffee."

"If you want to take a shower, I'll make a pot." He headed for the complimentary hotel coffee.

I nodded and grabbed a clean towel. The shower did make me feel better, but I soon realized that my headache was almost as much a result of my punched-up face as it was Bob. When I stepped out, still wearing yesterday's pants and socks, but with clean shorts and a fresh T-shirt, I did feel much improved.

As I brushed my teeth, I surveyed my reflection in the mirror. Damn. My face looked worse than it did yesterday. My eye was swollen and purple. My elbow ached where I'd fallen on it during the chase last night. My split lip throbbed.

But the Zuraxx were kicking in and the coffee was hot, and by the time TJ and I finished watching Matt Lauer interview some self-help author, I was finally ready for that breakfast.

We returned to the IHOP, where I had a more sensible breakfast of fruit and yogurt. I also decided now was the time to take the latest dose of my antiseizure meds. Just as we signed the check, which we split, my cell phone rang. TJ and I exchanged a look before I answered it.

"Hello?"

"Mike? It's me. Arlene. I have the money."

I grabbed a few things out of my truck and we took TJ's car. If Alomar and his goons were on the prowl, they were probably looking for my truck, which had spent the night in front of the 7-Eleven and was now safely hidden in the private Rainbow Arms lot. They wouldn't expect me to be tooling around town in a canary yellow Jetta. Although it might keep them off our tail, as inconspicuous transportation, it left a bit to be desired.

We drove to the Florida Mall, where we parked and strolled casually into a JCPenney department store. As arranged, we met Arlene in the linens.

Without a word she walked up to TJ and clutched him in a relieved embrace. Her cool façade cracked and I glimpsed the fear and worry that had obviously been bubbling inside her. TJ responded in kind, visibly relaxing, returning the embrace. They held each other for a long moment before separating.

Arlene swallowed and wiped her eyes. "Are you okay?"

"I'm okay," TJ said.

She patted his face to reassure herself. Satisfied, she turned to me. "What about you?"

"Good." An optimistic assessment and she knew it.

She nodded and put a hand on the large tote bag slung over her shoulder. "So, what do I do? Just hand it to you?"

"Yeah." I took the bag.

"It's all in there. One seventy-five."

I nodded. "Any problems?"

"No."

"Thanks. I'll get this back to you. Somehow."

Arlene waved me off. "We'll talk about that later." She looked between TJ and me. "What do you do now?"

"We wait," I said.

We bid Arlene good-bye and she gave TJ another emotional hug. She clearly wasn't comfortable with his agreement to be part of my plan, but she didn't try to talk him out of it.

TJ and I found a Bentley's luggage store, and I picked out a suitable briefcase for the drop. I made sure that the cash would fit inside and that it had the kind of pocket and easy catch latches that I needed.

"How much cash do you have?" I asked TJ as we exited the store.

"You mean in my pockets?"

"No. At the hotel. How much could you get within an hour if you needed it?"

"I'm not sure. A pretty good chunk. I've been using cash to pay for everything."

"Could you get ten grand?"

"Yes."

"We need to add that to the one seventy-five. It's a gesture. An apology for the trouble."

"So you're really going to give them the money?"

"Hell yes. At the end of the day these guys are businessmen. They care about money over all else."

We returned to the Rainbow Arms and loaded the briefcase, adding in another ten grand from TJ's stash. Arlene had done well, getting her withdrawal in mostly large bills, fifties, hundreds, and a few twenties. TJ and I rehearsed the scene a few times—at least how I thought the scene might go. I instructed TJ where to stand depending upon where we made the delivery.

My guess was that it wasn't going to be a dead drop, where I leave the money in a specific location for someone else to pick up. That would be a more traditional kidnapping scenario. These guys weren't typical kidnappers. Plus, they wanted TJ. The only way they could get him was if I delivered him personally. They might even suspect that I would have to drag TJ in by force.

When Day-Glo's call came, I assumed it would be instructions for me to personally bring the money and TJ somewhere, and that I would have face-to-face interaction with Alomar or his goons. Probably Alomar himself would be present because this was his mess and he would be encouraged to clean it up himself.

After rehearsing the possible scenarios a few more times, we ordered lunch from room service and watched TV. It was strange. After looking so hard for TJ with no success, I had found him within a few hours of receiving the twenty-four-hour deadline. Now that I had him and the money, there was nothing for me to do until my time ran out.

I wasn't going to take any chances, so we agreed to stay in his room at the Rainbow. We watched cable news and *Oprah*. I took two more Zuraxx and another dose of antiseizure meds.

As the afternoon wore on, my anxiety ratcheted up. I couldn't afford to make a mistake. Jennifer's life literally depended on it. My mouth grew dry and I couldn't sit still. To make matters worse, I felt a welling dizziness in my head, an intermittent and unwelcome side effect of my seizure pills.

I lay down on the bed, trying to stop the spinning gyroscope in my inner ear. Closing my eyes offered little solace.

"Mike?" asked TJ. "What's wrong?"

Before I could answer, the trilling ring of my cell phone pierced the room.

I sat up and looked at TJ, then at the clock: 6:25. This was it. I found the phone. The caller ID read UNKNOWN. I took a deep breath and pressed ANSWER.

"Garrity here."

"Mikey," came Mr. Day-Glo's filtered nasal voice through the receiver. "I do hope you've been busy."

CHAPTER 35

"Where's my daughter?" I demanded.

"You have my money?"

"My daughter."

"My money."

"I got it."

"And the cousin?"

"Yeah."

"No shit? You lyin' to me, Mikey?"

"No lie."

"We'll see." Day-Glo chuckled. "I gotta admit. I didn't think you'd do it. All it took was some incentive, right?"

"Where's my daughter?"

"First things first. Pay attention now, this is important. Bring the money and the cousin to the Palm Court Motor Lodge on 192. You know where that is?"

"No."

"East of I-4. Next to a Perkins restaurant. Come to room 126. Knock five times. Got it?"

"Yeah."

"You got exactly forty-five minutes. One minute late and we'll know you're bullshittin'. No funny business, Mikey. You hear me? I got watchers all around. If I even think I smell a cop within a mile of here, it's over for you and your girl."

He abruptly hung up.

TJ stared at me, his eyes wide and expectant.

"Showtime," I said. "Let's go."

. . .

I was still dizzy, so TJ drove. We took his Jetta because it would allow us to get closer without being marked. We drove quickly, but didn't push the speed limit dangerously. We couldn't afford to get pulled over.

Twenty-eight minutes later we pulled off I-4 and exited onto U.S. 192. We passed the ramp that led to Walt Disney World's Magic Kingdom and entered an entirely different world, a land populated by motels, T-shirt shops, and fast-food restaurants. Tourist World.

"There," I said, pointing. "The Perkins."

"I see it."

Directly behind the restaurant was the Palm Court, an independently owned motel whose street sign advertised its low rates as being even lower than those of the Econo Lodge across the street. Compare and save.

TJ pulled into the parking lot and I glanced around, searching for Mr. Day-Glo's watchers. I didn't see any, but I knew that didn't mean anything. Any one of these parked cars could have been hiding a pair of eyes.

Room 126 was at the back of the property, opening up onto a thin strip of parking lot abutting a shallow drainage canal and a view of palmetto scrub. It was the most isolated part of the motel. A few cars were parked on the cracked asphalt of the lot, but there were more empty spaces than filled.

TJ parked in front of room 126 and cut the engine. Neither of us said anything for a moment.

"You ready?" I asked.

"I think so."

We both got out. As we had discussed, I held the briefcase. TJ remained a step behind me and just off to one side. I paused, resting a hand on the hood of the Jetta.

"What's wrong?" TJ asked.

"Dizzy. I'll be okay." It was almost seven o'clock in the evening but the summer sun still hung fat and hot in the sky. Sweat was beading on my forehead and upper lip. I closed my eyes and took a breath, calming my nerves, forcing down the nausea. In all my years on the job, charging through doors, dicey moments during my undercover work on the previous Alomar operation, I had never been as nervous as I was now. My hands trembled. My heart pounded in my ribs. Never before did I have so much riding on my actions.

I took another deep breath and straightened. TJ followed me to the door. As instructed, I knocked five times. For one long, horrible moment, nothing happened. Then I saw the door's peephole go dark.

The door opened to reveal my pal Slick from the Escalade, his face looking even worse than mine. His broken cheek was a deep, swollen purple, the massive bruise ringed with an angry red border. He didn't look too happy to see me. The feeling was mutual. I braced myself for another fist to my chops. Instead, Slick took one step back and allowed me to move into the doorway. He frisked me roughly and thoroughly. He also pulled up my shirt to make sure I wasn't wearing a wire.

"He's clean," Slick said, and allowed me to step to the side of the door. TJ took my place in the doorway and was subjected to the same search. "Okay," Slick said, and gestured for us to enter.

It was a small, shabby room with a thin orange carpet and peeling wallpaper. A large, brown water stain decorated one corner of the ceiling. I smelled mildew and Lysol. Besides Slick, three others were in the room. Day-Glo stood in front of the television smirking at me, his unnaturally dark hair reflecting the room's artificial yellow lamplight. Alomar stood between the two double beds, arms folded, hostility seeping from every pore in his body. A guy I recognized as the driver of the Escalade stood in the far corner near the bathroom.

"That him?" Alomar said, nodding his head at TJ. The question wasn't meant for me. The guy in the corner held up a *Tiger Beat* magazine and studied it for a second. He looked back at TJ, then back at the magazine.

"Yeah," the guy said. "That's him."

Alomar nodded and addressed TJ. "You think you're real funny. Think you can play games with me, huh? I don't care who you are. Nobody fucks with me." TJ remained silent, following my instructions, but I saw the nervous movement of his eyes, the rapid breathing.

"Where's my daughter?" I asked.

"You don't ask the questions!" Alomar snapped. "I ask the questions! Where's my fucking money?"

I held up the briefcase. "I want my girl first."

"You don't make the rules," Alomar said.

"Let me see her."

Day-Glo shifted his weight. "You don't think we'd bring her here, do you? C'mon, Mikey, you insult us."

"Where is she?"

"One step at a time. You done good so far. You found the cousin. Let's see the money."

I placed the briefcase on the near bed and looked at Day-Glo for confirmation.

He nodded. "You open it, Mikey. Toward yourself."

The others in the room watched intently as I flipped the latches on the case. I raised the lid slowly and stood up. Then I rotated the open case toward Alomar and Day-Glo. The stacks of cash were arranged in neat rows.

"It's all there," I said. "One seventy-five. What Eddie owed. Plus an extra ten for the trouble." I felt the floor shifting slightly under me as a wave of dizziness washed over. I swallowed and took a breath, fighting through it. "Now, where's my daughter?"

Day-Glo narrowed his eyes, the hint of a satisfied smile on his face. "You done real good, Mikey. Real good. You can leave now. We'll call you and tell you where to pick her up."

"No. You tell me now." I didn't trust these guys for an instant and knew that if I walked out of this room now, Jennifer had an equal chance of living or dying. Those were not acceptable odds.

"Don't push it, Mikey," Day-Glo said. "I told you you done good. Now get out."

"What about him?" I said, nodding at TJ.

"He stays," said Alomar.

"Why?" I asked.

"None of your fucking business."

"Like hell. This is all my fuckin' business now."

Day-Glo sighed. "Look, Mikey, this is business. We got rules.

He played us and he's gotta pay. Don't worry. He's not gonna get what Eddie got."

"What're you gonna do?"

Day-Glo's eyes shifted to the credenza, where a pair of garden shears sat. Slick picked them up.

"What are they for?" TJ cried, no longer following my directions, his voice panicked. I could sense his body tensing to bolt.

"Now, c'mon, Mikey, you don't need to see this," DayGlo said, taking a half step toward TJ.

"No—," I said, feeling the room start to spin.

"Get out, Garrity."

I looked at TJ's ashen face. His saucer eyes implored me to help.

"No," I repeated, feeling myself listing as my balance wavered.

"Out, Garrity!" Day-Glo barked. "Now, or we take your thumbs, too!"

"Oh my God!" TJ yelled, and he turned to run.

In that instant, when everyone in the room focused on TJ, I thrust my right hand into the document flap of the briefcase's inside lid. My fingers slid in quickly, just as I had practiced in TJ's room. Alomar saw me and opened his mouth to shout. My hand came up quickly, brandishing my nine-millimeter Glock. Alomar yelled to the others, who were now reacting to me instead of TJ. All three were reaching for weapons hidden under shirts.

My other hand whipped out and snatched Alomar's collar, pulling him onto the near bed, bouncing the briefcase onto the floor, wads of cash tumbling out. Words were coming out of my mouth, a cop's voice, yelling unambiguous instructions to get the fuck down and don't fucking move. I jammed the muzzle of the Glock into Alomar's neck and kept pulling, dragging him over the bed by his collar.

The other three were all pointing weapons at me now, fury in their eyes. More commands came from my mouth, ordering them to stay the fuck back or I would blow a hole in Alomar's neck. Adrenaline surged through my body, my vision tunneled, my heart raced. The dizziness was overwhelmed by the endorphins.

I had no idea if TJ was still with me or if he had bolted out the door never to be seen again. I registered sunlight in the room and dragged Alomar to the open doorway.

"*Nobody moves!*" I shouted. Alomar struggled and I adjusted my hold, bringing an elbow around his neck and pressing the Glock hard into his temple. "Don't move, Juanito! I'll blow your fuckin' head open!"

"Not smart, Garrity," Day-Glo said, his pistol leveled at us. "Not smart."

"I don't care what happens to me," I said. "But if I find one hair out of place on my daughter, Juanito here loses his brains. I swear to Christ."

I jerked Alomar out the door and kicked it shut. I kept the gun wedged against his head so hard I knew he would have a small, circular bruise for several days, provided he lived.

"You're a dead man," Alomar croaked, his voice strained by the pressure on his throat.

I dragged him backward to the curb where—thank God—I found TJ in the Jetta with the engine running. As directed, he had opened the back door. I pulled Alomar into the backseat with me and yanked the door shut.

"Go! Go!" I yelled to TJ.

The car lurched backward and then squealed through the parking lot, careening around a parked station wagon. I pressed the gun harder into Alomar's head, leaning my weight on top of him in the backseat. I quickly frisked him and, satisfied he was unarmed, I leaned my mouth next to his ear.

"Where's my little girl?" I hissed, and closed my free hand around his windpipe.

CHAPTER 36

Alomar responded by spitting at me. I raised the pistol and whacked it solidly on his head, resulting in a satisfying thud of metal on bone. Alomar emitted an involuntary grunt.

"Where is she?" I repeated.

"Where do I go?" TJ called from the front seat. He had reached U.S. 192.

"Which way, Juanito?" I asked, squeezing Alomar's throat until my knuckles turned white. I fought down the unbridled rage coursing through me, forcing restraint on myself. In that instant, I wanted nothing more than to squeeze the life out of Juan Alberto Alomar Jr.

"East—," Alomar croaked. TJ spun the steering wheel and charged across traffic, turning left.

"Where we goin'?" I said.

"Shopping center—"

A phone rang suddenly, a ring tone I didn't recognize. After two rings I determined the ringing was coming from behind Alomar. I reached under him and produced his cell phone. I answered it.

"That's a bad move, Garrity," Day-Glo said as a greeting. "You, of all people, should know who that boy's friends are."

"I want my daughter. Now. You won't put her on the phone. You won't let me see her. I don't even know if she's still alive. You've given me nothing to trust you. This is my insurance."

"You know that even if you get her back, this won't be over. Alomar's a hothead. He's gonna put a price on you."

"Hey, I got cancer. I already got a price on me."

"Look—okay. Maybe we didn't handle this right. Maybe we

shoulda let you talk to her. Just let him go now and I'll see what I can do. Maybe we can just keep this between us."

"I'll let him go when I get my daughter back. Tell me where she is."

I heard him exhale in frustration.

"If you don't tell me right now," I said, "I'm gonna assume she's already dead and that you bastards were playin' me the whole time. Then I'm gonna drive out into the swamp, unload my clip in Juanito's head, and leave him for the gators."

Silence on the other end of the phone. My finger tightened on the trigger.

"I got my answer—"

"Wait. Okay. Just wait. There's a shopping center five miles east of here. She's in a blue minivan in the parking lot in front of a Chinese restaurant."

"What's the restaurant's name?"

I heard him ask someone else "the name of the fucking Chinese restaurant." He came back on the line. "Golden Dragon."

"You call whoever's holding her and tell him to get her out of the van by herself. If we drive by and see anyone standing with her, Alomar gets a bullet in the foot."

"Fuck you!" Alomar shouted. I pressed the Glock harder into his forehead.

I continued into the phone, "If we drive by and I don't see her standing by herself outside the van, I'm gonna know you were lyin' and we're headin' for that swamp."

"How am I supposed to get that message to the van? He's got no phone in there."

"That's bull. You call him now because we're almost there."

I hung up.

I relayed the directions to TJ and leaned more heavily on Alomar. I debated the odds that I was being lied to, that it was a setup. What would I do if we pulled up and saw no van? What if we pulled up and saw a van but no Jennifer? What if Jennifer is there but when we pull up the van's doors slide open and three guys lean out with Uzis?

I had no idea what I'd do. But I was about to find out.

"There it is," TJ said. "Golden Dragon."

It was across a wide intersection from where we waited at a red light. The signal seemed to last an hour.

"Do you see the van?" I asked, emotion straining my voice. I was about to learn the fate of my daughter.

"I . . . I can't tell," TJ said.

The light finally changed and we pulled through the intersection and into the restaurant parking lot.

"Do you see it?" I urged, anxiety charging my voice.

"No. Wait—yes! There. A blue minivan."

TJ swerved the car across the lot and up to the minivan. Only half the van was visible from the angle we approached, but we saw no one. Not Jennifer. Not some Mafia goon. Not even a goddamn customer for the restaurant.

"Keep going," I said to TJ, urging him to roll forward so we could see the other side of the van. The Jetta inched past the van's tail.

"You better pray she's there," I said to Alomar, tightening my hold on his throat. The other side of the van came into view.

No one was there.

The world suddenly fell away under me and I tumbled headlong into a murky abyss. She wasn't there. My mind spun, rocked by the unimaginable realization of what this meant.

"No . . . ," I muttered. "No . . ." I blinked at the blank space before my eyes and found my vision filled with the face of Juanito Alomar. "No. You son of a bitch. No. No!"

Circuits were sparking in my brain, misfiring. I squeezed Alomar's neck as hard as I could. His eyes bulged. Unable to speak, he was reduced to stuttered choking sounds.

"You son of a bitch," I repeated, positioning the Glock between his eyes, tightening my grip.

Somewhere, far above me, I heard my name.

"Mike!" It took a second for me to recognize TJ's voice.

"Mike!"

TJ . . . I was in the backseat of his car. We were still in the parking lot . . .

"Mike—the door!"

Robotically, I turned my head and saw the minivan's back door slide open. A figure stepped out and blinked at the setting sun. A girl.

"Open the door!" I shouted at TJ. "Open it!" He leaned across the empty front passenger seat and swung the door open. *"Get in!"* I screamed.

Jennifer stared anxiously at the unfamiliar car for a moment and stole a glance back into the van.

"Jennifer! Get in!" I shouted again. "It's me! It's okay!"

She spotted me in the backseat and almost burst into tears.

"Get in!" I ordered.

She made her feet move and quick-stepped into the car. TJ mashed his foot on the gas and the car rocketed out of the parking lot. I saw a man's face peering from inside the open door of the van.

Jennifer was crying in the front seat, holding herself tightly.

"Are you okay?" I barked at her. "Jennifer—are you okay?"

She nodded.

"Did they hurt you?"

She continued crying.

"Did they hurt you?"

She shook her head.

"Thank God. Thank God . . ." I loosened my grip on Alomar. He coughed and gasped for breath. "Okay, Juanito," I said, surfacing completely from the abyss, taking a deep breath. "Okay."

"Where do I go?" TJ asked. Still crying, Jennifer now looked over at her driver. It took a moment, but I saw the recognition wash over her. Unbelievably, she was being driven by TJ Sommerset. She turned and looked back at me. I still held the gun to Alomar's head. It was all too much for her and she erupted into a fresh set of terrified sobs.

"East," I told TJ. "Drive east."

We unloaded Alomar about twenty miles away, at a gas station halfway to Melbourne. He spewed a torrent of threats, mostly directed at me. I hardly heard him.

I helped Jennifer into the backseat, but when I started to climb into the front passenger seat, she held my arm.

"Stay," she said in a tiny voice. "Please, Dad."

I settled in next to her and she buried her face in my chest. She cried again, but not as uncontrollably. These were sobs of relief. She put her head on my knee and closed her eyes. I held her and stroked her hair and reassured her that everything was okay now. I flashed back on a distant memory of a four-year-old girl lying in my lap after a nightmare, me stroking her hair and telling her everything was okay.

She didn't ask about the police or what had happened to her. There would be time for all of that later. She only asked once where we were going and, when told, didn't even ask why. She kept her head on my knee and her eyes closed.

TJ drove for the first two hours, heading north on I-95. We stopped at a mall near Daytona, and we all bought a fresh set of clothes and some toiletries. Jennifer wanted to change out of her mall work outfit, which she had been wearing for two solid days. Then I got behind the wheel and we hit a Wendy's drive-through for dinner.

Now that she finally felt safe, Jennifer stole glances at TJ from the backseat. Eventually, she worked up the nerve to speak to him.

"Your hair's longer."

He smiled at her, the same smile from the cover of *Tiger Beat*, but more radiant in person ... more charming ... more sincere. "Too long?"

She considered. "No. It looks good."

"Thanks."

"I'm Jennifer."

"I know. I'm very happy to meet you, Jennifer. I'm TJ."

She smiled a shy grin. "I know." She turned to me. "How long till we get there?"

"Not sure," I said. "Twelve hours. Maybe more. You might as well relax."

"How 'bout some music?" TJ offered, and flipped the passenger visor down. A half dozen CDs sat snugly in slotted holders.

"Yeah," Jennifer said. "Music would be good."

It was just after dawn when we crossed into North Carolina. It took another couple of hours to reach Wayne's cabin. We called before we arrived and Becky was more than a little surprised to hear we were on our way.

"Good Lord, Mike," Becky said when she opened the door and saw my swollen face. "What happened to you?"

I told Becky everything. I knew she would have a nuclear fit and she didn't disappoint. It took three waves of tirades, but once she got her initial anger at me out of her system, she was rational enough to be grateful for our daughter's safety. I asked her not to call the authorities yet and told her why, describing what I still had left to do.

She didn't want to wait a single nanosecond, but she understood what was at stake and eventually relented, especially when I told her that Jennifer would be staying with her and Wayne for a while. She grabbed Jennifer's hand and squeezed it tightly.

When she was ready, Jennifer recounted what had happened.

She was at work and took a break to use the restroom. When she started back to the food court, two guys jumped her and pulled her out a service door into an alley behind the mall. It all happened so fast. They covered her mouth so she couldn't scream and tossed her into the van.

They threatened to hurt her and told her that if I didn't come through on a job for them, it was going to be bad for her. They didn't give her enough to eat and didn't let her use the bathroom as often as she needed, but other than that, she was treated okay. She spent most of the time blindfolded with her hands bound so she never knew where she was. She was moved at least three times in the minivan, always blindfolded. She was only allowed to open her eyes when she was in the bathroom, which was always windowless.

She described her emotions throughout the ordeal. The abject fear. But she said that deep down she knew that I would come through. She didn't know what I was supposed to do, but for the first time in her life, she had confidence I would deliver. I caught Becky looking at me when Jennifer said this.

Jennifer excused herself to take a shower in the master bath, and TJ did the same in the guest bath. The exhaustion hit me hard, after the adrenaline of the day's events and all the coffee I'd poured into myself for the drive to North Carolina, combined with the little sleep I had gotten the last few nights. I had been awake and charged for most of the past several days.

I crashed in a spare bedroom and spent several hours in a deep, dreamless slumber. When I awoke, it was getting dark. I padded downstairs and found the others eating dinner. Wayne offered me a glass of water and some grilled chicken, both of which I accepted.

Considering the frightening circumstances that had led Jennifer, TJ, and me there, plus the tongue-lashing Becky had delivered earlier, the meal was actually quite pleasant. Wayne even offered to take Jennifer and TJ out on the lake in the morning.

I thanked him and Becky for dinner and stood up. "I gotta go."

"Tonight?" Jennifer asked.

"Yeah."

"You still want my car?" TJ asked me.

"Yeah," I said, pocketing the keys. "If all goes well, I'll have it back to you by tomorrow night."

It was at least a two-hour drive from Wayne's cabin to the Butner federal correctional facility, and I wanted to get there before it got too late.

CHAPTER 37

I found a Motel 6 in Butner and took a room. I stood in a scalding shower for a long time, letting the hot water massage me, the white-knuckle stress of the past few days washing off my skin like a greasy film.

I set the bedside alarm clock for 8 a.m. and lay back on the bed. I exhaled deeply, releasing what felt like a week's worth of held breath. I could finally breathe again.

There, alone in the dark room, I reevaluated my relationship with Bob. In every relationship I've ever had in my life, even my two marriages, there came a time when one of us realized that things just weren't working out. Both parties in a relationship need things. For some it's attention. For others it's financial support. For others it's unconditional acceptance. Whatever. Everybody needs something in their relationships, and when they stop getting it, the relationship is doomed.

What was I giving Bob? That was fairly obvious: real estate in my head. But I was also giving him a large amount of attention. His needs were being met.

But what was Bob giving me? An excuse for self-pity? A lazy man's means for suicide? As odd as it sounds, those had been valuable gifts. I had clung to them. Desperately. Subconsciously, I was grateful to Bob because he allowed me to hide behind him, to define myself through him. I could continue to do so until I eventually became him completely in the instant before my heart stopped beating altogether.

However, I wasn't so sure I still had the same needs anymore. It happens. Two people come together but grow apart. When they finally part company, they do so as very different people. I was no longer the same person as when Bob had come into my life.

Bob and I were gonna have to talk. *It's not you. It's me.* Should I take him to a restaurant to avoid a big scene? How should I break the news? I decided to wait to do anything, at least until after my visit tomorrow.

The last thing I remembered thinking before I drifted off into a blissful sleep was the absolute absurdity of naming my brain tumor Bob.

"This is highly unusual, Mr. Garrity."

"Yeah. I know. I appreciate it."

"I'm just saying, it's highly unusual."

The warden of the Butner federal correctional facility walked me down a stark white hallway. He was in his early fifties, African-American, and carried himself more in the manner of an insurance agent than the head of a prison.

"Wait here, please," he said, indicating a small conference room. I did as instructed.

The Butner Federal Correctional Complex was situated in rural central North Carolina and consisted of three distinct complexes: a medium-security prison for midlevel and/or dangerous federal crimes; a low-security prison for lesser offenses; and an administrative federal prison hospital, which was secure but designed primarily to treat patients rather than prisoners. With the demise of the manufacturing industry and the current political drumbeat against tobacco, the prison was the backbone of the local economy. The motel where I'd stayed last night caters mostly to visiting family members of the incarcerated.

The administration wing where I now sat was military clean, and the entire operation seemed efficiently run. Of course, I was comparing it quite favorably to the Orange County lockup on a typical Saturday night. No urine was streaming out from under doors here.

Fifteen minutes later the warden returned with a guard whose nametag read GOMEZ.

"Officer Gomez will escort you," the warden said.

"Thanks," I said.

"This is highly unusual, Detective. We have official visiting hours. And approved lists. Not being on the list or coming at the wrong time means you have to turn around and go home."

"But you make medical exceptions."

"Sometimes. That's the only reason you and I are still talking."

I followed Officer Gomez down the hall and through a series of autolock doors until we stepped outside onto a sidewalk that bordered a large open-air courtyard. The courtyard was surrounded by a high electrified fence topped with concertina wire.

Gomez lowered himself into a golf cart and I sat next to him. We drove on the sidewalk around the perimeter of the courtyard. A few prisoners in light blue jumpsuits strolled idly around the courtyard, casting predatory sidelong glances as we cruised past.

Gomez parked the golf cart and grunted for me to follow him. We passed through another set of autolock doors and checked in at a guard station just inside the hospital building. I signed in and followed Gomez down the hall.

We rode a shiny elevator up two floors and exited into what looked, on the surface, to be a typical hospital ward. Upon closer examination, however, I saw that the orderlies wore billy clubs and sidearms.

"Visitor for 303," Gomez mumbled at the nurse/guard desk.

The male nurse crinkled his thick brow at us. "Who's he?"

"Visitor," Gomez elucidated.

"He ain't on the list," the nurse said.

"Medical exception," Gomez said.

The nurse shook his head in annoyance. "Never tell me shit." He turned to me. "You got fifteen minutes."

"Okay," I said.

Gomez planted himself in a hallway chair and closed his eyes. I followed the nurse down the hall to room 303. The nurse shook his head and muttered to himself as we walked. When we reached 303, he fumbled with a set of keys and finally unlocked the door. The tiny window in the door was obscured by a sliding shade.

"When you want out, pound on the door. If you wanna guard outside, tell me now."

"Do I need one?" I asked.

The nurse snorted. "You tell me."

He swung the door open and revealed an old, frail man lying motionless in a bed. Oxygen tubes ran over his ears and under his nose. His thin, white hair hung limp around a blotched, pink scalp. I heard his labored breathing even across the room. His eyes twitched toward us, a motion that seemed to take all his strength.

"I'll be fine," I said, and stepped into the room. The door thunked shut behind me. With the exception of the locked cell door, this looked like any private hospital room. A large picture window sat in the center of the opposite wall, allowing warm sunlight to flood in. A television sat on a wall-mounted stand. A telephone rested on the bedside table.

"Hello, Juan."

He wheezed slightly louder, which I assumed was acknowledgment of my greeting.

I came around the bed and pulled a chair up next to him. I sat in the pool of sunlight and considered him for a minute before continuing. He considered me right back.

"You remember me?" I asked.

He nodded.

"You know why I'm here?"

He made a shaky, one-shouldered shrug, a gesture that implied he knew but wanted me to tell him anyway. So I did. I explained how his son, Juanito, had made some bad business decisions, extended credit to the wrong guy. Despite efforts to stay out, I got mixed up in it. I told him how they kidnapped my daughter and threatened to hurt her if I didn't do what they wanted. I informed him that I found their money, plus an extra ten large for the trouble. That should have been it. That was business. But Juanito doesn't understand business. He made it too personal. He gave me no assurances of my daughter's safety. I did what any father would have done. But I embarrassed Juanito. I explained that I was afraid that Juanito didn't think it was over.

Alomar said nothing for a moment, just struggled to get air in and out of his lungs. As I watched him labor to breathe, I had a vision of myself, one year from now, lying in a bed just like this, cancer swirling throughout my body. My breath coming in ragged gasps.

"You," he rasped, ". . . betrayed me."

I was about to respond.

Alomar held up a pale, trembling hand. "I'm dying. . . . What . . . what do you . . . want from . . . me?"

I leaned close to the bed. "I want your word. As a businessman. As a father. I want your word on the lives of your children. This is over between your son and me. He got his money, plus consideration. As a businessman, you understand that. You respect it. I did what I had to do to protect my daughter. As a father, you understand that. The slate is clean. From this moment forward, if I happen to notice someone followin' me or catch someone peekin' at me over a newspaper, then I make sure your wife and your daughters all get audited by the IRS every year for the rest of their lives. And if anything happens to my daughter—if I even *think* something might happen to my daughter—I'll make it my life's mission to hunt down and kill your only son in the most painful manner possible. He stays away from her, he stays away from me, he stays away from everyone I know. Everyone I ever met. He stays away, or he's a dead man."

Alomar sucked in a long, rattling breath. "I heard . . . you're sick. . . . I heard . . . you're dying."

I leaned in close to him. "Not anymore." I fixed my gaze on him. "That's what I want. Your word that it's over. You call Jersey or wherever you need to make sure Juanito knows it's over." I pressed a hand on his shoulder. "Do I have your word?"

He glared at me and held his breath. The room became eerily silent.

I pressed his shoulder harder. "Do I have your word?"

He nodded and exhaled a wet, gurgling breath. A terrible weariness seemed to descend on him like a fog. He nodded again and closed his eyes.

I stood and moved to the door, pounding on it to call the guard. Alomar's wheezing snagged somewhere in his chest, and he erupted into a racking coughing fit. His frail body convulsed with each spasm. Thin lines of blood stretched from his lips to his starched white linens. The door opened and the nurse stepped in. Alomar continued hacking, blood and spittle dotting his gown and sheets.

"Jesus," the nurse said, and strode into the room. He pulled an oxygen mask from a nearby tank and held it over Alomar's nose and mouth. After a moment, the coughing subsided. Alomar collapsed back on his pillow, his bony chest heaving up and down as he sucked in the oxygen.

I turned and walked out of the room, looking only where I was going, not gazing back. I kept my focus forward even as I drove away, refusing to even glance in the rearview mirror.

CHAPTER 38

"Check it out, G." Jim Dupree slid a manila folder across the booth table at me.

I opened it and whistled. "Damn."

We sat in an Orlando Denny's four days after my visit to Butner, drinking coffee and eating breakfast. Big Jim had two softball-sized banana-nut muffins on his plate. I had yogurt and fruit.

"It hits the news later today," Big Jim said.

I held an Orlando Police Department Internal Affairs report. In it were listed three officers who were on the new Alomar payroll, including the deputy chief. There was also evidence that Mr. Day-Glo's claims of federal graft were also true. If I had gone to the cops when Jennifer was kidnapped, the deputy chief would definitely have been in the loop, and Jennifer would now be dead. I suppressed a shudder at the thought.

Before I'd left North Carolina, I'd called Jim and told him the whole story. I gave him everything I could, including fingering Mr. Day-Glo as Eddie's likely killer. I spent much of the first two days of my return giving statements and being interviewed, as did Jennifer and TJ.

Apparently, OPD Internal Affairs already suspected that one or more officers had been compromised, but didn't have specifics. My story clicked a few tumblers into place and unlocked their investigation. They nailed one of the dirty beat cops and leaned on him. Within twenty-four hours he gave up his partner and the deputy chief. Later today, the story would become a public scandal that would probably last for months.

Big Jim told me that Alomar and his entire operation had vanished. Juanito's mother and sisters were still in town, but they claimed no knowledge of his whereabouts. Naturally, Mr. Day-Glo had also disappeared. The theory was that they knew the heat would be on after the stunt with Jennifer, and they'd planned all along to pull up stakes. But they needed their money first. The conventional wisdom was that Alomar and his crew went underground in San Juan. Alomar Sr. still had a loyal network of contacts back in Puerto Rico who could help Juanito hide and also continue to allow him to run his operation. As long as the boys in Jersey got their cut, they probably didn't care where he was. Besides, after screwing up in Central Florida with Eddie Sommerset, the boys in Jersey were likely eager to move Juanito out until things cooled off.

The dude I had been calling Mr. Day-Glo was almost certainly Victor Karidakus, a second-generation Greek American from Staten Island. Victor's father owned an import/export business that allegedly fronted for the Angelino crime family. Young Victor was introduced early into the business and rose quickly through the ranks as a ruthless enforcer of Angelino policies. He had been around a long time and was a trusted member of the Angelino inner circle in Jersey. Nobody was surprised to learn that Victor had been dispatched to Florida to clean up Juanito's mess.

The FBI was working the case now, as well as ferreting out which agents, if any, were on the take. No one was particularly optimistic that they could make a murder charge stick to Victor. He was suspected in at least a half dozen other executions over the past ten years, and none of those crimes had produced enough physical, or even circumstantial, evidence to arrest him. The investigation strategy was to go after Juanito. He was impulsive, and that made him vulnerable. The Feds' main fear was that the Angelinos would neutralize him themselves before the FBI could get to him.

I slid the file back to Jim and sighed, sipping my coffee.

"So, G," Jim said. "Whaddaya gonna do now? I know this case got your juice flowin' again. I tole you I been keepin' your desk warm."

"Thanks, bro. But I think I'm done bein' a cop." I stirred a spoon in my mug. "You know I haven't thought much about long-range plans lately. . . . But, who knows? As I was drivin' back from North Carolina, I actually had an idea. I thought I might apply for a PI license."

"What?" Big Jim put down the fistful of muffin that was halfway to his mouth.

"Yeah."

"Doin' what? Peepin' at husbands gettin' some strange? Video-tapin' worker's comp claims? Damn, G . . . you're better than that. We need you doin' real police work."

"Well, I'm not gonna worry about it now. I'm focused more on short-range plans."

Big Jim nodded. "Yeah . . . you just take care of business now. Then we'll talk. Till then, I'll just keep my ass on your desk."

I chuckled. It had been a long time since I had laughed in any capacity, and this small chuckle felt strange, like seeing an old friend I barely recognized.

"You do that," I said.

The waitress appeared and asked if we wanted more coffee. Jim nodded.

"No thanks," I said. Then to Jim: "I gotta go."

"Whay-uh?" he said, his words muffled by the huge bite of muffin rolling around in his mouth.

"Executive Airport. A friend of mine is goin' on a trip."

It was a surprisingly subdued group who waited in the leather-appointed passenger lobby of Executive Charters Inc. Holden and Ben were planted in front of a big-screen TV, playing some sort of NASCAR video game.

Miguel was standing by himself, hands in pockets, looking out the window at the tarmac. When I came in, he turned. Realizing it was only me, he offered a small, sad smile and turned back to the window.

A half dozen other Global Talent and record-label staffers milled around the free buffet. I walked up to Miguel. We stood in silence for a moment, watching a stark line of gray rain clouds recede across the brilliant blue sky, like a sodden blanket being slowly pulled away.

"Hey," I said.

"Hey."

"You okay?"

Miguel nodded. "I don't know how you did it."

"I didn't. It was my daughter. Jennifer. She can be very persuasive."

"She must really be something."

"Yeah," I said.

I felt a big hand on my shoulder.

"Mikey," George Neuheisel said. "Glad you could make it."

"Wouldn't miss it," I replied.

George pulled me aside. "Listen . . . he's coming, right?"

"That's what I was told."

"If he doesn't . . . ," George muttered to himself. Then, back to me: "Eli has started shifting the promotion to TJ's big farewell tour. Y'know, come and say good-bye. Advance ticket sales have already gone up. The kids are eating it up." He looked at me expectantly.

"That's nice," I said.

George reached into his back pocket and awkwardly produced a sealed envelope. "Here. Your payment."

"I thought Eli canceled the deal."

"Nah. He's a hothead, sure, but he's thrilled you came through. He keeps his word." A shaky smile. "You did come through, right?"

"That's what I was told."

"Right . . ." George shoved the envelope into my hand.

At that moment the door swung open and in walked TJ and Arlene.

The open doorway seemed to suck the air from the room. For an instant there was absolute stillness. Even the video game became mute.

"You're late," Ben said, barely glancing up.

"Yeah," TJ said, running a hand through neatly cropped hair. "Sorry about that."

The air and noise rushed back into the room, and several staffers descended upon TJ with papers, forms, itineraries, schedules, interview requests, and whatever else was necessary before a concert tour.

I caught Miguel watching the scene, pain hidden behind his eyes, but visible if you were looking for it. For just an instant—a half second, maybe—TJ glanced up and caught Miguel's eye through the crowd of people. In that instant TJ gave him a wink and a lopsided grin. I was a few steps away, but I thought I heard Miguel's breath catch in his throat. He turned back to the window suppressing a smile of his own.

As I was watching this, I felt another hand on my elbow. A smaller hand. A softer hand.

"Arlene," I said by way of a greeting.

"How's Jennifer?"

"Good. Things are finally gettin' back to normal."

Arlene nodded. She, too, had gotten a haircut, her light brown locks styled into a short bob that framed her face. She looked ten years younger.

"Eli actually decided to pay me," I said. "Give me a few days and I'll get you back the one seventy-five."

She shook her head. "No. That was Eddie's debt. A family debt. Besides, I can afford it. Put your money towards Jennifer's college fund or something."

"Thanks."

We watched TJ talk to the Global Talent and record-label staff for a few seconds.

"So . . . are you ready?" Arlene asked.

"Yeah," I said. "I guess."

"It's the right decision."

"Yeah."

She placed a hand tenderly on my cheek, patting it softly. Then she leaned over and kissed my other cheek.

When I looked up, I saw TJ watching us. His face was expressionless until the hint of a smile crept in. He gave me a *Hey, there* nod with his chin. I nodded back.

Arlene and I watched TJ excuse himself from his attendants and step over next to Miguel. As TJ approached, Miguel's hand involuntarily reached up for him, but he caught himself and brought it back down. TJ gave him a chaste pat on the shoulder, but their eyes betrayed the emotion of their reunion. I felt sorry for them and their self-imposed restraint for the sake of image. They clearly wanted to embrace but couldn't in this public forum.

"What's he gonna do after this?" I asked Arlene.

"Not sure. Take some time off. Try to cut a solo album, maybe. He has time to figure it out."

I nodded. "I hope so. If there's one thing we could all definitely use, it's more time."

Thirty-five.

That's the number of acoustic tiles in the ceiling of the pre-op room. It's amazing that a mindless activity such as counting ceiling tiles could be so engaging. Ah, the amazing entertainment powers of really good drugs.

I was lying on my back, contemplating my next diversion, feeling my body relax into seminumbness, when the door opened.

"Hello, Michael."

"Hey." My words came out slurred, drunken.

Father Luis Sanchez sat next to my bed and put his hand on my arm. In his black shirt and pants, he was a stark contrast to the white-clad nurses and orderlies who had been attending to me thus far.

"I was told you wanted to see me," he said in his slightly accented voice.

"Yeah. Sorry . . . I'm a little loopy. . . . They gave me some drugs to relax."

"That's okay. Take your time."

"Time . . . ," I mumbled to myself. "Can you . . . hang out? I mean, in case?"

"In case?"

"Yeah . . . y'know. In case . . ."

"In case something goes wrong?"

"Yeah . . . just in case . . . I wanna have last rites."

Father Sanchez nodded. "Of course."

"They're takin' the top of my skull off. . . . Anything can happen when a guy gets the top of his head removed, y'know? . . . They tell me I've only got a fifty-fifty shot of gettin' the whole tumor. . . . And even if they do get it . . . there's a good chance I could end up a vegetable. . . . And if somehow they get the tumor and I don't wind up a vegetable, it'll probably grow back as an even worse kinda tumor."

Sanchez nodded again. "What, then, are the odds that everything will turn out the way you want?"

"Dunno . . . five percent?"

Sanchez smiled and squeezed my arm. "You'd be amazed at the things that God can do with just five percent."

I nodded, closing and opening my eyes in a slow-motion blink.

"Michael, did you know that there are four beautiful women sitting in the waiting room for you?"

"Yeah . . ." I smiled, picturing the scene of Becky, Cam, Arlene, and Jennifer all sitting in the family waiting area, trading stories about me. In other circumstances I might have been horrified. But instead, today, I found it both amusing and reassuring.

"You must be very loved, to have four such ladies come down here at six in the morning."

"I must be."

Sanchez reached into his pocket. "Your daughter gave me this for you."

He handed me a folded note. I opened it. In Jennifer's round, adolescent handwriting were four simple words: *I love you Dad.*

"Thanks," I said.

The door opened and an orderly entered. Father Sanchez blessed me, and then I was rolling. In a surreal, drugged daze I watched doorways and ceiling tiles flash by in a staccato montage of hospital scenes. The inside of an elevator. The scent of alcohol. A garbled intercom announcement. I closed my eyes and felt the motion of my wheeled bed traveling the corridors.

I didn't know what the rest of my life held or how many days it would last, but I knew I would spend it without Bob. It was time to evict him from the rented room in my head. So I bid a silent farewell to Bob, but not before thanking him. By threatening me with death he had given me a second chance at life. I planned not to waste it.

I stopped moving and then felt hands lifting me, moving me from the gurney to the operating table. I heard muted tones of classical music.

"Morning, Mike." A man's voice, colored with a slight Indian accent. The anesthesiologist. He attached something to the IV tube in my arm.

"Okay, Mike. Do me a favor. Count backwards from one hundred."

"Yeah . . ." I swallowed. "One hundred . . . ninety-nine . . . ninety-eight . . ."

I felt my body relaxing. My mind relaxing. My head felt lighter, as if Bob had already given up and shriveled away. Live or die. Vegetable or not. Either way, I knew I was doing the right thing. I realized that, for me, the choice to live was far more important than if I actually did. No matter what happened here today, no matter what happened tomorrow, for the first time—perhaps ever—I was truly at peace.

"Ninety-seven . . . ninety . . . six . . . ninety . . ."

With a smile on my lips, I felt myself slip gently into a warm, dark slumber.

RESOURCES

We all have our cancer stories.
Whether it was a friend, family member, or yourself,
cancer has probably touched your life.

For resources, support, and information about how you can help,
visit the American Cancer Society at www.cancer.org.

A valuable resource for me during the writing of this book was
the Web site of the American Brain Tumor Association (ABTA).
I would be remiss if I didn't recognize them here
and encourage you to support their efforts at http://hope.abta.org.